ABDUCTED

ABDUCTED

A NOVEL BY

PETER S. BERMAN

Published by Merseyside Press
For information: merseysidepress@gmail.com

AUTHOR'S NOTE

This novel is a work of fiction in its entirety. All characters, settings, dialogue, incidents and other story elements are wholly imaginary, as are the personalities of my characters. Following an old literary tradition, I have honored some of my friends by using their names to identify fictional characters, but there is no connection between my imaginary characters and my real-life friends. Any resemblance between the fictional contents of this book and real people, companies, institutions or places is strictly coincidental.

This story is dedicated to my two grandchildren,
Maxwell and Charlotte.
You are the gift that makes my growing old both
bearable and delightful.

***

It is also dedicated to the men and women of the LAPD
Robbery-Homicide Division who work tirelessly each and every
day to track down those who prey on the innocent.

It is a pleasure to be allowed to work with you all.

"Risk comes from not knowing what you're doing."

—Warren Buffett

"If knowledge can create problems, it is not through ignorance that we can solve them."

— Isaac Asimov

"Every addition to true knowledge is an addition to human power."

— Horace Mann

ABDUCTED

ONE

ALEXANDRIA, EGYPT
DAY ONE   7:06 PM

Still waters run deep, and that was certainly the case when it came to Doctor Angela Disler, for to look at this diminutive woman, one would never suspect that she was in possession of an IQ that put her in the category of genius. But blessings often come with a curse, and that was true in Angela's case, for while she had a tendency to be singularly focused when it came to her area of specialty, she was blissfully ignorant of the much bigger picture.

She was seated in *The Bleu Bar,* an outdoor terrace on the third floor of the fifteen story *Four Seasons Hotel* in Alexandria, Egypt. The bar was on a large patio that overlooked the Mediterranean Sea. Between the hotel and the water was the *El-Gaish Road,* a main thoroughfare, miles long, that was lined with hotels, high-rise apartments, and stores of every description.

She took a small bite of pasta with tomato sauce from a bowl full of *Kushari,* the Egyptian national dish. She chewed it slowly while she savored this moment in time.

For the past eight hours, she had taken part in a series of roundtable lectures at an international medical conference on cancer and virology. Her area of interest was communicable diseases, and in addition to hearing from other experts, she had successfully delivered the keynote speech. It was only now that she was starting to unwind from the weeks of stress she'd undergone while getting her notes ready for her presentation.

A waiter arrived with the martini that she'd ordered, and after he had walked away, she took a large, celebratory sip.

To everyone's relief, the setting sun was finally poised on the edge of the horizon where it was ready to surrender its day-long dominance to the inky blackness of the nighttime desert sky. A cooling wind would soon creep into the city from out of the North; a godsend for the millions who suffered throughout the days and nights without the luxury of reliable air conditioning

From her table by the edge of the balcony, Angela could just make out a large swath of the beach across the highway where it meandered along the coastline. She watched with a growing fascination as thousands of beachgoers, who had called it quits for the day, gathered up their families to head home for a late evening meal.

When the sun disappeared, the initial promise of the gathering darkness was replaced by a ribbon of lights that turned on automatically to illuminate the route of the *El-Gaish Road*. She marveled at such a beautiful sight; the way the lights were reflected on the open sea like electrified golden glitter. For a few moments, it truly rivaled the ocean of stars that slowly appeared in a broad, twinkling swath across a carbon black desert sky.

She was fifty-two years old, petite, and having the time of her life. Alexandria was the center of Egyptian culture and trade, a true crossroads of the Middle East since it's founding by Alexander the Great in 332 BC. The city was huge—a population of almost four million people—and perpetually alive, as evidenced by the constant traffic on the highway which produced a constant syncopation of horns and squealing tires. The city was literally bursting at it's seams; teeming with life both day and night. For Angela, spending time in Alexandria was a way to feel alive, to be a part of an endless, living tableau, where one's senses were constantly bombarded with the sights and smells that made her life back home in Los Angeles seem terribly tame...*and boring.*

She took another sip of her martini. Since this was her last night in Egypt before the long flight home, she was bound and determined to make the best of it. Her plan was to finish dinner, do a little souvenir shopping for the kids and her husband, and if she was really lucky, she might even run across a street vendor selling an inexpensive knockoff of the *Leiber Precious Rose Handbag*, a photo of which she carried in her purse after tearing it out of a fashion magazine that she found on her flight from the states.

She was about to take another bite of her pasta when a man walked up to her table and gave her a tentative smile.

"Dr. Disler?"

He didn't wait for her reply.

"Please allow me to introduce myself. I am Dr. Andre Petrov, from the

Ministry of Health of the Russian Federation." He spoke perfect English. "I wanted to tell you how much I enjoyed your presentation today. It was most enlightening."

"Thank you," she replied. There was a moment of awkward silence, but she quickly recovered. "Are you a member of the GVN, Dr. Petrov?"

"Not yet, but I believe that the *Global Virus Network* is an excellent organization, and assuming there are no political impediments to prevent us from joining, I intend to recommend to our Minister that we seek membership just as soon as I get back to Moscow."

He looked longingly at the empty chair at her table, and Angela soon realized that he wanted to sit down. Not wishing to appear to be impolite, she invited him to join her, and he quickly settled in.

"Do you come to the Middle East often?" he asked.

"It's my first time. With all of my duties back home, I'm afraid I don't get out very often."

Petrov laughed a deep chuckle. He was a very attractive man, middle aged with jet black hair, a dark complexion, and piercing black eyes. Tall and athletic looking, but polished and stylish, he kept his nails well manicured, his hair neatly trimmed, and his suit—an Armani—was impeccable. His watch was gold, probably a Rolex, and a gold pinky ring worn on his right hand was inlaid with a single, large sapphire.

Angela studied him carefully.

"Petrov? That doesn't sound Russian to me, doctor. What is your parental nationality?"

Petrov smiled.

"I'm Bulgarian by birth. After medical school in Switzerland, I accepted a position at the Institute in *Irkutsk, Siberia,* where I was given a research grant by the Russians to study the genetic modification of viruses."

She slowly leaned back in her chair.

"How interesting? That's also an area I'm interested in."

"I know, and that's why I was so pleased to learn that you would be presenting at this conference." He smiled broadly. "And I must say, I was not at all disappointed."

They spoke for a few minutes more about the institute where he worked and about his research on the BRCA, a breast cancer susceptibility gene. Angela was enjoying his company, so when he ordered them a round of drinks, she looked at her watch, but did not turn him down, as staying for a while longer would not alter her plans for the evening. She decided she could take a little time to make friends with this interesting man and still have a chance to get her shopping done before the nearby mall closed down.

He seemed comfortable with small talk, and soon she found herself laughing at his stories. He talked about Siberia, the hospital where he worked in Irkutsk, the horrible freezing weather he had to endure to work there, and his burning desire to visit the United States.

She was telling him a story about one of her daughters when she had the sensation that she was slurring her words. To be feeling this hammered after only a couple of martini's seemed weird. She tried to apologize for the effect it was having on her, but the words only came out jumbled.

Her head began to spin, and she mumbled something unintelligible about not feeling well and needing to go to her room.

She put down her drink while he got to his feet and helped her to stand, then watched as she struggled to maintain her balance. He offered to take her arm, but she brushed him off before staggering from the table and out the restaurant door to the lobby in front of the public elevators.

Her mind seemed as sharp as a tack, but her motor coordination was failing.

Dr. Petrov again appeared out of nowhere, and while she was certain that he was trying to talk to her, his words were completely indiscernible. Her hearing had failed; either that or she was no longer processing sounds in the usual way. What she suspected to be his words came through as nothing more than a series of tonal sounds that bounced around inside her head.

Am I having a stroke?

It was her last conscious thought.

She pitched over face-first and crashed to the floor.

*****

TWO

LOS ANGELES, CALIFORNIA
DAY FOUR   4:00 PM

Detectives Jennifer Donahue and Shari Thompson parked their car in the large circular driveway of a lavish home in Cheviot Hills, a suburb on the Westside of Los Angeles. The house was Spanish in design, built in the early 1920s, but it was impeccably maintained by the lucky few previous owners who over the years had called it home. The red tile roof and thick stucco walls kept the house cool in the summer and warm in the winter, and with over five thousand square feet of living space for a family of four, that meant a considerable amount of savings on utility bills.

Donahue was a tall blond, mid-thirties, with shoulder length hair, liquid blue eyes, and a face that was all the more attractive because of her disdain for heavy makeup. She was physically fit, smiled easily, and had an even disposition regardless of the situation. A fourteen year veteran of the force, she'd been working homicides for four straight years, the last two of which were with the Robbery-Homicide Division as a Major Crimes specialist. On a daily basis, her girl-next-door beauty seemed to work for her as an asset, and when she found herself glamming up, usually for a date or a night on the town with her girl-friends, she was magically transposed from the girl you wanted to cover your back to one you couldn't take your eyes off.

Her partner, Shari Thompson, was also a blond, albeit from a bottle, and as the shorter of the two she more than made up for the height discrepancy with a chest that garnered frequent admiring looks from the majority of men who weren't blind or already dead. She was in her late thirties, or so she claimed, and liked to wear her hair in a low, loose ponytail.

For those men whose eyes rose above her chest, they were treated to a stunningly beautiful face, one that also frequently went without makeup. Her eyes were emerald green, particularly light and bright, with a faint bluish cast. But since her recent divorce, more often than not, they contained a hint of sadness. With three young boys to raise at home, she often made no bones to Donahue about how happy she was to again be single, and how exciting it was to sample the current crop of available men now that she was out there and dating again.

For the moment, getting tied down in a long term relationship was the last thing Thompson wanted to do.

They climbed out of their unmarked Crown Victoria—a motor pool relic that was a particularly gaudy shade of lime-green—and slowly made their way up the Spanish tiled pathway to the ornate, heavy, wooden front door.

"Nice digs," Thompson said, and Donahue smiled. *Nice* was a major understatement. The house was a veritable mansion.

The weather was breezy, and both women were wearing overcoats. No rain was in the forecast, but the winds—and with them, the clouds—were coming down from the North, an indication of a shift in the jet stream, so for the next few days there was always a hoped-for chance for intermittent sprinkles.

Donahue pushed the doorbell which was answered almost immediately, and once they presented their credentials, they were quickly ushered inside and into the living room by a man who appeared to be mid-fifties.

He was tall, over six feet, with light brown hair flecked with gray, a broad forehead, and a thin, angular face. He wore a pair of black framed glasses, a long sleeve green and white plaid shirt, and a pair of light brown corduroy pants.

Once they were settled on a couch, a nervous appearing Henrik Disler caught Thompson's eye.

"You said you're from Robbery-Homicide?" he asked.

"That's right, Mr. Disler."

Thompson studied him carefully, then suddenly realized that the name of her division was likely contributing to his apparent anxiety.

"Don't let the name of our unit worry you," she said. "Your call to the Mayor's office was directed to our division. We have the experience and the resources to work on international cases. That's why they sent us over. We're just here to get some basic information."

"So you haven't found her body or anything like that?" he said, not really accepting her explanation.

Thompson shook her head. "She's probably fine, Mr. Disler." She attempted to use her most soothing voice. "Why don't you start by telling us what happened? Just start at the beginning."

He visibly relaxed while Donahue took out a small notebook.

"Angela, my wife, is a genetic virologist. She works in Santa Monica at a research facility called *Zurich Pharmaceuticals*. She was in Alexandria, Egypt, speaking at an international medical conference for the *Global Virus Network*, a worldwide authority, and resource for the identification and control of viral diseases; you know, like the Bird Flu? The kind that poses a possible threat to all of humanity."

"When did she go to Alexandria?" Thompson asked.

He ran his hand through his thinning hair.

"Almost a week ago."

"And when was she supposed to return?"

"Three days ago."

"And you've heard nothing from her since she was due back in LA?"

Disler hugged himself with his arms. He was noticeably anxious again, and both detectives studied him intently.

"She called me just before she presented her keynote speech. She was nervous. That was the day before she was scheduled to fly home. I called the hotel, but the people I spoke to at the front desk said that her room was prepaid, so they presume she checked out online and went directly to the airport."

He looked from one to the other.

"I checked with the airlines. She never made her flight."

He started to tear up, so Thompson gave him a moment before asking the next question.

"Any chance she might have just wanted to stay over a little longer? Maybe go to a different hotel?"

"I know what you're thinking," he said, holding her glance. "That she may have met someone and gone off with him." He shook his head. "My wife and I have a great marriage. We've got two beautiful daughters that she adores. There's no way she'd hook up with someone else. She's too responsible for that."

Thompson shrugged. "You do understand that we have to ask these kinds of questions?"

Disler nodded.

"What kind of work do you do, Mr. Disler?" Donahue asked.

"I'm a physician at UCLA. Internal Medicine is my specialty."

Donahue nodded, duly impressed. She spent the next twenty minutes getting Angela's hotel and airline information, as well as her cell phone number, work address, and the names and contact information for her close friends as well as co-workers.

When she and Thompson stood up to leave, she asked him, "Can you give us a current photo of your wife?"

Disler walked over to the fireplace mantle and removed a photograph from a small frame.

"My wife and our daughters," he said as he handed the photo to Donahue. "This was taken last month."

Donahue studied the photo before handing it over to Thompson who also studied it carefully. Angela Disler was an attractive, petite woman who appeared to be slightly younger than her stated age of fifty-two. Her hair was dark and cut short, her eyes were pale brown, and her figure was still good. She looked to be genuinely happy when posing with her daughters.

Thompson put the photo in her purse, then said, "Would it be possible to get a DNA sample for your wife? Perhaps hair follicles from a hairbrush or comb, or something like that?"

Disler's eyes widened. "You think she might be dead?"

"She might have had an injury of some kind. Perhaps she's in a hospital and unable to communicate. If we get a DNA sample processed now, we can have it handy just in case we need it sometime in the future. It's just a precaution, Doctor. We don't need to get it right at this moment, but if you do have something we can use, I'd appreciate a call."

She handed him her business card and swallowed hard. Disler wasn't buying it. He was clearly intelligent and understood that she was trying to soft peddle the remote possibility that his wife might already be dead.

He studied her briefly, put the card in his shirt pocket, then nodded.

"If you want, I can look around right now?"

He left them seated in the living room and returned a few minutes later with a hairbrush in his hand.

"This should do just fine," said Donahue. She placed it in a clear plastic bag that she pulled from her purse.

They thanked him and promised to keep him in the loop before making their way back to their car.

Once they were settled back in their undercover unit, Donahue said, "I doubt if she's dead. Someone in Egypt would have notified the State Department if her body had turned up."

Thompson nodded in agreement as she fastened her seatbelt.

"So how do we handle this?"

"I'll give the State Department a call. They're better equipped to look into this than we are."

"Good idea, but in the meantime, should we start looking into her background?"

"Let's wait until we hear back from State. Maybe she's just having a fling or something? So there's no sense putting a lot of work into this until someone on the scene takes a read of the situation."

Thompson looked over. "If we do get around to checking her out, we should find out if she went over there alone of if somebody else went with her?"

"You mean like a co-worker? I was just thinking the same thing. A good looking guy; perhaps a business getaway to an exotic location? She wouldn't be the first."

"Are you speaking from experience, Jen?"

Donahue threw her head back and smiled.

"I'm not going to dignify that with an answer."

"So...*you have!*" Thompson had a gleam in her eye. "Who was it? Wait! I know! That Lieutenant we met at the Homicide conference in Las Vegas? The one from New Orleans? You remember, his first name was Rocco but we started calling him *Lieutenant Dan* because he looked like that actor from *Forrest Gump!*" She laughed. "I'm right, aren't I? I'll bet you hooked up with him the night I went to see the *Cirque de Soleil*?"

"Oh, *please!* You're joking, right? He wasn't my type, a total narcissist and way too full of himself."

"So you really aren't going to admit it? Even to me, your best friend?"

"You're so perceptive."

Thompson looked out the windshield and put on her sunglasses. Without looking over, she said, "Just to set the record straight, Lieutenant Dan had a particularly interesting talent that you shouldn't have missed."

Donahue's mouth dropped open.

"*Oh my god, Shari!* You didn't?"

Thompson winked.

"Sorry, Jen, but I'm not going to dignify that with an answer."

*****

THREE

ALEXANDRIA, EGYPT
DAY FIVE   10:30 AM

Dan Taylor entered the front lobby of the *Four Seasons Hotel,* in Alexandria, Egypt, and made his way to a bank of elevators that provided passage to the upper floors. It was brutally hot outside, and the coolness of the air conditioning within the hotel was a godsend.

Once inside, he used a key card to access the panel that covered the upper floors. He pushed the button for the ninth floor, and when he arrived, he made his way to a room that looked out over the front of the hotel.

He knocked softly on the door and was granted entry into the suite by a beefy agent in a dark blue suit. Several other agents were standing around, but he ignored them all. He made his way to the inner door that connected to the adjoining hotel room. He knocked again, and this time he was met by Richard Watt, age forty-six, a twenty-year veteran of the FBI.

Like old friends who had worked together before, their mutual greeting was warm.

"I came as soon as I could," Taylor said, extending his hand.

"Glad you could make it, Dan." Watt took the proffered hand. "We've got something here that might interest you?"

Watt was a good looking man with piercing blue eyes and thick black hair. His face was smooth, clean shaven, and wrinkle free. He led Taylor over to a window and away from a small group of agents who sat at a dining table where they worked on laptop computers.

Taylor glanced out the window. He would never get tired of the view of the Mediterranean Sea and the meandering coastline.

He was a tall man, almost six foot four, with dark hair, a kindly face, and a broad, warm smile. He'd been an undergrad at Princeton, majoring in political science, when he was first approached by the CIA to consider working as an analyst. He'd taken the job right after graduation but found that working ten hours a day behind a desk was something he had no interest in. He applied for a transfer to field work, and once he was accepted, he began to excel. He had a knack for recruiting agents, and before long he was assigned to work in the Middle East. After five years of field experience, including stints in Libya, Morocco, and Jordan, he was promoted to *Head of Station* in Egypt, a role that kept him out of the daily grind of the field while allowing him to oversee all of the important operations.

Taylor was single, never married, and he preferred it that way. It was all but impossible to develop a lasting relationship with his particular career, and as a realist, he supposed it was better that way. If you were going to work in the Middle East, a wife and kids could prove to be a liability.

"Angela Disler," Watt began. "Know anything about her?"

"Should I?"

"She's a genetic virologist. Made a huge discovery of some kind having to do with cancer or something like that." He shrugged. "I've been told that she's on the shortlist for a Nobel Prize in genetics."

Taylor still had no idea who she was, so Watt continued.

"She was attending a conference in this hotel that was sponsored by a group called the *Global Virus Network,* or GVN. Apparently, it's an international group set up to coordinate information on viruses." He shrugged. "Go figure? Anyway, she collapsed about a week ago out by the elevators down on the third floor. She was taken away by ambulance, and no one has seen or heard from her since."

"When did you get called in to investigate?"

"Twenty-four hours ago. We got an inquiry yesterday from the State Department after they got a call from the Los Angeles Police."

"And you've checked with all the hospitals?"

"Nothing under her name, and no Jane Doe's that fit her description."

Taylor rubbed his chin.

"Did you check with our contacts at GIS?"

Watt shook his head.

"We wanted to bring you guys on board before we notified Egyptian Intelligence."

Taylor nodded. It was a perceptive decision. These days, the Egyptian *General Intelligence Service*, often referred to as the *Mukhabarat*, was not completely trustworthy. Until they knew more about Disler's disappearance, and whether or not it might be terrorist related, it was best to keep everything close to the vest.

"I saw some cameras when I entered the hotel. Is there anything useful there?"

"We've got the digital recordings transferred onto our computers. Want to take a look?"

They made their way over to one of the computer terminals, and once the agent who'd been working on it gave up his seat, Watt called up the hotel security video.

The first image on the screen was taken from a camera that covered the lobby on the third floor. It showed a well-dressed woman coming out of the restaurant. She was stumbling and clearly intoxicated. A man followed closely behind, and just before she reached the nearest elevator, she collapsed onto the carpeted floor. The man quickly checked her breathing, then checked her neck for a pulse.

A male and female who were obviously members of the hotel security detail ran up a short time later, and after talking briefly with the man, both pulled out phones and made calls. One minute later, the elevator doors opened up, and a pair of medical attendants arrived with a portable gurney. The woman was quickly strapped on, then placed on an elevator being held on that floor by the male from hotel's security staff.

The scene then shifted to the view from the cameras on the exterior front of the hotel. An ambulance was parked there with its emergency lights flashing, and Angela Disler was rolled to the back of the ambulance and quickly placed inside. One medic climbed in with her, while the second ambulance attendant got into the driver's seat. The ambulance then drove off and out of the view of the rest of the hotel's security cameras.

In total, the tape lasted less than seven minutes from the time she collapsed until she was driven away.

Taylor rubbed his jaw again in thoughtful contemplation.

"That ambulance crew…seems to me they got there awfully fast?"

"You noticed that, too? Take a look at this."

Watt resumed playing the digital camera feed, and to Taylor's surprise, a second ambulance pulled up at the hotel five minutes after the one carrying Disler had left the property.

"So the first crew was in on it?" Taylor asked.

"Looks that way. The second crew was the one dispatched to the hotel pursuant to the calls made by hotel security."

"Who was the man that was with her?" Taylor asked.

"His name is Doctor Andre Petrov. We took a freeze frame from the video and ran it through our facial recognition program. Born in Bulgaria, he's a virologist working at an institute in *Irkutsk, Siberia.* He was here attending the virology conference as a representative of the *Ministry of Health of the Russian Federation.*"

"Did he sound the alarm when she collapsed?"

"No."

"Then who called hotel security?"

"Apparently, they were already watching the security cameras, and when she hit the floor, a heads-up security man dispatched their people on his own to see how bad it was. When she didn't immediately respond to Doctor Petrov's efforts to revive her, they made the call for an ambulance."

"Did you run the phony ambulance attendants through facial recognition?"

"We did."

"And?"

"No hits. We've sent their photos on to our allies, but so far we've heard nothing back. But take a look at this."

He started the tape again, and let it run through Angela's collapse on the floor. He pointed out the actions of Petrov who checked her pulse then looked back over his shoulder into the gathering crowd.

Watt froze the tape on a single frame.

"Watch this."

He ran the tape forward and backward, and it appeared to both men that the doctor was indeed giving a barely perceptible nod to a man in a suit who was standing just behind him.

He then froze the tape again, and using a computer program, he focused in and enlarged the face of the man in the crowd.

"He's on a cell phone," said Taylor. "Do we know who he is?"

Watt smiled. He reached for a manila envelope that was on the desk, opened it up, and took out a handful of glossy eight by tens.

"It turns out that he's an Iranian named *Ali Niroomad,* a First Colonel in the *Iranian Quds Force* and a member of a special operations unit charged with overseeing their out-of-country intelligence and direct action operations."

He handed Taylor the file photograph of Ali Niroomad.

Taylor knew the name. As the CIA station chief assigned to the Embassy in Cairo, he was familiar with most of the Iranians who were active in this region of the world.

The Quds Force was very active in Syria, providing logistical support and weapons to Bashar al-Assad's government in their attempt to crush the rebels in the country's active civil war. But their actions in Egypt had been minimal, so it surprised him that they'd been so brazen in their efforts to kidnap an American citizen.

"Any idea where Niroomad went after the woman was spirited away?"

"He got into a black SUV parked in front of the hotel. He paid the valet extra to keep it there; said he wouldn't be long. But the car had no plates, so while we could see it drive off, we have no idea how to track it down."

"And the other guy? Doctor Petrov? The Bulgarian?"

Watt handed Taylor a blown-up photo of Petrov made from the digital tape feed.

"He walked out of the hotel behind the ambulance crew, and once they drove off with Disler, he got into one of the black and orange Alexandria cabs. We got the vehicle number, and traced the trip that night down to the docks in the Port of *Ad Daerah Al Gomrokeyah,* about five kilometers from here."

"How about the ambulance that picked her up?" Taylor asked. "Any leads on that?"

"We found it, or rather what was left of it. Somebody torched it; burned down to the frame. But you'll never guess where we found it?"

"Down by the *Port of Ad Daerah*?"

Watt nodded.

"We checked with the Port authorities." He handed Taylor a photo of a cargo ship that was docked somewhere in Egypt. "Turns out there was a hundred and fifty-ton freighter berthed there that night called the *Cargo Star,* one of several to set sail that evening. It cleared the harbor at just after midnight."

Taylor studied the photograph. "Do we know where it is headed?"

"It's scheduled to deliver a cargo of food goods to the port of *Shahid-Beheshti* in *Chabahar*, Iran. But before it gets there, it's going to pick up some additional items at *Aden Port*, in Aden, Yemen."

"You're kidding?"

"Nope, and with a little digging, we discovered that the ship in question was initially called the *Vali-e Asr.* It was owned by the *Islamic Republic of Iran Shipping Lines.* The name was changed to the "Cargo Star" and re-registered in *Tuvalu*, a Polynesian Island in the South Pacific which is largely subsidized by Iran."

Taylor smiled.

"New owners in name only, huh? An Iranian attempt at obfuscation?"

"A rather feeble attempt," Watt replied with a tight grin.

"So why not just fly her out of Egypt directly to Iran or wherever they're going?"

"With the sanctions we currently have in force against Iran, the air carriers are not a viable source of transportation, so more than likely, Disler was spirited out of Egypt on that boat instead of by plane."

"What about chartered flights?" Taylor asked.

"We keep track of the charters that work in this region of the world. If they land here, we check 'em out. If they've done business with Iran in the past, they don't get to leave the ground until we're sure they're adhering to the sanctions."

Taylor smiled and clapped him on the shoulder.

"You put this all together in less than twenty-four hours?"

"I work with some really competent people."

"Well, anytime you get tired of working for the Bureau, you give me a call. Perhaps we can make it worth your while."

"I'll keep that in mind."

Taylor took a look around the room.

"Is this the room where she was staying?"

"No, we're holding it as a crime scene. It's just across the hall. We've got a forensic team in there now, looking for prints. We want to know who, if anyone, may have entered her room while she was here or shortly after she was gone."

"What happened to her belongings?"

"We've got 'em, but so far nothing of significance. But our people haven't finished with her laptop yet, so I'll let you know if something shows up."

Taylor looked at his watch, then locked eyes with Watt.

"They're gonna want you to give a presentation on this case tonight at seven p.m., which is ten a.m. stateside, eastern time zone. Type something up that can be sent to them, finish up here, then get to the secure video transmission room at our embassy in Cairo. My people and yours will have questions, so be ready with specifics."

Watt nodded once, then said, "I was afraid you were gonna say something like that."

"You know how this works, Rich. You're the guy on point, so you have to give the briefing."

Watt sighed. "Will you be there?"

"I'll try."

Taylor started for the door, then turned back around.

"Something about this isn't right, Rich. Why would the Iranians make use of a Bulgarian doctor currently working for the Russian's? Why not use their own doctor to slip her a drug, if that's what he did?"

"The Russian's have long been an economic partner with Iran," Watt told him, "so a joint operation is not out of the question. Still, I know what you mean. Why do they want her in the first place? We didn't turn up a reason yet. Maybe ransom, or maybe they just want to do a trade of some kind. I figure you guys might have a better take on that then we do?"

Taylor shrugged, then left the room.

*****

FOUR

SANTA MONICA, CALIFORNIA
DAY FIVE   11:00 AM

It almost goes without saying that *Zurich Pharmaceuticals* was head-quartered in Zurich, Switzerland, but they operated research facilities in a number of locations around the world. Angela Disler worked at their United States facility in the city of Santa Monica, California, so when the detectives were informed by the State Department that Disler's disappearance was thought to be a legitimate kidnapping, they were asked to conduct an initial interview with the Medical Director, a virologist named Darryl Lum.

Forty-eight and still unmarried, Lum was a Chinese American geneticist who completed his clinical and research fellowships in infectious diseases and tropical medicine at the *Walter Reed Army Medical Center.* He also worked for a time at the *Institute of Human Virology* (IHV) at the University of Maryland before accepting a position as a Director with Zurich Pharmaceuticals at their Santa Monica facility.

It was during his stint at the IHV that he first became aware of Angela Disler and her abilities as a researcher, so when he found himself in charge at the Santa Monica facility, his first course of action was bring her onboard.

Donahue and Thompson showed up on time for their appointment, but they were kept cooling their heels in the reception area for more than twenty minutes. When Lum finally invited them into his office, he profusely apologized, explaining that he'd been on the phone with Henrik Disler who was still beside himself with grief and worry.

Lum had clearly been affected by the phone call from Henrik. He seemed to be nervous and mildly distracted.

Donahue caught the vibe and began the interview slowly by asking about Disler's record of attendance.

"She's never missed a day," Lum told them. "She's very organized, very methodical, an excellent researcher, and a wonderful human being. I knew there was something wrong as soon as she didn't show up."

"What was the conference about?" Thompson asked.

"The conference is one that's held at various locations worldwide every other year. This time it took place in Alexandria, Egypt." Lum looked from one to the other, then smiled. "The purpose is to keep virologist around the world aware of recent discoveries being made in the field. And, of course, the potential of threats from various viral outbreaks that occur with astonishing regularity throughout the world."

He briefly closed his eyes and rubbed the bridge of his nose.

"We heard that she made an important discovery?" Donahue said.

"Angela is multi-talented. She was able to work on several projects at the same time, but the discovery you're referring to, the one that's made her famous, was the result of a compilation of two different procedures. First, she genetically altered a harmless cold virus to enable it to attach itself directly to a chemotherapy drug molecule. Then, with further genetic adjustments, she got the virus to attach itself to a particular portal on a colon tumor cell."

When Donahue and Thompson both looked lost, Lum smiled and continued.

"By piggybacking a chemotherapy drug onto the harmless virus, she was able to deliver the chemotherapy agent directly to the tumor cells, thereby allowing the chemo agent to kill the tumor cell while avoiding any damage to a patient's healthy cells."

His pride in Angela's accomplishment was evident. He was like a father bragging about a talented child.

"Think of it this way," he continued. Her accomplishment was a way to avoid the harmful side effects that usually accompany chemotherapy treatments. She deserves a Nobel prize for her work."

But his jubilant mood quickly disappeared when he remembered why they were meeting like this.

"I don't understand how the hell she could just go missing like that? She's such a wonderful person."

"We don't know, Dr. Lum," said Donahue. "But we intend to find out."

"How was the state of her marriage?" Thompson asked.

Lum looked surprised.

"It was all right so far as I know. Why do you ask?"

"Because we have to rule everything out," Thompson replied. "By any chance, did she have a boyfriend on the side?"

"Not that I'm aware of." Lum frowned and his tone became sharp. "And if you'll permit me to say so, you're barking up the wrong tree. Angela and Henrik are very much the perfect couple, and they've got two charming daughters."

"Well, as I said, Doctor, we have to eliminate every possibility so that we can focus our resources in the proper direction."

Donahue asked, "Did anyone go with her to the conference?"

"She went alone. Angela works all the time, so before she left she told me that she was going to make full use of the spa and the pool. I'm sure she planned to treat this as a mini-vacation."

Donahue closed up her notepad, got to her feet, then handed him a business card.

"Well, thank you, Doctor. If you hear anything from her, anything at all, please give us a call." Her eyes narrowed. "And, if possible, for the time being, please don't mention her disappearance to anyone. It's been our experience in these international kidnapping cases that publicity can undermine efforts to get her back."

"Kidnapped?" Lum's mouth flew open. "You think she was *kidnapped*?"

Donahue and Thompson exchanged a glance.

He didn't know.

Donahue said, "We don't know that for sure, Doctor, but it's a theory that must be considered."

****

In the car, on their way back to the station, Donahue glanced over at Thompson.

"So what are you thinking?"

"I'm thinking about lunch. You up for a little sushi?"

"That's not what I meant. But yeah, sushi would be great."

Thompson smiled.

"Let's go to *Sushi Sushi* in Beverly Hills. It's on the way back and they've got a great lunch special."

"That's fine," Donahue said, but her tone grew more serious. "But what do you think about the Disler case?"

Thompson sighed.

"The Feds think she was abducted, so I think Lum is right. There's nothing to suggest she ran off with someone, and it seems like the marriage is on solid footing, so I guess our involvement is probably over."

Donahue slowly nodded in agreement, then said, "Were you surprised that Lum didn't know that she was kidnapped?" she asked.

"Yeah, I was, especially since he says he was speaking to her husband."

She suddenly turned to face Donahue.

"*Shit!* You suppose the Feds haven't told Mr. Disler that his wife's been abducted?"

"My guess is they didn't."

"Why not? If I were in his shoes, I'd sure want to know?"

"Me too," said Donahue, with a sigh, "so I think I'll give Henrik a call." She made a show of careful deliberation. "We said we'd keep him up to speed, so I see no reason why he shouldn't be told that we were informed that his wife's been abducted. Henrik deserves to know what we know, even if it isn't much."

Thompson looked over at Donahue and cocked her head.

"Just to change the subject, and while I'm thinking about it, there's a guy I met last night at my kid's school. An attractive man, about six feet tall, one-eighty; intelligent, age appropriate, divorced, and he's got a really ass. You think you might be interested?"

Donahue glanced over.

"Setting the 'great ass' part aside, if he's all those other things, then why are you trying to pass him off?"

"Fine. Be that way. I was just trying to be helpful."

"I'm sure you were, so I'll ask again. What's wrong with him? Is he in his nineties? Have a criminal record? Unemployed? *What?*"

Thompson tried to keep a straight face.

"Did I mention he's got four kids?"

"Four?" Donahue threw her head back and laughed. "You can't be serious?"

"A ready-made family—"

"Four!" Donahue looked over and held her glance.

"Four?"

Donahue was laughing so hard that tears began to form in her eyes.

Thompson shrugged.

"So, I guess that means you're not interested?"

*****

FIVE

CAIRO, EGYPT
DAY SIX   8:00 PM

Situated on a large triangular plot of land near the Nile River, the United States Embassy in Cairo, Egypt, was a walled compound; a virtual fortress. As the largest US diplomatic physical presence in the Middle East, it served as a clearing house for information from a host of missions throughout the Arab world.

After making his way along the fourth-floor hallway, Taylor caught a security elevator and proceeded down to a basement conference room that was completely shielded from electronic eavesdropping. As he got off the elevator, he spotted Richard Watt standing alone in the hallway. He was putting the lid on a styrofoam cup of coffee from a nearby carafe that someone had thoughtfully set up for their use.

"How'd it go?" he asked Watt.

"Fine, I guess. They had a few questions, nothing earth shaking."

"Some of the Embassy staff are planning an impromptu steak fry up on the third-floor patio. You wanna stick around here for a late dinner?"

"Wish I could," Watt said with a shake of his head, "but I can't. I need to get back to Alexandria and check in with my team."

"Maybe another time, then. I'll catch up with you later."

Taylor watched him go, then entered the conference room, sealed the door behind him, and once he took a seat at the large rosewood conference table, he notified a technician in a nearby room to connect him by video conference call with an eleven a.m. meeting that was currently in progress in Langley, Virginia.

When the sixty-inch screen lit up, he could see a group of men and women who were seated around a large conference table. The location of this particular meeting was in the CIA's Operations Center.

Present at the meeting were members of the CIA's Office of Middle

ABDUCTED

East and North Africa Analysis (MENA), various members of the military's
Joint Special Operations Command (JSOC), the Federal Bureau of Investigation
(FBI), and the Central Intelligence Agency (CIA). But only two of the men
present were of real interest to Taylor. One was Hamilton Granger, age sixty-
four, Director of the CIA. He was Taylor's immediate superior. And the other
was Henry Creighton, age sixty-seven, the current director of the FBI.

"It's good to see you, Dan," Granger said. He was looking at Taylor's
image on a similar TV screen. "Before you begin your report, we've had time to
review the written report you sent to us from Richard Watt, and we just finished
listening to his verbal presentation. Please convey to him how impressed we are
with what he's accomplished in such a short time frame."

"I will," Taylor responded. He had already arranged for the delivery of
a bottle of thirty-year-old *Johnny Walker* Scotch to Watt's hotel room back in
Alexandria; a little gift he knew his friend would greatly appreciate.

"Mr. Taylor," said Creighton, "has any effort been made to determine
the current whereabouts of the *Cargo Star*?"

"Yes, sir, I've been in touch with the *Air Force Satellite Control Network*. They routinely track shipping in the Middle East. Our latest information is
that the ship is presently docked at *Aden Port,* in Aden, Yemen. It's scheduled to
sail tomorrow morning at 4:00 a.m. Aden time." He looked at his watch. "That
would be 6:00 p.m. your time."

"Is she on the ship?" Creighton asked.

"We still don't know, sir. We just learned of the ship's location this
morning, and we don't have any assets established in that port to monitor what's
been going on."

Creighton folded his arms across his chest.

"So, we don't know for sure if she was ever on that ship? Or, for that
matter, if she was taken off in the port of Aden? Is that your assessment?"

"Yes, sir. It is."

Taylor steepled his hands in front of him on the table. At this
moment in time, he thought about mentioning his intent to discuss the matter
with his opposite number in the Israeli *Mossad,* but then he thought better of it.
He had no idea who was seated around the table with the two agency directors,

25

so he decided he would wait until he could talk in private with his boss, Hamilton Granger, before bringing the subject up.

Granger cleared his throat. He glanced at the other faces around the table.

"It seems pretty clear to me that we need to search that freighter. If Disler is on board, then we can get her back and deal with the Iranians later. If she's not on the ship, then I suppose we'll need to regroup and decide what our next move is going to be."

"One small problem, Hamilton," said Creighton. "We can't search the ship while she's in port. The Yemeni government would never agree."

"Why not?" Granger locked eyes with Creighton. "We've been working closely to assist them with their *Ansar al-Sharia* problem. It seems to me a little reciprocity on their part wouldn't be too much to ask for?"

Creighton rubbed his chin.

"Well, Hamilton, I can think of a couple of reasons why they won't cooperate. For one, the Iranians are the big boys in the neighborhood, and while the Yemenis are willing to let us deal with our common enemy—the Ansar al-Sharia—they're not about to risk their tenuous financial position with a country that has no qualms about supporting terrorist groups throughout the Middle East.

"Then again, there's the question of the precedent it would set if they allowed us to search a foreign freighter in their port. Most countries would never tolerate such a practice. I know we wouldn't. So the Yemeni's will never jeopardize their income from shipping by allowing us to encroach upon their territorial integrity."

Granger realized he was right. As a former US Attorney and a short stint as Federal Judge, Creighton's role as Director of the FBI carried a lot of weight when it came to any discussion of the intricacies of international law. To demand an immediate search was an untenable proposition. He was going to have to resort to a fallback position, so he returned his attention to the television screen.

"Dan? How long would it take to mount an operation if we wait for the *Cargo Star* to reach international waters?"

Taylor thought that over for a moment.

"Well, sir, we have naval assets prepositioned in the Arabian Sea, and there's a SEAL contingent onboard the *USS Enterprise,* so I would imagine we could board the ship within the next twenty-four hours. Of course, that depends on the weather in the region and the tactical considerations that the SEALs would demand."

Granger looked around the table.

"Anyone have any problems with that?"

A lone hand came up. It was an Undersecretary from the State Department, a forty-something Princeton grad with ambitions far beyond his current station.

"Sir, if she's not onboard the ship, the Iranians will use the incident as justification for their claim that America is harassing them and that the remaining sanctions are overly broad and unwarranted. It could undermine our support with our UN coalition partners."

"The Iranians can go suck an egg," Granger said.

Surprised laughter broke out around the table, and Granger gave the young man a withering look.

"They've abducted an American citizen, son. We'll have no trouble selling our reasons for the search to our coalition partners."

He glanced over at Creighton who still had a smile on his face.

"Will you sign on, Henry?"

Creighton nodded, then said, "I'll run it by the President later this morning. He'll listen to me."

Granger thanked him, then addressed Taylor's image on the TV screen.

"In the meantime, I'll put you in charge, Dan. Call JSOC, fill them in, then get on out to the *Enterprise.* Once the President gives the okay, I'll notify the Joint Chiefs and we'll get everyone here on board."

Taylor knew that such an operation would require at least the tacit approval of the members of Congress in leadership positions. They'd be lucky if things got off the ground within twenty-four hours, but if they did get the go-ahead, he intended to be ready.

Granger looked around the table.

"Does anyone have anything else to add before we adjourn?"

Creighton coughed, then said, "I'm wondering why the Iranians and this doctor who's working for the Russians would go after Disler? From what I've been told, she's a viral geneticist who made a discovery that's going to help cancer patients."

Granger smiled tightly. There was a twinkle in his eyes.

"Perhaps the Ayatollah has been stricken with cancer?"

There was another round of laughter from around the table, and Creighton joined in.

"We should be so lucky," he finally said.

Granger nodded, pleased that his little joke had elicited such a unanimous response. Then, he said, "To be serious for a moment, Henry, this could be nothing more than a ransom attempt by a criminal element within the Quds. If it is a government sponsored operation, then my analysts believe they might be holding her as bait for a trade. Perhaps they're after concessions related to the embargo or a swap for someone we might be holding in custody."

"Are we holding someone of importance?" Creighton asked.

"The answer is yes. Several years ago we picked up a few of their agents in Thailand, and I know of almost a dozen we arrested here in the States for export violations. And let's not forget that the Iranians blame us for the disappearance of a former deputy minister, a guy named *Alireza Asgari,* who went missing in Turkey back in 2009."

"Then I guess we better hope that we find her on that freighter," Creighton said as he got to his feet.

The meeting was over.

When everyone was gone, Hamilton Granger, who had stayed behind to speak privately with Taylor, addressed him through the video screen.

"Are we clear on what you're going to do, Dan?" he asked.

"Yes, sir."

Taylor then put forth his proposal to make contact with the Israelis to see if they could be of assistance.

Granger thought it over.

"That's an excellent suggestion, Dan. Their sources are far more extensive than ours, and I'm sure I don't need to remind you that if they do end up helping us out, there will be a *quid pro quo* down the line. So be mindful of what you agree to do for them in exchange for any offer of help."

Taylor smiled. "So I guess you don't want me to agree to support the Prime Minister's position on settlement expansion?"

Granger laughed.

"That's what I've always admired about you, Dan. You always get it."

He gathered up his notes which were on the table in front to of him, then said, "Anything else before I go?"

"Yes, sir, there is. Is there anything we haven't been told about this Disler woman?"

"I'm afraid I don't understand the question?" Granger said. He stifled a yawn. "What are you asking?"

"It's just that it doesn't make sense for the Iranian government to snatch a civilian of ours in a foreign country when she's not connected to the current political situation. And the involvement of the Russians? That seems to me to make even less sense."

"I agree. It does seem unusual, but those people are crazy, and from time to time they like to give us a poke in the eye. They might not need a reason, Dan. Maybe they're just bored?"

He got to his feet, signaling that the meeting was over.

Taylor stared openly at the screen. Granger had not come up in the intelligence world, so his naivety was somewhat excusable. But it was hard to believe that a man in his position would ever think that the Iranians would do anything as significant as this on a whim.

"I'll let you know if I learn anything else," Taylor finally said.

*****

SIX

THE GULF OF ADEN
DAY SEVEN   5:00 AM

The two HH-60 Seahawk helicopters had been in flight for close to an hour and a half before the pilot of the first one reported that he had "eyes on the target." The Seahawks, which were modified Blackhawks used for water-based operations, were part of the *Helicopter Sea Combatant Squadron* (HSC-8), an air detachment assigned to handle the ocean-going missions of the Special Operations Forces (SOF).

On-board the helicopters were members of Naval Special Warfare Group 2, one of four teams normally based on the East Coast of the United States. This particular team, designated SEAL Team 2, was composed of a twenty man troop made up of two officers and eighteen enlisted men. They were specialists in taking down oil rigs and ships at sea. They had been tasked with securing and searching the *Cargo Star,* and since the ship had just entered international waters, the risk of provoking a major political incident was now dramatically reduced.

When the two-minute warning was given, the SEAL's began their final preparations. The two doors were pulled open, weapons and radios were checked, helmets adjusted, and night vision goggles were slipped into place. Words were unnecessary. The ritual was routine.

The sky was cloudless but dark and the seas were relatively calm. The weather was cooperating nicely with the overall mission plan.

Seahawk Alpha approached the ship from the stern and came to a hover approximately thirty feet above the rear upper deck. When the pilot gave the command to go, the SEALs used ropes to rappel to the deck below. In less than twenty-seconds, the first members of the team were already moving silently across the deck and into the shadows. The first order of business was to protect themselves and the rest of the team on the helicopters, while the second important objective was to take control of the bridge.

Seahawk Beta took up station above the starboard side of the ship. From there, the crew was in a position to provide an overview to the search team, and once Alpha was finished disgorging it's boarding party, it took the overwatch position to allow Beta to take its place over the rear quarter deck where the unloading process was quickly repeated.

The men were organized into five separate four-man fire teams. The SEAL team leader, Lieutenant Commander (LC) Eric Brandlin, made his way straight to the bridge with two of his men. Upon arrival, they entered the control center and took captive the Chief Officer, the Chief Engineer, and the Third Officer—all of whom were taken by complete surprise.

The rest of the men moved swiftly through the ship, encountering little or no resistance. The Captain was located in his cabin, and twenty minutes later, when the entire crew had been rounded up, the Captain was interviewed in private while a detailed search for Angela Disler was begun in earnest.

"Captain, my name is Wycroft."

Brandlin was not about to give his real name, but the use of a pseudonym was commonly used by the men of the team to make things seem a bit more personal, thereby increasing the odds of getting the Captain to talk.

"I understand you speak English, sir. Do you know why we've boarded your ship tonight?"

The Captain slowly shook his head. An Iranian by birth, he was not a fan of his country's current form of government, but he was not about to say anything to these men until he learned exactly why they had boarded his ship.

"We're looking for a particular woman, Captain. Her name is Angela Disler. She's an American doctor who was brought on board this ship while you were berthed at the Port of *Ad Daerah, in* Alexandria."

Brandlin studied the Captain intently, assessing his reaction and looking for any telltale signs that might indicate that he was deceptive.

But the Captain had no intention of lying to these men. In fact, he visibly relaxed. He knew the woman would mean trouble for him when she was first brought on board, but it wasn't his fault. It was those bastards from the Quds. They threatened his family members in Tehran if he didn't do exactly what they told him to do.

"I believe I know who you are referring to," he finally said. "She boarded my ship in Alexandria, but she is no longer here."

Brandlin exchanged a glance with his second in command. They suspected as much, but the search would continue just the same.

"Where did she get off?" Brandlin asked.

"In Aden," he said as he looked from one to the other. "I was informed that the lady was ill. She was brought aboard in a wheelchair and put in one of our cabins. She didn't come out until we arrived in *Hodeidah.*"

"You say she was ill? Was she traveling with anyone?"

"Two male nurses and a doctor. They alternated taking care of her, but when they were off duty, they never spent any time with my crew or me. They took their meals in their cabins, and when they weren't with the woman, they spent their time separately up on deck."

"What about the lady? Did she come out of her cabin?"

"No, sir, she must have been very ill."

Brandlin frowned. He reached into a pocket on his tactical vest and pulled out a photocopy of a family photograph—one that showed Disler and her two daughters—one that he'd received directly from the State Department who, in turn, had obtained it from the LAPD.

"Is this the woman you transported?"

The Captain looked at the photograph.

"I couldn't say. When they brought her on board, she was wearing the *Hijab*, and her face was covered by the *Niqab*. When they left the ship in Yemen, they had her covered the same way, and she was in a wheelchair, so we never did get to see her face."

"Are you saying that she was dressed like a conservative Muslim woman?"

The Captain nodded.

"Then what makes you believe it was the American if you never got a look at her face?"

"There was only one woman who boarded the ship in Alexandria, so I assume that's the one you've been asking about."

Brandlin tried to keep the frustration off his face. He'd made a mistake by telling the Captain that it was Disler who had boarded the ship in Alexandria. Since the man had never seen her face, Disler's presence on the ship was still uncertain.

There had to be another way to get confirmation.

He showed the Captain a photograph of Ali Niroomad. "Is this one of the men who was with her?"

The Captain looked at the new photograph and began to sweat. This was the man who had threatened his family to get his cooperation. His hand began to shake. If he identified this man, there would be repercussions.

Brandlin could immediately sense that the Captain had recognized Niroomad. The man was clearly afraid, his hands were shaking, and he sensed that he had likely been forced to take her onboard the ship against his will.

"I know that you know him, Captain," Brandlin said. "I can see it on your face. Was he one of the two men who traveled with the woman?"

The Captain looked with pleading eyes from one to the other. He didn't want to answer directly, but he really didn't have a choice.

"He looks like the man who was with her when she came on board, but I can't be certain. He got off before we sailed. I only saw him once, and that was only for a few short moments."

That was enough for Brandlin. He could push the Captain, even threaten him with harm, but for what purpose? He was clearly terrified, which meant that he knew that Niroomad was directly connected to the Quds.

In that situation, who wouldn't be afraid to talk?

The interrogation continued for another twenty minutes, but it produced no further useful information. The Captain had no idea what the plan was for the woman, or whether or not she was headed to a destination that was outside the country of Yemen. Brandlin turned to go, then remembered the third photograph he had in his pocket.

He pulled it out and showed it to the captain. It was a grainy blowup of the face of the man who claimed to be a doctor when Disler collapsed.

"I know this man," the Captain said. "He's a doctor. He came on board with the woman and the two male nurses, but he also got off in Aden."

Brandlin had the confirmation that he wanted. The Captain had just identified Andre Petrov, the Bulgarian doctor.

He left the Captain confined to his cabin and proceeded with one of his men to the stateroom where Angela Disler had been held against her will.

It was small, cramped, and contained four bunks. There was barely any room to move around.

His team had finished their search of the ship, which confirmed that she was not onboard, and a forensic unit had searched her cabin, but even though they'd printed every likely surface, no lifts of any kind were obtained.

The cabin had been thoroughly wiped down.

He went up to the upper deck, and using his *Silynx Communications* headset, he placed a satellite call to his boss, Navy Commander Terry Lawson, who was based on the *USS Enterprise,* now on station far out in the Gulf of Aden.

"Echo Two-One Actual, this is Echo Two-Six, over…"

By using the term "Actual," he was requesting to speak directly to his Commanding Officer and not to the person manning the radio communication.

Lawson, who was seated at a communications console on the USS Enterprise, quickly responded.

"Echo Two-One Actual, over…"

"Two-One Actual, the package was offloaded three days ago at the port of Hodeidah. ID is circumstantial but ninety percent conclusive. Three male escorts handled the off-load. One, a Bulgarian doctor, was positively ID'd. We have an ID on target, but he did not sail with the ship from Alexandria. Situation contained. No casualties. Returning to base. Over…"

"Echo Two-Six affirmative. Echo Two-One Actual…over and out."

****

Commander Terry Lawson, a career officer and graduate of the Naval Academy, whose call sign was "Echo Two-One Actual," turned in his seat to face Dan Taylor who was sitting nearby at an old, metal desk.

Taylor had flown out to the carrier five hours earlier to be present during the SEAL operation.

"She was taken off in Aden, Dan. Looks to me like you Agency boys are gonna have your work cut out for you."

Taylor stretched.

"At least your man got an ID on Niroomad back in Alexandria, so the chances are good it was her. But you're right. We seem to be one step behind these bastards. We need to catch a break."

"The team will be back here at 07:30 ZULU Time. Do you want to attend the debriefing?"

As a former Marine, Taylor understood that ZULU meant Greenwich Mean Time (GMT). When it came to operational matters, because events could occur in multiple time zones, and to avoid the resultant confusion, GMT was the standard for all military personnel no matter where they were in the world.

Taylor studied his watch and made the time conversion. They would be back on board the ship at 10:30 am. He nodded. It wouldn't hurt to get a first-hand account from the men who'd been on the scene.

But he was dead on his feet, and his mouth tasted like crap from drinking too much coffee in an aborted effort to deal with all the time zones he'd flown through on his way to the *Enterprise*. He briefly reviewed his present situation, then slowly got to his feet.

"I'm gonna catch a nap. Have someone wake me when the boys are ten minutes out." And then, as an afterthought, he added, "And if you can get me a fast ride to Tel Aviv right after the briefing, I'd be much obliged."

Lawson shot him a smile.

"You're in luck, son. We've got a T-45A/C Goshawk on board; a jet two seater. You won't have to ride in the pilot's lap."

Taylor grinned.

"Sign me up."

*****

SEVEN

JERUSALEM, ISRAEL
DAY 7   5:00 PM

The white Jerusalem taxi pulled up at the Lions Gate on the eastern perimeter of the Old City of Jerusalem. Dan Taylor climbed out of the backseat, paid the driver, then passed through the gate on his way to the Western Wall. Along the way, he paid careful attention to the people around him. He was still early for his meeting, so several times he doubled back, making carefully planned detours through narrow alleys filled with the usual assortment of shops —from foodstuffs to antiquities—all the while scanning the area to see if he could detect any surveillance. When he was finally convinced that he was not being followed, he made his way to the Temple Mount, arriving at the large plaza in the Jewish Quarter, the portion that fronted the Wailing Wall.

It was unseasonably warm, and the plaza was filled with tourists. They arrived by the busload, and like little ducklings following their mothers, they lined up behind the tour guides to listen to the history of the temple and it's later destruction.

To blend in with the tourists, Taylor was wearing a pair of cargo shorts, a short sleeve button shirt—which was stuck to his back by perspiration—short white socks and a pair of Nike tennis shoes. On his head he wore a green safari hat and a pair of dark aviator sunglasses.

In any major US city he would have stuck out like a sore thumb, but because this was Jerusalem, he looked like any other tourist from any one of a dozen western European countries.

He bought an ice cream from a vendor in a nearby shop, one that fronted on the plaza, then made his way over to a bench, on of many made available to tired tourists who were having trouble dealing with the heat. Once he was seated, he studied the crowd of several thousand again, looking for stragglers or anyone else who might be paying him particular attention.

He noted the heavily armed military and local police who moved through the plaza in groups of twos and threes. They were on the lookout for terrorists, but also to ensure the protection of the tourists should a dispute break out among the many competing religious groups who used the plaza as a conduit to get to the various Christian, Jewish and Muslim holy sites that made up the bulk of the Old City.

The plaza itself, in front of the wall, was divided into two sections: one for Jewish women and one for Jewish men.

He finished his ice cream and was looking for a place to dump the stick and his paper napkin when he spied a particular tour group arriving at the plaza. Led by a young man in his early thirties, the group consisted of about forty people, all obviously from the United States. Most of them were stopping along the way to snap pictures of the wall and the surroundings while ignoring the tour guides efforts to keep them all together.

The group he was interested in stopped in the center of the plaza, and he watched as the tour guide gave his charges a small presentation, occasionally pointing out certain features of the wall. A minute or two later, he looked at his watch and informed the group that they would have thirty minutes to look around before meeting him back in the center of the plaza.

The group soon scattered into smaller contingents, moving off in a myriad of directions. The guide wiped at his brow with a handkerchief, then slowly made his way over to the Western Wall before passing through a stone archway in the corner of the plaza that led into a building attached to the wall that was exclusively reserved for men of the Jewish faith.

Taylor made his way over to the archway, covered his head with a *Yamaka* that he obtained from a box made available to tourists, and went inside.

He was immediately struck by how cool the air was inside the building. The large stones that made up the walls of the first room kept out the heat of the day, and the movement of cooling air, subtle as it was, meant that the room he entered had access to the excavated tunnels that ran underground along the edge of the wall.

He saw the guide standing next to a door that led into an even smaller room. He walked past several Orthodox rabbis who were praying near sections of the wailing wall that were exposed and accessible, then followed the guide into the smaller room. It was lit by a single lightbulb, and once the door was closed behind him, they greeted each other like brothers.

"It's good to see you again, Dan," said Mordecai Ben-Gurion. "However, you must let me take you to a tailor friend of mine who can provide you with something more stylish to wear."

"Ah, Morty, you just don't understand the meaning of disguise."

Taylor gave him a hug, then Mordecai led him over to a nearby table where both men quickly sat down.

"I know you're working today, so I'll get right to the point." Taylor leaned forward and lowered his voice. "We need your help."

"Is this an official request?" Mordecai asked.

Taylor nodded.

"We're trying to locate someone; a first Colonel in the Iranian Quds named Ali Niroomad. Ever hear of him?"

As an Intelligence Officer with the Mossad, Mordecai had at least a passing knowledge of most of the senior players and field operatives in The Ministry of Intelligence of the Islamic Republic of Iran, (VAJA).

Mordecai had grown up in Tel Aviv, done his compulsory military service with a border patrol unit before being recruited into the Mossad for his ability with languages. Of Eastern European lineage, he discovered at an early age that he had a natural ability with words. In addition to Hebrew and English, he became fluent in Arabic by the age of ten. A word from his rabbi to a friend in the intelligence circles first brought him to the attention of the Mossad. They met with his parents, encouraged a broadening of his remarkable talent, and by the time he was of age for his compulsory military service, he spoke half a dozen middle eastern languages.

He was tall, lean, and strong as an ox. His tan skin, dark eyes, and black hair enabled him to blend in with almost any of the numerous Middle Eastern populations. The military used him to work the borders where he cultivated informal relationships with members of the neighboring military services.

He spent a year along the frontier with Egypt; then he did a stint in the Golan Heights at an outpost that overlooked the Syrian border. But his most useful contacts were made during a two-year period when he worked with the

Jordanian Intelligence Service. His ability with various languages enabled him to work closely with them during tracking operations against the many nomadic Bedouin tribes who traveled freely through the Negev desert on drug smuggling routes that were centuries old.

He then joined the Mossad, and after extensive training, he spent two years working undercover while stationed in Tehran. After that, he was brought back to Jerusalem to work as a tour guide. It was a front for his work as a handler, and it enabled him to maintain a plausible connection to his many foreign operatives, while he moved without suspicion throughout the state of Israel.

Mordecai's motivation for staying in the intelligence service was not complicated. He wanted the state of Israel to be around for his children and all future generations.

"Why do you want him?" Mordecai asked.

"That's confidential, Morty."

Mordecai shook his head.

"We don't work that way, Dan, but you already know that." He smiled broadly. "So now that you've given me the official party line let's discuss this matter as friends."

Taylor had played this little game with Mordecai before, and the result was always the same. The Agency took the position that intelligence was currency and should not be given out without a quid pro quo. It was incumbent upon him to try and get what they wanted without giving back, but that never worked with the Mossad. What little the Agency could ever develop on its own was nothing compared to what the Israeli's already knew. This was their little corner of the world, and their very survival depended on what they knew and when they knew it. It would be foolish to ever hold back, especially when he wanted to get something in return. So he smiled back, as Mordecai knew he would, and began to tell him what they knew.

He described the kidnapping of Disler at the hands of Ali Niroomad, her removal from the ship at the Port of *Hodeidah* in Aden, Yemen, and the boarding of the ship and the subsequent search of the boat in international waters by SEAL Team 2.

"Niroomad was last seen when he put her on the ship in Alexandria. We have no real assets on the ground in Yemen, so if she's there, or if he ended up joining her, we were hoping you might be in a position to help us track either one or both of them down."

"Who is this Angela Disler?" Mordecai asked. "And why do the Iranians want her?"

"To be honest, Morty, I don't know. My people say she's a possible candidate for a Nobel prize in genetics for her work on the use of viruses to deliver chemotherapy agents, so maybe they want to use her as bait for a trade? I'm told we don't know."

Mordecai nodded, but he wasn't buying in. The Americans might think that was all there was to it, but he'd made a study of the Iranians methods. An action like this was brazen. No, make that foolhardy. To kidnap a possible Nobel laureate? That didn't make any sense. If made public, the rest of the world would likely condemn the kidnapping, and in retaliation, Tehran would end up facing unified sanctions once again that would hasten the destruction of their economy.

He shook his head. They were smarter than that. To take a woman of that caliber in such a manner meant that something more important had to be a stake.

Mordecai scratched his chin in thoughtful contemplation.

"You know something, Dan? I'm wondering if maybe she got a patent for her genetic alteration of the virus cell?"

"What difference would that make?" Taylor asked.

"If her alteration created a new cell to carry chemo, she could get a patent on the genome. She'd own it. And if drug makers want to use her transporting cells, they would have to pay her royalties."

"You think it could be something as simple as that?" Taylor asked.

"Why not? There's probably a lot of money at stake for anyone holding the patent for such an important breakthrough technique. That's something the Iranians would be interested in."

"You might be right," said Taylor, now warming up to Mordecai's theory. "I'll run that by my folks at Langley and see what they have to say."

Mordecai nodded. He intended to run it by his people as well. He was sure they would want to get involved in the search for Disler, if for no other reason than to figure out why the Iranians would risk doing something so brazen.

"I'll bring up your request for assistance with Eli this evening," he said. "You staying at the usual hotel?"

Taylor nodded.

Mordecai got to his feet and shook Taylor's outstretched hand.

"There's more to this than meets the eye," he cautioned Taylor. "These Iranians...they mean to destroy both of our countries. I'll call you later at the hotel."

Mordecai checked his watch then turned on his heels and quickly left the room.

*****
EIGHT

EASTERN JERUSALEM, ISRAEL
DAY SEVEN   7:00 PM

Mordecai stepped off the city transit bus and slowly walked the two blocks to his flat on a quiet street in Eastern Jerusalem. Stopping along the way to check for surveillance, he soon satisfied himself that he was not being followed. He moved quickly into the building, climbed the stairway up to the third floor, then let himself in.

The sun was still up and the heat of the day had hardly diminished. A warm breeze blew in from the West, and the streets were full of people out socializing while they walked off the calories from their evening meals.

He checked his watch and confirmed that he was running late. He entered into his bedroom, stripped off his clothes, and donned the garb of a conservative Hasidic Jew: dark black trousers, a white shirt, and black shoes.

Once dressed, he walked over to a mirror and opened up his commercial makeup kit. Among his peers, he was a recognized expert in disguises. He darkened the skin under and around his eyes, used a spirit gum to glue a false beard to his face, and slipped on a black haired wig, complete with side curls that extended down below his cheekbones. He finished the disguise with a long, black cloth jacket called a *rekel,* and a broad-brimmed black fedora, the hallmark of a *Lubavitch Hasidim.*

Satisfied that he now looked like any other adult Orthodox Jewish male in a neighborhood of many such men who all dressed the same way, he made his way down a flight of stairs on the back of his building and out through a gate at the rear of the property to avoid the possibility of unwanted surveillance.

He walked a total of five blocks to a small neighborhood *Shul,* a house of prayer. He entered the building and walked into the main sanctuary where he was met by three large men who quickly got to their feet in protective mode. He walked up to the nearest one, gave him a smile and said,

"Levi. You don't recognize your *chaver hachi tov (best friend)?"*

Levi stared at him in confusion before the light of recognition appeared in his eyes. He started to laugh.

"Morty, you've really outdone yourself this time."

The others started to laugh while Levi gestured with his thumb to the door that led to a private reading room.

"He's waiting for you." Levi's eyes narrowed playfully. "And he's not too pleased that you're late."

Mordecai put his hands together as if he was praying, jiggled them up and down, and in his best imitation of a rabbi said, "Only ten minutes, *chaver* (friend). Give him a glass of warm milk. It will work wonders for his disposition."

The three bodyguards laughed as Mordecai entered the small reading room. In the center was a library table and six chairs on a threadbare Turkish carpet, and seated at the head of the table was Eli Ben-Jehuda, the acting director of the Mossad.

He had risen to the leadership role after thirty years in the intelligence service. He came up through the ranks, having worked in the Collections Department for more than a decade where he was tasked with many aspects of conducting espionage overseas. He did assignments under various covers, including diplomatic as well as unofficial. He ran the *Political Action and Liaison Department* for more than five years. He was responsible for coordinating actions with allied foreign intelligence services and with nations that had no regular diplomatic relations with the state of Israel. He was a natural leader; intelligent, quick of wit, and deadly serious when it came to issues of security affecting his country.

He stared at the man who entered the room, then started to laugh.

"You kept me waiting, *bubby,* but now I see why. It must have taken you quite a while to put on that getup?"

"Not so long, Eli. I wanted to try it out on you first before I use it in public."

Eli gave him an admiring look.

"Well, you had me fooled. But let's get down to business. I'm late for another meeting. What did you want to see me about?"

Mordecai took a seat at the table and proceeded to tell him about his meeting with Dan Taylor. He covered the kidnapping of Angela Disler, the involvement of Ali Niroomad, the tracking and boarding of the *Cargo Star,* and the formal request for help in locating either Disler or Ali Niroomad.

Eli listened quietly, all the time assessing the information he was being given while noting the questions he needed to have answered. When Morty finished, Eli leaned back in his chair, folded his arms across his chest, and sighed heavily.

"The Americans have committed a lot of resources to get this lady doctor back. What do we know about her?"

"She's a medical doctor," said Mordecai with a shrug."A genetic virologist. Taylor told me that she's being mentioned for a possible Nobel prize. Something about using an inert virus to deliver chemotherapy directly to tumors."

"Nothing more?"

"Taylor says that's all he knows, but if there is something more, they haven't let him know what it is."

"Very strange? What do you suppose the Iranians know that the Americans aren't saying?"

Not waiting for an answer, Eli pulled out a satellite telephone, one that had a built-in signal scrambler. He made a quick call, mentioned a few names, then hung up the phone and placed it on the table.

Mordecai studied his boss for a moment, then smiled.

"You're looking thinner, Eli. Have you been working out?"

Eli frowned. He was seriously overweight, had been for years, and probably would be for the rest of his life. His weight was a sensitive issue, and while he knew that Mordecai was just offering encouragement, he had no plans to make it a topic of conversation.

"Are you still seeing the nurse? What was her name? The one with the long curly hair and the beautiful smile who worked at Hadassah Medical Center?"

"Are you referring to Rachael?" Mordecai asked.

"You were seeing more than one nurse?"

Mordecai shook his head. He knew Eli was getting back at him for having brought up the topic of weight. It was a tit-for-tat, and Eli was going to remind him that his social life was once again the subject of a modern Greek tragedy.

"We broke up almost a month ago, Eli, but of course, you already knew that, didn't you?"

"I heard something like that." Eli shrugged. "Too bad, she was very beautiful."

Mordecai shrugged. What could he say? Rachael was stunning and special, but she hadn't been thrilled by his choice of careers. All she knew about him was that he worked as a tour guide, and she had hoped, no *demanded,* that he aspire to be something more. And while he wanted to tell her about his real profession, he was forbidden to do so until the relationship was firmly cast in stone. So he kept her in the dark, she'd given him an ultimatum, and when nothing changed, she told him good-bye.

He thought about telling the Old Man the truth, but before he could speak, Eli's phone began to ring.

Eli answered it quickly, listened for a while, then thanked the caller before hanging up.

He returned his attention to Mordecai.

"Niroomad flew to Aden five days ago from Alexandria on a false passport."

Mordecai was not surprised. Israel's human intelligence gathering had expanded dramatically over the last decade, and monitoring the activities of known foreign intelligence agents, particularly when they moved about in other Arab countries, had become a top intelligence priority.

"Do we still have him under surveillance?" Mordecai asked.

"He's being watched, but not by our people. We passed him off to the Jordanian's who have the necessary assets on the ground in Yemen."

Mordecai smiled. Taylor would be pleased.

"So, I should tell the Americans?"

Eli nodded, then leaned forward and lowered his voice.

"I want you to pass him on to your friend in Jordan. It's time they met, and I'm sure the Jordanian's will welcome the introduction."

Mordecai got to his feet.

"I'll set it up."

"Hold on." Eli studied him for a moment. "Inform the Americans that in exchange for the introduction, we insist on being kept in the loop. I want you to be an integral part of any operation. There's more going on here than meets the eye, and since this is happening in our backyard, I want to know what it's all about?"

Mordecai nodded and smiled to himself. He was getting bored with guiding tours and would welcome a chance to get back in the field.

"I'll do my best to keep you informed. Is there anything else before I go?"

Eli nodded, then pointed with his finger.

"Give that girl Rachel another chance. I know she's too good for you, but if she has a weak moment, and if you tell her the truth about your profession, she just might agree to take you back."

Mordecai was speechless. All he could do was stare, open-mouthed, until Eli waived him to go.

As he left the *shul*, he shook his head. The Old Man's sources and his ability to learn all about one's personal life was remarkable, as was the tacit permission he'd just been given to tell Rachael about his work for the government.

This had certainly been an interesting day.

*****

NINE

BETHLEHEM,
THE PALESTINIAN TERRITORIES
DAY NINE   2:00 PM

Bashir Harb, known as "Bryan" to his family and his American friends, slowly sipped his double shot of espresso while he poured over the headline stories in an issue of *Al-Ay yam*, a Palestinian Arabic newspaper, one of three local dailies that covered events both within and outside of the Palestinian territories. All three led off with the latest clashes between Israeli soldiers and demonstrators who were protesting a recent Israeli decision to resume the building of settlements in territories claimed by the Palestinians as part of their plans for a Palestinian State.

Periodically, he raised his eyes and looked around, carefully noting those who came in and out of the coffee shop.

This was part of his usual routine. He'd been coming to this particular location for the better part of a year. The attraction for him was a small group of Palestinian men, all retired from business or the military, and all still connected through friends to elements of the PLO and Hamas. From what he'd come to learn, these men had been gathering together every afternoon for at least the past several years to drink coffee and sample the sugary pastries that were baked fresh each day by the owner's wife.

A chance remark in this very shop uttered more than a year ago by one of the men and overheard by Bryan while he was standing in line, caused him to come back several days later and with even greater frequency shortly after that. As a group, these men had turned out to be particularly well informed about the ongoing *intifada*. During their daily discussions, which Bryan would casually overhear, they often tried to impress each other—as old men are inclined to do—by occasionally disclosing the names of their sources and by dropping little tidbits of inside information. It was the kind that had quickly convinced Bryan that these men were obviously knowledgeable and a veritable gold mine, full of high quality, actionable intelligence.

Bryan was Lebanese by birth but raised and educated in Connecticut when his father moved the family there to reconnect with relatives who had emigrated to the States a generation before. His father was a cook, and within a year of their arrival, and with the assistance of his already established family members, he opened up a restaurant. Ten years later, his three locations were considered to be among the best around for authentic Lebanese food.

And by that time, the entire family had become American citizens.

They were prosperous, happy, and the epitome of a true American success story.

Bryan, an only child, attended Georgetown University where he graduated from the Department of Arabic and Islamic Studies with a minor from the School of Languages. At home, the family spoke both English and Lebanese, so as part of his minor, he developed a fluency in Arabic, Hebrew, and Persian, and this brought him to the attention of the CIA.

He was introduced to a recruiter by one of his professors, but after politely turning him down, he went to work in one of his father's restaurants, fell in love with a young woman that his family approved of, and shortly after that, they became engaged.

On September 11, 2001, he was scheduled to meet his parents and his fiancee for breakfast at the *Windows on the World* atop the North Tower of the World Trade Center in New York City. But he was forced to work late at one of the families restaurants the night before, so he had failed to get up right away when his alarm clock first went off.

He was thirty minutes late and was caught up in traffic when the first plane struck the North Tower. A hundred and two minutes later, he watched from the sidewalk several blocks away when the building and everyone that he'd ever truly loved came crashing down to the street.

Twenty months later, he did his first tour of duty in Iraq as a US Marine. A sniper by training, he served in downtown *Ramadi*, often referred to by the Marines as *the most dangerous neighborhood in the most dangerous city in the world*. His kill ratio was impressive. In less than six months, he had twenty-seven confirmed kills and thirty-four other possible kills. He achieved the rank of Lance Corporal, and he had every intention of re-upping for a second tour when the CIA decided to pay him another visit.

This time he listened, and they convinced him that he could do more for his country by becoming an intelligence operative. As a further inducement, they promised him that initially, his focus would be strictly on *al-Qaeda* and the individuals responsible for the destruction of his family.

Bryan signed on and was posted to Afghanistan where he worked with a specialized group that was charged with tracking down *Ayman al-Zawahiri.* While they never found him during his tour, he did play a significant role in the capture or killing of dozens of senior terrorist figures, including the drone strike in December of 2012 in the tribal zone of North Waziristan, Pakistan, that killed *Abu Zaid al-Kuwaiti*, al-Qaeda's second in command.

After the success of that operation, he was reassigned to work in Israel. There was a growing concern about the connection between the senior leadership of Hamas and their sponsors in Tehran. The smuggling of a dirty bomb into Tel Aviv was a possible scenario, and knowing that Bryan would need substantial lead time to establish his operation, Taylor gave him the green light for operational status to get a read on Hamas before the situation turned into a full-blown crisis.

What he needed to establish was their smuggling routes, funding sources, and the names of their Iranian based handlers.

Bryan took to the assignment like a fish in water. He secured forged passports from a number of different countries, set up safe houses throughout the various Middle Eastern states, and began to establish identities for himself within each region of operation.

In the West Bank of Palestine, he was known as the successful owner of a clothing store. Everything was funded by the Agency, and while he rarely had any personal dealings with any of his store's employees, he would drop in often enough to establish believable credentials.

The group of old men that he'd been casually watching began to break up, so he redirected his attention back to the newspaper until the last one walked away from the courtyard. Then he got to his feet, ordered a tasty pistachio baklava to go, wished the cafe owner the blessings of Allah, then left the cafe and set off down the street.

It was the hottest time of the day, so many people were already in their homes taking an afternoon nap.

Bryan scanned the street, carefully noting who was out and what they were wearing. It was part of his training: he was always on guard.

He was in the city of Bethlehem, within the West Bank, in a zone that was administered by the Palestinian Authority. He wore dark jeans and a T-shirt, and on his head, he wore a black and white checked *Keffiyeh,* a traditional head-scarf that denoted an affiliation with *Fatah*. It lent him a certain air of credibili-ty, and it helped him to move freely throughout the various neighborhoods where loyalties were key to survival.

He was on his way to a restaurant on *Manger Street,* one that was known for exquisite food. It was three blocks away from the border crossing on a route that led directly to the checkpoint that existed in the Israeli-built security fence known as the *barrier wall*.

The restaurant was a gathering spot for the PLO border checkpoint sol-diers who often used it as a place to get a bite to eat before reporting for their shifts at the crossing. It was another of his eavesdrop locations, one he privately referred to as *a fishing hole*, and he was looking forward to having a great meal there when he was suddenly startled by the ringing of his cell phone.

He answered the call, listened for a few moments, then slipped it back into his pocket.

He looked at his watch.

He was going to have to hurry. He had less than an hour to pass through the checkpoint, change out of his disguise, and meet with Dan Taylor at the des-ignated rendezvous spot.

*****
TEN

JERUSALEM, ISRAEL
DAY NINE   3:00 PM

Bryan made his way up the pathway and through the entrance gate at *Yad Vashem*, the official memorial to the Jewish victims of the Holocaust, established in 1953 and built on the western slope of *Mount Herzl* on the *Mount of Remembrance* in Jerusalem. It's an exceptionally large facility, containing such sites as the Children's Memorial and the Hall of Remembrance. There is also a garden called *The Righteous Among the Nations*, a place that honors non-Jews who at great personal risk saved Jewish lives during the Holocaust.

Bryan had been to the museum on a few occasions. As a place that honored the innocent dead, he felt a strong connection because of what had happened to his family. And while the tragedy of his own loss had destroyed his faith in God, he still wanted to believe in something, and the contentment that he felt in the *Hall of Names* gave him a renewed sense of hope; that somehow his loved ones were not abandoned in the bigger scheme of existence, and that hopefully, there might be something post-death after all.

He ambled along with a large group of tourists along the public pathway through the Garden of the Righteous Among the Nations, stopping several times along the way to watch for a tail. He was dressed as a tourist in a flower print shirt and a baseball cap, and his eyes were concealed by dark glasses.

When he got to the Hall of Remembrance, he split off from the group and made his way around the side of the building to an exterior concrete stairway that led to a floor below street level. He used a key to get in, and once inside, he made his way to a small storage room that they'd used on previous occasions.

Dan Taylor was waiting for him inside the room. He had taken a seat in one of three chairs and was smoking a cigarette.

"I don't think they allow that down here," Bryan said.

Taylor nodded, but he didn't put it out.

Bryan pulled up a chair.

"You wanted to see me, sir?"

"It's Dan, Bryan. You don't have to be so formal."

"Yes, sir," he replied.

Taylor laughed. "Once a Marine, always a Marine! Is that it?"

Bryan smiled back. "I guess so, sir."

For the next twenty minutes, Taylor proceeded to tell him everything he knew about the kidnapping of Angela Disler. No notes were taken because it wasn't safe, and besides, Bryan had the uncanny ability to commit everything instantly to memory.

When Taylor finished his recitation, Bryan asked, "You think they're gonna hold her in Yemen?"

"Our analysts back home have concluded that there's an eighty percent chance they plan to move her overland and into Iran."

"Eighty percent?" Bryan smiled. "I'm not gonna even ask what kind of voodoo they had to use to come up with that number."

"My sentiment exactly, but I think we have to accept that pronouncement as our working premise."

"So why not just fly her there?"

"Two reasons. The number of flights directly into Iran is severely restricted by the sanctions. Between the other Western intelligence services, we have physical surveillance and record checks on every flight that travels there."

"Even from the Russian Republic?"

"Especially from the Russian Republic."

Bryan shifted in his seat.

"You said two reasons. What's the second?"

"We have to assume that by now they must suspect that we're looking for her. We boarded and searched that freighter of theirs, but she was already gone, so it looks as though they anticipated that we would be coming. But more importantly, if they tried to move her by air in a private plane, they'd run into the airspace restrictions imposed by our Middle Eastern allies." A slow smile spread out from the corners of his mouth. "And it's my understanding that we're tracking all flights in the region, so if they try to move her that way, we'll know."

Bryan was skeptical, but he decided not to push the point. Nevertheless, it caused his line of thinking to move forward in the obvious direction.

"So why are the Iranians and the Russians so interested in her?"

Taylor was silent for a long moment.

"To be honest, Bryan, I just don't know."

"You said she's a virologist and a geneticist? Maybe it has something to do with her work?"

"We're looking into that, but she's being considered for a Nobel prize for her work in dealing with cancer, so I think it's a stretch to believe that's the reason for their interest."

Bryan had a lot more questions that he wanted to ask, but he knew the answers would be speculative, so he looked at his watch and shifted his sitting position.

"So what'd you have in mind?"

Taylor began to answer, but his cell phone started to ring. He checked the caller ID, then answered it with a "Taylor here."

He listened for a few minutes, then hung up the cell and pursed his lips.

"Apparently, the Russians have begun discrete inquiries with Egyptian Intelligence. It seems that a doctor of theirs has gone AWOL from the virology conference."

"Petrov?" Bryan asked.

"How'd you guess?"

Bryan nodded slowly. "So he hooks up with the Iranians and goes rogue? That's a big red flag, sir."

"Maybe so, but then again, maybe it's just a ploy by the Russian's to throw us off. If they know we're looking for Disler, perhaps they're publicly trying to distance themselves from Petrov in case something goes wrong."

"Wheels within wheels." Bryan shook his head. "Doesn't thinking like that exhaust you?"

"Just keeping all the possible scenarios in mind, Bry. You'd be wise to do the same."

Taylor was right, of course. He was possibly paranoid, but he was certainly right.

"So what do you want me to do?" he asked.

"I want you to go to Aden. See what you can find out. With you in the region, if we come up with something, you'll be right there and ready to go."

"Weapons?"

"Once we know where you're bunking down, we'll see that you get what you need."

"Should I ask how you plan to accomplish that?"

"It's Yemen, Bryan. As we speak, the items you're gonna want are already in transit."

"Are our people involved?"

"My understanding is we're working on this with the Jordanians. And speaking of that, I almost forgot to tell you. You're going to be joined on this operation by an Israeli agent named Mordecai Ben-Gurion."

"I work better alone, sir."

"Not this time, Bry. The Israelis have connections and sources we could never pull together by ourselves. The request to have him join you came from no less than the head of the Mossad himself."

Taylor studied him carefully.

"As a bonus, Mordecai intends to introduce me to one of their Jordanian sources. That's an opportunity we can't pass up."

"Don't take this the wrong way, Dan, but we seem to be moving heaven and earth to find this woman, yet no one can put forward a believable reason as to why the Iranians would want to target her." He shook his head. "There's something else going on here, sir. You need to find out what it is."

"When I do, Bry, you'll be the first to know."

The two men shook hands, and Bryan made his way over to the door.

"Stay safe," Taylor whispered to his back.

*****

ELEVEN

EILAT, ISRAEL,
ON THE BORDER WITH AQABA, JORDAN
DAY TEN   9:40 AM

Mordecai stood at the front of the bus, a microphone in his hand. It was burning hot outside, nary a trace of wind, and the bus was full of American tourists on their way from the city of Elat, Israel, to the border crossing with Jordan. The plan was simple. They'd get out of the bus on the Israeli side, walk across the no man's land to the Jordanian border station, then get on a bus that is staffed by a Jordanian tour guide, one who would escort them to and from the ancient city of *Petra*. It was one of the true remaining human-made wonders of the ancient world.

"All right my friends," Morty said. "This is as far as your driver and I are allowed to go. Once you get off the bus, you're to proceed through the Israeli station, then walk on the road for about three hundred yards to the Jordanian passport control office. Once they make sure that you have the necessary visa, they'll pass you through into Aqaba. At that point, you'll be met by your Jordanian guide, her name is Maryam, and she will put you on one of their buses. She will watch over you and answer all your questions on your way to the magnificent city of Petra.

"I will see you back here later this afternoon. Please be sure to take all your belongs, and grab a bottle of water from the cooler in the front of the bus. It's going to be very hot today, close to 112 degrees in Petra—"

His announcement was interrupted with a chorus of groans.

"And even though your Jordanian bus is air conditioned, you're going to be spending quite a few hours out in the sunshine. So don't forget your hats and remember…*please…*to stay hydrated."

One of the passengers, an attractive, middle-aged African-American woman from Windsor Hills, California, raised her hand.

"Can we get drinkable water on the Jordanian side if we run out?"

Mordecai smiled.

"Of course, Ms. Meyers. They'll have everything you need to be safe and comfortable."

But she wasn't through.

"Are there bathrooms where we're going?"

Mordecai struggled to keep from laughing.

"Of course there are. You can use the one at the border station if you have to go now, and I have it on high authority that there's a bathroom on the bus. And the town just outside the ruins where you'll be getting off has a number of hotels and restaurants with sparkling clean restrooms. You'll be just fine."

The bus came to a stop and the passengers filed off, all except Dan Taylor who sat at the back of the bus in the very last row. He was dressed like a typical American tourist; a wide brim safari hat, a lightweight long sleeve shirt, and lightweight cargo pants. He wore brown lace-up hiking boots that had seen better days.

Mordecai made his way back to where Taylor was sitting and together the two of them watched as the passengers lined up at the entrance to the Israeli border station.

"I don't know how you can do this every day," Taylor said with a forced smile. "You've got a lot more patience than I have."

Mordecai grinned.

"My job is to make contacts and gather intelligence. For example, that woman who was asking all the questions? She's a prominent government prosecutor in Los Angeles. By the time she's completed this trip with us, we'll have another strong voice in support of our survival."

"I see your point, and I completely understand what a fantastic opportunity you have here for gathering useful intelligence. I'm sure Ms. Meyers will be only too happy to report to you on the state of the cleanliness of the bathrooms in Jordan."

Mordecai chuckled.

"You'd be surprised what I learn from the Americans. They notice things, and they love to talk."

He looked over at the checkpoint and realized that most of the passengers were already well on their way through the no man's land.

He turned back to Taylor.

"I think we can cross now without arousing suspicions."

They were quickly escorted through the Israeli checkpoint, thanks to a senior officer who was familiar with Mordecai's real role. They made the long walk to the Jordanian side on a long paved road that was secured on both sides with a chain link fence that was topped with six strands of barbed wire. All along the route, Taylor noted a several abandoned cement bunkers and decrepit machine gun emplacements, the remnants of a distant, troublesome past.

They walked through a sliding, waist-high guarded gate that was stretched across the road. An archway above the gate said *Welcome to Jordan,* in both English and Arabic. Mordecai led Taylor over to a whitewashed, wooden building, adjacent to the Jordanian passport control office.

When they went inside Taylor was introduced by Mordecai to the sole occupant of the room.

Saleh Refal was a director in the Jordanian General Intelligence Directorate (GID). His area of responsibility was counter-terrorism.

He was dressed in a dark blue, well-tailored Armani suit. A crisp white shirt and light gray tie completed the outfit. He wore high-end aviator sunglasses, and his dark black hair was short, neatly trimmed, and worn with a part. His light brown face was clean shaven, but the thickness of his facial hair gave him a perpetual five o'clock shadow. The room they were in was not air conditioned, but Saleh was not sweating at all.

On the other hand, Taylor was literally dripping. He pulled a handkerchief from his pocket and wiped his face.

"Let me get you some hot tea, Mr. Taylor," said Saleh. He walked over to the door and spoke to someone nearby before turning back to his guests.

"I'll tell you what," Taylor said as he wiped his brow. "I'd actually prefer a little cold water if you have it?"

Saleh smiled.

"Try the tea instead, Mr. Taylor. You'll discover that drinking hot fluids on a hot day will make you feel very much cooler." He looked over at Mordecai. "Would you care for some, too?"

Mordecai said he would, and when the tea appeared, Saleh poured three cups and passed them out.

When all three were comfortably seated in straight back wooden chairs, Mordecai opened the meeting by turning to Saleh.

"Before we begin, Saleh, Eli has asked me to inquire as to the health of your son?"

Saleh threw back his head and laughed.

Mordecai smiled. Eli told him that Saleh's child had been stricken with a cold, but as was the custom between these two men, they liked to demonstrate to each other how deep their sources were and how much they really knew.

Saleh straightened his tie and smiled politely.

"Please thank Eli and tell him that my son has recovered nicely. And while you are at it, please mention to him for me that the box of cigars he recently received from his Russian counterpart are not really from Cuba. They're knockoffs made in Panama."

Mordecai struggled to suppress a laugh. Eli was going to have a fit when he learned that his cigars were from Panama.

Saleh put down his teacup.

"Mr. Taylor, it is a pleasure to finally meet you. Your reputation for integrity is well known."

"Thank you, Mr. Refal. And you're right about the tea. I feel much cooler already."

"Please, call me Saleh. We heard about what happened in Alexandria, and Mordecai has briefed me on your subsequent efforts to find Mrs. Disler. How can we be of service to you?"

Taylor put down his tea. The small talk was over. It was time to get down to business.

"I'll be frank with you, Saleh. We do not have sufficient assets on the ground in Aden. We have learned that Ali Niroomad flew to Aden from Alexandria and that he arrived there before she did. We believe that he's the key to getting her back, and I understand from Mordecai that you have a substantial presence in Yemen, so if there's any way you can help us locate him *or her*, we will be in your debt."

Saleh lifted his cup to his lips and took another sip of the tea. When he put it down, he said, "Perhaps we can help each other out."

Here it comes, Taylor thought. *The quid pro quo.*

Saleh crossed his arms and leaned back in his chair.

"We have the information about him that you desire, however, we are not in a position to carry out an action on your behalf."

The Jordanians were perfectly capable of mounting a special operations mission, but for political reasons—perhaps the delicacy of their current relationship with the Republic of Yemen—they had already decided that in this particular situation, the American's would have to be on their own.

"That's fine," Taylor replied. "We'll be happy to handle any capture operation. We just need to know where he is."

"We have him under surveillance."

Taylor waited, but when the information was not forthcoming, he realized that Saleh was expecting him to make a similar offer to be of assistance.

"Forgive me for not asking sooner," he began, "but how can we be of service to you?"

Saleh's eyes brightened. Taylor was proving himself to be a quick learner when it came to the art of negotiating in the Middle East. He leaned forward in his chair.

"There is a Yemeni who has been meeting with Niroomad. His name is *Fahd al-Quso.* I think you know who he is, yes?"

Taylor felt his heart begin to pound. His hands became sweaty. Of course, he knew al-Quso.

He quickly nodded.

"I believe your people have been looking for him in connection with the *Cole* bombing and other terrorist acts. He is a key player in *Al Qaeda in Yemen,* the *Ansar al-Sharia.* He is a threat to you and a major irritant to us, and we would like you to take him out."

"I would like nothing better, Saleh, but for the sake of both of our countries, wouldn't it be better to take him alive? He could be an intelligence gold mine."

Saleh shook his head.

"If you take him alive, actions will be carried out to try and force you to release him. This man has a powerful reach. He needs to be killed."

What Saleh was asking for was going to require approval from the highest of levels, but he knew all about Fahd al-Quso, and he was confident that his people would sanction the hit.

Taylor nodded. He did not want to have his voice on record in case the meeting was being bugged.

Saleh nodded back.

"There is also the question of the reward. I believe your people have been offering five million dollars?"

If he was surprised by Saleh's inquiry, Taylor didn't show it. He didn't care if the man was motivated by money and not by the idea of doing what was right. It was certainly unfortunate, the Middle East was full of such men, but it was something they would have to contend with if they wanted to do business in this cultural milieu.

But surprisingly enough, he decided that the payment of this reward directly to Saleh could have an unexpected silver lining. As a senior intelligence officer in the Jordanian GID, Saleh would be putting himself in a delicate position by accepting the money. If his superiors were ever to discover what he'd done, it would cost him quite dearly. By taking the money, Saleh's actions could easily become a leverage to be exploited at sometime in the not-so-distant future.

Taylor slowly nodded his head.

"If we get him, I see no impediment to paying you the money."

"You misunderstand me, Mr. Taylor." Saleh held his hands up in protest. "I do not want the money for myself. On the contrary, once he is dead, I will send you an account number where the money can be wired. And since I know you will check on the account, I will tell you up front that it is an account that my government has established to aid the Syrian refugees who have been flooding into our country. You see, Mr. Taylor, the money will go to serve a good purpose, a sort of balancing of the scales."

Taylor smiled. Saleh had actually surprised him.

"You have yourself a deal," he said.

Saleh nodded in appreciation. He like this man. He now believed that he was someone they could trust and do business with.

Taylor pursed his lips.

"Well, now that we have got that settled, can I ask you a question, Mr. Refal?"

"Please, Mr. Taylor. Call me Saleh."

"Okay, Saleh, as long as you call me Dan. My question is this. Since you know where al-Quso is hiding out, and since he's such an irritant to your country, why don't your people just take him out?"

Saleh winked at Mordecai.

"Our friend here is about to get his second lesson in Middle East negotiations."

Mordecai laughed as Saleh shifted his gaze back to Taylor.

"Two reasons, Dan. Your President can always use another success in the war on terrorism. We owe him that much. And secondly, why should we do it when you are willing to pay us for the privilege?"

Taylor flushed, then laughed out loud. He hadn't thought of it that way. He still had a lot to learn about the art of negotiation with men like these.

"Niroomad is staying at the *Mercure Hotel* in Aden, on the shore of the Arabian Sea," said Saleh. "He's been mixing his business with pleasure. He and Fahd al-Quso have been sampling the local cuisine and the Russian prostitutes, but you'll have to hurry if you want to pick him up. In twenty-four hours he's scheduled to board a commercial flight to London."

"Thank you, Saleh. We'll do what we can to deal with our mutual problems and to help you deal with the Syrian diaspora."

"I can ask for no more."

For the next twenty minutes, Saleh provided Taylor with a contact in Aden and the details of the precise location where Niroomad was staying.

When Taylor finally crossed back over the border to Israel with Mordecai, he knew that he'd just made a very important contact within the Middle East.

For his part, Mordecai was thrilled with the way the meeting had gone, and he was surprised by how much he'd learned. He was going to have to meet again with Eli, and they were going to have to map out their strategy for staying in the loop.

*****

TWELVE

ADEN, YEMEN
DAY ELEVEN   2:00 AM Local Time, 11:00 PM GMT

Off the coast of Aden, Yemen, lying just below the horizon in international waters was the carrier *USS Enterprise* and its entourage of support vessels. At precisely 1100 Zulu, the fleet changed course to head directly into the wind.

A few moments later, two drones were launched from the deck of the Enterprise, and once they were high above the city of Aden, they went on station, patrolling the skies, endlessly searching for anything that might compromise the intended mission.

With the drones in place, two rigid hulled inflatable boats were launched from one of the carrier's support ships. The boats were a cross between rubber life rafts and high-powered speedboats. Each craft held eight Navy SEALs, and because the sea was calm that night, they moved towards their target at a speed that was just under forty-five knots.

The population of Aden was close to one million people. It lay on the eastern approach to the Red Sea. Its ancient, natural harbor, called *Front Bay,* was situated in the crater of a dormant volcano on a peninsula that was joined to the mainland by a low-lying isthmus.

On that isthmus sat the *Mecure Hotel.*

When the two fast boats were within eyesight of the shore, the engines were cut, and fourteen of the sixteen SEALs quietly slipped into the water. The swim to the beach was uneventful, and once they were on shore, their CO, Lieutenant Commander Eric Brandlin, had them strip off their wetsuits and don the extra clothing they carried that would enable them to blend in with the Yemeni population.

At 3:29 a.m. local time, one minute before the scheduled rendezvous time, a single male approached their location. Code words were exchanged, and after the male was quickly searched, he was taken to meet with Brandlin.

Asef Ahmadi was a handsome Jordanian intelligence operative. At twenty-three years old, he had been working undercover in Aden for the past two years. He welcomed this contact with the Americans, and when he was taken to Brandlin, he was quick to extend his hand.

Brandlin shook it, then asked, "Is Niroomad at the hotel?"

Ahmadi pointed to the Mecure which was several hundred yards away.

"He is in the bar on the first floor, just off the lobby. He is sharing a drink with one of my operatives, a young Russian girl who knows the score. Once you are ready, I'll give her the signal and she will walk him outside to the upper patio that overlooks the coastline on the backside of the hotel."

"What about surveillance cameras?"

Ahmadi nodded, then smiled. "My contact in the security office has been paid quite handsomely to see that they're not recording."

"You trust him?" Brandlin asked.

"I trust *her* completely."

Ahmadi smiled, and Brandlin could sense that there was more than money involved in the Jordanian's connection to the security girl. He smiled back and nodded his understanding.

"How about the Yemeni?" Brandlin asked in a whispered tone. "Is he still with Niroomad?"

"He's in the hotel, but he went to bed. He's in room 327, apparently asleep, but he has six bodyguards who are with him. They sleep next door, in 329, but two are always on guard in the hallway in front of his room."

Brandlin considered the information. They'd run through the many possible scenarios in advance, and taking him down in a guest room was one of them. But with six armed bodyguards, the odds of successfully assaulting the hotel room would be minimal and could have serious complications. He wanted to avoid collateral damage, so in all likelihood, they'd have greater success if they went with the plan designed to lure him out into the open.

But now was not the time to make that decision. At the moment, their primary target was Niroomad, and if all went well, he would soon be in their custody and they would deal with the Yemeni after that.

"You stay close to me," Brandlin said to Ahmadi. He then turned to his men, and using a hand signal, he gave them the order to move out.

****

In parallel, single file lines, the men made their way to the hotel. Each of them had a specialty, and redundancy of talent was part of the operation. As they moved through the sand along the beach, Brandlin directed his two snipers to break off from the group to proceed to a spot that overlooked the rear of the hotel.

Once the snipers were in position, the rest of the group split up into smaller teams and took up predetermined positions around the hotel grounds. First and foremost was their safety, and after that, the goal was to contain the target if he came outside.

Ahmadi remained with Brandlin, and when all of the teams were in their positions, he used his cell phone to send a coded text to the Russian girl in the bar with Niroomad.

The night was cloudless, warm, and quite dark. The quarter phase moon had already disappeared below the horizon. Security lights were placed strategically throughout the hotel grounds, but they were few and far between, and those that were near the concealed SEAL teams were quickly shot out with a pellet gun brought along precisely for that purpose.

They waited and waited for what seemed like an eternity, and Brandlin was beginning to consider the option of entering the hotel. He turned to Ahmadi and was just about to speak when Ahmadi pointed to the hotel's rear entrance.

Brandlin looked over just as a young, brunette girl with very long legs in a very short skirt came out to the upper patio, arm in arm, with an older, dark-haired male.

"That's him," Ahmadi whispered.

Brandlin watched him for a few moments before speaking softly into his radio.

"The package is out on the landing. It's a go! Hold positions until they reach the beach."

The girl led the man away from the building and toward a long staircase that went down to the sand. But the man was resisting. He wanted her without further delay. He grabbed her around the waist, pulled her close and tried to raise her skirt, but she gently resisted. When she whispered something into his ear, he smiled broadly, then let her lead him by the hand down the staircase towards the beach.

They stopped several times along the way to kiss and fondle, but when they finally reached the bottom of the stairs, a pair of SEALs, dressed as civilians, moved out of the shadows and approached them from behind.

Niroomad was clutching the girl and didn't hear them coming. He was dressed in slacks and a collarless, short sleeved shirt. He had his arms completely around the girl and was so involved in what he was doing that the SEALs were upon him before he turned around.

He was hit with the darts from a Taser, a fifty-thousand-volt jolt, and he immediately dropped like a stone. The girl stepped back, straightened her clothing, smiled at the soldiers, then made her way back up the steps and into the hotel.

A second team arrived and the designated medic gave Niroomad an injection of sedative, one guaranteed to keep him down for at least another hour. A SEAL took photos of his face and another ran a set of his fingerprints.

Brandlin and Ahmadi joined the team that was putting Niroomad onto a field stretcher. The lateness of the hour had been perfect for the mission. There was no one around and no one else came out of the hotel.

Brandlin watched as the last of the man's fingerprints were scanned and transmitted by encoded satellite to the Enterprise. In less than two minutes they had their confirmation that the man in custody was Ali Niroomad.

Brandlin gave the order to begin the withdrawal, so two SEALs picked up the stretcher and carried Niroomad down to the waterline. They were joined by six others who covered the retreat as they headed to the spot where they'd come ashore. What remained of the Team then gathered around Brandlin and Ahmadi to await a decision on the rest of the mission.

Brandlin turned to Ahmadi.

"The girl? Will she be safe?"

"She'll be on a flight to Amman first thing in the morning."

ABDUCTED

"Can we trust her?" Brandlin asked.

Ahmadi looked confused, then realized the source of Brandlin's confusion.

"You think she's a prostitute?" He shook his head. "She's GID. She's one of us."

Brandlin smiled. With an operative like her, there was no limit to the intelligence that could be gathered.

"Well, that solves our problem," he said.

Ahmadi said, "What about Fahd al-Quso? I was told that you would deal with him for us?"

Brandlin looked at his men who were gathered around. An assault on the hotel room would be quick and efficient, but there would be a level of risk to the team. On top of that, the issue of collateral damage weighed heavily. There were innocents staying in the hotel who could end up being injured or killed if everything suddenly turned to shit.

He made his decision; caution won out rather than expediency. And what the hell? Inevitably, the result would be the same.

"Here's what I want you to do, Ahmadi. Go back to the hotel. Get yourself a coffee and find a chair. No matter what you hear or see in the hotel, do not get involved and do not go outside. Stay in the hotel where you'll be safe. Don't leave until everything's over."

"How will I know when it is over?" Ahmadi asked.

"Trust me. You'll know. Just keep your ears open."

Ahmadi returned to the hotel and Brandlin turned to his men.

"Move into position while I get the okay."

Several members of the team then turned away and headed for the front of the hotel. They would take up concealed positions of surveillance where they could watch the front door and the valet parking service while others continued to cover the back.

Brandlin pulled out his encrypted satellite phone and placed a call to Terry Lawson, his CO on the Enterprise.

"Echo Two-One Actual, this is Echo Two-Six over."

Commander Lawson was quick to acknowledge the call.

"Two-One Actual, over."
"Two-One Actual, the package has been wrapped and is ready for pickup. No casualties. Requesting permission to implement Phase Two? Over."

Lawson only briefly considered the request. Pre-approval had already been given by the JSOC and the President back in DC.

He responded quickly.

"Echo Two-Six. Affirmative on implementation of Phase Two. Will contact you again when Alpha and Beta are on station. Two-One Actual out."

****

Six minutes later, Brandlin received the call.

"Echo Two-Six. This is Two-One Actual. Eyes-in-the-sky on station. Phase Two now in play. Two=One Actual. Over."
"Affirmative Two-One Actual."

One of the SEAL's who remained with Brandlin took out a cell phone, and when Brandlin finished advising the rest of the team that they were ready to proceed, he gave the SEAL a nod. The SEAL then placed a call to the hotel switchboard. In perfect Arabic, he requested to be connected to room 327.

The phone rang through and was finally answered by a very sleepy voice that responded in Arabic with a curse.

"The Americans are here!" the SEAL whispered in Arabic.

"Here?" The man, now completely awake, sat bolt upright."What are you saying? Who is this?"

"A friend," he whispered. "They came by helicopter. They are on the outskirts at the northern end of the city and they are coming for you. You must get away quickly or you will be killed."

He disconnected the call, then he and Brandlin made their way to a position of greater concealment where they could await what was coming.

Less than five minutes later, a heavily armed group of Yemeni men came running out through the front door of the hotel. They ran directly over to the valet parking lot where words were exchanged with a sleepy attendant who noticed their weapons before nervously presenting them with several sets of keys.

The group ran over to two white Toyota Land Cruisers and quickly climbed in. One behind the other, the two SUV's raced out of the lot.

From a place of concealment near the parking lot, a SEAL with the nickname of *Brown Bear* softly spoke into his headpiece.

"Target confirmed," he whispered. *"He's in the second white Toyota with four others. The lead white Toyota contains two. They're heading east on the Sahel-Abyen highway, the N4 on your map."*

****

Lawson smiled with satisfaction when Brandlin advised him that the targets were now on the move. He picked up a nearby satellite phone.

"Black Dog One. Did you copy that?"

Black Dog was the radio call sign for the Unmanned Aerial Vehicle (UAV) operations supervisor at Cannon Air Force Base in Clovis, New Mexico. Part of the 3d Special Operations Squadron (3SOS), he oversaw the five-man team that was piloting the two drones flying over the city of Aden.

Black Dog's team had been linked in by radio and video since the SEALs first arrived on the beach.

"Copy that, Echo Two-One Actual. We are tracking with video and au-dio."

The drones assigned to this particular operation were *MQ-1 Predators* which were used by the CIA for their missions in Yemen.

The Predators were known to loiter on station for as long as fourteen hours, and each one was equipped with a Multi-Spectral Targeting System, a color nose camera used by the pilot for flight control, a variable aperture day-TV camera, and an infrared camera for low light and night surveillance. A laser designator was also part of the Predator package for use in the guidance of missiles to targets.

These two particular Predators, designated by their operators as Alpha and Beta, were armed with a compliment of AGM-114 Hellfire missiles, and because of that, and with an overwhelming sense of satisfaction, Lawson relinquished control of the mission to Black Dog One.

"Black Dog One, this is Echo Two-One Actual. We are relinquishing command and control of this mission at 0100 Zulu. Gods speed Black Dog One. Two-One Actual out."

Black Dog One looked over at the five expectant faces of the members of his team.

"You heard the man," he told them. "The ball is in our court, so don't fuck it up!"

****

Lawson made his way to a satellite communications room where he joined half a dozen other senior naval officers who were there to watch the Predator's live satellite feeds. A channel had been established to monitor the radio chatter between the various members of the Black Dog team, and while the sound feed had been turned on, what was said was being drowned out by the excited conversations that were going on around him.

Lawson poured himself a cup of steaming hot black coffee and settled into a chair. His men on the ground in Aden were all accounted for and were now on their way back to the ship in their armored speedboats with Niroomad in tow, so there was nothing to worry about on that score. All that mattered now was the drone strike, and if Black Dog's team could pull it off without killing a bunch of innocent civilians, he would consider the mission a wild success.

The plan was to hit them out on the highway, once they were clear of the civilian population. Lawson glanced at the screens. Both trucks were still traveling together, and the houses along the road appeared to be getting farther apart, so he knew it was close to zero hour, the time of the attack.

He turned to a nearby Lieutenant Commander.

"John, can you turn up the audio?"

The LC walked over and turned it up, and the room immediately went silent. The lights were dimmed and the men stopped talking and took their seats.

The show was about to begin.

****

In the fire and control center at Cannon Air Force Base, Black Dog's team was focused on the images as they appeared on two large television screens. Each Predator was focused on one of the Toyota's, and using the low light sensors, they had the ability to detect body heat signatures from an altitude of just under ten thousand feet.

Because the Black Dog team was so small and because everyone was in the same room, the radio call signs were based on nicknames and transmissions were not as formal. But everything spoken now was being recorded and would later be scrutinized by senior personnel, and for that reason, they stuck to protocol for everything related to the firing sequence.

"Farm Boy to Reaper Six. My target, vehicle two, is almost clear of the city."

"Roger that Farm Boy. Drop down to five thousand. Packer Two, hold at ten thousand and give us eyes on the road ahead."

While Predator Alpha dropped down in altitude, the pilot of Predator Beta adjusted the variable aperture lens on the Predator's low light camera to bring up the landscape ahead of the two Toyota's.

Lawson studied the feed and it appeared to him that the two SUV's would reach a long and unoccupied stretch of highway in less than another two klicks. He was suddenly aware that he was holding his breath, so he forced himself to relax and breathe. The room was completely silent. Everyone knew the moment was at hand.

"Reaper Six? I'm picking up five HT's (human targets) in vehicle 2, two in the cab, three in the bed. All appear to be armed. Can you confirm?"

"Copy that Farm Boy. I also count five. Thirty-seconds 'till shoot. Packer Two, drop down to five thousand and maintain eyes on vehicle 1."

"Roger that Reaper Six."

From what he was hearing, Lawson understood that Reaper Six was the call sign for the Fire Control Operator. It was his responsibility to take the shot. Above him, in the chain of command, was Black Dog One, the failsafe voice of reason; the one with the power to cancel the kill if anything appeared amiss. He would have to weigh in at some point before any of the missiles were fired.

Lawson was glad that he didn't have to make that call. He didn't know Black Dog One personally, but the responsibility for assuring that there was no collateral damage from a high explosive drone strike was as tough a position as one could be in. Everyone in the chain of command was expecting the shot to be taken, and the pressure on Black Dog One to go with the flow would be intense. But to have the strength to call it off, if he even suspected that anything was amiss, took a special kind of person. He could only hope that Black Dog One would turn out to be that kind of man.

Lawson watched as the two Toyotas sped down the highway. They finally cleared the last building and were now passing through an agricultural zone.

"Packer Two, this is Black Dog One. Give me the eyes-on overview

once again."

Lawson breathed a sigh of relief. Black Dog One was requesting the second drone to give him a shot of the open road again so that he could look for oncoming traffic. It would be the final check before he authorized the shot.

The view on the B screen became all open road, and everything suddenly went into overdrive.

Farm Boy turned on the laser targeting sight. He lined it up on the speeding truck and held it steady. On the screen that Lawson was watching, it was a large cross-hair that was projected directly on the moving truck. The missile, when fired, would follow the beam which would take it right down to the target.

"Farm Boy to Reaper. Do you show lock on?"
"That's affirmative, Farm Boy.
"Farm Boy to Black Dog One. Reaper Six has lock on and is requesting permission to fire."

There was a final moment of radio silence.

"Black Dog One to Reaper Six. Take the shot. Repeat. Take the shot."
"Roger that Black Dog One. Confirmation received."

One moment later, he fired the missile.

"Fox One away," said Reaper Six, and Lawson was surprised by the lack of any emotion in the man's voice.

A few seconds later, as Lawson watched the screen, a crosshair on the moving truck was suddenly engulfed in a blinding flash of light. The Hellfire missile had obliterated the target and the vehicle and it's occupants vanished in a cloud of dust and smoke that concealed the devastation brought about by what could only be described as hell on earth.

There was no verbal reaction in the room. No cheers, no high five's, no slaps on the back. To the witnesses present, such a cold blooded ending of life was difficult to process by men who valued life, even when the enemy deserved it. And on top of that, it would be considered bad form to celebrate the mass killing of combatants who never had a prayer of survival.

On the other hand, Fahd al-Quso more than had it coming, so for the group at large, despite the horror of what they'd witnessed, there was a sense of satisfaction that the man had finally met his end.

But the mission wasn't yet over. They still had to deal with the lead SUV.

The camera on Predator A had once again focused on the remaining truck, and the laser targeting device was activated.

"Farm Boy to Reaper. Do you show lock on?"
"Affirmative Farm Boy."

Then, in a voice that carried no emotion, Reaper Six asked Black Dog One for permission to fire.

Black Dog One wasted no time mulling over his decision.

"Roger that Reaper Six. Take the shot. Repeat. Take the shot."

The lead Toyota had come to a stop in a ditch on the side of the road. The two occupants inside could be seen through the heat sensing optics. They appeared on the screen as solid masses of white in human form set against a cold, dark background.

Lawson watched the screen with fascination. It was as if he was looking at a video game that was playing out in real time before his eyes.

Once the terrorists grasped what had happened to the other Toyota— that the explosion that wiped it out had rained down from the sky—they jumped from the bed of the truck in an attempt to scatter in different directions.

But their efforts to run were for naught.

When the missile arrived seconds later, both of their lives came to a quick and very violent end.

*****

THIRTEEN

GULF OF ADEN,
OFF THE COAST OF YEMEN
DAY ELEVEN   7:30 AM

Ali Niroomad attempted to open his eyes. It was like coming up from the bottom of a pool of water. Everything was a blur. He tried to move his body, but it felt as if it was encased in cement. His hearing seemed to be working, but he could not understand the words being spoken around him. He knew the language was Arabic, he'd spoken it since childhood, but that had no bearing on his ability to make sense of what happened to him. He was still too far gone from the effects of the sedation to have any real comprehension of where he was or why everything felt so sluggish.

If he'd been in control of his facilities, he would have known right away that he was in a conference room aboard the USS Carrier Enterprise, and that the people around him were putting together a plan that was guaranteed to break him and force him to talk.

The extensive preparations had taken hours to set up. Four Persian speaking men from the CIA had been flown in to handle the illusion. The walls had been draped with large dirty sheets to conceal the whereabouts of this tableau. Written on the bedsheets, in drippy spray paint, were various phrases in Persian about freedom and justice, the kind of poetic rhetoric so common since the *Arab Spring* among members of the youthful Persian population.

Niroomad was seated in a straight back wooden chair. He was bound securely and his mouth was gagged. Around his neck was a hangman's noose, the rope leading high above his head, and to his immediate left was a photographic blow-up of his own face, one taken somewhere else at a much better time, but discovered and reproduced by the CIA to give credibility to their operation.

When the agent-videographer in the group completed the lighting for his set up, he stood behind the camera which was mounted on a tripod and motioned to the other three CIA agents that he was ready to begin. The room was cleared of the nonessential personnel while the men donned black bala- clavas that covered their faces so that only their eyes were showing. They then armed themselves with AK47's that were favored by terrorists throughout the world.

When the actors were suitably gathered around, the videographer framed the camera to tighten the shot. Niroomad would be at the center, sur- rounded by the three posed freedom fighters. Where the rope was secured above his head would not be a part of the shot.

When everyone was ready to begin, a doctor stepped forward, with- drew a syringe, and gave Niroomad the antidote to bring him up to full con- sciousness.

****

Lawson and Taylor were seated in the conference room. The two men were glued to one of the screens which were giving a live feed from the video being shot next door. They were getting a preview of what the rest of the world would see once the tape was released to the media.

Niroomad was now fully conscious, but he was not reacting well to the situation. He was painfully aware that he was being held captive by armed men, and while he had no idea who these terrorists were, the eventual outcome seemed to be beyond doubt. His eyes moved wildly back and forth as he tried to take in his surroundings. He shook his chair, tested his bindings, and realized once and for all that there was no way to escape. The look on his face conveyed the impression that he was completely helpless, paralyzed by fear, and complete- ly afraid of what was going to happen.

He tried to yell but the gag in his mouth made his words come out like screams. To those that would later watch the tape, it would look like just another one of the many kangaroo trials in the Middle East that would certainly end bad- ly for the focus of their hate.

One of the CIA's agents picked up a portable microphone and started to read a prepared statement in Persian, the translation of which would later run across the bottom of *Al Jazeera's* broadcast screen.

"We are The United Iranian Front for Justice. We have captured Ali Niroomad, a First Colonel in the parasitic Quds Force. While this man is purported to be responsible for organizing, training, equipping, and financing the Syrian military, he and others like him have been systematically looting the wealth of our country for their own personal use. We have questioned him and he has disclosed to us information about others within the hierarchy of the Quds who have amassed vast fortunes at the expense of the people of Iran. Among the biggest offenders is Ahmadinejad, the dog who at one time was purportedly our leader. He has been building up his personal wealth through the sale of our oil reserves on the black market.

"Niroomad has been tried by his military peers and found guilty of betraying the people of Iran. The sentence is death by hanging. Let his death serve as a warning to others in the Quds Force who steal from the people. We know who you are, and you will meet the same fate.

"Allahu Akbar."

He put down the microphone, turned to the other mock terrorists who were flanking Niroomad, and gave them a nod.

The two men released the ropes that bound Niroomad to the chair and got him to his feet. His hands were still tied to a strap that ran around his waist and his legs were crudely bound together. They held him upright while Niroomad squirmed and twisted and screamed through the gag. His eyes betrayed his fear. He was going to be hanged.

Lawson and Taylor watched with fascination as Niroomad was yanked off his feet and up into the air. In the frame of the video, he was only visible from the waist down. The impression conveyed was that he had been hung by his neck. His legs, while tied together, kicked wildly for a while, but eventually, he ceased his struggle, and at that point, the show was over and the screen went dark.

****

Lawson turned to Taylor. "So what do you think?"

"You've got me convinced, Terry. I think it's gonna work."

They walked together from the conference room down a nearby flight of metal stairs to the room where the mock hanging had taken place.

Niroomad was alive and well. He was once again seated and strapped into the same chair. Two of the members of SEAL Team 2 had just finished removing the harness from under his clothes, the one that had supported the weight of the lift when he was supposedly hanged. The harness had been wired up to a large eye hook on a metal crossbeam that allowed them to raise him without the slightest bit of strangulation, and by only showing his feet on camera, the illusion that he had met his end was completely realistic.

Other SEALs were tearing down the sheets and breaking down the set. The four supposed terrorists still wore their masks, but that was strictly for Niroomad's benefit.

Niroomad was staring wildly around the room. By now he knew he was on a ship, but he still couldn't grasp what was going on. About the only thing he did know for sure was that he was in a shitload of trouble.

Lawson looked around the room. Brandlin was standing with a small group of SEALs off to the side and some distance away. They were all armed and all were now dressed in mission fatigues.

He and Taylor walked over and Taylor introduced himself to the group. Congratulations were given all around.

Brandlin locked eyes with Taylor.

"Can I ask you a question, sir?" He pointed over at Niroomad. "What was that all about?"

Taylor smiled.

"That was Mr. Niroomad's death tape," he said, under his breath. "It's going to go out anonymously to *Al Jazeera Arabic* later this morning. That way, when he does cooperate, the Iranians won't know that he's still alive or what he's doing."

Brandlin smiled. "And on top of that, they'll be wasting a lot of time looking for a group of radicals that don't exist." He nodded to himself. "Pretty slick."

Taylor pulled Brandlin aside and lowered his voice.

"I've been intending to speak with you privately, L.C. I've been talking with Commander Lawson and he's under the impression that you might have the right stuff to work for me once your present tour is over."

Brandlin was floored. Was he actually being recruited by the CIA? Admittedly, it was just a feeler, but it was flattering none-the-less.

"Well, thank you, sir. To tell the truth, that might be something I'd be interested in."

"Good! Why don't you go with Commander Lawson upstairs to the ready room? I'm going to have a little talk with Mr. Niroomad in a couple of moments, and I can arrange to have it screened live for the two of you up there."

Taylor noticed the look of concern on Brandlin's face, then added, "It's not what you think, LC. I know there have been stories about our use of water-boarding, but that's a thing of the past. We've taken to using the *Boogie Man* approach."

Brandlin frowned in confusion.

"Sorry, sir, but I've never heard that term used that way."

"The Boogie Man, LC. No one has ever seen him, but we instinctively know from childhood that he lurks in the dark recesses of our bedroom and means to do us harm. The concept crosses all cultures, so we just tap into our subject's greatest fear."

Brandlin smiled.

"This I've got to see."

*****

As the room emptied out, Lawson led Brandlin to the ready room, leaving Taylor and Niroomad alone. When sufficient time had passed, Taylor stepped out of the shadows and walked over to Niroomad and carefully removed his gag.

"I understand you speak English, Ali. Do you know why you're here?"

Niroomad was normally a cautious man, but his fear was momentarily replaced by anger.

"There will be hell to pay for what you've done," he barked.

The two men locked eyes, but it was Niroomad who blinked first.

"I don't think so, Ali. By tomorrow your people will believe that you are dead. They will see what we want them to see, that you have been hanged by a group of Iranian dissidents who've told the world that you were corrupt and stole from the people. No one is going to be looking for you."

Niroomad squinted and tried to get his bearings.

Taylor began to pace. "That means, of course, that you belong to us, Ali. And we can do with you what we want. Has that sunk in yet?"

Niroomad struggled against his bonds, but he was strapped in tightly to the chair. He wasn't going anywhere.

Taylor smiled at his efforts.

"There are many things we want to discuss with you, Ali, but I'd like to start with the present whereabouts of Doctor Angela Disler and the reasons behind her kidnapping."

So that was it!

Niroomad almost smiled. They were looking for the woman. By telling him that now he had a bargaining chip.

"I don't know what you're talking about," he said with a sneer.

"Ali... Ali." Taylor shook his head. "Don't take that approach. We both know that once this little dance is over, you're going to cooperate and give us what we want."

Niroomad did not respond, but even though the man appeared calm and sure of himself, Taylor could tell he was dreading what was to come.

Taylor stopped in front of Niroomad and moved in as close as he could until their faces were only six inches apart. He lowered his voice to a whisper.

"Right now, you think that somehow you're going to be able to keep from telling us what we want to know." He smiled tightly, stepped back, and paused for a moment to let his words sink in.

"I understand you were once an interrogator when you were coming up in the Quds, so I'm sure you know first hand that sooner or later *everyone* breaks."

In brotherly fashion, he rested his hand on Ali's shoulder.

"I know you're having trouble coming to grips with the fact that you will soon find yourself on the receiving end of the process, instead of being the one in charge. But that's life Ali, so I'll make this as simple as I can for you by spelling out your options.

"First of all, you can tell us what we want to know right now, without coercion, in which case there just might be a chance for you to trade what you know for your *eventual* freedom. That can save you lots of grief, Ali. You should give that option some very serious consideration."

Taylor stepped back a step, then smiled tightly.

"The second and only other option is to resist giving us the truth, in which case, we will get what we want from you anyway, but you will end up paying a terrible price for your lack of cooperation."

Up to now, Niroomad had assumed all along that the hanging video would not fool his people. They would figure out soon enough what had happened, that his death had been faked, and then, through diplomatic channels, they'd find a way to get him back. But now he wasn't so sure. The Americans appear to have gone to a great deal of trouble to fake his death. If their plan worked, no one would ever come looking for him, and he'd be at their mercy until he was dead.

He tried to assess what might happen to him. The American's were no longer involved in their infamous rendition operations. Once they were exposed, they'd been forced to stop. Now they were all about playing by the rules, at least that was their public posture, so if that was the case, what's the worst that could happen? They might send him to Guantanamo Bay, where Muslim brothers were led around with hoods on their heads, confined to open air cages, and deprived of most of life's pleasures with nothing to do but pray and read the Koran. It wouldn't be fun, but if he was totally honest with himself, it might just be the best thing that could happen. He'd been going against the Prophet's teachings for quite a while now: drinking, whoring, killing, lying… the list of his sins was endless. Perhaps he could use a period of confinement to get his immortal soul back in line? If he went to Guantanamo, then sooner or later they would have to set him free.

America tended to suffer from short term memory, and they had no real stomach for prolonged oppression, so he was fairly confident that when they finally sent him home to Iran, he would be honored by his people as a national hero.

But he was letting his imagination run away with him, and he knew it. They could just as easily kill him now and no one would ever know the truth.

He swallowed hard, on the edge of real panic, when his captor's smile unnerved him even further.

"If you agree to cooperate, we will begin debriefing you within the hour. But if you choose to remain silent, then you will be put to sleep and taken to a location where you will be turned over to friends of ours—" The smile widened. "—where what will happen to you, Ali, will be beyond your wildest comprehension."

Oh, no! He's talking about extraordinary rendition!

"I promise you, Ali, we *will* get what we want."

A thin line of perspiration appeared on Ali's forehead. It was the demeanor of this man, so confident and so self-assured, that it had him realizing that he'd grossly underestimated his current situation.

"You're bluffing," he said in a shaky voice. He wanted to say more but he didn't want his captor to know how scared he really was.

"No, Ali, I'm not bluffing. Have you heard of *Al Jafr?*"

Ali had.

Al Jafr was the most infamous prison in the Middle East. Located in the Southern Jordanian desert, it was run by the Jordanian secret police, the feared *Jordanian Mukhabarat.*

The change in Ali's demeanor was quickly apparent. His pupils dilated and his breathing became rapid. His mind was conjuring up every conceivable horror story that he'd ever heard about that notorious prison. He tried to swallow, but his mouth went dry. His situation was worse than he ever imagined.

Taylor stood upright.

"I want you to think about your options. I will give you five minutes. And to be honest, it makes no difference to me what you decide to do, because in the end I'll get what I want from you...one way or another."

Taylor held up his hand, made the outline of a scissors with his fingers, then slowly gestured as if he were snipping.

Niroomad felt like throwing up. They had to be bluffing. There was no way they'd ever turn him over to the *Mukhabarat.* He'd heard stories about the castrations, done slowly, with acid, which was used first to burn off—"

No! Stop it!

He couldn't let his mind go there. It was just too awful to contemplate. But he couldn't control his thoughts, and his mind started racing again. It appeared as thought they really were going to send him to Al Jafr. This guy was as serious as a heart attack. There had to be some way out of this, but what that might be didn't quickly come to mind.

Ali was sweating profusely now. He managed to look up and lock eyes with Taylor.

"You turn me loose now, destroy that tape, and I'll tell you everything I know about the woman."

Taylor shook his head.

"Not good enough, Ali, this is not a negotiation. There are no preconditions. You will tell us everything about everything, or you'll be on your way to Jordan in twenty minutes."

"But what if I don't know the answers to everything you ask?"

"We'll discern if you're telling us the truth. Your body will give you away if you're lying. And just so you know, we have flown in a team from Jordan. They're right next door, just waiting for the chance to take you away." Taylor shook his head. "I wouldn't want to be in your shoes."

Niroomad finally relented.

"What happens if I tell you what you want to know?"

Taylor's face remained blank. He had him.

"If you tell us the truth, you'll survive. If you don't, you're going to learn what it's like to be in a place that even Allah has completely forgotten."

He stepped back, ready to end the conversation.

"I'll leave you now to gather your thoughts and to think about what I've told you. When I return, I'll need your answer. And I hope with all my heart that you do decide to cooperate. I really do, Ali. You see, we've done this before. It's our little secret. And honestly, no human being should ever have to go through what the Jordanians are going to do to someone like you."

He started for the door.

"I'll be back in five minutes for your answer. May Allah have mercy on your body and your soul."

****

Up in the ready room, in front of the closed circuit TV, Brandlin exhaled slowly. He'd been holding his breath.

What a performance!

He turned to Lawson.

"*Jesus Christ,* Sir! He's really good. When he made that scissors gesture, I swear my nuts crawled up into their secret hiding place."

"He's good, all right," Lawson replied. "Niroomad is known to be a player, so Taylor just preyed on his greatest fear."

"Do the Jordanians really do stuff like that? You know… snip a guy's balls off?"

Lawson allowed himself a grin at Brandlin's expense.

"I don't know if they do or not, LC, but right now, if I was Ali, and if my hands were free, I'd be safely clutching my junk while selling out my mother and everyone else."

Brandlin smiled sheepishly. He had moved his own hand protectively down to his package, a gesture not missed by his boss.

Lawson said, "Why don't you catch a little sleep, LC, and try not to worry. I'll make sure that the *Mukhabarat* are not lurking around in the shadows of your room."

"I'm not worried, sir. I plan to sleep with one eye open…and I'll be wearing a protective cup."

He gave Lawson a salute, smiled broadly, then smartly walked off.

*****

FOURTEEN

LOS ANGELES, CALIFORNIA
DAY ELEVEN   9:30 AM

Jennifer Donahue was seated at her desk in the Homicide squad room working on some paperwork when her partner, Shari Thompson, hung up the phone and leaned over the top of the waist-high partition.

"Captain wants to see us," she said.

"Are we next up?" Donahue asked.

Thompson, who was busy checking her lipstick in a small, gold compact mirror, said, "Not that I know of."

Donahue rolled her eyes. She had an important first dinner date set for tonight, and the last thing she wanted was to get hooked up with another major case.

She got to her feet and fell in behind Thompson who was already headed to the Captain's office.

Captain Tom Elwood was a large, formidable force on the Department. A former Marine, he was six feet four, two hundred twenty pounds, with the build of a professional athlete. On the streets, he could throw a punch with the best of them, but since first making rank, he'd left that style of policing behind.

He had a boyish face, an easy going smile, and a neatly combed head full of light brown hair. But the gray at the temples was a dead giveaway that he was older than most folks imagined. He had twenty-nine years on the job and was seriously considering pulling the pin. Because of his experience, he could leave the Department, walk away with a pension, and pick up a Chief's job in some small department. If the right opportunity came along, he'd probably take it, but for the time being, he planned to keep on doing his job.

Thompson knocked on the door and heard the Captain yell out for them to come in.

She swung open the door and the first thing she noticed was that the Captain was sitting behind his desk. In front of the desk, with his back turned to them, was an African-American male dressed in a dark blue suit.

The man got to his feet when they came through the door and shook their hands while Elwood made the introductions.

Elliot Davis was a ten year veteran of the FBI, currently assigned to the Los Angeles office. He was ruggedly built with an angular face, dark brown eyes, a clean shaven face, and ebony skin. Of Haitian background, he received his law degree from Southwestern School of Law in Los Angeles before joining the FBI.

He smiled quickly upon meeting the detectives, and when everyone was seated, Elwood leaned back in his chair.

Davis said, "A joint task force has been set up to work on the Disler kidnapping case. Because it occurred on foreign soil, it's being run out of Washington DC. I've been asked to coordinate the LA connection to the investigation."

He shifted his gaze back and forth between the two women.

"The task force is made up of the Bureau, the CIA, the State Department, and others. I understand that you folks did the initial interviews with the husband and the employer, so I thought I'd come by and get your impressions; you know, any stuff you didn't put in your report?"

"It's all in there," Donahue said, pointing with her chin towards a copy of the reports that Davis held in his hand. "The husband had no idea his wife had been kidnapped until we spoke to him the second time. He was clearly in shock and couldn't imagine why anyone would want to do that to her."

"He said they had some money in savings," Thompson added, "but not the kind of money that would make her a worthwhile target."

"We've had no word from the kidnappers," Davis said, "but at some point we expect them to make a demand."

"How'd it go down?" Donahue asked. "No one bothered to give us any details."

"I'm afraid I can't help you with that, detective. I don't have them myself. All I've been told is that the CIA feels that any leak about the kidnapping or any of its details could severely hamper our chances of getting her back."

"I can understand being worried about leaks," Donahue said, "but when we work on a case, we always try to make sure that everyone involved knows what we're facing."

Davis nodded that he understood, then shrugged.

"I wish we worked that way, but I'm just the low man on the totem pole in this investigation. I've been asked to go over the statements you took and see if the husband or the employer have anything to add."

It occurred to Donahue that Davis might be telling the truth. The federal way of doing things was built on a culture of secrecy, and while she'd seen that philosophy in action on numerous occasions, it had never occurred to her that the same secrecy rules might apply within their organization.

No wonder their investigations always took so long to come together. If the people working the cases didn't know all of the facts, how could they possibly know what questions to ask?

"Well, I wish we could tell you more, but we put everything we got into our reports," she said. "I think it's fair to say that our first impression was that she might be having a fling with someone, but the husband and her employer were both adamant that she was not that type of woman. Other than that, I don't know what else we can tell you?"

Davis nodded. He was already pretty sure that everything they knew was in the report, but it was going to take another visit with both the husband and the employer to make sure that there was nothing else that they'd neglected to say.

"Since you've already handled the initial interviews, would you consider going out to the family's home to introduce me to the husband? It would go a long way towards breaking the ice."

Donahue thought it over. In spite of her reservations about working with the Feds, the Disler family was hurting. There were two young girls without their mother and a husband who had nothing to do with her disappearance. She made up her mind. If taking Davis out there would help the transition for the family, then she would do it.

"Sure, I guess so." She looked at her watch. "We can go now if that's okay? I've got plans for later that can't be changed, but if that doesn't work for you, then we can do it sometime tomorrow?"

"Now would be okay," Davis said. "The family must be going out of their minds with worry, so if they see a united front, it might help them to cope in some way."

Donahue nodded. He was thinking about the family. Perhaps he wasn't so bad after all.

"You wanna go with us?" she said to Thompson.

"Absolutely!" She turned to Davis. "You wanna ride with us?"

"I've got my car, and since they live out near my office, I'd rather not come back downtown afterwards if I don't have to."

"Not a problem, you've got the husband's address in our report, so we'll see you out there in… say an hour?"

Davis thanked them, then made his way out of the office. Elwood asked the two of them to stay behind.

"I don't want you to get too involved in this case. It's strictly a federal operation, so introduce him to the husband and let it go at that."

"What about the employer?" Thompson asked.

Elwood shook his head.

"I can see where you two could be a help in dealing with the family, but I don't see any upside for holding his hand with her boss." He locked eyes with Thompson. "He's a big boy. He can handle that by himself."

"Suits me," said Thompson, "but I'm kinda surprised that they wanted us involved at all?"

Elwood smiled then leaned back in his chair.

"It's a task force, Shari. They love to get others to do the work so they can take all the credit later when things fall together."

Donahue smiled. It was fair to say that the Captain shared her sentiment about working with the feds.

"Well," she began, "I guess we can work with them…just as long as they don't expect us to fetch their coffees."

*****

FIFTEEN

CHEVIOT HILLS, WEST LOS ANGELES
DAY ELEVEN   10:45 AM

Jennifer Donahue pulled the Crown Vic up to the curb in front of the Disler family home in Cheviot Hills. The drive from downtown LA had been uneventful. In fact, they had breezed through traffic, arriving there in only forty-five minutes. There was no sign of Davis, so they decided to sit in the car and wait for him to show up.

The sky was gray and overcast with a thick marine layer, but according to the latest weather reports, rain was not on the horizon. Still, the temperature was hovering in the mid-sixties, and both women were wearing light-weight coats.

Donahue checked her watch.

"Relax," Thompson muttered. "We'll be out of here soon."

"We better be. I was hoping to leave a little early this afternoon. I was planning to get a Brazilian blowout on the way home."

"Your hair looks fine, kiddo," Thompson said with a wry smile. "It's a lot more important for you to make sure that your Brazilian wax job is still holding up."

Donahue rolled her eyes.

"You're impossible, Shari. It's just a first date, so that's not on the agenda."

"Don't tell me you've got an ironclad rule about not doing a man until after the third date or something ridiculous like that?"

Donahue didn't respond. Instead, she checked her watch again.

Thompson leaned against the door.

"So? Who's the guy?"

"A civil attorney, you don't know him. We met at the supermarket last week."

"You're kidding? The supermarket?" Thompson shook her head.

"You end up meeting the most interesting guys in the most unlikely places." She cracked the window and took out a cigarette. "I always end up meeting the ones that want to be lawyers or doctors. The trouble is, they barely got their GED's, and they're actually plumbers or delivery truck drivers."

"At least they're employed," said Donahue with a smile. She reached over and plucked the unlit cigarette from Thompson's fingers.

"I'm allergic to second-hand smoke," she said.

"Since when?"

"Since you said you were going to quit."

But while she spoke, Donahue was staring at a green Jeep Cherokee that was parked in the driveway of the Disler home. She picked up her portable radio and ran the license plate.

"What's happening?" Thompson asked, sitting up.

Donahue looked over and met her glance. "I don't remember seeing that car here the last time. I'm wondering if the family's got visitors?"

But the Jeep turned out to be registered to Henrik Disler, so Donahue put her radio down.

"At least he's home," she said. "We probably should've called before coming out here."

Thompson gestured down the street with her chin and Donahue followed her gaze. Davis was just pulling up to the curb in a new black Chrysler sedan.

"Right on time," Thompson said as she opened her door to get out. "I'll say one thing for the FBI. At least they get to drive decent cars."

Donahue climbed out on her side and closed the driver's door.

"I hear they're not allowed to eat in their shiny new cars, so maybe that's the tradeoff."

They met with Davis on the sidewalk, and then the three of them made their way up to the front door. Donahue rang the bell, but no one responded. She knocked a second time, but still no response.

While Thompson walked up the driveway to see if someone was out in the back yard, Donahue walked over to the living room bay window and took a look inside.

What she saw caused her pulse to quicken. The room was disheveled. There was an overturned chair, a broken vase, and a table lamp lying on the floor.

Donahue pulled her gun.

"What the hell?" said a very confused Davis. He was still standing on the porch by the front door.

"The house looks like it's been ransacked," Donahue replied. "You stay here and cover the front. I'm going to get Shari."

She ran around the side of the house leaving Davis busy scrambling to get out his gun. She found Shari returning from the back of the house.

"Something's wrong," Donahue said. "The front room has been trashed."

Thompson pulled her gun from her holster.

"Do we go in?"

Donahue nodded.

They slowly approached the back door. Donahue had her eyes focused on the nearby windows when Thompson tapped her on the shoulder.

"Is that blood?" she whispered.

Donahue followed her pointed finger and noticed what appeared to be blood drops on the cement. When she looked down the driveway, she could see other spots leading out towards the street.

"It looks dry," Thompson said. "We better call it in."

Donahue pulled her Rover off her Sam Browne belt and put out a call for backup while Thompson moved away from the door to cover the back of the house. Donahue walked back out to the front yard, told Davis what they'd found, then waited for the black and whites which pulled up two minutes later.

With uniformed officers now covering the front and back of the house, Donahue, Thompson, and Davis made entry by breaking the glass on a French door off the back patio. They cleared the downstairs first, then allowed the additional responding patrol units to take over the search upstairs. When the all clear was given, the officers huddled outside in the back.

Donahue turned to a Sergeant, the senior officer overseeing the patrol units that responded to the call for backup.

"Sarge, I think we've got a crime scene here. There's a blood trail lead-ing from the front room through the kitchen and out here towards the street. Can you get your guys to run the tape? We need to secure the entire property."

"I'll take care of it," he said. "Any idea what went on here?"

"This may be related to a kidnapping were working that occurred to another family member."

She looked around at the faces of the patrol officers who had gathered around to get instructions.

"The occupant of the home is one Henrik Disler. He has two young teenage daughters that live here too. We don't know if any or all of them are victims. All we've got at the moment are signs of a struggle and a blood trail. I'm going to get the lab out here, and I'm going to need a few teams to go door to door to see if any of the neighbors noticed or heard anything unusual?"

"Who's car is in the driveway?" the Sergeant asked.

"It's registered to Henrik Disler," she told him.

The Sergeant began handing out assignments to the patrol officers while Donahue, Thompson, and Davis returned to the street in front of the house.

Donahue put out a call for the crime lab team, then turned to the others.

"Anything else we should be doing?"

Davis nodded.

"I'm going to notify my boss who'll pass this on to the task force. I'll let you know what they have to say."

"Tell you what," said Donahue. "We're gonna be primary's on this in-vestigation, so whatever your task force decides, you clear it with me first."

"But this is related to the task force investigation—" he said, but Don-ahue cut him off.

"If that's the case, then you're gonna have to fill us in on what hap-pened in Alexandria and how that's connected to this case? Otherwise, as I see it, you have no federal nexus, and therefore, no jurisdiction to assume the role of primary."

Davis didn't respond. He walked off, ostensibly to make the notifica-tions.

Thompson turned to Donahue.

"Nexus? Really? Where'd you pick up that little gem?"

"Scrabble." Donahue smiled. "But if they think we're gonna take the case over, then they just might decide to fill us in on exactly what happened to the wife."

"How's that gonna help us with this case?"

"Look, Shari. Mom gets abducted, and now the husband and daughters go missing after a struggle and some injuries? I'm not a big believer in coincidence. It has to be related to her disappearance."

"Hold that thought," Thompson said. She turned and walked over to a citizen who was standing behind the yellow crime scene tape, waving at them to get their attention.

"Hi, there!" Thompson said as she lowered her voice. "Can I help you?"

She was speaking to a woman of about sixty: well dressed, expensive clothing; she was likely one of the neighbors.

"It might not be important, but I saw something—"

Thompson stopped her mid-sentence.

"Hold on. Come with me."

Thompson led the woman under the crime scene tape and over to an unlocked black and white unit. Once they were both in the back seat, she introduced herself to the neighbor, a woman whose name was Iris Waxman.

"So what did you see, Iris?"

"Two nights ago, about eight p.m., I was walking my dog and I noticed a van arrive at the Disler's house. Several men got out; I think three. Because of the lateness of the hour, I thought they were probably plumbers or something like that."

"Were there any markings on the van?"

"The van was white, but I don't recall seeing a company name or anything like that."

"How about the men? Can you describe them for me?"

"I'm not too sure. As I say, I thought they might be plumbers, so I didn't pay much attention."

"Well, were they white? Black? Hispanic? Any idea?"

Iris closed her eyes in an effort to recreate what she'd seen in her mind.

"I think they were Caucasians. I'm not certain, but I do know they weren't African-Americans."

Thompson smiled inwardly at the political correctness of Iris's choice of words. It had been a subtle way of correcting Thompson, and if she had to put money on it, she would guess that Iris had once been—or still was—a school teacher.

"Tell me something, Iris, did the Disler's get along okay? Any problems with the marriage?"

"Not that I was aware of. They are good neighbors and terrific parents, too. I've never heard them quarreling or anything like that."

"They have any problems you know of with any of their neighbors?"

Iris shook her head again.

"Okay, Iris." Thompson closed up her notepad. "Which house is yours?"

"I'm just a few houses up the street."

She gave Thompson her street number and other personal information, including the fact that she was a retired teacher.

Thompson smiled at that.

"Okay," she said, "I'll have an officer come by later to get a detailed statement from you. Thanks for coming forward. We'll be in touch."

After Iris had been escorted back to the area outside the crime scene tape, Thompson tracked down Donahue who had been giving directions to the head of the Crime Scene Unit who'd just pulled up in a van.

"You get anything important?" Donahue asked.

"Two things of interest. First was a subtle reminder that educated people use words like Caucasian and African-American for white and black—"

Donahue smiled.

"—and secondly, a white van showed up two nights ago with three men, likely *Caucasians,* definitely not *African-Americans.* She thought they might be plumbers because it was eight p.m. However, she doesn't recall any markings on the van."

"The blood in the house and on the driveway is dry, so that's probably about right." Donahue looked around. The neighborhood was wealthy, and large homes often meant owners with decent security systems.

"We'll need to get someone to walk the block and see if we can come up with any security cameras that might have been focused out towards the street."

"I'll set that up." Thompson glanced at her watch. "This is gonna go on for a long time, Jen. If you wanna take off, I can handle things here."

Donahue frowned. "I already called and told him that I have to cancel the date."

"How'd he take it?" Thompson asked.

"No problem, but that's what they all say the first time it happens. It's once you reach the third or fourth time that you start to get a sense of how soon it won't fly anymore."

"I hear that," Thompson replied, "which just goes to prove my point. Dump the three date rule, Jen. Otherwise, you'll never get laid."

Donahue cocked her head.

"Care to share how you arrived at that pearl of wisdom?"

"Of course. Life's too short, so don't waste any golden opportunities, 'cause you never know when the job is gonna get in the way."

"You're right, Shari," she said in a voice that was dripping with sarcasm. "I'm convinced, and if I'm ever fortunate enough to have a teenage daughter, just remind me to pass that on to her, too."

Donahue looked over the neighborhood, then sighed heavily. A hint of sadness crept into her voice.

"I'm really concerned about the Disler's daughters. I think I'll start with their schools and see if they showed up yesterday or today. I guess we can only hope that one or both are staying with friends."

Thompson nodded. "I just wish to hell we knew what this is all about. I feel like we're working in the dark."

"I feel the same way. I'll have a talk with the Captain first thing tomorrow morning. Maybe he can put some pressure on the people running the task force to let us know what the hell is really going on?"

*****

SIXTEEN

ADEN, YEMEN
7:00 PM   DAY TWELVE

Bryan made his way on foot down a dusty paved street in the Sheikh Othman district, a former oasis in Aden, Yemen. He was dressed in a long white robe, worn over a pair of new pants and a button down white shirt. His head was covered in a traditional Yemeni headscarf, and on his feet, he wore an inexpensive pair of sandals. Around his waist was a wide, decorative belt, covered in white beading, and tucked into the belt was a ceremonial curved dagger. He sported a full black beard, one that had been made especially for him shortly after a training class presented by the CIA on the use of disguises. For all intents and purposes, he could pass as a typical Yemeni male from the northern desert area.

Two nights previously, he had received a call from Taylor letting him know that Niroomad had been captured and that Fahd al-Quso, a Yemeni who was wanted for his role in the bombing of the USS Cole during a refueling stop in the harbor of Aden in October of 2000, had been killed in a drone attack. What Bryan was surprised to learn was that al-Quso had been meeting with Niroomad. It gave him his first substantial lead.

With Niroomad in custody, he could concentrate on finding Angela Disler.

The worst heat of the day had passed. It was close to the dinner hour, and many shops along the road had been closed during the afternoon. They would soon reopen again, and many of the restaurants would remain open until late in the evening.

The people of Aden were surprisingly sophisticated. In part this was due to the British occupation in the southern end of the country. They had adopted the habit of eating the dinner meal late in the evening, a custom they picked up from the Europeans. However, this tradition stood in stark contrast to the customs observed by the poorly educated and religiously conservative tribes that populated the northern and the eastern ends of the country, where meals were eaten early and people were quick to retire for the night.

He stopped along the route several times to look at the street from the reflection of store windows. He crossed the street multiple times and doubled back on occasion, all to determine if he was being followed. He checked his watch. The restaurant he was seeking would be open within the hour.

The sun was setting, but it was still quite warm outside, with a gentle breeze that offered little in the way of relief, so in spite of his overall adaptation to the climate in the Middle East, Bryan found himself beginning to break a sweat.

He crossed the street mid-block, dodging cars and motorbikes that paid him no attention. The old family restaurant he was headed to was nestled between a closed tailor shop and a small little market that stayed open all day long.

He knocked on the front door and waited a few moments until it was unlocked and he was invited in.

Once inside, the owner of the restaurant shut and bolted the door behind him, pulled down a window shade to prevent prying eyes, then turned to Bryan and offered a smile.

"Good thing you called. I wasn't planning to work this evening, but for you, I've changed my plans."

Mansoor Ali, an urban Yemeni with no tribal affiliation, was fifty-seven years old, although his weather-beaten face and long gray beard made him look considerably older. He was dressed in a light colored tunic, but without the ceremonial belt. He was relatively short, but significantly overweight, a sign among the less fortunate that he was prosperous and living well.

"*As-salamu alaykum*'" Bryan said by way of greeting.

Mansoor bowed his head slightly.

"And to you. Be at peace together with God's mercy." He smiled at Bryan. "Let us speak English. I do not get a chance to do so very often."

Bryan nodded.

"How have you been?"

"I am well." Mansoor put an arm around Bryan's shoulder. "Come, Hakim. We will go in the back and I will get us some tea."

Mansoor knew him as Hakim Al-Shaqqaf. This identity was part of a carefully constructed legend that Bryan used whenever he was in the country of Yemen. Everyone he dealt with knew him as Hakim; very few knew he worked for the CIA, but Mansoor was the rare exception. And while he suspected that Hakim was not Bryan's real name, Mansoor embraced the fiction as part of the reality of working in the world of intelligence gathering.

Bryan was taken to a small table in a back room just off the kitchen area where a full staff of people was cooking dishes in preparation for the evening crowd. Mansoor quickly disappeared, then returned a few moments later with a steaming pot of tea and two small glasses on a small tray. He poured the first cup of tea from high above the table, used it to rinse Bryan's glass, then poured it out and refilled it again, this time handing it to Bryan. He repeated the process for himself, then shut the door to give them privacy before taking a seat at the table.

The two men sipped their tea for a while, then Bryan put his cup down and started to speak.

"A few days ago, a ship called the *Cargo Star* arrived at the Port of *Hodeidah.* A rather precious item was offloaded and I am trying to track it down." He studied Mansoor. "You know anything about it?"

Mansoor smiled. He had been working with Bryan for several years and knew that the man was stingy with information. He was going to have to show patience if he wanted to get him to reveal more facts.

"There are many cargos unloaded in that port, my friend. What was the nature of the item you are seeking?"

Bryan decided on the spot that it wouldn't hurt to tell him.

"It was a woman, an American. She was taken off the ship in a wheel-chair."

"A woman?"

Mansoor ran his hand several times through his beard. He had thought the cargo Bryan was interested in might be drugs or weapons. But a woman? That was really strange.

He racked his brain to think if there was anything he'd heard that might be of assistance. The restaurant was a gathering place for wealthy Yemeni businessmen, most of them traders and importers. Mansoor had a habit of listening in when they discussed their businesses, but he had to admit to himself that he heard nothing at all about a woman in a wheelchair.

He told Bryan as much, and he could see the disappointment on his face.

He had been an informant of Bryan's for several years, the result of a chance encounter when Bryan—who made frequent trips to Aden, and who posed as a Lebanese importer pursuant to his *legend*—had entered his restaurant to grab a bite to eat.

Business was slow that night, and Mansoor had been quick to engage his customers in conversation. Bryan had watched him work the room, and he realized that the man would likely have a good measure of the pulse of the community. When Mansoor stopped at his table to inquire about Bryan's satisfaction with the meal, Bryan invited him to join him for a drink, and over the course of the next few hours, a discussion ensued that enabled Bryan to conclude that Mansoor would be amenable to a more formalized approach. And after three more such visits and many hours of conversation, a level of trust was developed, and shortly after that, Mansoor became one of Bryan's trusted informants.

Their personal friendship quickly blossomed after Bryan learned more about Mansoor's family life.

Mansoor's wife died after giving birth to their only son, a boy named *Murad*. Mansoor had raised him to adulthood by himself, and he'd seen to it that the boy received a good education in London before returning to Aden to open up an import business. But his son ran afoul of the Ansar al-Sharia, those ignorant fanatics who wanted to see life return to what it was in the Middle Ages. On a business trip to the North, Murad was kidnapped and held for ransom. But something went wrong before the ransom could be paid, and the dogs had murdered his boy.

Later, when the body was discovered, it was formally determined that the killers had subjected him to physical torture.

The group responsible was never officially identified, but Mansoor took the time to befriend individual members of the differing regional tribes in hopes of one day getting a lead on the killers. As time went on, the political situation changed again, and when the government began working with the Americans to target leaders of the Ansar al-Sharia, most of his contacts went underground.

Mansoor hated the religious fanatics. They were mostly ignorant tribesmen, hardly better than ordinary criminals. But he kept what contacts he could with members of that group, and when Bryan learned that they shared a common enemy, he recruited Mansoor with a promise that if they ever got a line on Murad's killers, he would see to it that they paid the ultimate price.

After that, the two men became fast friends.

Bryan said, "My people tell me that the man responsible for kidnapping this woman and bringing her here is a member of the Iranian Quds. She was snatched in Alexandria, and the man responsible was recently seen meeting with Fahd al-Quso, here in Aden."

Mansoor's eyes widened.

"But al-Quso was killed two days ago, out on the highway?"

Bryan nodded.

"That's what the papers say, but even if that's true, I'm thinking that the Iranians might have been planning to move her overland, hence the connection with al-Quso and the Ansar al Sharia."

Mansoor closed his eyes, deep in thought. To Bryan, he looked to be falling asleep.

He suddenly opened his eyes.

"Hmm, I wonder…?"

"What?"

"If al-Quso arranged for transportation, then I think I know what he might have done." His eyes landed on Bryan. "Three days ago, a large caravan left from the city of *Al Habilayn.* My understanding is that some of the tribes-men involved with the caravan are aligned with the Ansar al-Sharia."

Bryan liked the sound of that. It would give strength to his theory of why Niroomad might have been doing business with Fahd al-Quso.

"Any idea what route they'd be taking?"

"My guess would be that it depends on the nature of the cargo. If it's weapons or drugs, I'm sure they'll stick to the deep desert routes. If it's animals or consumer goods, they'll use the more populous routes."

"And if they've got the American with them?"

"The deep desert, for sure. Especially if she's disabled."

Bryan nodded. It made sense. He reached into the pocket of his robe and pulled out an envelope containing money which he passed across the table to Mansoor.

"That's not necessary," Mansoor told him. "We are friends, and I've done little to assist you." He made an effort to push it back, but Bryan refused to take it.

"You have given me the best lead I have, Mansoor. You've earned it."

Mansoor sighed.

"I will accept it only if you agree to let me serve you dinner."

Bryan smiled. Mansoor's restaurant was one of the best in Aden.

"Are you serving *saltah* tonight?" he asked. It was a national dish of browned stew meat, chili peppers, tomatoes, garlic and herbs ground into a salsa.

Mansoor smiled and winked.

"You know we are. God willing you brought your appetite, Hakim, for tonight you will feast!"

As Mansoor left for the kitchen, Bryan began to contemplate his next move.

*****

SEVENTEEN

RESTON, VIRGINIA
DAY TWELVE   9:00 AM

Dan Taylor came out of a basement room in a CIA safe house in Reston, Virginia, and quietly closed the door behind him. He walked down the hallway, climbed the stairs, then walked into the library where he was able to get a satellite signal for his encrypted phone.

The safe house was nestled in the middle of fifteen forested acres. The nearest neighboring homes were far off in the distance, which afforded those who used the location complete isolation and guaranteed secrecy.

A winter storm arrived with the jet stream, bringing snow to the eastern seaboard, and outside the safe house, the grounds were covered with almost half a foot of fresh powder. When he last looked at the outdoor thermometer, it was twenty-nine degrees, so there was little chance that the pesky snow would be melting anytime soon.

Taylor punched in the number, listened while it rang several times, then heard the click as the call was answered.

"Granger here," said the Director of the CIA. He was seated at his desk in the headquarters building in Langley, Virginia.

"Niroomad has broken."

"That's excellent, Dan! Congratulations!"

Taylor squinted and pinched his nose.

"He's admitted that he was responsible for orchestrating the snatch of Disler from Alexandria and putting her on the boat. He flew ahead to Aden where Disler was taken off to be transported across the Yemeni desert."

Granger leaned forward and put his elbows on his desk, resting his head in his free hand.

"Did he tell us where they plan to take her?"

"Yes, sir! They're taking her to Iran."

"Did he say where in Iran?"

"He said he doesn't know specifically, but I'm convinced he's still holding back." Taylor began to pace. "He's a lot tougher than I thought he'd be, but we'll get the truth eventually."

Granger nodded to himself. He let out his breath and began to relax.

"Concentrate on finding out where they're taking her, Dan. That's what we need to know."

"I can do that, sir, but I think it's critical that we find out why they took her in the first place?"

"That's secondary, Dan, just keep him talking, and perhaps he'll tell you where they've got her?"

"I don't agree, sir. Beyond using Fahd al-Quso to set up her transportation across the desert, he claims he wasn't made privy to the specific details of her movement. He also said he was never told where Disler would be going once she got to Iran, or who would be taking her back from the *Ansar al-Sharia* operatives who were going to move her from Aden to the coast."

"Ansar al-Sharia? My God! Are you telling me that the Iranians are using *them* to handle her movement through the desert?"

"That's what he's saying."

Granger leaned back in his chair to think this through. Would the terrorists try to move her along the coastal highway? The remnants of the Yemeni government was working hand in hand with the US Navy to target known members of Al Qaeda in Yemen. There were government roadblocks set up along the highway to prevent the easy movement of fighters and weapons. If Disler was being moved in that way, then the chances were good that they could run into a checkpoint. If they did, and if a shootout ensued, Disler could end up dead. Would the Iranians want her to be transported that way? Granger doubted it. They had too much riding on the success of the operation to allow it to fail because of a chance encounter at a roadblock. No, it was far more likely that they'd be staying off the main roads, and if they tried to move her directly through the deep desert, the going would be a lot slower. They might still be en route, in which case satellite's or drones might still have a chance to pick them up.

He allowed himself a half smile. If they picked them up before they got to the coast, he could order a special operations action which would greatly improve the chances of getting her back alive.

"Let's put up the drones and re-task a satellite," he said. "Maybe we can spot them out in the desert."

"I've already put that in motion, sir."

Taylor wasn't entirely confident that they'd be able to locate them that way, but it was certainly worth a try.

"Well, keep me up to speed on what you learn from Niroomad," Granger said. "And by the way, what caused him to break?"

Taylor smiled.

"We primed him to think that he was going to end up in the hands of the *Mukhabarat*, and when he tried to call my bluff out on the ship, we brought him here, under sedation. The specially constructed room we've got him in has been heated to 110 degrees. I've got my Arabic speaking guys handling the interrogation, and he's convinced that he's at *Al Jafr* prison in the Jordanian desert."

"That's all it took?" Granger asked. It seemed to be awfully easy.

Taylor momentarily debated whether or not to say anything more, then decided that it really wasn't a secret.

"Rumors have run rife through the Middle East that the Jordanians at *Al Jafr* get the prisoners to talk by pouring acid on their testicles before castration with a dull knife."

Granger was truly shocked.

"My God! That's absolutely barbaric!"

Taylor laughed. "It's an unfounded rumor, sir, but the Jordanians and we have managed to use it to our advantage. Niroomad has been sleep deprived, and because of the rumor, he's been primed to believe that if he isn't forthcoming during the interrogation, his *"Jordanian guards"* won't hesitate to turn him into a eunuch."

Granger gave a sigh of relief. The use of mental torture, while still frowned upon, was certainly preferable and more defensible than the use of physical coercion.

"How long do you anticipate holding him there?" Granger asked. A decision would have to be made at some point as to what to do with him when the questioning was over.

"I suspect we're going to have to hold on to him for at least the next six months. Because of his role in the Quds, there's a lot of other activities they're involved in that we want to talk to him about, so it's gonna take some time."

"Who's handling the interrogation?" Granger asked.

"Chris Rooney. He's assigned to *PSYOPs (Psychological Operations).* A good man. If anyone can get him to tell us what he's holding back, Rooney's the one."

"All right. Just keep me up to speed, but do whatever it takes to break this guy and get her back. We can't let the Iranians get away with this."

Granger hung up, and Taylor sighed. Scanning the desert was like searching for a needle in a haystack. It wouldn't take them long to get her to the coast, a few days, not much more, if they were actually even out there in the first place.

If they were moving her by van on the highways, it might already be too late to do an intercept. So in spite of Granger's desire to keep the focus on the physical search for Disler, Taylor was firmly convinced that finding out why the Iranians had taken her in the first place was the likely key to where she would end up.

He punched a number into his phone and held it up to his ear. It was time to pass on to Bryan what little they'd gleaned from Niroomad.

*****

EIGHTEEN

AL HABILAYN, SOUTHERN YEMEN
10:00 AM   DAY THIRTEEN

Bryan drove the white Toyota pick-up truck the fifty-five miles north from Aden to the city of *Al Habilayn* in the province of *Lahj*, in Southern Yemen. He made the drive in just over an hour and was pleasantly surprised that he hadn't encountered a military checkpoint. To do so would have been both dangerous and time-consuming. On the other hand, he was disappointed to know that if Angela Disler had been transported this way, her captors would have reached Al Habilayn without any challenge by the Yemeni military forces.

The city itself was a hotbed of separatist activities and had been since the unification in 2009 of Northern and Southern Yemen. The separatist movement had been continuous, and over time it had become progressively more violent, including bombings and attacks on security forces both in and around Al Habilayn. On several occasions, most recently in January of 2011, the town had been shelled by military forces intent on crushing dissent. When the troops were later withdrawn, the area was infiltrated by *al-Qaeda in Yemen* forces who saw an opportunity to gain an important tactical foothold. And since that time there had been an ongoing cat and mouse series of confrontations with governmental forces intent on getting rid of the threat that was posed to the national security interests.

Bryan made his way through the city in search of the camel market. His Toyota was dirty and beat up, exactly what he needed to avoid unnecessary attention. He was dressed as he had been in Aden, so he blended in quite easily with the local population.

He stopped once to ask a street vendor for directions, and a short time later, the market was in sight.

He smelled it well before he arrived.

Camel markets were common throughout the Middle East. The ones in Aden and *Sana'a,* the capital of Yemen, were enormous and centuries old.

From what he could see from the cab of his truck, the one in *Al Habilayn* was considerably smaller than either Aden's or Sana'a's, which should make acquiring the information he wanted that much easier to get.

He climbed out of the cab and slowly walked over to a man who was sitting on the ground near two scrawny camels whose feet were hobbled to keep them in place.

The area was little more than several acres in size, with camels lined up and tethered by a rope to posts that were placed in the ground. Laid out around the camels were piles of dates, grasses, and grains, including wheat and oats. The size of the piles was entirely dependent upon the wealth of the various traders.

The smell was difficult to take, particularly in the heat of the day, and Bryan soon found himself rigging a scarf to cover his nose and mouth.

He walked up to the seated man and gave him the traditional greeting of peace in Arabic. The man responded in kind, and as was the custom, his response was considerably more effusive.

Bryan squatted down to make sure that he and the old man were on the same visual plane.

"Pardon me, my brother, but I am seeking a little information."

"Are you from the government?" the old man asked.

"I am just a trader, like you. My name is Hakim. The information I seek concerns a caravan which left here several days ago. I'm trying to determine if my brother was part of that group?"

"I would not know about such things," the old man replied. He was obviously reluctant to provide any information to someone he did not know.

"I understand your concerns," Bryan said. "I am a stranger, and these are difficult times, but my heart is pure, and my intentions are honorable. My mother is dying, and before she joins Allah, she wants to see her second son one more time. If he left with a caravan, I must try to track him down. It's a question of honor. I'm sure you understand."

The old man seemed to consider this for a moment before pointing to a group of men who were gathered together under a tree farther into the market.

"Ask for Jamil. He may have the information you seek."

"Peace be upon you, my brother." Bryan smiled and shook the man's hand. "May Allah grace you with years of happiness and fortune."

He stood upright, approached the group on foot, and because he was a stranger, he went through the same skeptical reception he'd received from the old man. He volunteered his story about a dying mother and withstood a barrage of questions from the group at large that were designed to elicit where his loyalties were given.

Bryan had a cover story prepared, one that flowed from his lips as if it were real, and after twenty minutes of give and take, one of the men identified himself as Jamil before walking Bryan away from the group so that they could speak with some degree of privacy.

Jamil was easily in his sixties. Thin, weathered, full beard, dark skin; he'd been a camel herder all his life. But age and illness had taken their toll, so no longer able to handle the arduous life of a Bedouin trader, he now sold camels in the city market and lived in a house instead of a tent.

"I was told that my brother was joining a large caravan that was heading for the coast. I was hoping that you might know if that's true? My brother is named Waled. He's about my size, an inch or two shorter, with one hand twisted up by a childhood disease. Have you seen him, my brother?"

"I'm sorry, but no one like that comes to mind."

Bryan made a big show of demonstrating his disappointment. He shoved his hands in his pockets and sighed.

"I don't suppose you could tell me if a large caravan left here the other day? It could be worth a little something for your trouble?"

Jamil smiled tightly. The discussion had finally turned in the direction that he wanted it to go. Information was a commodity, and commodities were always to be sold. He nodded to Bryan and casually held out his hand.

Bryan now knew that he had him. It would simply be a question of how much he was willing to divulge.

He pulled a large wad of bills and peeled off 5000 Yemeni Rial's, about twenty-three US dollars. He slipped the money into Jamil's outstretched hand.

"A caravan did leave here two days ago. It was headed for Oman."

"Do you know their tribe?" Bryan asked.

Jamil put out his hand, and now realizing how this game would be played, Bryan pulled another series of bills from his pocket and placed them in Jamil's hands.

It took two more transactions for Bryan to discover that the route to be taken was unknown, but he learned enough about the men involved to make an educated guess about their likely use of traditional routes. While there was no certainty that he would be right, it was, at least, a good start.

He thanked Jamil, made his way back to his truck, and quickly got back to the highway. He didn't trust Jamil as far as he could throw him, and he was quite certain that if he remained in the area that within hours, he would have been confronted by armed robbers.

****

Back at his hotel in Aden, Bryan stuffed his dirty clothing into a hotel laundry bag and left it outside his bedroom door to be picked up by the hotel's cleaning service. The next order of business was a shower and a good scrub to get the smell of the camel market off his skin and hair.

Once he was dry and dressed in a pair of jeans and a western style collared shirt, he pulled out a laptop computer from the hotel safe and set up a satellite link. He then began to research the basic information he received from Jamil, and thirty minutes later, when he had what he wanted, he composed a message to be posted on a site that Taylor would be checking every hour on the hour.

When his message was ready, he surfed his way through the internet to a comment board on a website in Jordan. Addressing his correspondence to *Hassan,* he presented a message in Arabic intended to be innocuous on its face.

Hassan,

I have done some research for you. Hope this helps with your term paper.

The Banu Abdul Qays tribe is predominately Shia from Bahrain and Oman. Some, in Oman, are herders, but while the Makki faction are still herding in caravans of up to fifty camels and using historical desert routes when they travel from Al Habilayn, a city just outside of Aden in Southern Yemen, most are involved in agriculture and shipbuilding, doing distinctive Dhow construction for trade from coastal Oman with the countries of Africa, Iran, Indonesia, and India.

Good luck with your paper.
Hakim.

He sent the message, closed up his computer, then lay down to take a nap.

*****

NINETEEN

THE DEEP DESERT, YEMEN
11:00 AM   DAY THIRTEEN

Angela Disler carefully opened her eyes then quickly shut them again. The room was spinning wildly; the disorientation was overwhelming. The nausea that followed struck with a vengeance and she could feel that her heart was racing. She was on her side, lying on the ground. The vomiting came in waves, but there was nothing in her stomach, so the heaves were dry.

If a doctor had been in attendance, he would have told her that she was severely dehydrated and suffering from the side effects of the sedatives they'd used to keep her helpless during the journey from Alexandria. And because of the heavy use of the drugs, her mind was fuzzy and her memory faulty. She struggled to recall what had happened to her, but she had no idea what was going on.

Slowly, the nausea subsided, and her dizziness abated, only to be replaced by a splitting headache. Her mouth was horribly dry, her lips were cracked, and she had to concentrate just to make herself swallow.

When the spinning abated, she slowly opened her eyes again. She was in a small room, still lying on her side, and her first unscrambled thought was that she was being cooked inside some kind of an oven. But as her mind began to clear, she realized that she was in a small room in a hut or a shed of some kind. There was no electricity, but light was seeping in through what appeared to be a partially open door. She tried to move her hands but discovered that they were securely bound together behind her back. She couldn't move her feet, and it took a few moments to realize that they were tied together as well.

She tried to remember what had happened, but it didn't come back to her easily. There were snatches of memory, disjointed fragments that popped in and out of her subconscious like individual scenes from a poorly edited movie. There were camels, a restaurant, riding in a wheelchair, the rocking motion of a boat at sea, covered faces of a man or men, needles sticking her in the arm, both arms, the sound of a ship's horn, and the sensation that she'd been wrapped in a cocoon of some type, suspended in the air and somehow attached to a camel.

A camel?

Things slowly started to come back into frame. She remembered the conference in Alexandria and being in the restaurant for dinner. A man had joined her, a doctor of some kind, and he bought her a drink. It was fuzzy after that, just broken pieces of memory.

The camel, the boat? *Were they nothing more than hallucinations?* Perhaps they were, but one thing was certain, her hands and feet were tightly bound. That was not a figment of her imagination. It was something real and tangible, and it did not bode well for her current situation.

She started to think about her physical condition. As a trained physician she began a logical assessment. She decided that she must have been drugged, for how long she didn't know, but the anesthesia they'd given her had caused her nausea and vomiting. The dry mouth, cracked lips, the bad headache? Most likely they were the result of severe dehydration.

She sighed. This was not good, not good at all.

The door, or what she perceived to be the door, was suddenly opened, flooding the room with the brightness of the sun which forced her to squint to protect her eyes. A lone figure came in, took a long moment to look at her, then turned around and walked back out.

Two things immediately came to mind. While she was initially blinded by the sunlight, she had finally seen enough to realize that she was in a tent of some kind and that the man had been dressed like some Middle Eastern tribesman; the kind of men she'd seen on the National Geographic channel.

First impression? *I've been kidnapped and sold to Bedouin slavers!*

Her thoughts turned quickly to her husband and her daughters. What would they think had happened to her? How long had she been here? Were they okay? Why was this happening to her?

The flap of the tent came open again, and a man walked in, followed by another. When her eyes adjusted again to the change in the lighting conditions, she could see that both men were dressed the same way as the one that she'd seen before.

"Ah! You're awake."

The man crouched down and studied her face.

Angela was momentarily relieved to realize that the man had spoken to her in English. She'd never mastered a foreign language, so this could have been much worse if he wasn't English speaking. The second thing that struck her was his smile. He was actually smiling at her.

"My name is Muhammed," he said.

He produced a sharp knife from his waistband and leaned over to sever the ropes that bound her hands. He then produced a goat skin bag that was used to carry water. He handed it to her and said, "Drink some of this, but drink it slowly, or you will be sick."

She awkwardly tried to sit up by herself, but couldn't. Muhammed grabbed her under the arms and raised her up into a sitting position. She greedily brought the goat skin up to her lips and tasted the water. It was cool and refreshing, and she was suddenly dying of thirst, so in spite of his warning, she gulped the water down.

Muhammad quickly grabbed the goat skin back.

"That's enough for now! You don't want to be sick. I will give you more in a couple of minutes." He studied her briefly.

"How do you feel?"

Angela shut her eyes tight. This is so surreal; it must be a dream. But when she opened them up, nothing had changed. The man was still there with his companion.

"Am I in Egypt?" she asked.

Her voice sounded strange and hoarse to her, which came as a complete surprise.

The man laughed. He turned to his companion and translated what she'd said into Arabic which made the second man laugh. Muhammad then told him to get her some solid food: a small piece of goat meat and a helping of brown rice.

The second man quickly disappeared from the tent and Muhammad returned his attention to her.

"You are in the desert in Yemen, just outside a town called *Yarim,* about two days from the coast. You are a guest of the *Ansar al-Sharia*, perhaps better known to you westerners as *Al-Qaeda on the Arabian Peninsula*. We will be giving you food, and you must eat it all to regain your strength. You still have a long journey ahead of you, and if you do not want us to sedate you, you must be able to travel as one of us."

Angela tried to process what he was saying.

Al-Qaeda on the Arabian Peninsula?

Is he saying that I'm in Yemen?

At heart she was a major news junkie. Each day she read all the international headline stories on a number of selected online websites including the BBC, CNN, the New York Times and the Washington Post. At times, she even read Al-Jazeera, so she knew a great deal about the AQAP.

They were a militant Islamist organization, primarily active in Yemen and Saudi Arabia. It was considered to be the most active of the Al Qaeda branches, and it boasted a strong foothold in Yemen because of the weakened central government and the *Houthi* revolt.

She shook her head slowly in disbelief. These people are crazy fanatics. They blow up ships and try to bring down airplanes. They kidnap people for ransom and murder government diplomats.

What am I going to do?

"I can see that you are in need of a change of clothes," Muhammad said, "and I'm sure that you would benefit from a bath. I will send in several women to help you clean up."

He gave her a curious smile. "You will need to wear our clothing for the rest of your journey."

She looked up and held his glance. "Where are you taking me?"

"You are going to see a very important man who will explain everything."

He turned to go.

"Can you at least untie my legs?" she asked.

He stopped, thought it over, then walked back and cut the cords that bound her legs.

"There is nowhere to run. You are out in the desert, and no one can help you. And, if you try to leave, you will have your head separated from your shoulders in a propaganda video."

He laughed when he saw the fear in her eyes, then he turned and walked out of the tent.

****

Muhammad walked over to a group of more than a dozen women who were preparing food for the rest of the caravan. After a short conversation, two of the women got up and carried bathing supplies and a change of clothing into the tent where Angela was being held.

Muhammad then approached the group of men who were seated around a campfire that was being used to boil water for the making of tea. The group was composed of elders from the *Makki* tribe, most of whom were from the country of Oman.

"She's awake and fit to travel," he told them in Arabic. He sat on the ground and joined the group. "We will break up into much smaller groups and take off as soon as it is dark."

"But their drones will be watching," said Murad, one of the senior elders and an informal leader of the group.

"All the more reason to split up. We must anticipate that they might figure out that she's being moved by caravan. By breaking up into smaller groups, and by taking many different routes, there will be too many of us for them to consider mounting an operation."

Murad wasn't convinced.

"But their camera's will see her in the sling hanging from the side of one of your camels?"

Muhammad shook his head.

"She will be walking with the other women, and she'll be wearing the abaya and the veil. She won't be discovered from the sky."

"It's a great risk, Muhammad," Murad cautioned.

"True, but the money they are paying us will make the risk worth taking."

*****

TWENTY

LOS ANGELES, CALIFORNIA
DAY THIRTEEN   9:00 AM

Captain Tom Elwood walked into his office, placed his briefcase on the floor, hung up his sports coat, then settled into his ergonomic desk chair, one that was specifically tailored to ease the problems caused by the bulging disc in his lower back. Yesterday, he spent the better part of the day at Kaiser Hospital where he went through a series of scans and exams related to his condition. And while his doctor recommended that he stay home in bed for a couple of days, he preferred to be at work, particularly when his subordinates were working on a major case.

He was barely settled in when both Thompson and Donahue appeared at his door.

"Got a minute, Captain?" Donahue asked.

Not waiting for an answer, she and Thompson entered the office and quickly took seats in front of the desk.

"I guess I can spare a few moments. Would you like to come in and sit down?"

He was being facetious, but Donahue didn't smile. She was in a sour mood and ready to start a rant.

"We're working blind, Captain. We need to know what's happened to the wife in order to know what we're up against."

Elwood grimaced then shifted slowly in his chair.

"As you know, I was off yesterday, so why don't you fill me in on what's going on?

"Is your back bothering you again?" Donahue asked when she noticed his discomfort. Her face reflected her genuine concern.

Elwood ignored the question, so Donahue explained that the crime lab lifted dozens of prints from the Disler residence, but that most of them belonged to family members.

"There were lots of smudge marks," she added, "which suggests to me that whoever took them from their home was probably wearing gloves."

"Do we know what time it happened?"

Thompson said, "The girls didn't show up for school the last two days, so we're working on the assumption that they were taken two nights ago. Plus, a neighbor watched three guys get out of a white van that pulled into the Disler driveway about 8:00 pm that night. She thought they were plumbers, but we're pretty sure they weren't."

"So we're dealing with three suspects?"

"She's not sure. There could be more."

Elwood's brow went up, but Donahue jumped in without giving him a chance to get off on a tangent.

"I did a neighborhood walk yesterday and found a home with a security camera pointed out at the street. We got a copy of their video from that night, and it shows a white van pulling into the driveway at just before eight. We had the license plate blown up, and it turns out to be a reported stolen from the Wilshire Division."

"Have we located the van yet?"

"We put out an APB, but so far, no luck."

Elwood made a notation in a notebook that he used for briefings just like this.

"What else?"

"There were signs of a struggle. Furniture overturned, food left on the table and stove, and Henrik Disler's wallet complete with credit cards and cash was found on the dresser in the bedroom. There was a blood trail which led from the front room out the back door and down the driveway. Drips mostly," Donahue added. "We don't know yet who it belonged to, but logic suggests that it's Disler's."

Elwood looked from one to the other.

"Well, that means he's still alive. They wouldn't bother to take him if he was dead."

"Small consolation," Donahue replied.

Elwood rubbed his chin while he pondered what he'd been told.

"So they took him and his daughters. The big question is why?" Donahue leaned forward in her chair.

"If the snatch is for a money ransom, who do they expect is going to pay it? The wife is missing, so she can't pay, and the husband is a doctor at UCLA, which means he's okay but not getting rich." She shook her head and leaned forward in her chair. "What's left? Are they gonna try to blackmail our government?"

"It wouldn't be the first time," Thompson said, which surprised them both. "Back in November of 1979, the Iranian hostage crisis, remember? They took fifty-two American hostages and held them captive for more than four hundred days."

Donahue tilted her head towards Shari.

"*Wow!* Where'd that nugget come from?"

"I looked it up last night," she replied with a smile. "The Iranians wanted the former Shah returned for trial and execution, but the Shah died after coming to America for medical attention. They demanded an apology for our interference in the internal affairs of Iran, and for the overthrow of the Prime Minister in 1953. They also wanted their assets in the United States to be unfrozen."

Elwood was stunned.

"You're just full of surprises today, aren't you?"

Thompson nodded.

"The point is, we gave in. They got what they wanted. So maybe the Egyptians who took her have simply dusted off a page from the Iranians playbook?"

Donahue locked eyes with Elwood.

"See. That's the problem we've got, Captain. It's natural to think that *Egyptians* took her, but we don't know that for sure, or for that matter, how the snatch went down?"

"I see your point," Elwood made another entry on his notepad.

Thompson cleared her throat.

"If the two events are connected—and how could they not be— shouldn't we assume that whoever did this knows that our government's policy is not to negotiate with terrorists?"

"But you said it yourself, Shari, this woman is apparently very important." He looked up and held her glance. "Maybe the kidnappers think she's valuable enough to force our government to negotiate for her release."

"Then why take the rest of the family?" said Donahue. "It doesn't make sense."

"We might be getting ahead of ourselves," Elwood told them. "This may be nothing more than a kidnapping for ransom by a criminal element."

"But the ransom for money angle doesn't seem right to me, Captain. These folks aren't super wealthy."

Elwood had been writing furiously. He put down his pen, leaned back in his chair, then lapsed into a contemplative silence.

A moment later, he said, "Right now all we're doing is speculating, and that's not gonna get us anywhere. We need to keep an open mind about everything. Off the top of my head, I can think of a couple of possible angles that you'll need to check out. Like…does Angela Disler have access to the company assets? Because if she does, they might be trying to force her to transfer money out of the corporate accounts."

Donahue slowly nodded. That was something she hadn't considered.

"And second, we shouldn't overlook the possibility that all of this might just come back to the husband. Maybe taking her was just a way to put pressure on him to do something?"

"That sounds a little far-fetched," Thompson said.

"Look. I'm not saying that's what happened; I'm just illustrating my point. We know nothing yet, so all options are on the table, including the fact that the husband might be the real target of whatever's going on. We need to put this family under a microscope, with emphasis on both parents."

"But we've already asked around, Captain," said Donahue. "Everyone says their marriage was solid."

"Then dig deeper, Jen. There's a reason behind all of this, and sitting around conjuring up theories is not gonna get us anywhere."

He looked over at Thompson.

"What about cell phones? Do we know if the husband has one? If so, we might be able to track him down using the *find my phone* feature or by pinging?"

"One tiny little problem, Captain," said Thompson. "We found his cell phone on the dresser next to his wallet. We have the sound lab going over it now to check the call log, and I plan to write a warrant later this morning to get the phone company to turn over his outgoing call records. We thought we'd see what calls he made both before and after his wife went missing."

"Good idea, and hit the work angle again. Somebody's got to know something."

Donahue managed a tight smile. "So, what about getting the Feds to fill us in on what happened in Alexandria?"

"Let me work on that," he said tonelessly.

****

On the way to their desks, Donahue said, "That stuff about the hostage takeover in Iran? That was very impressive. You must have spent all night memorizing those details."

Thompson gave her a wink. "It was pretty good, wasn't it?"

"I'll say. I was convinced you were speaking from personal memory. How old were you when that happened? Sixteen? Seventeen?"

"Bite me, Donahue. Your jealousy is showing."

Donahue laughed.

"So, are you gonna do the search warrant for the phone records now?"

Thompson nodded. "Yeah, it won't take me too long. How about you?"

"I'm gonna start a background check on the husband. Why don't you take Angela Disler when you're done with the warrant?"

"Fair enough." Thompson looked pensive. "You think the Captain will get the Feds to give us a briefing?"

"If anyone can do it, he can."

But Donahue wasn't convinced that Elwood would make any headway. It was beginning to look like the whole situation was covered by a veil of secrecy that was well beyond their pay grade.

*****

TWENTY-ONE

WASHINGTON, DISTRICT OF COLUMBIA
DAY THIRTEEN   2:00 PM

Dan Taylor finished reading the entry on the Jordanian website, thought about it for a moment, then read it again, this time making notes on a piece of paper that would later be destroyed. He leaned back in his chair as a small smile spread quickly across his face. Once again, Bryan had pulled the rabbit out of his hat, or in this case, his head scarf. He was worth his weight in gold. With few exceptions, he could put him on the ground by himself in any Middle Eastern country and Bryan would come up with some form of actionable intelligence. In this case, he had significantly narrowed down the search for Angela Disler.

Taylor was still in the States, in his hotel room at the Grand Hyatt Washington on H Street. It was a little pricey, but it was a convenient location for all the running around he was doing. Between the trips back and forth to the safe house for updates on the prisoner interrogation, and a seemingly endless series of meetings out at Langley, the location of the Hyatt made good sense.

He hooked up his cell phone to a portable signal scrambler and made a quick call to his boss, Hamilton Granger.

Granger answered on the fourth ring.

"Yes?" he said.

It was brusque, and it was exactly what Taylor had expected from the man whose grouchy disposition was frequently at the core of his subordinate's complaints.

"Sir? It's Dan Taylor. I've got an update on Angela Disler's whereabouts."

Back at his home on the Potomac, in Maryland, Granger sat upright. He'd been in the middle of a late afternoon nap, a practice he engaged in whenever possible.

"Go ahead, Dan." He was now wide awake.

"Sir, our agent in Aden has confirmed our belief that Ali Niroomad was working with Fahd al-Quso to transport Disler through the Yemeni desert to coastal Oman. He believes that the method of transport is a large camel caravan that originated in *Al Habilayn,* a city just north of Aden in Southern Yemen. The men doing the transport are from the *Makki* faction of the *Banu Abdul Qays* tribe. They are *Shia* traders from Bahrain and Oman. Our agent believes that once she reaches the coast of Oman, she will likely be transported by a Dhow across the Arabian sea to a port somewhere in Iran."

"So how do these tribesmen fit in with al-Quso?"

"The Makki are known gun smugglers. They've been providing weaponry to Al-Qaeda on the Arabian Peninsula for the past five years. They use the desert routes to avoid the government checkpoints."

"How solid is the information?" Granger asked.

"I can't answer that with any degree of certainty, sir. Our agent is well connected in that part of the world, so he must be relying on his sources. But the scenario makes sense. Niroomad meets with al-Quso who has the contacts and the organizational skills to get her overland to the coast. They can't fly her in because of the sanctions, and they can't move her by tanker beyond Yemen because they know we'd board the ship once we figured out what they were up to. And if they tried to move her by vehicle on the highways running through Yemen, they'd have to deal with the government or rebel checkpoints, and while they might be able to get through the checkpoints by spreading around a lot of money, there's a greater chance for successfully getting her to Oman by moving her through the desert."

He paused for a moment to marshal his thoughts.

"I think we're on to something here, sir. Plus, it's the only real lead we have."

Granger began to get out of his bed.

"Our eye's-in-the-sky should have no trouble picking them up," he said, reaching for his robe.

It should be that simple, Taylor thought. Unfortunately, he was going to have to give Granger a lesson in Middle Eastern cultural history.

"Actually, it's a little more complicated than that, sir. The routes through the desert have been used for thousands of years. Caravans from all over the middle east use the same routes because they have all been developed based on the location of water holes. I know it sounds crazy, but at any given moment, there are hundreds and sometimes even thousands of small groups of these nomadic traders on the move using these ancient highways. The only clue we've got to work with is that the caravan we're looking for started out with approximately fifty camels. That, at least, should help us narrow down our initial search."

Granger thought that over. It didn't sound too bad. How many caravans would be that large? He suspected the answer was very few.

"Make the call. Let's get a couple of drones on it right away. I'll notify JSOC and see if we can get their satellites tasked to take a look as well."

He paused for a moment to consider if he was overlooking something obvious.

"Do we have a plan of action worked up in case we find the caravan?"

Taylor had given some thought to the possible rescue scenarios, and only one seemed suited for their purpose.

"We can keep an armed drone on station to provide backup support, but we're going to need a Special Operations Team to go boots on the ground to get her back."

There was an uncomfortable silence between them, and for a moment Taylor wondered if he'd lost the satellite signal.

"Sir?" he said.

"I'm thinking," came the reply.

Taylor waited him out. Granger was a political appointee, a one-time corporate executive and a former United States senator from Michigan. In the past, he might have been a good businessman and an excellent politician, but he was completely out of his element when it came to foreign affairs and intelligence operations, and this weakness was never more obvious then when a quick decision had to be made.

"Let me think about that for a while," he finally said. "I'll get back to you later. In the meantime, let's see if we can locate her first before we bring a Special Forces team into the picture. Tell your source he's done a good job, and call me back if you come up with any further information."

Granger hung up the phone and Taylor shook his head in disbelief.

If a SEAL team was going to be used, the sooner they knew about it and could develop a formal operational plan, the better it would be for the troops and Disler.

They were running out of time. If the kidnappers ever got her to the shores of Iran, the chance of getting her back using a military operation in Iranian territory was highly unlikely. An action like that would presage an invitation for an all out war with the Islamic Republic of Iran.

No, the SEALs would have to be given as much lead time as possible, for if they found the caravan, they would need to move quickly.

He would make the call to tip off the SEALs himself, and if Granger later called him on the carpet, he'd just have to deal with it then.

*****

TWENTY-TWO

CLOVIS, NEW MEXICO
DAY THIRTEEN   3:30 PM

Packer Two, true name Matt Gleason, was seated at his flight action console in the 3d Special Operations Squadron command center in Clovis, New Mexico. He was drinking from a can of *Coca-Cola* and killing time until his EOW, another forty minutes away.

It had been a long shift, and he was ready to call it quits. Endless hours of patrolling the night skies over the Arabian Sea, looking for anything that seemed out of the ordinary, waiting for a hot lead on some wanted terrorists that never seemed to materialize. He would have given anything for a break in the monotony, but the night had gone like many others; ninety-nine percent of the time just hanging around on station, endlessly patrolling the skies, being ready for anything. And for what? For that one percent experience, the adrenalin rushing chaos that comes with tracking a target and wiping it off the face of the earth.

He would never admit it to the team he worked with, but he had mixed feelings about what he was doing. It wasn't that he was opposed to the concept of drone strikes, in fact, he believed in them as a legitimate facet of the war on terrorism. By carefully targeting enemy combatants, they could effectively reduce the risk of collateral causalities, and in this era of unconventional warfare, where the enemy blended in with the innocent civilian population, it was an ethical imperative that they do what they could to avoid the slaughter of innocents. But what caused him to lose sleep was the fact that he was the one who had to pull the trigger, the man who did the actual killing.

He was okay if he didn't think about the deaths he was responsible for, and most of the time, that wasn't a problem. He learned to compartmentalize his feelings, and when he was sitting behind the console, seeing what the drone was looking at, he was all business. If a target was spotted, and if the green light was given, it was as if he was playing a video game. Being one step removed from the physical consequences of what he was doing made the process seem somehow unreal, and he preferred it that way. But during his down time, when he wasn't at the console patrolling the skies, he would sometimes think about the enormity of what he'd done, the dozens and dozens of lives he'd taken, and he would begin to question his role in what was going on.

He was pretty sure his problem stemmed from the value he placed on human life. A church-going Christian, he could think of nothing more wonderful and special than the gift of life in a physical universe so full of randomness and chaos. The human being was so special, so evolved as a species, that it was able to explore and contemplate the concepts of space and time, as well as having a fundamental understanding of the building blocks of life itself. To him, the complexity of existence was so amazing that the taking of life seemed completely unforgivable. And yet, it was something he did with growing frequency.

His wife was aware of his feelings, and she was pushing him to pay a visit to the base psychologist; or at the very least, the unit Chaplin. But he was leery of taking that step. They might decide he was unsuitable for his work, in which case, he could end up with a medical discharge, and if that were to happen, how would he support his wife and the children that they wanted to have?

These thoughts were weighing heavily on his mind when the call came into Black Dog One from JSOC that they were to shift their area of surveillance from the coastline along the Arabian Sea to the desert of eastern Yemen.

"What are we looking for?" Packer Six asked.

"We're looking for a camel caravan that set off from *Al Habilayn* a few days ago. It's headed for the coast of Oman."

"Are they kidding?"

Packer Two put down his soda can and punched in the coordinates that would effectively change the course of his Predator drone, moving it from high up over the city of Aden to the area above *Al Habilayn.*

"With all the Bedouins moving around out there, we need to find a way to narrow things down," he said.

Black Dog One, the team leader, leaned back in his chair. His console overlooked the consoles of the other four members of the team. He glanced down at Packer Two. Of all of the people on his team, he was the one most suited to the work. He had a unique sense of mission about him; always looking for the edge that would make their tasks that much easier to accomplish.

"We're going to be looking for a large one," said Black Dog One. "Possibly fifty camels, but they want us to note the latitude and longitude of any group out there, along with the observable direction of travel in case we have to relocate them later for a possible land operation."

Packer Two looked back over his shoulder at Black Dog One.

"Oh, I get it! With the position and direction of travel, we can overlay on a trail map and determine where they came from and where they'll be at any given moment. Very cool."

Black Dog One smiled. The kid was sharp, and one day soon he would be ready to run his own team.

At the console next to Packer One, Reaper Six had already made the course correction for his drone. He had been farther inland from the city of Aden, so he had a head start and was already much closer to *Al Habilayn* and their new area of operation.

Reaper Six turned his head and gave Packer Two a smile.

"Five bucks says I'll find the big one before you do."

Packer Two smiled back. "You're on, homey."

Long gone were the thoughts of the right and wrong of raining down death from the skies. Instead, Packer Two was mentally calculating the average distance a camel could travel in a single day, a calculation that could be extrapolated to give him a likely starting point for conducting his search.

His confidence level now high, he was sure he was going to win the five dollars.

****

After two hours of searching the deep Yemeni desert with drone operated cameras and satellite imagery, no caravans even close to fifty camels were found. In fact, very few were spotted in the twenty to thirty camel range. It was a moonless night in Yemen, but infrared cameras were able to pick up individual body heat signatures, so counting camels had not been a problem. It took a while to accept the fact that while the search would continue in earnest, it was possible— even probable—that the caravan they were looking for had already broken up.

Packer Two was relieved of duty by Green Eyes Four. He got to his feet, stretched his legs, then walked over to the supervisory console still being manned by Black Dog One.

"Hey, Dog," he said. "You got a minute?"

Black Dog One nodded. He never took his eyes off his computer screen.

"What's up, Matt?"

"I've been thinking. We know the caravan left *Al Habilayn* three days ago, right?"

"That's what they tell me."

"Well, I think I figured out what's going on."

Dog turned to give him a look. The kid had brains. If he had an idea, it was certainly worth a listen.

"A couple of months ago, I was tracking a caravan, and I was bored, so I tried to figure out the speed at which they were traveling. I also noted that most of the desert traffic takes place at night, too hot to be moving during the day. Anyway, it's my guess that these caravans travel at about the speed of a walking man, which translates into 5 kilometers, or 3.1 miles per hour."

Dog was interested.

"You figured that out all by yourself."

Matt smiled.

"Not exactly. I did a little research on the internet just to make sure my computations were accurate, but it also appears that most of these caravans have people walking along with the camels. So in this case, I have the feeling that we can extrapolate how far they go in a day, times three days—make that four if we count tonight—and by mapping it out as an overlay on our satellite desert photos—you know, the high altitude ones that show the desert trails that have been hard packed from use into the surface of the earth—we might be able to determine where this particular caravan should be. And then, if they've split up, as it appears they might have done, we can identify all of the smaller groups within the projected zone."

Dog was absolutely speechless. Matt's idea was sound. In fact, it was more than that. It was brilliant and consistent with his reputation as a thinker.

"I like it, Matt. I know you're off duty, but would you be able to stick around and oversee the workup?"

"My wife will kill me, but yeah, sure. If I can help, I'd be glad to do it."

Dog turned to Farm Boy whose replacement had just taken over. He was getting ready to go EOW.

"Jose, I need you to work a few hours overtime."

"Aw, boss, I'm really beat—"

Dog cut him off.

"That's an order, son. We've got an idea and we need your valuable assistance."

Jose smiled. "Well, when you put it that way, how can I say no."

"You can't," said Dog. "I want you to pull out our satellite blowups of the eastern desert, the ones that show the desert trails being used by the caravans."

He turned to Matt.

"Do your calculations for eight, ten, twelve, and fourteen hour days of travel, times four. We'll pinpoint each of those locations, start with the ones farthest out from *Al Habilayn,* and we'll work our way back. We'll focus on caravans using the most likely trails towards Oman, and then we'll spread out from there."

He stood up and stretched his legs.

"Your idea is brilliant, Matt. If it works, we won't forget who gets the credit."

Matt smiled.

"As long as I'm on your good side for the moment, can I ask you for a favor?"

Dog wanted to smile, but he couldn't. It wouldn't do to show a crack in his reputation as a gruff, authoritative figure.

"I'm listening," he said with a scowl.

"Could you call my wife and tell her that you're making me stay over?

I wasn't kidding. She's gonna kill me if she thinks this was my idea."

In spite of his best efforts not to laugh, Dog couldn't help himself.

Matt, who was embarrassed to have asked, soon joined in.

"Give me your home number and your wife's name, son." He winked at Matt. "By the time I'm finished, she's gonna treat you like a national hero."

*****

TWENTY-THREE

SANTA MONICA, CALIFORNIA
DAY THIRTEEN   4:30 PM

Donahue and Thompson pulled up to the curb in front of the Zurich Pharmaceuticals facility in Santa Monica, California. Having gone around the block twice, and not finding an available parking space, Thompson opted to park in a red zone.

"We're in Santa Monica," Donahue warned her. "They might give us a ticket."

Thompson turned off the engine and removed the keys from the ignition.

"Have a little faith," she said. "We're brothers in arms. They won't write us up." And just to be on the safe side, she dangled the microphone cord over the rear view mirror so that any half-blind ticket writer would instantly know that the car belonged to the police.

They made their way into the building, and after identifying themselves to the receptionist, they were led to a back corner office where Darryl Lum was seated at his desk and on the phone. He waved them in, quickly ended the call, and got to his feet.

"Any news on Angela?" he asked.

They could sense the sincerity in his tone.

"Sorry, doctor," said Donahue with a shake of her head. "Still no news. We just came by because we had a few more questions to ask you."

Lum nodded dejectedly. He gestured for them to take seats while he returned to his chair.

"We were wondering if you or anyone working at Zurich's headquarters in Switzerland have been contacted by the kidnappers?"

Lum shook his head.

"No one has contacted me, and if they did, I would have called you right away."

"How about at the home office?" Thompson asked.

Lum looked at her. "You told me not to say anything?"

Thompson smiled tightly.

"But we both know you notified your superiors, didn't you?"

Lum winced and hung his head.

"I had no choice," he explained. "If I didn't let them know, I could have been fired."

"But they haven't heard anything, have they?" Donahue asked.

"I check with them every day. They're just as mystified as I am."

Donahue leaned back but maintained eye contact with Lum. He seemed sincere enough, but how would he react to news of the family's disappearance?

"Have you talked with Henrik Disler in the last couple of days?" she asked.

"I haven't spoken with him since the last time you were here. I don't know what to say to him. This whole thing is just so awful."

Donahue cleared her throat.

"I'm afraid the situation has gotten worse. Henrik and their two daughters have gone missing."

"Missing?" Lum swallowed hard. "I don't understand. What are you saying?"

"Did he mention anything to you about going out of town?" Thompson asked.

"No! Why would he want to leave? What if Angela tried to call him and he wasn't there?" He studied Donahue's impassive face. "What's going on, detective? Are you suggesting that he might somehow be involved in her disappearance?"

"Not at all, in fact, there were signs of a struggle at the Disler's home, so it's entirely possible that they've been kidnapped, too."

"What?" Lum blanched. *"Dear God! What is going on?""*

Both detectives exchanged a glance. If facial expressions were any indication, it was clear that Lum wasn't faking his surprise or distress.

"Tell me something, Doctor," Donahue said bluntly. "Does Mrs. Disler have access to any financial accounts here at Zurich?"

Lum shifted his weight and shook his head. He needed a moment to frame his answer.

"She holds a partnership share in this operation, but she's not on any accounts as a signatory if that's what you're asking."

"We're trying to discover a reason why someone would want to kidnap her, and since the family's not wealthy, we thought she might have access to corporate money, and if that was known to the kidnappers, it might explain why she became a target?"

"I see what you mean, but the answer is no. I'm the only person around here who can authorize an expenditure of funds."

"And of course, you'd tell us if you were approached?"

"Yes, detective," he said as his eyes narrowed, "I certainly would."

Donahue looked around the office. It was comfortably furnished and functional. No expensive furniture, no "wall of fame" displaying his plaques or awards. It was pretty clear to her that Zurich and Lum as an individual didn't waste their money on frivolous accouterments.

Thompson shifted uncomfortably in her chair.

"So, doctor, if Mrs. Disler doesn't have any access to corporate money, do you have a theory as to what they might be after?"

Lum was slow to answer.

"To be honest, I have no idea."

"How about her work? Could someone be interested in that?"

"Angela is known *only* for her cancer breakthrough work," he said stiffly, "so I can't imagine what possible interest that could have for a kidnapper?"

"Money, doctor," said Thompson without hesitation. "A big, important breakthrough like hers must come with certain financial rewards?"

"What she hit upon was *a process*," he said, "a way of delivering chemotherapy agents directly to tumor cells while avoiding any risk to healthy cells."

"How is that accomplished, doctor? And if you don't mind, can you tell us about it in layman's terms?"

Lum summoned a smile.

"Perhaps the best way I can explain it is this. Angela was working on another project when she inadvertently hit upon a way to genetically alter a virus. It was then that she realized that she could use a harmless virus to deliver chemotherapy to tumor cells."

"But how does that work?" Thompson asked. "I'm trying to understand the process."

Lum nodded.

"Currently, a chemotherapy drug attaches itself to a tumor cell, then kills that cell when it divides in half. But it also attaches itself to normal cells, and it will kill those cells as well. Angela was working with colon cancer cells, and what she developed was a way to encase the chemotherapy molecule inside a harmless virus. She then altered the DNA of the virus to attach itself only to a specific portal on a colon tumor cell, one that's unique to that particular cancer cell, but one that does not exist on normal cells."

"So you're saying that because it only attacks the tumor cells, you avoid the harmful side effects, like nausea and hair loss, which can come with the regular infusion of chemotherapy?"

"Exactly!" Lum managed a smile.

"I understand it too," said Donahue, "and I can't help but think that the process itself must be worth a great deal of money?"

"For sure, detective, it is, but not to Angela—at least, not directly. Because she works for Zurich, they hold the rights to the patent for her gene splicing technique and the genetically altered cells. Zurich will reap the rewards when other drug companies have to pay them for the right to use the patented technology."

"So she gets nothing?" Thompson asked.

"I didn't say that. Angela will benefit indirectly. As a partner, she's entitled to a percentage of the profits, but that's a long way down the line. The process has to go through three stages of human testing before it can be approved for general use. After that, there would be licensing agreements drawn up with other companies, and negotiations like that take time. And if I were a betting man, I'd say we're talking years, maybe even ten or more before anyone at Zurich ever sees a dime."

"So what if the people who took her did so to learn her technique? Could they profit from that?"

"Only if they could beat Zurich to the patent office, and so far as I know, Zurich has already filed an application for a patent outlining her technique with the US patent office."

Donahue sighed. If Angela didn't have access to any real money, then kidnapping her for ransom appeared to be out of the question. And if that was the case, why take the rest of the family?

"Tell me about Mrs. Disler," Thompson asked. "What was she like at work?"

"She was a complete professional. Very dedicated to her work. She was a thinker who liked to work outside the box." His eyes moved from one to the other. "In fact, her discovery, the one that might land her a Nobel prize, was initially a technique she developed during work on another project." He leaned back in his chair and smiled brightly. "That's the kind of thinker she is, detective, always looking for ways to make things better. And in this case, she found an application for her work that could be used in the fight against cancer."

He shifted his gaze to Donahue.

"I sincerely hope she ends up with the Nobel Prize. She truly deserves it."

Donahue nodded ever so subtly. He was certainly proud of Disler's accomplishments, but what about her personal life?

"I know we already asked you about her relationship with her husband, but has anything at all come to mind since the last time we spoke?"

Lum vigorously shook his head.

"As I said before, they have a great relationship. Whatever's going on here, I can't believe it would be about that."

Donahue got to her feet, and Thompson followed suit.

"Okay, doctor. I think we've taken up enough of your time. You know the drill. If you learn anything, call us right away. Okay?"

"I will, and please let me know if you hear anything at all."

Donahue and Thompson made their way out of the office, and on the way out, they stopped in the building's foyer.

"I think he's being square with us," Thompson said, "so what do we do, now?"

"We do what the Captain said. We put the husband under a microscope and see if anything turns up."

"I think we should go through her home computer. I had the evidence tech's book it when they processed the scene. Maybe her emails will tell us a little more about her personal life?"

"You still think she's got herself a boyfriend, don't you?"

Thompson managed a small, frustrated laugh.

"I don't know about you, Jen, but I'm not buying all this goody-goody stuff. She sounds too perfect to me; loving wife, mother, brilliant researcher, devoted to her family," She shook her head. "No one is perfect, Jen, and that mean's the lady's got to have a blemish of some kind, and what's the old saying? Still waters runs deep? People like her always have a secret, and I'm betting that hers is a man."

"Why not a *woman*?" Donahue asked.

Thompson's brow furrowed. "You think...?"

"I'm being facetious. The Feds said she was kidnapped, Shari, so we will have to accept that at face value. But I can see your point. It can't hurt to go through her emails. I'll get Mitzi to do it for us. Her pinky finger knows more about computers than either one of us could ever hope to learn."

They left the building by way of the front door and made their way down the front steps towards the sidewalk. It was Donahue who first spotted the parking ticket on the front windshield.

"Brothers-in-arms, huh?" She pointed it out to Thompson.

Thompson saw it and flamed out.

"Get in the car," she ordered as she ripped the ticket off the windshield. "We're gonna track down that stupid idiot and I'm gonna shove this citation down his scrawny little throat."

"And if it's a her?" Donahue asked with a grin.

"No way! A sister-in-arms wouldn't do this. This has to be a male paper pusher who's pissed off because he can't get anyone to hire him as a real cop."

Thompson started up the car while scanning the street, looking for the ticket writer.

Donahue fastened her seatbelt.

"Take a deep breath, Shari. Hunting him *or her* down won't solve the problem. Instead, you're going to take me back to the station, and then you're going to call the watch commander at Santa Monica PD and ask him if he'll cancel the ticket? And if he says no, then you're gonna have to pay it and *we'll* chalk this up as a lesson learned."

Thompson looked over at her expectantly.

"I notice you said '*we'll*' chalk this up. Does that mean you're gonna split the cost with me if the WC decides not to cancel it out?"

"In your dreams, babe," Donahue replied.

Thompson started up the car and slammed it into gear.

"So much for the concept of sisters-in-arms."

*****

TWENTY-FOUR

THE SAN FERNANDO VALLEY, LOS ANGELES
DAY THIRTEEN   6:00 PM

Henrik Disler hugged Carrie, his youngest daughter, then slowly stroked the hair on her head with his free hand. He was seated on a carpeted floor, holding her in his lap. He told her not to worry, that they were doing fine and that everything was going to be okay.

Carrie wanted her mother, and Henrik tried to sound encouraging by telling her that mom was still at the conference and that soon they would all be together again.

Carrie seemed to accept what he was saying, although she was having trouble reconciling her father's assurances with her perceptions because it didn't address their current situation as hostages, nor the men with masks who kept them in this room.

Henrik looked over at Sienna, his oldest daughter. She was his rock, refusing to panic or give up hope. From the moment they'd been taken by these men, she had been the one who'd taken care of his wound—a badly broken nose that was caused by a gun stroke—while keeping Carrie's mind occupied with games and stories. She was certainly her mother's child; strong-willed, full of confidence, and fearless. But deep inside he knew that she was hurting, too. She had a way of burying her emotions, and as a physician, he was deeply concerned that at some point the pressure would be too much and she was going to have a break.

While he held his youngest daughter, he looked around the room for the hundredth time, hoping that an idea would miraculously come to mind; an idea that might give him a way to get his daughters out of harm's way.

The floor was covered with a cheap nylon carpet. It was a bedroom in a tract house of some kind, probably built forty or fifty years ago. There was no furniture in the room, and only a single overhead light fixture with a single bulb, probably 75 watts. There were three windows, but they'd been covered over on the inside with sheets of 3/4 inch plywood which were screwed in tightly to the window frames. There was a single wooden door on a very small closet, but when he examined it carefully, he found that there was no trap door that could lead them to the attic and a possible route of escape.

For bathroom bodily functions they were given a plastic bucket. Very quickly they learned to keep it in the closet, the use of which afforded Henrik and his daughters a measure of personal privacy. It wasn't much, but it was better than the alternative.

There was a single door that led from the room. The men kept it locked on the outside with a metal hinge and a padlock, Three times a day the door would be opened and one of the men, wearing a ski mask, would bring them something to eat. Usually, it was McDonald's. Henrik assumed that there must be one nearby. Once the food was delivered, the men allowed Sienna to carry the bucket from the closet to a real bathroom adjacent to their room. She would empty the bucket into the toilet, rinse it out with water from the shower, then bring it back and return it to their closet.

From what he'd been able to deduce, there were three men holding them captive, likely the same three that entered his home under the guise of being from the Gas Company. All of them were young, probably in their early twenties. He'd only seen one of them without the mask, but that look had been brief because the man had struck him in the face with a handgun and the blow had knocked him unconscious. They put a hood over his head, bound his hands behind his back, and when he was conscious again, they walked him out to a vehicle, likely a van. He wasn't sure of their nationality, but he had a gut feeling from the sound of their accents that they were from the Middle East. He never saw the faces of the other two when they entered his house, but they took turns bringing in the food, and from the appearance of the skin on the back of their hands, he was convinced that all three were Caucasians.

From what Sienna had told him about her trips through the hallway to the bathroom, he had a pretty good sense of the layout of the house. Two bedrooms, one bathroom, a kitchen, a dining area, and a living room. He wasn't sure what neighborhood they were in, but he was fairly confident that they hadn't been driven too far from his house on the night that they were taken.

He still had his wristwatch which turned out to be a blessing. He was able to discern that the men who were keeping them were holding to a very strict schedule. The meals were served at eight, noon and six, like clockwork. He wasn't sure what purpose that information might serve him, but he tucked it away, hoping that somehow he'd be able to use it sometime in the future to help them get away.

He looked at his watch. It was five minutes to six. Dinner would be arriving any minute now.

"They're going to bring us dinner in a couple of minutes," he said to his girls.

"Not McDonald's, I hope," Sienna said. "I'm sick of hamburgers."

"I'll talk to him, honey. Maybe they can bring us something else?"

A couple of minutes later the door was unlocked, and a man walked in with a bag containing three McDonald's cheeseburgers, three bags of fries, and three *Coca-Cola's*. He placed it on the floor about five feet away from Henrik and motioned to Sienna to go and get the bucket.

Henrik was nervous about saying anything to the man. He did not want to raise an issue that might piss them off and only make things worse. But the girls were reaching the point where they were barely eating, so he had no choice.

"Excuse me," he said to the man. "I was wondering if it would be possible to get something else to eat besides hamburgers and fries?"

The man stared at him for a while, then snarled, "If you don't like it, you don't have to eat it."

"I know," Henrik said, "and it's very kind of you to feed us as you do, but they have other things to eat at McDonald's, like fish sandwiches and salads. I'm a doctor, you know, and it's important to eat different kinds of foods to stay healthy. So, for the sake of my daughters, if you could get something different tomorrow, we'd be really grateful?"

He'd read somewhere that if one could develop a relationship with one's captors, it would make it more difficult for the kidnappers to see you as just an object. The hope was that they'd have to think twice before deciding to hurt him or his girls.

But the man chose not to respond. Instead, he turned towards the closet and yelled out to Sienna to hurry up.

Henrik tried again.

"Is there any chance you can tell me why we're being held like this? If it's money you want, I have a little savings I could let you have?"

"We don't want your money," the man said with an unfamiliar accent, but when he didn't elaborate further, Henrik decided to push forward.

"If it's not money you want, can you tell me what you're after?"

The man studied him for a moment while Sienna came out of the closet with the bucket.

"You'll find out soon enough," he finally said.

He opened the door and motioned for Sienna to follow, which she did. He shut the door, but Henrik could tell that he hadn't locked it.

When Sienna returned, he would have to ask her if she spotted the other two men in the front room? If they were gone, it would suggest that only one was present at dinner time, and if that was their pattern, and if he didn't lock the door, he might be able to surprise the man and hold him off long enough for his girls to escape through the front door of the house.

But he would have to establish a pattern to have any chance for a successful attack.

He continued to hold Carrie in his arms. They would wait for Sienna to return before breaking out the McDonalds.

*****

TWENTY-FIVE

THE EASTERN DEEP DESERT, YEMEN
DAY FOURTEEN   4:30 AM

The two Seahawk helicopters lifted off from the deck of the USS Enterprise and made their way inland off the coast of Aden at an altitude of 500 feet. The two helicopters contained a full team of twenty members of SEAL Team 2, all of whom were mission ready and looking forward to an assignment; any assignment that would break up the monotony of endless training.

Based on intelligence received earlier that evening from JSOC, an analyst from somewhere in the States had run a computer simulation to determine the likely position of a desert caravan that the CIA had been searching for. Unknown to the SEALs, the position of the convoy was first determined by the Black Dog crew in New Mexico using satellite photos of the desert and the fixed coordinates of known caravans making use of the ancient and established trading routes. Once a likely target was identified—a group of about twenty camels; the biggest in the area based on distance and time projections—the information was passed on to the CIA who then did their own computerized simulations before concluding that the New Mexico projections were highly accurate. After that, a series of briefings were conducted with senior administration officials before approval for the mission, which called for a physical interdiction, was given by no less than the President himself.

The helicopters were being guided by an AWAC's Boeing E-3 Sentry that was operating as the *Airborne Command and Control Center.* In addition to the AWAC's, two F16 fighters were on station over the Arabian Sea, available to interdict any threat from the air. Accompanying the two Seahawks was a Boeing AH-64 Apache gunship which would monitor the SEAL mission from just below the horizon in case the operation ran into unexpected trouble.

Lieutenant Commander Eric Brandlin was once again leading the operation. Their target was a caravan that had been traveling during the night and would likely make camp just before daylight. Drone intelligence identified the group in question as being composed of twenty-two camels and sixty men and women.

The mission plan was simple, at least it was on paper. They would interdict the caravan and search for the missing American woman. Deadly force was prohibited, unless, of course, they were obliged to defend themselves. But Brandlin knew what every other combat veteran found out the first time they went out on a mission. Nothing ever went as scripted. There was always an X-factor that changed everything.

His men were ready. Their current tour was almost over, and most of them were starting to think about going home. Brandlin had worked hard to keep them focused. It wasn't easy, but they were professionals, and once they climbed aboard the Seahawks, all thoughts of home were quickly forgotten while his men settled in and allowed the mission to become the focal point of the moment.

The Seahawks landed deep in the Yemeni desert, about two miles east of the caravan camp. They approached their LZ from the East, taking advantage of favorable wind conditions to keep their presence a secret. When the boots hit the ground, the team formed up, and once they were ready, they set off on foot on a hard packed trail, made so by centuries of caravan usage.

The men arrived within sight of the campground just minutes before the sun's first rays would begin to bring light to the waning darkness of the desert sky. Using their night vision scopes, the SEAL scouts were able to locate three heavily armed guards overseeing the camp. This wasn't unusual. Most caravans had to protect themselves from bandits, or worse, but considering their deadly force limitations, it made the SEALs operation more difficult. Stealth would be required to take out the guards with non-lethal force.

The SEALs began a slow creep up to the edge of the encampment, and by using saps, the three caravan sentinels were silently rendered unconscious without incident. The next phase of the plan was to round everyone up, making sure they were unarmed, before conducting a detailed search for Angela Disler.

As his men began to enter the unguarded tents, a single *Makki* tribesman came out of one of them, ostensibly to relieve a full bladder. He took one look at what he believed were members of the Yemeni military forces heading in his direction, ran back into his tent, then popped out again with an AK47, managing to fire off a burst of shots before one of the SEALs fired back, putting him down.

After that, the scene became one of total chaos. With men charging out of tents, guns blazing, a full-scale firefight was soon underway.

Unfortunately for the Makki, they'd never faced warriors of the caliber of the SEALs who brought with them the might of the US military. Had they known at first exactly who they were facing, they might have thought twice before engaging these particular opponents.

The SEALs had the upper hand from the start. They took covering fire positions that enabled them to engage the tribesmen from two different sides without any risk of getting caught in the crossfire. On top of that, they were all wearing night vision goggles, which allowed them to see the tribesmen who weren't in a position to see them at all.

The Makki were easy targets, and most of the shooters went down quickly, but the group was well armed, and surprisingly, they had a lot of firepower behind them. Their AK's were set on full automatic, and they tended to empty their clips into the dark with only a general understanding of where their targets might actually be. But that was not to say that they didn't get off a few lucky shots because, at the height of the battle, two SEALs were hit. Neither one, it turned out, was seriously injured, but the very fact that it happened was nonetheless disconcerting.

The fight appeared to come to a quick resolution when the Apache gunship made a low altitude pass right over the battlefield, the intent of which was to distract the Makki as well as to intimidate. It had the desired effect because as they circled around and prepared to open up with their M230 Chain Gun, Brandlin noticed that the few remaining Makki males were laying down their weapons.

He radioed the gunship and told them to call off their run, then gave the order to his men to move in and take the Makki as prisoners.

When the dust settled, and the camp was pacified, it was determined that thirteen of the Makki tribesmen were KIA, another six wounded, and another twenty-three taken prisoner. Eighteen women and two infant children were rounded up, and fortunately for all concerned, none of them were hurt.

As dawn broke, a careful search was conducted of the campground, but there was no sign of Angela Disler. Several of the Makki were pulled out and interviewed, but none of the tribesmen would admit to speaking Arabic or English, so Brandlin suspended the attempts, pending a decision on what to do next.

The evacuation of the wounded was made using one of the Seahawks, and the first two placed onboard the helicopter were SEALs, neither of whom was in critical condition. The Apache hung around on station in the sky above to provide cover for the troops on the ground should anything unexpected occur that might threaten the safety of what remained of the operation.

An LZ was established, and once the wounded were in the air, the second Seahawk arrived and waited on the ground for Brandlin to give the order to evacuate. While the search for Angela Disler had come up dry, it had still been productive in other ways. A large cache of weapons was discovered, including dozens of AK's, RPG's, and C4 explosives with electronic timers. The Makki weren't talking, but Brandlin was sure that the weapons were intended for the terrorist groups in eastern Yemen and possibly for Oman and other parts unknown. He was also convinced that all or some of the Makki were members of the Ansar al-Sharia.

He called in a situation report to Commander Terry Lawson, who agreed with his assessment and passed the details on to JSOC. A decision was made, and because the Makki were transporting weapons, and because of their possible connection to the Ansar al-Sharia, the Yemeni Republican Guard was notified and they readily agreed to take custody of the prisoners and to oversee the intensive interrogations that would be held once the survivors of the caravan were transported to a military base in the city of *Sanaa*.

When Lawson got back to Brandlin, he filled him in and advised him to return to the ship once the Yemeni Republican Guard arrived at the scene.

While Brandlin spoke to his men, Bryan Harb wandered off to make a call by satellite phone directly to Dan Taylor. He'd been ordered to accompany the SEALs on the raid, and if Angela Disler was located, it would have been his job to conduct an on-the-scene debriefing to determine if she was made privy by her captors as to the reason why she was abducted in the first place. But the fact that she wasn't there, and that the raid had turned into a shooting war, would likely mean that the CIA had lost the opportunity to interdict her before she reached the coast. There were just too many small caravans to put boots on the ground and inspect them all. They would have to try something else if they wanted to track her down.

"Hey, Dan," he said. "It's Bryan."

"Did you find her?" Taylor asked.

Bryan filled him in on the details of the operation, about the firefight and the casualties, and Brandlin's belief that the Makki were aligned with the Ansar al-Sharia. He ended with the JSOC decision to involve the Yemeni's in the prisoner interrogation.

"The Yemenis are gonna be focused on the weapons, Bryan, where the Makki got them and where they were headed, so we need to have you on scene to make sure that they question the males about Disler. Maybe someone there knows something we can use?"

"I'll see to it, sir, but I've got to say I don't think we're going to get anywhere with these searches. It truly is like looking for a needle in a haystack. By now, if they moved her during the day as well as night, she could already be at the coast. We need to rethink what we're doing and take a different approach."

Taylor, who was seated at his desk in Cairo, leaned back in his chair.

"What do you have in mind?"

"I think we should keep up the drone surveillance, we might get lucky, but I want to go directly to the coast of Oman. Considering what's happened here, I think our best chance is to try and intercept her there."

"You might be right." Taylor gave it some thought. "You go ahead and go on to Oman. Maybe we'll have better luck. Call me as soon as you get settled in. As I mentioned to you before, the Israeli's want you to team up with one of their operatives, so once you tell me where you're staying, I'll have him meet you at your hotel."

"I don't work well with anyone, sir. I'm better off alone."

"We've been through this, Bry. He's one of their better men, and I promised the Israeli's that we'd keep them in the loop."

"He'll just get in the way, sir."

"I can personally vouch for him. He's former military, got connections everywhere, very intelligent, and like you, he's good with languages and can blend in with the Arab populations. He's a specialist, Bryan. He has extensive experience on the ground in Iran."

Bryan sighed. It looked as though he had no choice in the matter.

"Fine. I'll let you know when I get settled."

****

Fifteen miles to the East from where Brandlin was standing, a small caravan of three camels and ten people slowly made it's way across the unmarked border into the country of Oman. Angela Disler was with the group, covered with garments head to toe with only her eyes showing. Once the anesthesia was out of her body, and once she resumed eating solid food, her strength returned quickly, and while she slept in a sling on the side of a camel for several hours each night, she managed to hold her own on foot with the other women in the group.

They had broken off from the larger caravan two days before and had no knowledge that the American's had just completed an interdiction of the largest of what was left of the initial group.

Angela hated cooperating with her captors, but she could sense that they meant business, and her only hope of seeing her husband and children again was to cooperate for the moment and hope that her nightmare would soon be over.

One thing was certain. She made a promise to herself that if she ever made it back home alive, she would never set foot in a god-forsaken desert again.

*****

TWENTY-SIX

LOS ANGELES, CALIFORNIA
DAY FOURTEEN   5:30 PM

Shari Thompson came into the squad room and went straight to her desk. First order of business was to take off her gun and holster, put them in her desk with her purse, then walk straight to the lunch room where she poured herself a cup of hot, black coffee.

The night before she intended to do a little research on her home computer. She wanted to see what she could dig up on Angela Disler, but her three boys had been anything but cooperative, so by the time she was finished feeding them, settling their disputes, and overseeing their completion of homework, it was well past ten p.m. She fought off exhaustion and managed to do a preliminary background search, but what she discovered was really disappointing.

When she woke up in the morning, after getting her three boys off to school, she spent the first part of the day searching every database for information about Angela Disler, but she came up with very little. So after lunch, she started a canvas of the Disler's neighborhood.

Three hours of going door to door, followed by visits to other neighborhoods to talk to friends of Angela's had absolutely wiped her out.

She walked back to her cubicle, settled into her chair, and took her first sip of the mediocre coffee.

"What's wrong?" Donahue asked from the adjacent cubicle.

"This coffee sucks," Thompson replied. She screwed up her mouth in disgust. "And on top of that, this Angela Disler woman has me stumped. I really had it wrong. She is Miss goody-goody."

Donahue, still seated, spun around, and without getting up, crab-crawled her chair around the partition and into Thompson's cubicle.

"So what'd you find out?" she asked.

Thompson sighed. She opened her desk, removed her purse, and pulled out a steno pad.

"Okay." She flipped through the pages. "She was born in Long Island, New York, to a working-class family of Italian immigrants. Her dad was a tailor and her mother a nurse." She looked up. "An only child, she picked up a BS degree in biology from Yale, and her MD from the University of Maryland, School of Medicine, in Baltimore."

She looked down at her notes again.

"She completed her residency at the University of Chicago, became a researcher at the National Cancer Institute, then worked at the Institute of Human Virology (IHV) at the University of Maryland before moving on to Zurich Pharmaceuticals in Santa Monica."

Donahue slowly shook her head. "That's quite a pedigree!"

"It gets better," Thompson replied. "At the IHV, she worked with Dr. Robert Gallo. He's famous for his role in the discovery of the infectious agent HIV, which we all know is responsible for AIDS."

Donahue sighed. "No wonder she had what it takes to make that Nobel quality breakthrough."

Thompson nodded. "According to all her friends, she's a devoted mom, a brilliant chemist, and desperately in love with her husband. In short, she's boring."

"Is that how you view unparalleled success?"

"Without a little rain, it's impossible to appreciate the sunshine fully." Donahue laughed.

"Where'd you pick that up? From a fortune cookie?"

"Well, it's true, isn't it?"

"If that's the case, then I guess I'd have to say that our Angela is now experiencing a full blown thunderstorm."

"Nice metaphor, Jen." Thompson took a deep breath. "So what did you learn about Henrik?"

Donahue opened her notebook.

"I didn't fare much better with Henrik. He did his undergrad at Princeton where he was cum laude with an AB degree in Molecular Biology. After that, he went to the University of Chicago where he met Angela, and coincidently, got his Doctor of Medicine. After they got married, he also went to the University of Maryland for his residency in Internal Medicine while she began her work at the IHV. When she took the job at Zurich, he transferred his practice to UCLA where he's a Clinical Professor at the David Geffen School of Medicine."

Donahue flipped to the next page in her notes.

"I did a check on the family's financials. The mortgage on their house is their only debt. They pay their credit card bills in full every month. Got money in the bank, drive nice cars; in short, we've got no hint of a scandal or impropriety."

She got to her feet.

"I guess I should fill the Captain in on what we know."

Thompson snorted. "I was hoping that something was gonna turn up, something we could latch on to, but I guess you were right. There is something else going on here, something we haven't hit on—"

"Sorry to interrupt, but have you guys got a moment?"

Mitzi Roberts walked up and corralled an empty chair from a nearby vacant cubicle which she pushed over to join their little group.

As a detective, she had no equal when it came to her knowledge of computers and electronics in general. Throughout her high school and college years, she'd played around as a hacker, never doing anything destructive, but just the same, she had walked a thin line when it came to legality. She enjoyed cracking codes and breaking through firewalls—skills that served her well with the LAPD.

She was a striking brunette with her black rimmed reading glasses, but her good looks were completely deceiving. Beneath that girl-next-door beauty and demure facade was a woman with an IQ of around 140; a formidable opponent in any debate, and one who was not afraid to tangle physically with male suspects who were twice her size.

She was known for her quick retorts and her easygoing smile which at the moment was on full display.

"What's up, ladies?" she said, taking a seat.

"Hey, Mitz." Donahue leaned back in her chair. "Great job on closing out that case of yours. I saw you last night on CNN, and you actually sounded like you knew what you were talking about."

Roberts had been giving interviews for the past several days on the case of a prolific serial killer that she'd been working on for several months. The man in question had already been linked by DNA to more than half a dozen murders throughout the United States, and there was a strong possibility that there were at least a half a dozen more.

Roberts winked at Thompson then focused her attention on Donahue.

"Considering that's coming from someone who *rarely* knows what she's talking about, I'll take that as a compliment."

Donahue snickered.

"Not bad, Mitz, but I've got a tiny little suggestion for you. Next time you're on the tube, lose the black rimmed glasses. They make you look…how can I say this…*too studious?*"

"For your information, Smarty, I was out partying the night before, so those glasses were strategically placed to conceal the dark circles under my eyes."

She gave Thompson a wink before returning her smile to Donahue.

"And by the way, Jen, you might want to consider getting yourself a pair of reading glasses. You could afford to look a little more studious."

Thompson laughed.

"If you two are finished sparring with the one-liners, is there any chance we can get back down to business?"

Donahue smiled broadly. "What'd you find out, Mitz?"

"Well, you asked me to go through her emails to see if there was something going on that was unusual or strange? Fortunately for us, she hoarded her emails. She'd read one and leave it in her mailbox as she moved on to the next. She never hit delete or put stuff in the trash."

"So…?" Donahue asked.

"So, there was nothing unusual going on. I went back almost nine months; almost fifteen hundred emails, and there was nothing! *Nada! Zilch!* It was mostly store advertisements and correspondence with girlfriends. Nothing jumped out as unusual or out of line."

"Well, that clinches it," said Thompson. "The lady is a now a certified saint."

Donahue shot Roberts a skeptical look.

"There was nothing unusual, Mitz? Nothing at all?"

"I didn't say that," she replied in her most pleasant voice. "I said there was nothing in the emails."

Thompson's eyes went wide.

"Out with it, girl."

Mitzi moved in closer.

"I pulled up her internet search history. It seems the lady never bothered to clear that either. Anyway, six months ago, she started doing a lot of research on viruses. In fact, it was pretty extensive, hundreds and hundreds of websites. If she read every page she opened, we're talking many months of hours."

"That's to be expected," Donahue said. "The lady was a genetic virologist. Viruses were her specialty."

"Maybe so," Mitzi replied, "but I thought you said she was a cancer doctor?"

"She is," Thompson interjected. "She developed a method to use harmless viruses to transport chemotherapy agents directly into cancerous tumors."

"Harmless viruses? Now that is interesting."

"What is?" Donahue asked.

Roberts cleared her throat.

"Her research was focused on deadly viruses, like Ebola, Bubonic Plague, Cholera, Anthrax... and at least a half a dozen more."

Donahue shot Thompson a puzzled look. That didn't make any sense, at least, not to her. She wasn't a science geek, but it seemed to her that if Disler's work involved using harmless viruses, then why would she be spending so much time reading up on the one's that were deadly?

Thompson was the first to speak.

"Hey, Jen, so you remember when we interviewed Lum? Didn't he mention something about how she made her discovery?" She struggled with her thoughts to get it right. "I think he said she was *'working on another project'* or something like that when she developed her technique. Maybe that other project has something to do with her kidnapping?"

"*Of course!*" Donahue rolled her eyes. "We were so focused on the cancer application we never asked Lum about the other project."

She got to her feet.

"What are you gonna do?" Thompson asked.

"Talk to Lum."

She slid her chair back into her cubicle and got on the phone. It took a few minutes, but after several transfers, Lum finally got on the line.

"Doctor? It's Jen Donahue. The other day you told us that Angela was working on another project when she made her big breakthrough. Can you say what the nature of that other project was all about?"

The silence was protracted…so long, in fact, that Donahue wasn't sure that he was still on the line.

"Doctor?"

He finally spoke.

"I'm sorry, detective, but that other project is classified."

"Classified? You mean as *trade secret* classified? Something like that?"

There was a long pause again before he answered.

"Not exactly! Angela was working on a classified government project. That's all I'm allowed to say."

*****

TWENTY-SEVEN

MUSCAT, OMAN
1:00 PM   DAY FIFTEEN

Bryan walked through the lobby and into the *Trader Vic's* restaurant at the *InterContinental Hotel* in Muscat, Oman. Vic's was an international chain of Tiki style restaurants whose claim to fame was their fruity rum cocktails.

It took a few moments for his eyes to adjust to the reduced lighting, but he was able to see that their lunch business was booming. He continued through the restaurant and out onto the terrace where the harsh desert daylight caused his eyes to squint.

He was dressed in a lightweight summer business suit, and in keeping with his CIA legend as a successful Lebanese businessman, he wore a gold Rolex watch (actually, a good Chinese knockoff) and a one carat, deep blue sapphire ring.

He glanced around, taking in the faces of the other diners, always on the alert for anything that didn't seem right. In his line of work, he tried to leave nothing to chance, but no matter how careful he tried to be, he knew that things could always go wrong.

He spotted what he was looking for, a male who was similarly dressed in a lightweight business suit with a white Keffiyeh on his head. His skin was well tanned, and he was bearded.

Bryan approached the table as the man got to his feet.

"*As-salamu alaykum'*," Bryan said, giving the man the traditional Muslim greeting of "*Peace be upon you.*"

Mordecai smiled. This man he was here to meet spoke excellent Arabic, so per the Islamic rule, he returned the greeting with an even better one.

"*Assalamu 'alaikum wa rahmatullahi wa barakatuh.*" (May peace, mercy and blessings of God be upon you.)"

The two men then shook hands, and per the custom in Arabia, they exchanged three light cheek to cheek kisses, alternating sides. Anyone watching them would have concluded that they were two Arabic businessmen about to have a business lunch.

During the exchange of kisses, Bryan whispered the prearranged code phrase, and Mordecai whispered back the correct response. Once that was out of the way, Mordecai invited Bryan to join him at the table, and as he did so, a very observant waiter came running over to offer the two of them cocktails. Bryan ordered the Scorpion, one of Trader Vic's signature cocktails, while Mordecai settled for his favorite, a *Mai Tai*.

Mordecai wore the Keffiyeh. He had a short, dark beard, and his skin had been brushed with an oil based tanning agent. The effect was to make plausible the legend he used as an important Arab businessman.

Once the waiter left to fetch their drinks, Bryan said, "I've been told you've already been brought up to speed."

Mordecai nodded. "Dan Taylor is a friend of mine. He filled me in last night."

Bryan looked around, then lowered his voice.

"Taylor says you have a lot of contacts here. Have you heard anything that might help us?"

"I only got here late last night, but after lunch, I thought I could start making the rounds."

Their drinks arrived a few moments later and they toasted to each other's good health.

"So, what's your take on the situation?" Mordecai asked.

"So far they've managed to stay one step ahead of us, but by now they have to know that we're on their trail, and for that reason, they're going to do whatever they can to get her over to Iran as quickly as possible. They could keep to the desert and try to make it to *Ras Al-Khaimah,* in the UAE, but if they did that, it would take a lot longer to get there, and that would give us more days to search for them by drone." He shook his head. "I wouldn't want to take a chance like that, so I don't think that they would either."

"So you think they'll come directly here? To Muscat?"

Bryan nodded. "The people they contracted to move her are Makki tribesmen. For the most part, they live along the coast of Oman. They're gonna stick to a route where they know the people and the government. And by coming to Muscat, they can more easily blend in with the population. In the UAE, they wouldn't be as invisible." He took another sip of his drink. "It's gonna be Muscat. I'm convinced of it."

"And where do you think they're headed once they're out on the water?"

"*Bandar-e-Abbas*. It's the home port of the Iranian navy and the closest main port to Muscat."

But Mordecai wasn't convinced.

"It would take them an easy twenty-four hours to go by sea to Bandar from Muscat. But if they sail out of Ras on the coast of the UAE, they could make the crossing at the *Strait of Hormuz* and get to Bandar in just a couple of hours."

Bryan didn't agree.

"At this point, I think they're not worried about making it all the way to Bandar. All they have to do is get into Iranian territorial waters, and they can take their time moving up the coastline. We didn't board their ship off the coast of Yemen until it finally reached international waters. The Iranians will assume that we'll act with restraint to avoid an International incident."

Mordecai thought it over.

"I see your point. They can leave from Muscat, sail straight across the Gulf of Oman, and be in Iranian waters in about five hours." He locked eyes with Bryan. "It makes sense. I think you might be right. So what do you want me to do?"

"We'll work independently," Bryan said. "You talk to your people and I'll talk to mine. That way, we can get twice as much done."

Mordecai smiled. That was a nice way of saying don't show me your sources and I won't show you mine.

"So how do we stay in touch."

"Satellite phone."

They exchanged numbers, then signaled to the waiter that they were ready to order their lunch. Once the orders were in, Mordecai turned his attention back to Bryan.

"Do your people have any idea why the Iranians want her bad enough to go to all this trouble?"

"I haven't the faintest. All I know is we're supposed to find her and get her back from the Iranians, and that's good enough for me."

Mordecai held his glance.

"I was briefed about your loss on 9/11. All I can say is that I'm really sorry."

Bryan was shocked that Mordecai had been made privy to that kind of personal information, and it showed on his face. Mordecai could sense that he'd made a mistake by bringing it up, so he quickly changed topics.

"I spent two years in Tehran on assignment for the Mossad, so if we don't catch up to her here in Oman, I've got a lot of good contacts there. Maybe one of them will know what's going on."

"You were in the military, right?" Bryan asked.

"I spent a year on the border with Egypt and two years up in the Golan Heights at an outpost that overlooked the Syrian border. But the best part of the job was my work with Jordanian Intelligence; tracking down nomadic Bedouin's who smuggled drugs and weapons through the Negev desert."

"Were you Intelligence during your time in the service?"

"No, that came after. I had a knack for languages, so they made me an offer I couldn't refuse."

For the first time in a while, Bryan smiled.

"Same here, I was a language prodigy, so after my military service, I also got an offer I couldn't refuse."

The two men laughed. Real linguists with time spent in the theater of war were worth their weight in gold.

"I was a Marine," Bryan added with a measure of pride. "I trained as a sniper."

"I also trained as a sniper," Mordecai said with a smirk. "But it's a skill set I seldom get to use."

After another thirty minutes of small talk, while they finished lunch, Mordecai picked up the check with his credit card. While he waited for the waiter to return with a receipt, he said, "I'm going to focus on the smaller harbors outside the city limits. Where will you be?"

"I'll stay within the city proper. I want to check out the ships in the harbor and talk to some of my sources. So, I guess I'll see you back here at the hotel tonight?"

"I'm on the sixth floor, room 624."

"I'm on the third. 342. Ring me up when you get back, and I'll buy the drinks."

"You're on."

*****

TWENTY-EIGHT

LOS ANGELES, CALIFORNIA
DAY FIFTEEN   9:10 AM

Donahue was on the phone with a DA at the Van Nuys courthouse explaining why the DA would just have to put the preliminary hearing on by herself without Donahue there to hold her hand.

"You don't need my testimony, Miss Rizzo. Detective Gibson was my partner at the time and he said he'd handle it for me." She listened politely as the prosecutor continued to whine, but she could tell that the rant was losing steam as the realization sank in that Gibson would be there to guide her through it.

It was then that she spotted her Captain coming in. He was on his way over to his office.

She put her hand over the mouthpiece on the phone and called out, "Captain? Have you got a minute?"

"Yeah, sure. Give me a bit to get settled."

Donahue nodded back. Elwood's daily business routine was a quick trip to the coffee room to get a cup and a search for any baked goods that might be lying around.

She returned her attention to the whiny DA.

"Is Gibson there with you?" she said into the phone, and when the DA said yes, she added, "Can I talk to him for a second?"

"You gonna show up?" he said when he got on the line.

"I can't Gibby. Shari and I are still working the kidnapping. You got it covered?"

"Don't I always?"

"I appreciate it. Rizzo seems to be wrapped a little too tight today. Just between us, I think it might be that time of the month for her, so don't lose your cool. Okay?"

"Oh, Jeez! That was way too much information, Jen."

Donahue smiled. Pulling his chain and throwing him off his game was a rare occurrence, but it was always so wonderfully satisfying.

She hung up the phone and looked around for Thompson but she still hadn't made her entrance, so she gathered up her notebook and made a beeline for the Captain's office.

Elwood was seated behind his desk with a steaming cup of black coffee in one hand and a plastic fork in the other. He was just about to cut into a Southern Red Velvet cupcake when Donahue walked in without knocking and took a seat in front of his desk.

She spotted the cupcake.

"Is that a Red Velvet from the *Vanilla Bake Shop?*"

Elwood was suddenly possessive.

"It is, and it's mine."

"Cut me off a little piece, will you?" she said, leaning up.

"No way! Go get your own."

"Seems to me the last time we had cupcakes from there I shared mine with you?"

Elwood was over a barrel. She was right, of course.

"There were a couple of others still in the box," he said lamely.

"But you took the last Red Velvet, didn't you?"

The fight was over and he knew it. He cut the cupcake in half with his fork and slid her share across the desk on a paper napkin.

"Knock yourself out," he told her, "but you can get your own coffee 'cause you're not getting any of mine."

"Gee, thanks, boss." She picked up the cupcake. "I think I'll save this for later."

She smiled to herself. He was already devouring his half of the cupcake and she knew that he would covet her half as long as it was uneaten.

Through a mouthful of frosting and cake, he said, "You came in here for something other than my cupcake, right?"

Donahue nodded. "Mitzi went through Angela Disler's personal computer and discovered that six months ago she was doing a lot of research on infectious diseases."

"So?" He took a quick sip of his coffee. "She's a virologist, right?"

"Exactly! We were looking at her work as a possible reason for her being kidnapped, but everyone was focused on her breakthrough, you know, the one that involved using a harmless virus to deliver chemotherapy to cancerous tumor cells."

Elwood nodded. His eyes shifted to her half of the cupcake.

"You gonna eat that?" he said.

She pulled it closer to herself.

"When I get back to my desk where I left my coffee."

"Okay," he said, eyes still on the cupcake. "Continue."

"Lum, her boss over at Zurich, told us that she made this great discovery while she was working on another project. So when Mitzi discovered her research on infectious diseases, I gave him a call to see if that was part of her other project. But get this. Lum said her other project was for the government *and that it was classified.*"

She waited to see if he made the connection, but a shrug of his shoulders told her that he hadn't.

"I still don't know where you're going with this, Jen. She's a virologist working with infectious diseases. What are you trying to say?"

"Biological warfare, Boss. I think the good doctor was working on a classified governmental project dealing with infectious diseases. Why else would the project be classified?"

"That's a pretty big leap, Jen."

"It's the only thing that makes sense. We've pretty much ruled out money as a motive, the family isn't exactly rich, and according to her boss, this significant discovery of hers relating to cancer won't pay off for almost a decade. It's got to be the government work. What else could it be?"

Satisfied that she'd made her point, she leaned back in her chair to give him time to absorb the import of what she was saying.

For his part, Elwood's mind was spinning. Donahue's conclusion made a lot of sense, but Disler's research on a computer six months earlier was certainly not proof of anything certain. In fact, it was tenuous at best. A good researcher—especially one working on a classified government project—would never use a personal computer to do their basic research. It wasn't secure, and it would probably violate a number of federal laws. And if she was doing research at home on infectious diseases, it could have been for any number of legitimate reasons, all unrelated to her work for the government.

But the more he thought about it, the more Donahue's theory seemed to add up.

He wiped his mouth with a napkin, then said, "I'm not completely sold on your theory, but I'm thinking we better let the Feds know what you've turned up."

Donahue gritted her teeth. "I'm glad you brought that up. Remember when we asked to be briefed on what happened to Disler in Egypt? Davis told us we were all out of the loop, and that the CIA was worried about the details of her abduction getting out. But someone in government must know what she was working on, and if it was a biological weapon, then maybe that's what they don't want getting out."

She shot him a smile. She'd finally arrived at a workable theory, and she could tell from his expression that he was giving it some serious thought.

"Either way," she added a moment later, "if that is the case, there's no way they're gonna share that info with us."

"Talk to Davis again," he said.

"I already did. I called him this morning. I didn't tell him what I suspect about her possible connection with biological weapons. All I said was we really needed some basic facts to pursue our line of investigation, but he sang the same old song: his hands are tied; they haven't told him a thing."

"You believe him?" Elwood asked.

"He might be telling the truth. I honestly don't know, but I can't help feeling that this goes way beyond Elliot Davis."

Elwood leaned back in his chair again, folded his hands into a steeple, and tried to review their possible options.

They could keep on working blind while they tried to unravel what had happened to Disler's family, or they could tell the Feds to shove it and do the case themselves. The latter would be the easiest way out of this mess, but Elwood felt an abiding sense of loyalty to the victims, as did all the members of his unit. Just because the higher-ups in the bureaucracy had their heads up their asses while they jealously guarded their territorial imperative, it didn't mean that he nor any of his people would ever throw in the towel.

They owed the Disler's their best effort, and if the Feds wouldn't cooperate, then they'd have to find a way to work around them.

Donahue interrupted his thoughts.

"I was thinking if she was doing biological weapons research, and if that's the reason why she was kidnapped, then the family might have been taken as leverage to force her to tell them what she knows."

Elwood nodded. Donahue's theory was making more sense by the minute.

"We need to know exactly what she was working on to be able to assess the risks to her family," she added, "and once we know that, it might help us to strategize what the kidnappers of the family might do to expose their whereabouts inadvertently."

Elwood rubbed his hand through his hair.

"Last time we spoke, I put a call into an old friend of mine who works in DC. I explained our situation, but I haven't heard back yet. You gonna be around the office today?"

Donahue nodded. "I got Gibby to cover my prelim in the Valley, so I'll be around unless something else breaks."

Elwood slowly shook his head and said, "What a cluster fuck." It signaled the end of their meeting.

Donahue got to her feet and started for the door.

"You forgot your half of the cupcake," he called out.

She wasn't about to tell him that she was the one who'd stopped at the bakeshop on her way in, or that she'd already secreted a *Red Velvet Cupcake* and a *Spicy Carrot Cupcake* inside a drawer in her desk.

"You can have it, Captain." She said from over her shoulder. "I don't need the extra calories."

"And you're saying that I do?"

He glanced down at his waist.

But she didn't answer. She just had a thought about what they might do to get a fix on Henrik Disler and his two missing daughters.

*****

TWENTY-NINE

MUSCAT, OMAN
DAY FIFTEEN   3:00 PM

Angela slowly opened her eyes as the effects of the drugs began to wane. She'd been conscious for almost an hour, drifting in and out of sleep. Sadly, she'd learned from experience that if she tried to move around too quickly, the room would spin and the dry heaves would begin anew.

This time, because she was taking it slow, she hadn't even felt nauseous, a welcome relief considering what she'd already been through. She had no sense of time, the nights and days of captivity all blended together. She assumed that it was nighttime. She couldn't tell because she couldn't see a window and there was no light inside where she was lying. She closed her eyes once more, counted to five, then opened them wide. It wasn't a dream; she really was still a captive.

She'd been awake long enough now that her mind was clearing. She knew she'd been drugged and kidnapped, put on a boat, then taken through the desert on a camel. She remembered walking for a while with a group of Arab women, but she'd become physically drained again, too weak to keep up with the pace, so she was drugged once more and put in a sling that hung down over the side of a camel. She had no real sense of time, so she had no idea how long this process had been going on. All she knew with any real certainty was that she wanted it to end, somehow, some way, because she wasn't really sure she could make it much longer.

She tried to assess her physical condition. She pinched the skin on the back of her wrist, and when it didn't bounce back fast enough, it confirmed her belief that she was still severely dehydrated. And her headache was still there; it seemed that she'd had it forever. That could also mean dehydration, or perhaps it was just a side effect of being pumped full of some kind of anesthetic drug.

She moved her hands and feet around. They seemed to work fine, but if she'd been able to see herself in a mirror she would have been shocked.

As petite as she was, she'd lost a good ten pounds since the day of her kidnapping, and on her slight frame, it was readily apparent.

She suddenly realized that her legs and arms weren't bound. Well, that was a first. She must be somewhere where they weren't worried that she would run away. She almost smiled at the thought. If she could run away, where would she go? She didn't even know what country she was in.

The air around her was completely still and *stale*, and she couldn't help but think about her home in West LA and the evenings she spent with her husband and daughters down at the beach in nearby Santa Monica.

What she wouldn't give to be there right now.

Her husband and her kids. What must they be thinking? That she'd just run off? That she didn't love them? Or would they realize that something was wrong?

She prayed to God that Henrik had already sounded the alarm, because if he did, then maybe someone would be looking for her.

She started to cry, but she was far too dehydrated to develop any tears. Then she heard a noise. It was off in the distance and it sounded like—

What? A ship's horn?

Am I somewhere near the coast?

There it was again. It was definitely the horn of a ship. Thank God! We must finally be out of the desert. But what coastline? *What country?*

She hoped to God she was still in Yemen. At least if she was in Yemen there were US forces somewhere nearby. Not that they would ever be looking for her, but at least there was always a chance that someone would see her and know that she wasn't a Yemeni woman and maybe that would get back to someone who could do something that would help.

She buried the thought. That wasn't going to happen. No one was ever going to find her now. These horrible people seemed to know exactly what they were doing. So if she was lucky, really lucky, then perhaps she would just get sick and die.

What could they want with her? She hoped it was something as simple as money. At least that would mean that she had a chance. But a nagging suspicion had slowly begun to percolate up from her subconscious, one that suggested that her predicament was somehow related to her work. And if that was true, she could no longer deny the real likelihood that her final destination just might be a country like Iran or Pakistan, the only two powers in the region sophisticated enough to desire or make use of her information.

If that was the case, she shuddered to think what she was going to have to endure. She would probably be tortured to get her to talk, and the thought of that was enough to make her physically ill. But that wasn't the worst of it. She would never see her family again because once they had what they wanted, they would never let her go. If she was forced to reveal what she knew, the consequences would be dire, for it would certainly change the balance of power throughout the entire world.

She decided she would never let it get to that. She would just have to find a way to kill herself before it ever got to that point.

A door to her left suddenly opened and someone threw a switch. A single overhead light came on.

Angela blinked rapidly, trying to see, hoping her eyes would soon adjust to the light.

Muhammad walked in and stood over her. "You're awake? I thought I heard you moving around."

"I'm sorry I've been such a burden to you, but I've been too weak to walk on my own."

Muhammad smiled again and slowly nodded.

"It won't be for much longer. You are almost at your destination."

He began to tie her hands, but she didn't struggle. Why bother? There was no way she could resist them anyway.

"Can you tell me where I'm going?" she asked.

Muhammad produced a syringe.

"Please, no," she said. There was panic in her voice.

"This will be the last time," he said as he stuck the needle into a vein in her arm.

She tried to fight the looming unconsciousness, but the fog of the anesthesia soon coursed through her body, and once again, she slipped into the void.

*****

THIRTY

LOS ANGELES, CALIFORNIA
11:00 AM   DAY FIFTEEN

Shari Thompson opened a refrigerated lunch bag and pulled out her mid-morning snack; a small bag of tiny pieces of celery, carrots and baby radishes. At home, she had mixed up a batch of ranch dressing, but she only brought along two tablespoons full, as any more than that would be too much temptation and would severely undermine what she hoped to accomplish. Years of experience had taught her that denial was the only successful way for her to lose a quick five pounds, so she dipped and then munched on a carrot while she used her computer to make a quick search of Amazon for a pair of skinny black leather pants.

Donahue arrived at her own cubicle and peered over the divider.

"Is that your breakfast?" she asked.

Thompson nodded. "I need to lose a couple of pounds."

"Sorry to hear that," said Donahue as she opened a small bakery box.

Thompson looked up, sniffed the air, then shook her head.

"You didn't?"

"Sure did."

Donahue smiled as she held up a Spicy Carrot cupcake. "I set one aside for you."

"Damn, you, Jen." Thompson turned back to the screen and clicked out of the Amazon site. "You are pure evil. How can you do this to me?"

"'Cause I love you. Try to think of it this way, Shari. You're eating raw carrots, and this is mostly baked carrots, so what's the diff?"

"The diff is the sugar," said Thompson. Her mouth was salivating.

Donahue dangled the cupcake out over the top of the divider.

Decision made.

Thompson took the cupcake, set it down on her desk, and put the veggies back into her cooler

"I didn't really want to eat that rabbit food anyway," she said as she took a small bite of the cupcake and smiled with pleasure.

"Mmm..."

She then got to her feet and looked over the top of the divider to watch as Donahue pulled another cupcake from out of the box.

"You want a part of mine?" Donahue held it up. "Red Velvet?"

Thompson smiled. "A fifty-fifty split, okay?"

Donahue nodded, and while the exchange was underway, Thompson's phone began to ring.

"Robbery-Homicide," she said when she answered it. "This is Thompson."

"Detective Thompson! Hello. My name is David Hatcher. I'm a senior staffer for Senator Jane Perribone. The Senator asked me to give you a call."

Earlier that morning and all on her own, Thompson looked up the Washington number for the office of the Chairman of the Senate Intelligence Committee. On a whim, she called the number, and once she identified herself, and to her great surprise, she was put right through to the Senator herself.

She explained to Perribone that she was working an active kidnapping case and that she was trying to learn whatever she could about any contracts that the government might have with Zurich Pharmaceuticals. The Senator expressed what sounded like genuine concern for the victims, and she graciously agreed to see what she could do to help.

Apparently, the call from the Senator's assistant was Perribone's response.

"Thank you for getting back to me so soon, Mr. Hatcher. Have you got any information that can help us out?"

Hatcher was at his desk in Washington DC. He leaned back in his chair and began to doodle on a notepad.

"The Senator asked me to check out any government research contracts we might have with Zurich, and I located three that we signed off on."

"Hold on for a second, Mr. Hatcher. Let me get a notebook and something to write with."

Thompson scrambled to get what she needed from her top desk drawer. "Okay. Go ahead."

Hatcher read from a list that he had compiled earlier that morning.

"The first two are contracts put out by the National Institute of Health (NIH). One was for the development of a drug to eliminate plaque buildup in Alzheimer's patients, and the second was for a drug to open up the blood-brain barrier."

Thompson was writing furiously.

"The blood-brain barrier? What's that?"

"Well, I'm not a scientist, but as I understand it, the blood vessels leading to the brain are very small and tightly packed together. Effectively, the tight packing creates a barrier that prevents larger chemical molecules from getting into the brain. The NIH wanted testing done on a drug that was developed by a neurosurgeon named Keith Black that would expand the blood vessels for a short period of time, enabling chemotherapy drugs composed of larger molecules to make it through the barrier and into the brain." He paused for a moment. "In the synopsis of the NIH proposal, the goal of the project was to verify the procedure as one that was medically safe for the treatment of *glioblastomas.* Apparently, that's a fancy name for a type of brain tumor."

Thompson sighed. She didn't really understand everything that she was writing down, but that was okay. She would look this stuff up on the internet once the call was over.

"How about the third project?" she asked.

"The third was a grant project, proposed by the Army and the CIA. It was to develop the use of inert viruses to transport chemical agents to particularized cells within the body."

Bingo!

Thompson sat up straight. That sounded exactly like the description of Disler's work as given to them by Dr. Lum.

She felt out of her league. She wasn't schooled enough in science to ask the right questions, but she tried anyway.

"You used the term *'chemical agents.'* Is that like using chemotherapy against cancer cells?"

Hatcher thought that over for a moment.

"That sounds about right. Although it says here the project is classified, so I can't say for sure that's what it's all about."

Hatcher looked at the time on his wristwatch. He was running late for a meeting.

"If that's all you need, Detective, I'm afraid I've got to ring off."

"Sure! I understand. Thanks for your help."

"No problem! Oh! The Senator asked me to thank you for your inquiry and she wants to wish you good luck in your investigation."

Thompson hung up the phone.

"What was that all about?" Donahue asked.

Thompson slid her chair backward so that they could both remain seated while talking face to face.

"I'm not really sure," she said with a sigh. "I'll show you my notes. Zurich got three projects from the government, but only one was labeled as classified. It came from the Army and the CIA. They wanted Zurich '*to develop the use of inert viruses to transport chemical agents to particularized cells within the body.* '"

She looked up from her notes.

"I'm confused. If that was the goal of the classified project, then what was Lum talking about when he said that her discovery was made while she was working on *another* project?"

"Maybe he just misspoke himself?"

"I don't know, Jen," Thompson said, shaking her head. "He said it a couple of times. Look, I'm just saying, if she was working on something else, then someone's holding out on us."

She handed Donahue her notes about the other two projects, and when she was through reading about them, she said, "So neither of these other two projects was classified, right?"

"That's correct, so what the hell is going on?"

"I don't know, but one way or another, we're gonna find out."

*****

THIRTY-ONE

SEEB, OMAN
DAY SIXTEEN   2:00 AM

Aseel Al-Lawati was dreaming. He was on a boat, hauling in his net, and for the first time in a long time, it was full of fish.

The sixteen-year-old was lying on a cot on the roof of a small house just across the street from a road that ran along a stretch of beach on the coast of the Gulf of Oman, in the area of *Seeb*, several kilometers to the north of the city of Muscat.

From the roof of the house, the view was of a protected cove that was home base for the local fishermen who plied the waters for a daily catch which they would sell on the beach each night as soon as they got back to the shore. Aseel was the son of a fisherman, and he worked with his father during the day tending to the nets and chumming the bait.

Aseel stirred, then turned over and went back to sleep. He always slept in the house unless it was unusually hot, in which case he preferred to be on the flat roof, on a cot, under a sky filled with stars where it was always a little bit cooler. But tonight he was there for a different reason, and while he did his best to stay awake, he lost the battle about two a.m. when his eyes just wouldn't stay open any longer.

The traffic on the nearby road at this time of night was all but non-existent, so the low growl of a motor pulled him out of his dream and caused him to open his eyes. It took him a moment to remember where he was; then he focused exclusively on the sound. It wasn't a car—too quiet and steady—and he never heard a truck with an engine like that.

He sat bolt upright and listened intently. In the still of the night, he decided that it had to be coming from the water.

He slid off the cot, put on his sandals, then ran to the stairway that took him down to the front yard.

The house was one of many that sat on the inland side of the highway.

He ran through the front yard, past his father's old car and down to the edge of the road. He looked both ways, then pulled up short when it dawned on him that it might be better to creep up on the sound rather than to run up exposed and out in the open.

He crossed the empty highway, then headed for a spot that was completely dark. A row of tall bushes lined the road, so he used them for cover as he headed north towards the cove and the moored fishing vessels that completely filled the little harbor.

The sound of the engine grew louder as he got closer. There was a low seawall ahead of him, so he crawled the last forty feet or so before he reached a point where he felt he could look without the risk of being discovered.

He raised up on his knees and peeked over the top of the wall. What he saw made his heart start to race. A high-powered, twin diesel fishing boat, maybe ten meters long, had made its way into the harbor between the rows of parked vessels. It was idling near the shore, and reachable only by a small rowboat.

A boat like that didn't belong in the harbor. This was a poor fishing community. There was no reason for such an expensive boat to be there.

Perhaps they were smugglers dropping off weapons or drugs. He heard stories about smugglers working the coast, but he'd never seen any in person. He wondered if they had already dropped off their load, but when he looked around, there were no people standing on the shore.

So why had the boat come into the harbor?

His question was answered a few minutes later when a small sedan approached the cove directly from the highway.

Aseel panicked. He dropped to his belly and tried to make himself as small as possible. What he worried about was that he might be seen in a flash of the oncoming headlights. But his fears were unfounded as the vehicle drove right into the parking lot and up to the edge of the water.

Aseel peeked up over the top of the seawall and watched the car as it came to a stop. Two men got out, then opened the rear door, and together they lifted out what looked to him to be an inert body.

Aseel started shaking. Could this be the woman the man was looking for?

He held his breath and continued to watch as the men carried the body down to the shore. One of the men called out. It was in a language that he didn't understand, but he recognized the spoken words as Persian.

He waited and watched as a small rubber dingy was launched from the port side of the idling fishing boat.

It seemed clear to Aseel that the body was going to be taken to the boat in the rubber raft. He wanted to run away, but common sense dictated that he should wait around a while longer to get a better idea of exactly what was going on.

The small boat reached the shore and the two men from the car, aided by the two men from the boat, lifted the body into the raft. After that, the two men from the boat sailed out of the harbor while the others returned to their car.

Aseel had seen enough. He made his way back along the seawall, crossed over to the trees, then hit the ground when the small sedan pulled out of the parking lot. He waited while it drove off, then ran along the tree line to an open spot where he sprinted across the highway.

He stopped in the front yard of his family home and reached into his pocket for his cell phone. It was then that he realized that he'd left it next to the cot where he'd been sleeping.

He ran for the house, climbed up the outdoor stairs and scrambled across the roof. He found his cell phone on a small end table and quickly made the call.

****

Bryan was dead to the world, fast asleep, a luxury in short supply since first getting involved in the hunt for Angela Disler, so it took him a while to come back into consciousness, and even longer to realize that the noise that brought him up was the ringing of his satellite phone.

Now instantly on alert, he sat bolt upright, reached over to the night-stand and brought it up to his ear.

"Yes?" he said.

"I'm on my way over," said Mordecai. The line went dead.

Bryan reached over, turned on the bedside light, and checked the clock. It was 3:00 a.m. He exhaled slowly, gathered his thoughts, then rolled out of bed and made his way to the bathroom. By the time he was done with his ablutions, Mordecai had arrived, so he had let him in while he finished getting dressed.

"I got a call from one of my sources," Mordecai said. "A kid I pay to keep his eyes open. He's in a small fishing village in an area called Seeb, a couple of klicks from here."

Bryan zipped up his pants, fastened his belt, and began to put on his shirt.

"I know the area," he said. "What did he see?"

"A twin- engine fishing boat pulled into the harbor around two this morning. Two men, Persian speakers, kept the boat idling. My source went to investigate. He saw a small white sedan drive up, and two men removed a body from the backseat. They put this body in a small rubber boat that was launched from the fishing boat, and the kid watched as they took the body onboard."

Bryan had stopped dressing. "A body? Alive or dead?"

"He couldn't tell."

"Man or woman?"

"Again, he couldn't tell from where he was hiding."

"But he was sure it was a body?"

Mordecai nodded. "The boat took off as soon as the body was aboard."

Bryan buttoned his shirt and began to put on his shoes and socks.

"What time did this happen?" he asked with a touch of urgency

"He called me just as the boat was leaving the harbor, maybe ten or fifteen minutes ago."

"Did he give you a description of the boat?"

"Ten meters, twin diesel engines, well maintained. Light blue or white in color, hard to tell because of the darkness." Mordecai held his glance. "Shouldn't be too difficult to find out on the open water. There aren't many boats out there this time of night."

Bryan walked over to the nightstand, picked up his satellite phone, and sat on the side of the bed.

"I think it's her," Mordecai said, "but it might just be too late to stop her."

Bryan didn't respond. He was too busy thinking about what he was going to say when his call was picked up.

****

Bryan's call was answered on the very first ring by a technician who was seated at a monitoring console at a top secret CIA facility in the community of Herndon, Virginia.

"This is Tyler," the young man said. He was in his early thirties, one of a select group of Air Force technical wizards and analysts whose job it was to assist the JSOC overseas operations.

"*Operation House Call,*" Bryan responded, giving the code name that had been chosen for the Disler operation.

"ID, please," the technician replied.

Bryan rattled off a series of numbers. The technician responded with a predetermined question, and when Bryan gave the correct answer, the young man replied with a polite, "How can I assist you, sir?"

"I'm looking for a fishing trawler that left the port of Seeb in Oman about twenty minutes ago, likely headed for Iranian territorial waters. Have we got a drone or a satellite up at the moment that could give us eyes in the sky?"

There was a moment of silence as the technician worked on his computer screen.

"We've got a geostationary satellite over the region, but no drones up top at the moment."

Bryan knew that any satellite in the region would be positioned in a geosynchronous orbit in the plane of the equator so that it would remain stationary in relation to a fixed point on the surface. The orbit was achieved at an altitude of 22,300 miles above the earth, giving it the leeway and ability to use powerful cameras to focus in on targets or points of interest far to the North and/or South of its position.

"Can I get you to task the satellite to find me that boat?"

"Affirmative, sir! Do you have the coordinates?"

Bryan sighed. "Negative. But can't you start with the position for Seeb and work your way east from there?"

"I don't see why not," the young man answered. "If I start right away, it'll take about thirty minutes to get her on line."

Bryan shook his head. The delay would mean that they'd be cutting it awfully close. If the boat was to enter Iranian waters, then a boarding operation might be out of the question without the approval of the Joint Chief's and probably the President himself. If they were going to get to Disler before that likelihood, they'd have to act faster than that.

"How long would it take to get a drone on scene?" Bryan asked.

"We could launch a drone from the Enterprise, sir, but that could also take up to thirty minutes. And I'm showing her current location in the Indian Ocean as two hundred miles south/southeast of your target's position, so at best, we could have it on station in—"

He paused to run the calculations.

"—just under two hours."

Again, they'd be cutting it awfully close. And even so, that didn't even factor in the use of SEALs to make the intercept. They'd need to be scrambled now to have time to develop a plan.

It was starting to look as if an intercept was going to be almost impossible, but there just might be time to set up a way to track her once she made it to land.

"Okay, Tyler. Here's what I want you to do. Task the satellite first; we need to watch that ship in real time. I believe they're moving an unconscious human cargo, so I need your people to watch in real-time for any kind of transfer, at sea or on land. That's critical, you copy?"

"Yes, sir," the technician replied.

"Next, I want you to launch a drone, same goal. We need to watch that ship, track her location, and watch for any movement of the cargo."

"Roger that, sir."

Bryan was struck by a sudden thought. "Will I need to get authorization for this?"

"No, sir, we were told to expect a possible operation. *House Call* has been given a priority clearance, sir."

"Thank you, Tyler. I'll be in touch."

He hung up and looked over at Mordecai.

"You may be right. We might not be able to get to the ship before it makes it into Iranian waters. Do your people have any assets in the area?"

Mordecai smiled. "Assets, probably, but it would take too long for me to get the necessary approvals to mount any kind of intercept operation, particularly when we have no idea what this incident is all about."

Bryan nodded. In their position, he would feel the same reluctance to get involved. He picked up his phone again.

"Who're you calling?" Mordecai asked.

"My boss."

"Want me to step out?"

"That's not necessary. I was told to keep you in the loop, so take a seat. This could take awhile."

****

Dan Taylor was sound asleep in his room at the embassy compound in Cairo when Bryan's call came through, and like most people involved in the war on terror, the ringing of the phone in the middle of the night was a sound that brought him instantly awake.

Bryan filled him in on the situation, covering the observations made by Mordecai's source, the call to the CIA monitoring station, and the re-tasking of the satellite and the launching of a drone. By the time he was finished, Taylor was already pacing the floor in his room.

"So we don't know for sure that it was Disler that was taken aboard the boat. Is that correct?"

"That's right, Dan. But who else could it be?"

Taylor didn't answer his question. He thought it was probably her, but there could easily be several other explanations for what was observed, including the Iranians capturing of a dissident, or the dumping of a body of an enemy. He could go on and on, but sometimes you had to go with your gut, and Taylor's gut was telling him that the odds were in favor of the Disler scenario.

"Assuming the guys in Herndon can get a fix on the boat, should we launch the SEALs?" Bryan asked.

"I'm not sure they could make it in time." Taylor scratched his head. His mind was spinning. "Given the head start these guys already have, by the time we could get a team on scene they could be well inside Iranian waters."

Bryan responded, "I've been looking at my Google map and it looks like the distance from Muscat to Iranian waters is only about a hundred and fifteen nautical miles. If we launched right away, we might just make it."

Taylor stopped pacing and pinched the bridge of his nose while he tried to review the larger picture. He could launch the SEALs from the Enterprise, but they might not make it in time. If they didn't, he'd have to go up the chain to get clearance to board the ship in Iranian waters, a decision that would not be readily forthcoming.

And what if they did board the ship in time? What if the cargo wasn't really a body? It might be nothing more then a dead goat or something that would prove to be equally embarrassing. But the real issue was even more severe than that. How far was his government willing to go to get back a kidnapped citizen whose value to those who took her was completely unknown? The people involved might not be acting on behalf of the government. They might be nothing more than common criminals.

Could Niroomad have been running his own little criminal enterprise?

Too many uncertainties, they would have to tread carefully.

"I'll give the order to launch the SEALs," he finally said to Bryan, "but on one condition. If the boat makes it into Iranian territorial waters before we can interdict, the mission is off. Any action of any kind in Iranian territory is going to require approval at the highest level, and I'm not sure we're certain enough about the integrity of our intelligence to take it up the ladder without additional verification."

"Fair enough," Bryan said. "Loop the SEALs directly into *House Call in* Herndon. "We'll stand down at this end until we see what happens."

"I'll get back to you later," Taylor replied.

His next call was to JSOC to have them launch the SEALs.

*****

THIRTY-TWO

LANGLEY, VIRGINIA
DAY FIFTEEN   7:00 PM

The below ground conference room at the CIA Ops Center at Langley was comparatively small. It could accommodate twenty people, but at the present time, there were only twelve. Included in the group were CIA Director Hamilton Granger, several members of his staff, four members of the Joint Chief's of Staff, and five representatives from JSOC, the Joint Special Operations Command, the group whose operation was now underway.

The room was filled with computers and four sixty inch flat screens which were mounted on a wall at the head of the table. The screens carried feeds from around the world. One of the feeds was from a high flying geosynchronous satellite in orbit over the country of Iran, and a second was from a high flying drone on station over the Gulf of Oman. For the moment, a third screen was dark, but the fourth carried the image of Dan Taylor who was in the secure communications room in the basement of the US Embassy in Cairo.

Taylor was also watching the same live feeds on a series of flat screens, one of which displayed the interior of the CIA conference room. This enabled him to see Granger and the others who were with him.

The screen displaying the satellite feed showed an overhead view of a fishing trawler as it moved through the waters of the Gulf of Oman. The view from the drone was a much tighter shot. Using a thermal imaging lens, they were able to pick up the heat signatures of two individuals on deck, but there was no way to know if there was anyone else below deck, and that was the nature of their problem.

They were also confronted with the distinct likelihood that the Seahawk helicopters launched from the Enterprise were not going to arrive at the scene on time.

A countdown was underway in an overlay display that appeared in the lower right corner of all of the screens. By plotting the ships real-time speed and course, a computerized program was coming out with an estimate of the time left before the trawler reached the safety of Iranian waters. On a second overlay, appearing in the opposite corner of the screens, a second real-time countdown was underway, this one showing the possible intercept time for SEAL Team 2 who were presently on their way to take down the trawler.

Granger looked anxiously over at the Air Force Major who was seated in the chair to his right.

"Will we make it?"

"If the ship stays on its present course without deviation, it looks like we'll fall short by about twenty minutes."

Granger looked up at the camera that was providing the feed to Cairo. He was visibly upset.

"We're not going to make it, Dan," he said.

Taylor leaned forward in his chair.

"I think we should go ahead with it, sir. Even if it enters Iranian waters, there will be fewer problems if we do it now as opposed to conducting a land operation."

Granger shook his head.

"Call me on a secure line, will you?"

He then got to his feet and walked over to a quiet corner of the room and waited for Taylor's call to come through.

"We can't do that," Granger told him as soon as they made a connection. "I ran it by the President this morning, and he said if she makes it to Iranian waters we have to call the team off."

"Doesn't he realize that we'll be mired in diplomatic wrangling for years while that poor woman is going to be kept in a cell somewhere?"

"I'm sure he does, Dan, and I agree with you, but it's not my call to make."

Taylor nervously ran a hand through his hair.

"But you know how this will play out. The Iranians will pretend a criminal element snatched her. They'll claim they are trying to find her for us, but it'll never happen until we rescind the rest of the sanctions, or make the trade, or do whatever it is they hope to accomplish by this brazen kidnapping."

"I share your concerns, Dan, believe me, but my hands are tied."

Taylor was furious. If history was any indication, the "kidnappers" would likely release a half a dozen videos showing her languishing in captivity, looking haggard and sickly, holding up signs that say...*Please help me!* or *Why won't you help me?* It would be a public relations disaster and might even put public pressure on the President to cave in to whatever demands there might be.

"Can't you talk to him again, sir? We're so close to getting her back. I can feel it."

Granger knew he could be right. It would be just like the Robert Levinson case, the retired FBI agent who disappeared in 2007 on the Iranian Island of Kish. The Iranian government repeatedly denied knowing anything about his disappearance, but their failure to do anything about his situation had most of the free world believing that they were the ones behind his captivity.

Captivity would be terrible for Angela Disler, but this was the real world, and innocent people frequently suffer. The President was a realist, and as a realist he would never risk an international incident that could kick off a war with the Iranians over the kidnapping of a lone American citizen, particularly when it could not be proven conclusively that the abduction was an operation sponsored by the Iranian State.

"As much as my heart grieves for her and her family, without a lot more evidence that the Iranians are involved, I don't see the President changing his mind."

"What about her family, sir? They've disappeared, too. Most likely abducted as well. And for what possible reason? The people around here are betting that it was done to put pressure on Angela Disler. Does *anyone* in DC have *any idea* exactly why this woman is so important to them?"

Granger bit his lip.

That was the question, wasn't it?

"She's a famous physician, Dan. Isn't that reason enough?"

Granger hoped that answer would suffice.

"I suppose it'll have to."

Granger pursed his lips. "Don't forget, Dan. We still don't know for sure that she's actually on that boat."

Taylor shook his head in disgust. This was a common theme in DC. No one was willing to act on gut instinct and common sense. Even when the subject was Bin Laden, many months went by while agents in the field sought concrete proof that he was in that compound in Pakistan. But in the end, they still had to take a calculated risk, one, it turned out, that really paid off.

Taylor softened his tone of voice.

"She's on that boat, sir. I'm as sure of it as I can be. We should go ahead with the operation, and if it turns out she's not onboard, we can claim that the boat was still in international waters—"

Granger was disappointed that Taylor wouldn't let it go.

"Your position is noted, Dan. Let's just hope our boys reach that ship before it gets to Iranian waters."

It's not gonna happen and he knows it.

"Sir, with all due respect, then we might as well call off the SEALs right now."

Granger thought it over. If he called it off now, there would be a chorus of criticism later that they'd squandered an opportunity by being too cautious. Yet it was highly unlikely that they would reach the boat while it was still in international waters. On the other hand, if he let them continue right up to the last minute, the complaints would be muted because they'd done everything they could while conforming to international law.

"It's never over until it's over, Dan. The boat might blow an engine or get lost or change course. Keep those choppers going until we have no choice."

"Yes, sir."

Taylor hung up the phone and walked back over to the table in the secure communications room to watch the rest of the drama unfold.

He considered the possible consequences of forcing the trawler off course. He could check and see if there were any naval military assets in the area, maybe a sub or a minesweeper? Forcing it off course just might give them the extra time that they needed.

He checked the countdown clock in the corner of the screen. If everything stayed the same, the boat would cross the imaginary line in just about fourteen minutes. He checked the second countdown clock and noted that the

SEALs were still a good ninety-six miles away.

They were never going to get there in time.

He got back on his satellite phone and rang up the technician at the monitoring console at the CIA facility at Herndon, Virginia. Tyler made him repeat the identification process, and then, in answer to Taylor's question, he told him there were no naval assets close enough to make an intercept that would delay the fishing boat long enough for the SEALs to interdict it in international waters.

Taylor rang off, then reluctantly called Granger again.

Granger's satellite phone rang, and when he saw that it was Taylor, he retreated once again to a quiet corner of the room.

"Yes?" he said when he answered the phone.

"I think we should call off the Seahawks, sir."

Granger frowned. "I already told you, Dan, we'll keep them on intercept until we have to call them back."

Taylor was doing a slow burn.

"Hear me out, sir. If we stay on mission, there's a good chance that the kidnappers will see our birds in the air. If they know we're on to them, we'll have no chance of tracking her once they get her on shore. But if we pull off now, we can use the satellite and the drone to locate their final destination. That way, if the diplomatic approach doesn't work, and if the President decides that a land assault is necessary, at least we'll know where they're holding her."

Granger thought it over. Taylor was making good sense. Something would have to be done to get her back, of that much he was certain. Diplomatic pressure hadn't worked with Iran in the past, and there was no reason to believe that it would work in this case. Also, once her true value to the Iranians was exposed, the President would likely move heaven and earth to get her back, or at the very least, he'd have to do the unthinkable to neutralize the situation, and knowing where she was being detained would certainly save time and minimize risks.

"All right. Call them off. But make sure the satellite stays on her until we have a chance to assess our options. And while you're at it, launch another drone. I want at least two of them up when they make landfall, and I'll want a game plan for placing intelligence boots on the ground by later this evening."

Taylor nodded. His mind was already working out a plan for an infiltration into Iran.

"I'll take care of it, sir. And thank you."

Reluctantly, he made the call to JSOC, telling them to order the Seahawks to turn around and return to the deck of the Enterprise.

He continued to watch the countdown screen, and five minutes later, the time to intercept went up as the SEALs were turned around. He couldn't help but wonder if history would view the inability of this mission with the same set of eyes that were being used to condemn the failure to capture bin Laden early in the war when they had him cornered in the caves at *Tora Bora*.

*****

THIRTY-THREE

LOS ANGELES, CALIFORNIA
10:20 PM   DAY FIFTEEN

It was dark outside and clear, but Los Angeles was in the grip of a cold front that had come in on the jet stream by way of Alaska. Donahue wore a black business suit and a dark wool overcoat, one that she'd inherited from her mother, but which she never got to wear because it rarely got chilly enough in LA more than one or two times each year.

She waited patiently on the fourth level down in an underground parking garage at a shopping mall in West Los Angeles. A glance at her watch disclosed that it was 11:15 pm, which meant that the last round of the evening's movies in the mall's fifteen Cineplex theaters was already well underway. The fourth level of the garage had room for almost two hundred cars, but tonight it was practically empty. Donahue counted twenty-one…make that twenty-two if she included the one she'd arrived in with Thompson who had parked several rows away so that she could monitor the meet just in case there was trouble. Still, even though this sub-basement level was all but deserted, the accumulation of residual heat from all of the automobiles that had used the structure throughout the day made wearing the heavy coat unnecessary and incredibly uncomfortable. She quickly took it off, then put it back on when she realized that there was no clean spot where she could put it down.

Donahue kept her hands inside her coat pockets. She looked around, wondering if the person she was meeting would arrive by car or if he would be coming down the escalator or in an elevator, both of which connected the five levels of the garages with the three upper levels of the mall.

Her Captain had come through. He'd made a call to a friend of his who worked at the CIA. He and his friend, whose name he wouldn't reveal, had served together when both were Marines. Donahue could only speculate about who his contact was, but she assumed the guy was a senior official in the organizational hierarchy, otherwise, he probably wouldn't have had any access to the kind of information that she was after.

Elwood had been cryptic about what to expect, but he told her to come to this location at this particular time to meet with someone who might be able to tell her what Disler's secret project was all about.

She checked her watch. It was now 11:20 p.m. Whoever she was meeting was already late.

A young woman suddenly appeared at the bottom of the escalator. She stepped out into the garage, took a quick look around, then made her way over to Donahue.

"Are you Donahue?" she asked after walking over.

"I am."

"Can I see your ID?"

Donahue pulled her ID card out of her purse and handed it over.

The woman studied it carefully, then handed it back.

"I wasn't expecting a woman," Donahue said.

"That makes us even. Neither was I."

She was Asian, likely Chinese, young, and a well dressed late twenty-something who looked more like a college student than an agent with the CIA. Her black hair was shoulder length, her skin was blemish free, and her almond shaped eyes were cautious and watchful.

"Your Captain's friend is back in DC, and since time is apparently of the essence, he briefed me today by phone and asked me to meet with you."

Donahue nodded. "I didn't get your name?"

"Does it really matter?" The woman smiled. "Tell you what. You can call me Charlotte, Annie, Keiko, or anything else for that matter. This meeting is off the books, and while you may use this information to help with your investigation, it must never come back to us."

Donahue smiled. She remembered the "Deep Throat" informant from the Nixon years, a man who turned out to be a senior FBI agent. If all went well tonight, she was about to learn secrets from her own "deep throat," and since there was no privilege on the books that would protect her from having to reveal the name of her source, she was going to have to be very circumspect about who, if anyone, she ever told this information to.

"Okay, Charlotte it is. I understand, and thanks for coming tonight. How do you want to proceed?"

Charlotte looked past her.

"Is that your partner sitting over there in the Crown Vic?" She gestured with her head.

"Yep, she's here to provide cover for both of us."

Charlotte smiled.

"No photo's, okay?"

"Of course not."

Charlotte turned in such a way that her back was now to Thompson who was watching intently from inside her car.

She's not taking any chances, Donahue thought. That's smart.

Charlotte was now all business.

"After your Captain called us, we did some checking on Angela Disler. But before I tell you what she was up to, I need to tell you what prompted her research."

Charlotte held Donahue's glance, then said, "I don't suppose you have a background in genetics?"

Donahue shook her head. "A biology course in college, but that's about it."

"That'll do. My background is in genetics, so if I start to talk over your head, you stop me, okay?"

Donahue nodded.

"How much do you know about viruses?"

"They make you sick?"

"There are more than 5,000 viruses known to mankind, and they are evolving every day. Modern medicine has been able to combat and eradicate some of the more dangerous ones, such as smallpox and polio, but there are thousands of others for which there are no vaccines.

"Viruses can be serious killers. In 1918, before there were any vaccines at all, there was a worldwide flu pandemic that killed between 20 and 50 million people."

Donahue's eyes widened. She'd heard of that particular pandemic, but she had no idea that it had been so deadly.

"Are you familiar with the bird flu virus?" Charlotte asked.

Donahue nodded. "It's been in the news. It made the jump to humans, right?"

"That's correct. The simplest way to explain this is to say that it was a virus that spread throughout the bird population, but only recently did it evolve and make the jump to humans. The thing is, the transfer to humans required direct contact with the virus. People who worked with chickens, for example, were the first ones to come down with the disease."

Charlotte studied her face. "You still with me?"

"I think so."

"Good! Well, several years ago, the genome, also known as the complete DNA structure of the bird flu virus, was mapped out by a group of researchers. By the way, that virus is known as H5N1, and it's a subtype of *Influenza A,* the common flu virus that comes around every other year or so. I mention that because it's nothing more than a mutation of the virus *Influenza A,* but because it is a mutation, we do not have a vaccine or immunity for that particular strain. Anyway, the researchers who mapped the genetic structure of H5N1 noted through further study of the genome that *airborne transmission* of the virus could be reached with only a few more mutations. This raised a huge red flag, detective, because, on its own, the likelihood of that happening seems inevitable, and that raises the specter of a pandemic outbreak within the human population."

Donahue nodded. This woman was making it easy to understand.

"Does that mean that if someone tampered with the genetic code, they could make the bird flu become an airborne disease?"

"That's right." Charlotte was pleased to see that Donahue was projecting beyond just understanding what she was being told.

"It's going to happen eventually through natural mutation, but genetic alterations in a lab somewhere could make an airborne bird flu virus a present day reality."

She shuffled her feet and let her eyes sweep over the rest of the garage.

"The bird flu discovery was a wake-up call. You see, most of the dangerous viruses—like Ebola or Lassa Fever—don't yet have vaccines. They're working on them, but slowly, because there's little or no financial incentive for American or Western European drug companies to expend the millions that it would take to develop the vaccines when those particular diseases don't really affect the people in our countries. And as unfortunate as that may sound, the countries that could use a vaccine for their populations don't have the technology nor the money to make the research financially viable."

Donahue knew that was true. The drug industry throughout the world was profit motivated, and unless there was a need within the United States, no one was going to worry too much about a disease that only seemed to break out in third world countries.

"Anyway, Zurich Pharmaceuticals received a grant from the Army and the CIA to map the genomes of various lethal viruses. The plan was to find a way to render them inert so that they could be used to produce a vaccine…and that's where Angela Disler comes in. She and her team mapped out several inert viruses in preparation for working with the deadly ones, and it was during that stage of her research that she hit upon the idea of using inactive viruses to transport chemotherapy agents."

Donahue's brow furrowed. "If that's the case, then why would someone want to kidnap her?"

Charlotte's expression turned deadly serious.

"The lethal viruses that Disler's team was working with were the genome's for *Marburg* and *Dengue Fever*. I'm told they were also scheduled to work on the genomes for *Hantavirus* and *Rotavirus* when the CIA ordered the project to come to a grinding halt."

"Do we know why they stopped it?"

Charlotte nodded.

"Do you know anything at all about the Marburg virus?"

"No, I sure don't. This is the first time I've ever even heard that name."

Charlotte sighed. That came as no big surprise. Most Americans were unfamiliar with this particular deadly killer.

"Marburg is a hemorrhagic fever virus that affects both human and nonhuman primates. It's extremely dangerous, and the *World Health Organization* rates it as a Risk Group 4 Pathogen, requiring biosafety level 4-equivalent containment. In the United States, the *Centers for Disease Control and Prevention* lists it as a Category A Bioterrorism Agent."

"Sounds to me like Ebola. Are the two similar?"

"Very good, Detective, and while I won't get too technical with you, both Ebola and Marburg require the same NPC1 cholesterol transporter protein to attach to cell-surface receptors."

Donahue grinned tightly. "You lost me there."

"Sorry, let's just say that there are two different genomes for the Marburg viruses—MARV and RAVV—and Mrs. Disler was working exclusively on the MARV genome at the time of her disappearance, trying to find a way to stimulate a mutation that would render it unable to bind with the NPC1 protein. The idea was to make the virus harmless because if it couldn't attach to healthy human cells, it couldn't invade them. But what she discovered instead was a way to use genetic splicing to turn the MARV into an airborne disease."

Donahue was shocked. "You mean she discovered how to spread it by a sneeze or a cough?"

"Exactly! In aerosol form, the disease could spread throughout the world like a prairie fire, and presently, there would be no way of stopping it. The disease begins with a sudden onset of an influenza-like stage, characterized by a general malaise, fever with chills, and chest pain. Nausea is accompanied by abdominal pain, diarrhea, and vomiting. Headaches, confusion, bleeding from the mucous membranes, fatigue, seizures and sometimes a coma. What kills the patients are multiple organ dysfunctions, and the fatality rate has been known to be as high as eighty-eight percent."

Donahue momentarily shut her eyes in an attempt to process the information.

"Still with me?" Charlotte asked.

Donahue opened her eyes and nodded.

"I guess I just don't understand why we would even want to mess around with such a horrible virus?"

Charlotte shifted her weight, then looked around the garage once more before returning her attention to Donahue.

"The old Russian Republic had an extensive offensive and defensive biological weapons program that included MARV. At least three different Russian research institutes had programs ongoing during the cold war, and while the data from those applications is still highly classified, we learned from a Russian defector named Ken Alibek that a weapon filled with MARV was tested at a base in Kazakhstan. That suggested to us that the development of a MARV biological weapon had reached advanced stages. And sadly, even though Gorbachev signed off on the dismantling of biological weapons production and testing, the Russians have remained prepared for future production." She took a deep breath and let it out slowly. " After the dissolution of the Soviet Union, we believe that the MARV research has continued to this day in all three of the major Russian research institutes."

Donahue shook her head. "So because they're still working on it, we decided we had to do it, too?"

"From what I've been told, our intent was to develop a way to render the disease harmless, and after that a vaccine. But once you start tampering with genetics, you never know what might happen. Mrs. Disler's discovery was an unexpected byproduct of her research, and that, unfortunately, has changed everything."

"Don't tell me our government is now going to use it as a biological weapon?"

"I wish I could say no, but as I said, everything's changed." Charlotte shook her head. "As soon as we found out about her discovery, we shut down the project, and from what my boss was telling me, both the Army and the CIA want time to consider the ramifications of what this all means."

"But aren't biological weapons banned by the Geneva Convention?"

"They are, and it has never been the intention of our government to weaponize any of these viruses. But now that we know that it can be done, we have to consider what other countries—particularly the Russians—would do with this type of information." Charlotte sighed. "If the technology is now available to weaponize something like MARV, it's only a matter of time before our enemies think about doing it too."

Donahue was nearly speechless. This was so much worse than she ever imagined.

"It's insane," she finally said. "Completely insane!"

Charlotte recognized the look of profound shock on Donahue's face.

"I'm just the messenger, detective, and I certainly don't condone what's happened, but the genie is out of the bottle, and the research on viruses is likely to explode in this country as well as throughout the rest of the world."

Donahue felt her stomach knotting up.

"So, if Disler was doing all of this classified work, how would the people who abducted her discover what she was up to?"

"Good question. My boss just learned about this yesterday, so we're still trying to get to the bottom of things. Maybe someone who's working at Zurich or in the CIA has turned. That's a distinct possibility, but another way would be for someone to hack their way into the computer system at Zurich. If their firewalls aren't completely secure, then some or all of Disler's research might be accessible to outsiders."

"If that's the case, if the research details were on her computer, then why take her?"

Charlotte shrugged. "You're asking me to speculate, Detective, but I would imagine that if they managed to hack her research, maybe some of it was encoded. Or maybe they want her to physically demonstrate her technique. But I'm just guessing here. There could be a lot of other reasons, too."

"When was her discovery made?" Donahue asked.

"Several weeks ago, and as far as I know, very few people inside the Agency or at Zurich know what Disler discovered."

I'll bet Lum was one of those who knew, thought Donahue.

She held Charlotte's glance. "Does your boss know that Disler's husband and her two daughters have gone missing?"

"What do you mean by missing?" It was Charlotte's turn to be surprised.

"We think that they've been kidnapped too."

Charlotte thought that over. "Sounds to me like someone wants to put pressure on Angela Disler to do something that she doesn't want to do." She nodded to Donahue. "I'll pass that on to my boss."

Donahue exhaled slowly. "If you find out how the kidnappers managed to target her, it might go a long way towards helping me find the people who took her family."

Charlotte nodded.

"Tell you what. If we find out how they got on to her, I'll let you know. Okay?"

Donahue thanked her, then, "Any chance I can get a number for you? In case I've got more questions?"

"I'll give you a number, but we don't talk on the phone. If you find out something or have any questions, you call that number and leave me a date and time for a meet back here. If I can't make it, I'll call you back. Otherwise, we're on. Okay."

Donahue smiled. "You sound a little paranoid?"

Charlotte smiled tightly.

"I'll let you in on a little secret, detective. Nothing is private anymore. Always assume that someone out there can hear or read anything you say or write. Just keep that in mind. Make it your mantra. *Nothing is private anymore.*"

*****

THIRTY-FOUR

WESTWOOD, CALIFORNIA
DAY SIXTEEN   9:15 AM

Donahue and Thompson pulled into the lot of the Federal Building on Wilshire Boulevard in West Los Angeles, and after parking their car, they made their way by elevator up to the 17th floor offices of the FBI. After presenting their credentials to a secretary who sat behind a counter with a bulletproof pane of glass, they were escorted by an agent to a small interview room located in a hallway behind the security door.

Shortly after they were seated, Elliot Davis walked in with a cardboard file folder under his arm.

"Detectives, great to see you. How's it going?" he asked as he took a seat.

Donahue folded her arms across her chest. "We thought it was time we had a little talk."

Davis, who agreed to meet with them on short notice, had been under the impression that they were there to give him an update on the progress of their investigation of the kidnapping of the Disler family, so he was somewhat taken aback by Donahue's tone of voice.

He leaned back in his chair and held her gaze.

"What did you want to talk about?"

"About your agency's failure to fill us in on certain information that has proven crucial to our investigation."

Davis looked from one to the other.

"I've already told you, I've given you what I'm permitted to divulge. There are national security implications. What else can I say?"

Donahue looked over at Thompson who was shaking her head.

"You hear that Shari?" she said. " He's given us '*what he's permitted to divulge.*' What do you suppose happened to...*they didn't give me any details?*"

"I'd say he's holding back, Jen."

Thompson leaned forward in her chair. She was offended by what she considered to be the prevalent attitude among FBI agents that local agencies couldn't be trusted. She decided it was time to put him in his place.

"We know about Disler's work on biological weapons, so why don't you just can the clearance bullshit and level with us on the details of what went down in Egypt."

Donahue gritted her teeth. Earlier, when she briefed Shari and the Captain on what she'd learned during her meeting with Charlotte, the three of them agreed that they would keep the revelation about biological weapons close to the vest. But Thompson had jumped right in with both feet, and by playing their trump card so quickly, the entire dynamic of the conversation was about to change.

But she was not prepared for Davis's reaction. He appeared to be completely taken aback by the revelation. All he could do was look back and forth from one to the other.

"What are you talking about?" he finally managed to say. He kept his gaze focused on Thompson. "What do you mean... *biological weapons*?"

"Oh, c'mon, Davis," Thompson snorted. "We're not fools."

But his face revealed his utter confusion. The man was genuinely surprised.

Thompson's eyes widened. She glanced over at Donahue.

"He's really in the dark."

"Apparently so."

Davis managed to regain his composure.

"Look, detectives, even if I did know a little something about what happened to her in Alexandria, my hands are tied. The CIA is running the show, and they've made it pretty clear to us that they don't want the details getting out."

Thompson shook her head. She looked over at Donahue.

"I knew he was holding back."

Donahue nodded. She leaned back in her chair and kept his confused stare.

"That's all well and good," Donahue said to him, "but we've got a family that's gone missing, and unless we know exactly what the hell is going on, our chances of getting them back alive are slipping away."

Davis swallowed hard.

"Look, I know how you feel about the Bureau, but if you know something that I can pass on to the task force in DC, then you need to put aside your feelings for the good of the victims and tell me what you know."

Donahue shifted in her chair. Thompson had struck a chord with Davis. Perhaps she could press the advantage by throwing her weight around.

"Sure, we'll tell you, but here's the deal. You get the CIA to fill us in on exactly what happened to Angela Disler, or we'll go public with what we know about the family's disappearance, and if that fucks up the DC investigation, then you can tell the CIA that they brought it on themselves."

It was Thompson's turn to be open-mouthed. Jen had really thrown down the gauntlet to Davis. That, and her use of an obscenity were quite a surprise. She sneaked a quick look at Donahue who flashed a quick tight smile while she waited for Davis to respond.

Davis cleared his throat.

"You really plan to go to the Press?"

"If you people don't trust us enough to give us what we need, then we have no choice."

"Can you at least tell me something more specific about what you know about biological weapons? It might go a long way towards convincing them to bring you on board."

"Not a chance," Donahue replied. "You guys have always been the black hole when it comes to information. All you do is take and never give back. So, like I said, if you want to learn what we know about biological weapons, then whoever's in charge of this so-called task force needs to bring us into the loop. Otherwise, you can figure it out for yourselves."

"And that means we want to know everything," Thompson added, thinking they might as well shoot for the moon. "No more of this *top secret* bullshit. Understand?"

Davis looked from one to the other before he got to his feet.

"Sit tight. I'll be right back."

He picked up his file and walked out of the room.

As soon as he was gone, Thompson turned to Donahue and whispered, "You were off-the-charts with that potty mouth of yours." A slow smile spread across her face. "I didn't know you had it in you?"

"*Shhh!* Not here."

Donahue was remembering Charlotte's warning about being cautious with what was said.

Thompson nodded that she understood. Both of them suspected that the Bureau was bugging the room.

****

Davis was not particularly bothered by Donahue's threat of disclosure. Donahue and Thompson were using the only leverage they had, and if he were in their shoes, he would probably play the same card. But what had him so upset was knowing that the CIA had intentionally failed to mention a connection to biological weapons. They'd kept the Bureau out of the loop, and that was breach of protocol.

If the information obtained by the detectives was accurate, it completely changed the scope of the investigation; not only the one going on in the Middle East, but especially the one underway in Los Angeles.

Davis considered himself to be a decent and ethical man, one who prided himself on being a team player. He had no personal reservations about sharing information with local agencies, and while he understood the history behind the Bureau's policy, it was one that he happened to completely disagree with.

In the distant past, some corrupt police departments had abused the Bureau's trust by tipping off criminals to sensitive Bureau investigations. It was certainly a legitimate concern, but so was the abuse of trust from within the Bureau itself. The fact remained that the policy was woefully outdated, and with a vast and respected agency like the LAPD, it was easy to see that there was more to be gained by cooperating with them rather than shutting them out.

He walked into the outer office of the Special Agent-in-Charge (SAC), and after getting a nod from the secretary on duty, he entered the inner office of Maxwell Colby.

At first glance, Colby, who was in his mid-forties, fit the profile of an old-school FBI Agent. He was Caucasian, a Mormon, married with four kids, had a tract home in the West Valley, and like most of his peers, he was thought to be politically conservative. But what set him apart from others of his ilk was that Colby was actually very progressive. He had a strong sense of right and wrong, and he was known for encouraging his agents to be independent thinkers, to push forward when appropriate, and to fight for what was right even when the methods used didn't fall within the rules of the FBI's playbook.

Davis took a seat in front of Colby's desk and in a voice devoid of emotion, he disclosed the conversation that he'd had with the two detectives.

Colby let him speak without interruption for almost fifteen minutes, and when Davis had finished telling him everything, Colby simply sat there while his mind was racing.

"Looks like they shut us out," he said, referring to the CIA.

Davis nodded. "I was given some details concerning the kidnapping in Egypt; details I was ordered not to share with LAPD, but no one ever said anything about biological weapons."

Colby concurred. "They probably decided that our involvement would be limited to a few interviews with her family and her employer. But once her family was taken, they should have told us what was really going on." He locked eyes with Davis. "Do we know for sure that the family was actually kidnapped?"

"It looks that way, and now that we have a possible motive for why they took her, it seems likely that the two events are connected. And if that's the case, we should probably get back the kidnapping case."

Colby was not a man to make rash decisions. If biological weapons were really at the core of this case, it was clearly a national problem, one that would require a coordinated effort at the highest levels of government. In short, it was not a case that should be left in the hands of the local office of the FBI, much less a couple of detectives from the LAPD.

"I can see why the Agency would want to keep a lid on this," Davis said. "If she really was doing research on biological weapons, this could prove to be a huge embarrassment for our country."

"That's of little interest to me, Elliot. What's important here is the intelligence value she presents to our enemies."

Davis nodded, sufficiently chastened. Colby was right. The only thing necessary now was determining how bad the situation really was and what could be done to resolve it quickly.

"So what do we do about the detective's demands?" Davis asked.

Colby frowned. If they told the detectives what they wanted to know, the CIA was going to go crazy, not to mention his higher-ups in DC. On the other hand, the fact that the LAPD had knowledge that the rest of the task force might not know about made them an integral part of the investigation, and therefore, indispensable.

Leverage. It was always about leverage when it came to coaxing information out of any federal agency, and at the moment, LAPD had them over the proverbial barrel.

"You go ahead and brief the detectives with what we know about the Middle East investigation into this case, and while you're doing that, I'm going to put a call into the task force, and we'll get to the bottom of this right now."

"You want me to mention the link to the Iranian Quds?"

"Absolutely! They need to know what's going on. But before you get started, get them to agree to tell us what they know about biological weapons."

"They're not gonna budge until they have what they want."

"Then that's the way it will be."

Colby got to his feet, signaling the end of the meeting.

"Get started now. Don't wait for me. I'll join you as soon as I can."

Davis left the room, and when he was gone, Colby pushed the button on his intercom.

"Liz, please get Dan Taylor on the line for me. Try him at our Embassy in Cairo."

****

When Taylor's phone rang, it was just after 8:00 p.m. in Cairo. He had just finished getting a quick bite to eat in the Embassy cafeteria and was seated at his desk, working on a plan to put Bryan Harb and other boots-on-the-ground in Iran.

"Yes?" he said, not recognizing the number on the caller ID.

"Dan? It's Max Colby. Have you got a few moments?"

Taylor and Colby had history together. They had been part of a joint agency task force that was sent to Yemen to investigate the October 2000 bombing of the *USS Cole* in Aden Harbor, in the Republic of Yemen.

"For you Max, anytime. What's up?"

"I'll tell you what, Dan. My team here in LA just learned that Angela Disler was apparently working on biological weapons at the time she was abducted, and I'm wondering why we weren't briefed on this when we signed on to work with your task force?"

Taylor rocked back in his chair.

"Where did you come up with that information?"

"The failure to brief us? I was there when you put the task force together, Dan. I know—"

"No, not that. What's this stuff about her working on biological weapons?"

Colby frowned. Was he also in the dark, or was he simply fishing for information that might help point to a leak at the CIA?

"The LAPD came up with a source. Which brings me to the second reason for my call. Right now, I've got two of their detectives in one of our conference rooms. They're handling the investigation into the kidnapping of the Disler family, and before they tell us what they know about her involvement with biological weapons, they're demanding a full briefing on the Angela Disler case."

"Hold on, Max."

Taylor's mind was spinning. He cradled the phone in his lap while he tried to process what Colby was saying.

Several things came quickly to mind, including the fact that if the information about Disler having worked on biological weapons were true, it would dramatically change the approach they were using to try and get her back.

The second point he needed to consider was how in the world the LAPD had learned this kind of sensitive information while he and his team had been kept in the dark?

He put the phone back up to his ear.

"In answer to your first question, Max, I was never briefed about any work on biological weapons."

"Are you saying it's not true?"

Taylor ran his hand through his hair.

"I'm not saying that at all. In fact, if it is true, it explains a hell of a lot. Have you given the LAPD any details yet?"

"I've got Davis doing it now, and don't tell me we shouldn't fill them in, because if this woman was actually working on biological weapons, this gets bumped to the very top of the Bureau's threat list, and I don't need to tell you what that's gonna mean."

A declaration of a national emergency would involve all aspects and all agencies of the federal government. If she was working on biological weapons, the danger to America by the disclosure of the details of her work was two-fold. If the rest of the world found out that America was working on biologicals, there would be outrage in all corners, including from their allies. The damage to existing relationships would be devastating. But of greater significance was the fact that if Disler had a working knowledge of biological advancements, and if that information fell into the hands of the Iranians, the risks to America and the rest of the world was the kind that could start a world war.

Taylor thought, *First things first. I need to find out if it's true?*

"I agree with your decision to fill them in, Max. Just make sure that they understand that any release of this will create terrible problems for our country and likely ruin our chances of ever getting her back."

"I'll try and coax them into telling me the source of their information, but I doubt if they're gonna say where they got it. According to Davis, they're very pissed off about being kept in the dark."

He left out mentioning their threat to go public with the details of the family's kidnapping. With the decision to brief them on Angela's disappearance, it no longer seemed to be a viable issue.

Colby added, "You know, if she really was working on biological weapons, I'm gonna have to pass that info up my chain of command."

"Let's not get ahead of ourselves, Max. Find out what they know. Once we have that, I can run down the info and see if it's true."

"You think it might not be?" Colby asked.

"Let's hope it's not."

But a knot in the pit of his stomach seemed to be telling him just the opposite, and that was a feeling he couldn't ignore.

****

The briefing given by Davis to Donahue and Thompson took almost twenty minutes. He went over what was known to have happened in Alexandria, the movement of Disler by trawler to Yemen, and the belief that she was still there and in the process of being moved overland by her captors. He touched upon the fact that the kidnapping appeared to be an Iranian Quds operation, and that one of the men responsible had been taken into custody and was in the process of going through a rather intense debriefing.

At the reference to *intense debriefing*, Thompson could only smile.

"I hope they're water-boarding the bastard," she said.

As the details unfolded, both Donahue and Thompson became painfully aware that they were involved in a case that had much greater significance than an ordinary kidnap-for-ransom, so when Davis was finished with the briefing, both women sat back in their chairs as they tried to absorb the details of what they'd just been told.

"Are we sure the Iranian government is behind her kidnapping?" Thompson asked.

"No one is sure," said Davis. "It was decided to keep their involvement confidential because keeping them in the dark about what we know gives us a tactical advantage when it comes to getting her back."

"Have we tried a rescue attempt yet?" Donahue asked.

"I've been told that we're tracking her whereabouts in Yemen, but that's being handled by the CIA and the military, so I can't really give you an answer."

"I'm confused," said Donahue. "Why not fly her from Alexandria directly to Iran?"

"The sanctions. The working theory is that they couldn't fly her out of Egypt, so they put her on a freighter, off-loaded her in Yemen, and are trying to transport her across the desert to the Arabian Sea for the final leg of the journey by boat."

Thompson caught his eye.

"What happens if she makes it to Iran?"

Davis shrugged. "The Iranians believe that we worked with the Israelis to assassinate several of their nuclear scientists who were building their nuke. So, if their government is involved, this may be an act in retaliation for their belief that we participated in those killings, and if that's the case, our chances of getting her back are slim to none."

Donahue shook her head in dismay.

"You realize that this changes everything," she said. "We were operating under the premise that she was abducted by Egyptians and likely being held for ransom."

"I know, and I'm really sorry, but the decision was made much higher up to keep everything on a need to know basis."

"And of course, we didn't need to know."

Thompson said it with an undisguised dose of sarcasm. She looked over at Donahue.

"Nothing ever changes with these guys, does it?"

"Apparently not."

Donahue was angry about having been left out of the loop for so long, but that anger paled into insignificance when compared with her disgust. The Disler's were in serious trouble, and the only hope they had for rescue lay in a meeting of the minds between agencies and an end to the dysfunctional hoarding of information.

She turned to Davis. "Now that you've told us what's really going on, it gives even more credibility to what we've been told."

Max Colby entered the interview room and was introduced to the detectives as the SAC of the Los Angeles office, and after he had settled in at the table, Donahue began her briefing.

She let them know up front that she was not about to name her source, but she did explain that the source was well-placed and completely reliable, which seemed to satisfy the agents for the moment.

She told them what Charlotte had learned about the nature of Angela's work, that she'd been looking for ways to genetically alter the Marburg virus to render it harmless when she stumbled across the DNA sequencing that would permit the virus to go aerosol.

Colby was the first to react.

"How the hell was someone who was working on such a sensitive project allowed to leave the country?"

"I think the bigger question is this. If it was such a top secret project, how did the Iranians find out what she was doing?"

Colby nodded.

"That's something I can assure you we'll be looking into."

That started Donahue thinking. The family was kidnapped for a reason, probably to put pressure on Angela to force her to reveal information about her research. Donahue wasn't all that knowledgeable about biological science, but it didn't take a masters degree to know that Angela couldn't possibly have all of the research information in her head.

Zurich's computers! The Iranians were going to try to gain access to her data!

And what better way was there to force Angela to cooperate than to threaten to kill her family.

If a threat to her family was made, she hoped that Angela would at least demand a proof life, and if she did, exactly how would that play out?

Donahue tried to use her common sense to think it through. They had to be planning to communicate with the parties who were holding her family. That would be essential. By phone or by the internet, it was the only sure way to put pressure on Angela, and if they wanted to get data from the Zurich computers, they would have to make use of the internet.

It was a weakness in their plan that might be exploited.

Charlotte's warning was prophetic. *Always assume that someone out there can hear or read anything you say or write.*

If that was really true—and she had no reason to doubt it—then perhaps there was a way to trace the calls back to their points of origin.

"Mr. Colby," she said, "I've given this some thought, and I think the kidnappers in Iran are going to call the people holding the family to give proof-of-life to Angela. Is there any way to trace calls coming into Los Angeles from the Middle East?"

Davis looked over at Colby.

"What do you think, boss? Can the NSA do something like that?"

"We can find out," Colby replied.

"Here's another thought." Donahue leaned forward. "Disler's research must be on a computer somewhere at Zurich. Can we get someone to monitor their computers and see if anyone tries to get in? If a probe like that could be traced back, we might find out where they're holding her?"

Colby nodded. Her ideas had merit and he was duly impressed.

"I'll get on the phone to DC," Colby said, "but first, I want to thank you both for providing this piece of the puzzle. It's going to make a huge difference in what goes on from this moment forward."

He shook their hands.

"And before I forget, Dan Taylor over at the CIA is the head of the task force, and for obvious reasons, he has asked me to stress to you the importance of keeping everything confidential."

Donahue nodded. Even though she'd made the threat, she never had any real intention of releasing what they knew to members of the press.

"He has also asked me to convey to you his apology for not seeing the wisdom of briefing you fully right from the start, and as far as he's concerned, you'll be kept up to date from this point forward."

Donahue couldn't resist a small smile. As far as she was concerned, she and Thompson had accomplished what they'd set out to do. They would no longer be deprived of the kind of information that they needed to work their case.

The meeting adjourned, and once they were back in their car,

Thompson looked over and smiled.

"Well, that went well."

Donahue nodded. "Better than I hoped."

Thompson hooked up her seatbelt.

"You really busted their balls in there." She turned in her seat and smiled. "And that threat to go public with our investigation? What was that all about?"

"I guess I did get a little carried away."

"I guess we both did."

Thompson put her sunglasses on and settled back in her seat.

Donahue started up the engine and pulled out of the parking lot.

"Let's get back to the station and find Mitzi. I've got a few questions to ask her about accessing mainframe computers."

*****

THIRTY-FIVE

WASHINGTON, DISTRICT OF COLUMBIA
DAY SIXTEEN   1:30 PM

After Taylor had heard back from Colby about Angela Disler's alleged work on biological weapons, he placed a call to Hamilton Granger's office in Langley, Virginia. When Granger finally came on the line, Taylor began the conversation with a question.

"When did you plan to tell me that Angela Disler was doing work on biological weapons?"

There was a long, uncomfortable silence before Granger finally spoke.

"I'd like to know where you heard that?" he responded slowly.

"That doesn't matter." Taylor's eyes narrowed. "Is it true?"

Granger leaned back in his chair. Apparently, what he'd hoped to keep under wraps was now out in the open.

"It's not what you think," he struggled to explain.

"What the hell does that mean?"

"It means that making new weapons was not the purpose of the project. Look, Dan, modern technology has made incredible progress in the last five years, and these days genetic alterations are being made all the time in the lab. The project at Zurich was intended to identify ways to protect our country from genetically altered viruses that could be used as weapons against us. Mrs. Disler was looking for a way to render the Marburg virus harmless. The plan was to develop a vaccine, but by tampering with the genome, she hit upon a way to make the damn thing airborne."

Taylor could feel his stomach knotting up again. "So what you're saying is we ended up with a brand new biological weapon?"

"Technically, we did, but that was never the intent of the program."

Taylor snorted. "But once she found a way to weaponize Marburg, everything changed, is that it?"

"We're not weaponizing Marburg, Dan." Granger stiffened. "The research was stopped because we need to consider where to go with this."

Taylor rolled his eyes. Of course, the government would want to re-assess its position. In light of such a frightening discovery, they'd have to. A weapon like that could change everything, even if it was never used. But none of that changed the fact that Disler's disappearance now posed a real threat to the nation's national security.

Or did it?

Taylor got to his feet and began to pace.

"How serious a threat are we facing by her kidnapping?" he asked.

"It's being assessed."

Taylor waited for more, but Granger's silence spoke volumes.

They don't really know!

"When did she make this discovery, sir?"

"Less than a week before she set off for Egypt."

Taylor stopped pacing. No wonder they haven't completed a threat as-sessment. This just went down.

He shook his head. "If you don't mind my asking, how many people know about this?"

"Perhaps a half-dozen. No one else has been cleared to know."

"So why wasn't I told?"

"It would have made no difference, Dan. I was on top of it, and we were already doing everything possible to find her."

Not exactly, Taylor thought. We just let her slip through our hands by the President's unwillingness to take down the trawler in Iranian waters. It was a golden opportunity squandered by a President who should have known better.

Taylor closed his eyes as if he was being reminded of a painful subject.

"The President should have let us take the boat down in Iranian waters," he said.

Granger cleared his throat again but didn't speak, and Taylor suddenly came to the realization that Granger hadn't bothered to tell the President.

"He doesn't know, does he? You didn't tell him about her discovery?"

When Granger finally spoke, all bravado had disappeared from his voice. He sounded subdued and beaten.

"It was my call," he said flatly. "I hoped we could get her back before it turned into a full-blown crisis. It was the only way I could see to keep her discovery under wraps."

Taylor was furious, but he wasn't quite sure exactly where to direct his anger.

Angela Disler should never have been allowed to leave the country, not with her classified knowledge, and certainly not without a security detail. And how did the Iranians come to know about her research? Was there a spy within our midst? Granger may have been a hot shot Senator before being appointed to run the CIA, but he knew nothing about intelligence or how to assess a threat to national security. His feeble efforts to oversee the rescue attempts—while keeping the President completely in the dark—had likely cost them their best opportunity to facilitate a rescue without the risk of going to war.

Granger was a dangerous fool who was completely in over his head.

Taylor looked at his watch. *Was there still time to turn the SEALs back around and stop the ship before it reached the shore?*

Taylor decided that he had to do what he could to salvage the situation.

"I would suggest that you advise the President *right now* and see if Disler's discovery changes his mind about intercepting that boat."

"It won't," Granger said with a sigh. "Before he would authorize such a breach of international law, he would need to know the extent of the threat that she presents, and conclusive proof that she's on that ship."

"Nevertheless, sir, and with all due respect, I would recommend that you wake him up and let him know exactly what is going on. At this point, a failure to advise him on such a serious, potential threat, borders on criminal malfeasance."

"Are you threatening me?" Granger asked. His mood had quickly changed.

"No, sir, I'm not. I'm simply stating for the record my disagreement with your decision not to advise the President, and I'm providing you with my best assessment of the potential consequences of your failure to do so."

Granger ran a hand through his graying hair. Taylor was probably right.

Perhaps he should have advised the President right away, but things had happened so quickly, and their leads on Disler's whereabouts made it very tempting to go it alone, thereby avoiding the fallout if word of her discovery ever reached the light of day.

"Perhaps you're right." Granger marshaled his thoughts. "I'll discuss the matter with the President once I get a full briefing from the military analysts who're working up a threat assessment. In the meantime, I would like your task force to develop a list of options that I can present to the President once we have a better handle on the extent of the threat."

A rescue from the fishing boat—if she really was on that ship—was now a thing of the past, and he needed to get past that screw up and quickly move on.

"Any restrictions on the options, sir?"

"All options are on the table, Dan. Are we clear on that?"

"Yes, sir, we are."

Taylor hung up the phone, then checked his watch and did the computations. It really was too late now to turn the SEALs around again, but it was now more important than ever to make sure that the satellite surveillance was kept on top of her minute-by-minute whereabouts.

He made a quick call to JSOC to ensure that the satellite was still tracking the progress of the trawler, then he decided that his next call was going to have to be to the military contingent attached to the task force. They were going to need a quick assessment of the danger presented to the country if Disler's information were to fall into the hands of the Iranians.

Taylor winced.

If he'd ever felt any sort of kinship with Hamilton Granger it was now ancient history. His failure to disclose the true nature of Disler's work in a timely fashion to the President and to everyone else involved had crippled an appropriate response.

He spent a few moments to gather his thoughts, then went in search of his secretary. He told her to arrange for him to catch an immediate flight back to Washington, DC.

Now was not the time to deal with Granger's incredible incompetence, and Taylor felt he could get more done if he went back to DC where the decisions were being made.

But one day soon Granger was going to have to face the music and Taylor planned to be there to lead the orchestra.

*****

THIRTY-SIX

WASHINGTON, DISTRICT OF COLUMBIA
DAY SIXTEEN   2:15 PM

CIA Director Hamilton Granger made his way past the Marine Guard posted at the outer door and through the scanners just inside that were manned by members of the Secret Service. Once he was cleared, he was escorted by a burly agent to the door of the Oval Office where he was made to wait in the hallway until the President was available to see him.

Henry Creighton, the Director of the FBI, showed up moments later, and the two men cooled their heels in the presence of a statuesque agent who silently stood post at the door.

"Hamilton," said Creighton, acknowledging his counterpart from the CIA. "I trust this won't go too long? This meeting of yours has played havoc with my schedule."

Granger shook his head. He was not about to give him an answer while they stood in the unsecured hallway.

Creighton sighed. He undid the buttons on his overcoat.

It was cold in DC; the wind was blowing hard and the forecast called for intermittent showers, and while his exposure to the elements was minimal— he was shuttled everywhere by a security driver—he still felt chilled to the bone every time he had to get into or out of the car.

He happened to look up and noticed what appeared to be a coin lying flat on top of the molding directly above the closed door.

"Excuse me, young man," he said to the Secret Service agent who was standing in front of the doorway. He pointed with his finger at the coin. The agent looked up, smiled tightly, then returned his glance to the visitors.

Creighton knew the man was embarrassed. The coin had likely been left there inadvertently by one of the agents on the night shift who had been standing post the night before. He'd long heard the rumors of a game that was played by the night shift agents who would stand with their backs to the door, before flipping a coin into the air, hoping to get it to land flat on the half inch wide strip of molding above the entrance to the Oval Office door. He could hardly blame them. Standing there for hours at a time had to be incredibly boring.

The agent listened to a voice in his earpiece, then reached for the handle on the door.

"The President is ready for you, gentlemen," he said as he opened it up.

Granger entered first with Creighton following close behind.

President Jamison Lindhurst was seated behind his desk and he was in the process of signing a document when the two men walked in.

"I'll be right with you, gentlemen," he said. "Please make yourselves comfortable."

Both Granger and Creighton had been to the Oval Office many times before, and they knew that it was the President's preference to conduct all meetings on the couches and chairs in the center of the room. Each man took a seat, mindful to avoid the chair that the President always favored.

Granger was suddenly nervous. On a previous occasion, he briefed the President on the kidnapping of Angela Disler and the plan to search the freighter when it reached international waters off the coast of Yemen. He briefed him a second time on the raid that was scheduled on the fishing boat that was headed for the coast of Iran, and it was then that the President had ordered him to call off the raid if they were unable to intercept the boat before it reached the Iranian territorial waters.

Granger realized now that he'd made a huge mistake by not telling the President about Angela Disler's Marburg discovery. Why he hadn't done so he wasn't quite sure. The project itself was legitimate. It was her inadvertent discovery that he failed to mention, and in hindsight, he realized that his reluctance to say it was done at the request of the military who needed time to consider the ramifications of such a discovery before the possibility of it going public.

He knew there were people on the military side who saw a huge advantage to having a weaponized virus, and while he didn't believe for a moment that either Congress or the President would ever approve the development of such a weapon, he had agreed to delay bringing it to the President's attention to give them sufficient time to develop a list of pros and cons.

He was convinced that the President was not going to appreciate being misled during the prior two briefings, and he could only hope that by the end of the meeting that he would still be able to hold on to his job.

The President walked over and greeted the two men with a handshake, then took a seat in his favorite chair and addressed his remarks to Granger.

"What's up, Hamilton?" He was chewing a piece of nicotine gum, a concession to his wife and children who demanded that he give up smoking cigarettes.

"Mr. President, I wanted to provide you with more information on the search for Angela Disler."

"Was she on that boat?" the President asked.

Granger shook his head.

"By the time we could get our SEALs into the area, the boat was well within Iranian waters, so we called them off before they were seen." He rubbed at his jaw. "I've been told that we'll be using a satellite and drones to monitor the offloading, and hopefully, we can confirm that it's her and if it is, where they're planning to take her."

The President sighed heavily. He had hoped that the SEALs would have been able to solve the problem before he had to resort to diplomatic channels.

"So we still don't know if it was her on that boat?"

"We're not positive, sir, but we think it is." Granger cleared his throat. "But there's more, sir."

"What is it, Hamilton?"

"Well, sir, during the course of Mrs. Disler's research, she inadvertently discovered a way to make the Marburg virus aerosol, which means that the virus can be passed from human to human through the air rather than by direct contact with infected blood or bodily fluids."

"What?"

Creighton, too, was astonished by the revelation.

The President studied Granger's face. The news of the discovery itself was shocking; so surprising, in fact, that the President hadn't yet realized the extent of the threat that Disler's kidnapping now presented to the United States.

As both a thoughtful and intelligent man, the President attempted to think it through. The discovery of a way to weaponize such a horrible virus literally left him speechless. It was nothing that would ever happen on his watch, but if she could do it, then others could do it as well.

And then it hit him, the cold hard truth. It was the intention of the Iranians to get the specifics of her method directly from her.

But how the hell did they know what she discovered when even I didn't know?

He stared at Granger. "When did she make this discovery?"

"About a week before she went to the seminar in Alexandria."

"And when did you learn about this?"

"The next day."

The President glared. "And you're just telling me about it now?"

Granger shrugged, and the President looked over at Creighton.

"Did you know about this, Henry?"

"No sir, I did not." Creighton's angry glance shifted over to Granger. "I'm hearing this now for the very first time."

Granger sighed heavily.

"General Mackey at the Joint Chiefs asked me to keep the information confidential until experts at the Pentagon were prepared to provide you with a formal briefing."

"Mackey made that request?"

"Yes, sir. He convinced me that the ramifications of such a finding should be explored so that you would be fully briefed before action of any kind was taken."

George Mackey, a three-star general, held the position of *Director of the Joint Staff.* He was the chief assistant to the *Chairman of the Joint Chief's of Staff* (CJCS), and his role as Director was to assist the Chairman with the management of the Joint Staff, an organization composed of approximately an equal number of officers from the Army, the Navy, the Marine Corps, and the Air Force, all of whom were assigned to assist the Chairman with the unified strategic operation of the nation's military forces.

The President was not pleased that Mackey had obviously overstepped his authority by making a unilateral decision to withhold this information from his Commander in Chief. But he would deal with Mackey later, just as he would have to think long and hard about Granger's role in acceding to Mackey's request.

"So this was put into play as an Army study?" he asked.

"It was a jointly set up by both the Army and CIA, Mr. President. The funding was approved by Congress."

The President was getting angrier by the minute, but he kept his emotions bottled up. They should have told him as soon as Disler made her discovery, but Granger's decision to postpone telling him at the request of the military implied that the military wanted time to give serious consideration to using the discovery to weaponize Marburg.

And as long as he was President, that would never happen under any circumstances...

In fact, the very idea of the possible release of a deadly virus and the risk that doing so posed to the world was an obvious anathema to basic common sense.

"Tell me something, Hamilton. Does anybody in your shop or in the Joint Chief's believe for a single second that I would consider the weaponization of a virus like Marburg?"

Granger cringed. That was certainly the obvious inference, but that was not the way Mackey had presented it to him.

"I don't think that's the case, Mr. President. General Mackey and his people are concerned that word of Disler's discovery might get out. They consider what she's done to pose a global threat, and they wanted time to evaluate her work and what options are available to us if similar discoveries are made by our enemies."

The President wasn't buying it. In the back of his mind he was confident that the temptation to make a case for weaponizing the discovery was really at the heart of the matter.

"For the moment, I'm going to ignore the fact that both you and Mackey and perhaps others chose not to advise your President of a significant discovery that significantly affects our national security. Instead, I want to know why this lady doctor was allowed to leave our country in the first place?"

"I believe I can answer that, sir," said Granger. "Apparently, she notified her supervisor who passed it on to the CEO of Zurich Pharmaceuticals in Switzerland. In turn, he notified his contact with the CJCS. By the time it got to Mackey, she was already in the hands of her captors. Apparently, her presence at the conference was set up months before the discovery was made, and I can only assume that she did not realize the risk that her going abroad presented to her safety and that of our country."

The President nodded. It wasn't much of an excuse, but given the layers of the bureaucracy at the Pentagon, it wasn't surprising that it had taken so long to get to the appropriate ears.

"Which brings me to my second question. Exactly how did the Iranians know what she was working on, or for that matter, what she discovered?"

"We're working on that, Mr. President."

"You're working on it?" He smiled facetiously. "Well, I'll tell you what, Hamilton. I'm very disappointed by the way this has been handled, and I mean to rectify that situation right now."

Granger hung his head. He'd made a mistake keeping the President in the dark, and since he served at the pleasure of the man, it was very likely that he was about to be asked to turn in his resignation.

He looked up to see that the President was still studying him.

Granger waited while the President turned to Creighton.

"Henry, I want the Bureau to find out how the Iranians learned about her discovery, and I want you personally to take the lead."

"Yes, Mr. President," Creighton replied.

The President then shifted his attention over to Granger.

"Exactly where is Mrs. Disler at the present time?"

"The trawler is currently approaching the coastline near the city of *Kolahi*. If you'd like, I can call the Ops Center and get you the exact coordinates?"

"That won't be necessary." The President shook his head. "For the time being, I want surveillance to continue. Don't lose sight of her. I also want you to prepare a complete briefing to be given to my Cabinet in exactly two hours. Do I make myself clear?"

"Yes, Mr. President."

"Do we have any intelligence assets on the ground in that part of Iran?"

"No, sir," said Granger, "but Dan Taylor is working on an Ops plan to put boots on the ground. Would you like me to include that in the briefing?"

The President could tell that Granger was clearly nervous. He was obviously worried about keeping his job, as he damn well ought to be.

"You know, Hamilton. If I'd known that she was in possession of such critical information, I would have authorized the SEALs to take that trawler down even if it was in Iranian waters."

Granger was thoroughly dejected. He should never have listened to Mackey and those fools over at the Pentagon.

"I'll have my resignation on your desk by tomorrow morning, sir."

The President ignored him. Instead, he walked over to his desk, picked up the phone, then hit the speed dial for his Chief of Staff.

"Mark. I want you to call an emergency meeting of the Joint Chiefs and the NSC at the war room in one hour. Advise everyone that the meeting is top secret and there's to be no notification to the press."

The President listened for a moment, then said, "No, I'm not going to say what it's about. Just tell them that the subject is completely confidential."

He listened again as his Chief of Staff informed him about the changes he would have to make to his already busy schedule.

"There's more, Mark. I want to call a Cabinet meeting in two hours. Same admonition, and after that, please ask the leaders of both the House and Senate, majority and minority, to meet me here in the Oval Office at—" He looked at his watch. "—let's say at five p.m.?"

He hung up the phone then returned his attention to the two men still seated on the couch.

"Henry, I'd also like the Bureau to investigate the kidnapping of Disler's family in Los Angeles."

Creighton said, "The LAPD has been handling all the leg work, but we'll step in and take it over."

"Keep them on it," the President said, "but let them know that it's a national security case and that secrecy, for the present time, is paramount."

"I'll take care of it right away, sir."

Creighton got to his feet and started for the door as Granger slowly stood up.

"Stay for a moment longer, Hamilton," the President said.

Granger slumped back down on the couch.

Once Creighton was out of the office, the President stood up and came around the desk. He walked back to his chair and took a seat.

"You've made one hell of a mess of this," he said.

"I know, sir, and I'm sorry. I really thought the military had a valid argument for keeping this under wraps until all possible alternatives were considered."

"It's my job to know about things like this as soon as possible, Ham. By not telling me right away, a situation that might have been resolved with a SEAL assault on the boat has now reached crisis proportions. We may be forced to go with boots on the ground into Iran, a nearly impossible task." He shook his head. "What the hell were you thinking?"

That was it. Granger had never heard the President swear, and it could only mean one thing.

Granger cleared his throat and repeated his offer.

"As I said, I'll have my resignation on your desk in the morning, sir."

The President shook his head.

"For the moment, that won't be necessary, but we will revisit the subject once this matter is resolved."

*****

THIRTY-SEVEN

LOS ANGELES, CALIFORNIA
DAY SIXTEEN   11:45 PM

Donahue and Thompson located Mitzi Roberts at her desk and asked her to join them in one of the interview rooms. Because the working area at RHD was open with only waist high walls separating the individual cubicles, every conversation that took place on the phones or in person was easily overheard by others who were sitting nearby. It was such a ridiculous situation that most of the detectives used their personal cell phones to make calls that they wanted to keep confidential. This meant that all day long, on every floor in the building—primarily in the hallways that led from the offices to the elevators—detectives and civilians alike could be found pacing up and down while having muffled conversations on their personal cell phones.

Once the three detectives were seated in the conference room, Donahue took over.

"We've decided to bring you in on our case, Mitz, but I need to tell you up front that it's highly confidential."

"Oh, goody," said Roberts with a smile. "A little intrigue. Keep talking."

"I'm serious, Mitz. This is heavy duty stuff, and once I tell you, you'll understand why."

Roberts looked at their faces and decided that Donahue really meant what she was saying. Her tone grew serious.

"Sorry, Jen, what's up?"

Donahue began by telling her the details surrounding the kidnapping of Angela Disler, followed by the supposed abduction of her husband and children. She then filled her in on Angela's discovery and its potential impact on national security. She finished with her theory that the family was taken to put pressure on Angela to reveal information of some kind or to do some form of action.

Roberts frowned. "You mean like turning over the details of her discovery to the Iranians?"

"That's exactly what we mean," Thompson said flatly.

"We need to pick your brain, Mitzi," said Donahue.

Roberts was silent for a few moments. It was not easy to stay focused when all you could think of was Marburg spreading around the world like the typical winter flu. She found herself trying to recall the mortality rate for that particular disease. Wasn't it eighty percent or something like that?

"You still with us, Mitz?" Donahue asked.

Roberts snapped back to the moment.

"Yeah, sorry. It's a lot to take in."

"I know. Welcome to our nightmare. So listen. I need some basic computer information, and you're my go-to expert." Donahue shifted her weight in her chair. "How would a company like Zurich store its information? On a computer, of course, but I guess what I'm asking is can the Iranians gain access to her research by logging on from a remote location?"

"Depends upon what security systems Zurich has in place. For example, if they store their research on a server that permits access from outside the facility, maybe her home computer or from another research facility, then access would be obtained by use of one or more passwords, depending on the redundancy of the security measures. If the server was not connected to the net, and by that I mean that it's a closed system, not accessible from any computers except those inside the facility, then the data is far more secure. That would require actual physical presence in the installation and the use of a password or passwords, again, depending on how many levels of security there are."

Donahue frowned. "So, if it is connected to the internet, they can force her to use one of their computers to get the data in the Santa Monica facility?"

"That's right." Roberts screwed up her face in thought. "Of course, if they're storing that kind of sensitive data on a server connected to the net, there are plenty of hackers out there who could get in, and using commercially available malware, they could get the password information and then steal the research data without anyone ever knowing."

"I'm confused," said Donahue. "How would they go about doing that?"

"There are *cyber espionage* groups—most notably in Russia and China

—that have been conducting a patient, multiyear effort to extract geopolitical and confidential intelligence from computers and network devices like routers, switches, and smartphones. They use malware that has been designed to extract files, e-mails, and passwords from PCs. They can also record a user's keystrokes, and they can take screenshots of what appears on your screen at any given moment. They also like to steal a user's web browsing history on commercial browsers, like the searches you or I might do on *Yahoo* or *Google*, and they can do that with searches that you or I make on our smartphones, too."

Thompson stared at her in horror.

"You mean to tell me that someone could put that malware stuff into my smartphone and they would know who I called and when I called them?"

Roberts nodded, then smiled.

"If you've got a little something on the side, Shari, then in the future, you might want to communicate your sexy text messages by hiring a bunch of carrier pigeons."

Roberts shifted her gaze over to Donahue.

"You can pretty much assume that anything that goes out over the airways can be collected if someone has the necessary equipment."

So Charlotte was right!

"So what if the data on the computer is encrypted?" Donahue asked. "Does that make any difference?"

"If a company is using a commercial encryption program, the hackers can read it. I read somewhere that hackers discovered that the European Union and NATO were using a classified software called *Acid Cryptofiler,* so these computer criminals then hacked the classified software and used it to read the information that they'd already stolen."

"Wow!" Donahue leaned back in her chair. This was a lot more severe and complex a problem than she had ever imagined.

"How do they get the malware onto someone's computer?" Donahue asked.

"It's called *spearphishing.* They send e-mails to people within a targeted organization that contains what are called malicious documents. Once opened, the malware gives them full access to the victims' machines."

Donahue leaned forward.

"So, is there a way to trace back the e-mails that contain this malware stuff?"

"Sometimes." Roberts looked over the top of her reading glasses. "But they'll use different domain names and several different server locations that are usually nothing more than proxies that are designed to hide the actual server's whereabouts."

"In other words, they can create a trail that can't be followed?" Donahue rolled her eyes. "This is not good, Mitzi, not good at all."

"Tell me about it," said Roberts. "And now that you can buy some of this malware on the underground market, almost anyone can hack their way into an ordinary person's computer with very little effort."

Thompson turned to Donahue.

"Well, I guess the first thing we need to do is call Zurich Pharmaceuticals and find out if their system is wired up to the net?"

"I'd be surprised if it wasn't," Roberts said. "Most corporations are."

Thompson got to her feet and started to leave.

"You can call 'em from the phone in here," Donahue said.

Thompson turned back and smiled.

"I need to get another cup of coffee, too."

When Thompson was out the door, Mitzi said, "Did you catch her reaction when she found out her phone could be hacked? She's probably out there now erasing all her naked photos."

Donahue laughed. Mitz was probably right.

As Roberts got to her feet, Donahue said, "Do you know much about the NSA?"

"A little, why?"

"I was told that they might be able to intercept calls from all over the world?"

"They have the ability to intercept phone calls as well as the internet, fax and satellite communications. But there are limitations, Jen, particularly when it comes to domestic surveillance. You might have to speak with a US Attorney to find out what you can and can't do."

Donahue nodded. "Thanks, Mitzi. I'll do just that."

*****

THIRTY-EIGHT

LANGLY, VIRGINIA
DAY SIXTEEN   9:00 AM

Dan Taylor walked through a basement hallway of the CIA headquarters in Langley, Virginia. When he arrived at the secure conference room, he held his identification card up against the reader, then submitted to a brief retinal scan before hearing the lock on the door click open. He entered the secure conference room, paused for a moment to let his eyes adjust to the low light, then made his way over to the conference table where he took a seat that had been reserved for him as the current head of the task force.

On one of the flat screens mounted on the walls was the view from a geostatic satellite in a low earth orbit over the Arabian Sea. At roughly six hundred miles up, it was set in a stationary position where it was used to monitor and photograph real-time activities in Iran, Saudi Arabia, Yemen and the Sudan.

In the ambient light of the television screen, Taylor was able to see who the other people were who were gathered around the table, all of whom were intently watching the screen on the wall.

The first person he noted was Hamilton Granger who was seated at the conference table with several military brasses from the JSOC. There was no sign of Henry Creighton, but considering the direction this investigation had suddenly taken, along with the Presidential directive that the FBI should handle the kidnapping of Disler's family, Creighton's absence from the table was completely understandable.

Taylor settled back in his chair and focused on the screen with the view of the suspect boat.

The satellite's abilities never ceased to amaze him. Even from the current altitude, the resolution of the camera was good enough to read a license plate on the ground. It was simply astounding!

The boat initially made a beeline to Iranian waters, then slowly made it's way up the coastline where it was now just tying up at a pier near the city of *Kolahi,* in Iran.

Taylor studied the harbor. It was surprisingly tiny, the size of a small marina, with room for only several dozen fishing trawlers. There were very few people moving around, and even fewer vehicles. A white van was parked nearby, and a man who was standing by the van appeared to be waiting for the men on the boat.

Taylor picked up a console phone, and in a soft voice said, "Can we get a closer shot of the people on the deck?"

A CIA analyst in an adjacent room in Langley who was monitoring the satellite coverage adjusted the cameras resolution, and Taylor got his first real good look at the two men on the deck of the ship.

The boat was tied off at a pier and the two men were standing out on the deck, apparently discussing their next move.

Both had short dark hair, well-trimmed, dark beards, and both looked to be in good physical shape. If he had to venture a guess, Taylor would have said that they were likely both members of a military unit.

One of the men waved at the man who was standing next to the white van. The man got into the van and drove it up to the side of the pier, right next to the now docked boat.

Both men on the craft appeared to look around, then they went below and a short time later they came up on the deck with a dark haired female who was staggering, as if under the influence.

A fourth person suddenly appeared on the deck. Taylor did a double take and leaned forward towards the screen for a better look.

"Is that a female?" he said to no one in particular.

"Looks like it to me."

The voice in the dark was Grangers.

"She might be a nurse or medically trained," Taylor said. "With the two males running the boat, they'd need someone with medical training to keep her sedated."

They continued to watch as the two men struggled to lift the woozy female over the side of the boat and onto the dock. The male from the van finally joined them, and with his help, they were able to get her safely off of the ship.

The two men then half-carried, half-walked her to the van before placing her in the back seat.

One of the men and the second female then off-loaded several small duffle bags which they put in the back of the van behind the seats.

"Stay with the van," Taylor said again into the console phone. "We need to know where they're taking her."

The satellite view shifted to focus on the van.

"Do we have drones on station?" Granger asked.

"No, sir," Taylor replied. "Too risky to let them go inland. The Iranians might pick them up on their radar."

Granger nodded, and Taylor thought to himself that the man should have known that without having to be told.

As the van pulled away from the pier, Taylor noted that the screen was displaying the GPS position of the van in real time as it made a turn out of the marina and started off on the highway.

Taylor leaned forward in his chair and once again spoke into the phone.

"Can we get a map overlay up on screen three that will track the van for us?"

A few seconds later the Langley analyst said, "I'll have it up for you in ten seconds, sir."

Taylor waited patiently, and when the map came up on the flat screen designated as number three, he noticed that the vehicle was headed inland, traveling on a two-lane highway, going north/northeast.

Taylor got to his feet and walked over to a small room that was attached to the main conference room. Inside the soundproofed chamber was a secure phone. He entered the room, sealed the door behind him, then punched a number into the satellite phone and waited for the call to go through.

"Are you ready to travel?" he asked Bryan Harb when the phone call was suddenly answered.

Bryan knew right away who was on the line.

"Yes, sir! What have you got?"

Even though the line was secure at his end, Taylor spoke in code as an extra precaution just in case the conversation at Bryan's end was somehow being monitored.

"We've received an order from a clinic in *Kolahi,* Iran. It's on the coast, just off the *Strait of Hormuz.* I'd like you to go there with your assistant and make sure that they're ordering the correct equipment for the work they have in mind."

Bryan sighed. Apparently, the ship had not been intercepted before making it to Iranian waters. He had hoped the hunt would be over, that the woman would have been successfully rescued, but from what Taylor was inferring, the hunt was now shifting to Kolahi, Iran.

Apparently Taylor now wanted him to go to Kolahi with Mordecai, the agent from the Mossad. The legend he created on several previous trips to Iran was that of a medical equipment salesman, and it sounded like Taylor wanted Mordecai to share the legend. But that might be problematical, as he was of the opinion that Mordecai did not possess the technical expertise necessary to successfully play the role.

He said to Taylor, "Sir, I'm not sure my assistant has been in training long enough to be of any value to me on this trip."

Taylor sighed. He expected Bryan to be resistant to working with the Israeli, but there wasn't sufficient time to put together a support team, and sending him in alone, when so much was at stake, was not a viable option. A second set of ears and eyes was always better and safer. And besides that, having the Israeli's involved in the hunt would keep their biggest Middle Eastern ally seriously invested in the search, and that would be a positive, because you never knew when that might prove to be important to the overall success of the operation.

Taylor said, "I may have a few additional stops that I want you to make along the way, so it's best if you take him along."

"You're the boss," Bryan said. He had nothing against working with Mordecai—the man's contact in Oman had proven to be quite valuable—but bringing in someone on such short notice to pose as an expert on medical equipment was risky, especially if they were questioned by Iranian immigration authorities when entering the country. But he supposed he could pass him off as a trainee, one who was simply learning the ropes, so maybe it wouldn't be all that bad.

Taylor said, "The travel agency we use will be sending you your tickets and other information by courier later today, so stay close to the hotel."

"Yes, sir. Anything else?"

"Actually, there is. I have further information to discuss with you, some rather important details relating to their choice of that particular equipment. So I'd like you to go to our local office there in Oman and give me a call a little later today so I can fill you in on the details."

Taylor had obviously uncovered something important about the victim that had made her the target for the Iranian Quds. Bryan rubbed nervously at the stubble on his chin. Taylor was insisting that he risk a trip to the US Embassy in Oman to get the information over a guaranteed secure communications link. It must be awfully important, because being seen going in or out of the US embassy by enemies of America could completely undo his carefully crafted legend.

But Taylor wouldn't be so insistent if it wasn't completely necessary so he would have to take a chance and risk it. He had no other choice.

Taylor cleared his throat. He wanted to tell Bryan right now about Disler's involvement with biological experiments, but even an encoded satellite phone was no guarantee that what they were saying was completely secure.

But just to make sure that Bryan understood the urgency of the situation, he added, "A sale like this is a big one, and it's critically important to the health of the company. So get on to it just as soon as you receive your travel information. We don't want this sale to end up in the hands of our competitors."

Bryan exhaled slowly. The urgency in Taylor's tone left not doubt in his mind about the seriousness of the situation.

"You can count on me, sir. We'll be in touch."

*****

THIRTY-NINE

LOS ANGELES, CALIFORNIA
DAY SIXTEEN   2:00 PM

Elliot Davis spread his paperwork out on the table of the conference room on the fifth floor of LAPD's Police Administration Building (PAB). Sporting ten stories and 500,000 square feet of cavernous office space, it was the workplace for approximately 2,300 employees, including the men and women of the Robbery-Homicide Division, whose offices took up nearly a third of the entire fifth floor.

The conference room was large, containing a table for ten and equipment that enabled a power-point presentation on a large screen that retracted into the ceiling.

Donahue and Thompson arrived together, and after greeting Davis and providing him with a large cup of dark black coffee, they settled into their respective chairs, ostensibly to listen to the results of inquiries made by the NSA.

Davis picked up a notepad that contained his notes from a meeting he had earlier that day with Max Colby.

"My boss contacted the head of the task force, Dan Taylor of the CIA, who's currently stationed in Cairo, but who is now in Washington, DC. He passed on your information, and he asked Mr. Taylor to make inquiries with the NSA."

He looked from one to the other, settling his gaze on Donahue.

"We heard back from Mr. Taylor about two hours ago, and I'm afraid the news is both good and bad."

"Why don't you hit us with the bad news first," Thompson said. "Then maybe we can end this meeting on a high note."

Davis nodded. "Okay. The information you provided to us was given in a briefing earlier this day to the President by CIA Director Hamilton Granger, and it's my understanding that my boss, Director Creighton, was in attendance. Anyway, the President has specifically directed the FBI to take over the investigation of both of the kidnappings. It's now believed that the two cases are connected, and because of the international aspects of both cases, the President feels that the FBI is the proper agency to handle the investigation."

"Well, *duh*," said Thompson. She locked eyes with Davis. "Took you guys long enough to reach that conclusion." She shifted her gaze to Donahue. "I guess that takes us out of the picture?"

"Hold on," he said. "Mr. Colby said to tell you that he'll assume responsibility for providing whatever manpower and assets the Bureau can make available, but he specifically wants you two to take the lead investigative role. He feels your knowledge of the case and your approach to the investigation cannot be duplicated by our agency in a timely manner, and because lives are at stake and time is of the essence, he wants you to continue to direct the investigation."

"Well, that's interesting," said Donahue.

"Of course, if a case is made, it will be prosecuted under federal law in federal court."

Both Donahue and Thompson were momentarily speechless, but it was Thompson who was the first to find her voice.

"Let me see if I've got this right? Your boss is asking us to lead the investigation, and your people will follow our directions, but if we crack the case and make some arrests, your agency will take all the credit?"

Davis nodded and smiled.

"Look at it from our standpoint. We have to assume responsibility for the case. We've received a direct Presidential order. If the investigation goes south, if God forbid some or all of the family members get killed, we're the ones who will take all the heat."

Thompson laughed.

It would be a cold day in hell before that ever happened.

Donahue leaned forward in her chair. While the two of them had been talking, she'd been mulling over the path of the investigation up to this point, and she concluded that the only real chance they had for solving this case lay in the ability of the NSA to help them track the family down. She cared nothing at all about credit for the investigation, and she knew that Thompson didn't either.

Shari just loved to stir the pot whenever it came to working with the Feds, and if the case wasn't so serious, Donahue might have gone along with the feigned outrage.

But lives were at stake, and here they were, wasting time, arguing who would get the credit if the case went well.

She shook her head. It was madness.

"Tell Mr. Colby we'll be glad to lead the investigation," she said.

She caught the sharp glance from Thompson, but she kept her gaze squarely on Davis. "You still haven't told us the good news."

Davis sat back and smiled.

"Mr. Taylor has provided us with a contact over at NSA named Susan Voake. Apparently, she's the go-to person who can get things done for us, and I've been told she's waiting for our call."

Donahue smiled. "Give me the number. I'll call her right now."

****

Five minutes later, she had Susan Voake on the line.

Voake was a twenty-three year veteran of the NSA and had reached the rank of a senior administrator. A short, compact woman, she was known as a workaholic who expected no less from her subordinates. Her office was at the headquarters of the *National Security Agency* (NSA) at Fort George G. Meade, in Maryland. Unknown to Donahue, the actual number of people working at the facility was classified data, but there were known to be more than 18,000 parking spaces at the facility that were visible from the air.

"I've been expecting your call, Detective Donahue. I've been given an overview briefing, so what can I do for you?"

Donahue, who was now back at her cubicle, leaned forward in her chair and consulted her yellow pad on which she'd already scratched out some notes.

"Can we talk about phone calls first?"

"Go for it," Voake said.

"We think the kidnappers of Mrs. Disler are going to attempt to get in touch with the people who are holding her family. We don't know where the family is, but if I had to take an educated guess, I would say that they're probably still in the greater Los Angeles area." She looked up from her notes and lowered her voice. "Is there a way to monitor all calls both in and out of LA if the other party is in the Middle East or Iran?"

Voake smiled to herself. For years, the US government had denied the very existence of the NSA, and by the time they admitted such an existence, misconceptions about the agency and what it was capable of had been exaggerated intentionally to make the agency seem omniscient. The truth was that the agency was essentially all-knowing, but to keep America's enemies guessing, a disinformation campaign had followed, one that was designed to conceal the true capabilities of the present NSA.

"The simple answer to your question is yes. In a city the size of Los Angeles, I would have to guess that there are many thousands of calls going both ways each day."

Donahue frowned. "Is there an easy way to sort through them all?"

"We have computers that do that for us," Voake said.

What she didn't mention was that the NSA was the world's largest single employer of mathematicians and was the owner of the world's largest group of supercomputers.

"How do the calls get organized?" Donahue asked.

"They're sorted in a number of ways. For example, if certain words are used during the conversation, like *bomb* or *al Qaeda,* the calls are flagged, translated, and transcribed. Once that process is complete, suspicious calls are reviewed in-house or sent to the CIA for analysis."

"So, if we came up with a group of words that were specific to our case, you could identify those calls and provide us with transcripts?"

"That's right," Voake said.

What she didn't add was that the calls would be run through a series of complicated algorithms that would further refine and sort any particular searches.

"That would be very helpful. So, I guess my next question would be is there a way to track the locations of the parties involved in the calls?"

Voake had suspected that this question would be asked. It usually was.

"The answer is yes and no. If a hardline is used, we can trace the conversation both ways. If a cell phone is used to enter the system, then sometimes we can, but sometimes we can't. In those cases where we can't, we might be able to locate the nearest cell tower carrying the call."

Donahue sighed. She had hoped that they'd be able to pinpoint with certainty the locations involved in any calls.

"I know that's not what you wanted to hear, detective, but there's more. When the number is called the first time, we can get the actual phone number called and work backwards from there. So, for example, if the phone has a GPS feature, and if it's activated, we have the capability to identify the actual present location of the phone."

"Well, that sounds pretty promising," Donahue said. "Would it take long to set up something like that?"

"A couple of hours at most, but you might have another problem. Have you ever heard of *ECHELON?*"

"I'm afraid I haven't."

"Okay. Well, ECHELON can monitor a large proportion of the world's transmitted civilian telephone, fax and data traffic. It's a project that's operated under the direction of UKUSA, which is a group composed of the NSA and similar agencies in the United Kingdom, Canada, Australia, and New Zealand. Each of these countries has strict limitations on the use of the system to collect or monitor information about their citizens. The US, for example, strictly prohibits the interception or collection of information about US citizens, entities, corporations or organizations, without the explicit written legal permission from the US Attorney General when the subject is located abroad. If the target is within the US, the *Foreign Intelligence Surveillance Court* must review and sign off on a warrant."

Donahue squinted. This whole situation was getting really complicated.

"Okay," she began, "I have a victim who's been kidnapped by foreign nationals and might currently be in Iran. And I have a family of US citizens who've been kidnapped in Los Angeles by people whose national identity is unknown. Who should we talk to so we can get permission to intercept their calls?"

"Are you working on this with the FBI?" Voake asked.

"Yes, ma'am. We are."

"They are familiar with the process, but I'd suggest you have them go to the US Attorney General for advice."

"That's a good idea," Donahue said.

"Were there other questions, detective?"

"Yes, if you have time?"

"I do. This matter is now a priority operation, so I'll be working with you for the duration."

"Then please feel free to call me Jennifer, or Jen if you'd like."

Voake smiled. "You can call me Susan. That ma'am stuff was starting to make me feel old."

Donahue smiled. "Okay then, Susan. My partner determined that the victim in Iran was working on a classified study, and after checking with her employer, we confirmed that the information she discovered was stored in a computer in Los Angeles that is connected to the Internet. Is there a way to determine if someone tries to get into the system? And if so, is there a way to trace them back?"

"Yes, and yes," said Voake. "What you're talking about has a name. It's *geolocation*. It requires special software, and if you really want to do that, I would suggest that the computers involved be disconnected from the net until they're swept clean of malware. Once they are, we can introduce our tracking software which should alert you if someone tries to hack their way in."

"What if our kidnap victim is forced to gain access to the information by using her own password?"

"We can track that back. We can locate the geographic location of the IP address and other embedded sources. But it can take a little time. The sophisticated hackers will probably use a trail of successive blind servers to throw us off, but with enough time, we can track them down."

There was a momentary pause while both women were thinking. Then Voake was the one who broke the silence.

"You should probably consider removing the sensitive information off the computer before you reconnect it to the internet. If you don't, some or all of it might get hacked into or captured by the bad guys while we're busy trying to track them down."

"I understand," said Donahue. The suggestion made good sense and would now be her top priority.

"So where do we go from here, Susan?"

"Get the US Attorney to okay your operation and I'll set everything up at this end," Voake told her. "Start working on a list of words that might come up during any conversation. The words should be unique, like the family names or something related to the classified information they're seeking."

"I understand. Can I call you back when we get organized at this end?"

"Anytime. You can get me at this number twenty-four seven."

****

Donahue and Thompson made their way into Elwood's office. He was seated behind his desk, pouring through a unit performance report which he quickly put aside as they sat down.

Thompson had already briefed him about their meeting with Davis and Colby, but Donahue wanted to tell him what was going on with the NSA.

She filled him in on her initial conversation with Susan Voake, then proceeded to tell him what she'd been up to since that initial call.

"I've spoken to Davis. They sent an agent in the DC office over to talk with a Deputy Attorney General. They got the AG's permission to monitor the calls in and out of LA, so Shari and I came up with a list of words they can use when they sort through the calls to hopefully identify the parties and locations involved."

"That didn't take long," Elwood said. "What words are we talking about?"

"We're going with Angela, Henrik, Disler, and the daughter's names, Carrie and Sienna. Then there are the usual words generally associated with terrorism. Susan Voake with the NSA provided those to us, and we added words like virus, Marburg, genetics, and any and all permutations of those particular words as well."

Elwood leaned back in his chair. "Sounds good. Have you given any consideration as to how you want to handle things if you do find out where they're being held?"

"We'd like to use the Metropolitan Division. I want to spread them out throughout the city. That way, if we get a fix on the location of the call, we can get someone into the immediate area right away while the other units converge on the neighborhood."

Elwood sat upright. "I don't want Metro to try and rescue the victims. If we need to make entry somewhere, SWAT is going to do it."

"No argument there," she told him, "but we might be getting a little ahead of ourselves. This is still a real long shot, boss. They may never call, and even if they do, there's no guarantee that we can pin any call down to an actual location."

"I'll keep that in mind."

"Tell him about the computer," Thompson said. She had a big smile on her face.

"What about what computer?" Elwood asked.

"We contacted Zurich in Santa Monica. They've taken their computers off-line while people from the NSA are going through their server to look for malware and bugs. Once it's clean, they're going to install a software program that will let them know if anyone is trying to access the information. It can pick up hacking attempts as well as anyone trying to get in using Disler's personal password."

"Can they trace back the source of the hacking?"

"Fifty-fifty chance, but we might get lucky."

Elwood nodded. It seemed like they had it all covered.

"There's more," said Thompson with an evil little smile. "Jen was talking it over with Davis, and she suggested that they keep Angela's research off the computer when it goes back online." She looked over at Donahue with genuine affection in her eyes. "Jen came up with the idea that they should substitute Disler's research work with other, non-classified research. That way, if the Iranians do get into the computer when it goes back on line, it won't do them any good, and it might help us buy the time we need to track them down."

"That's smart, Jen. What did the CIA say?"

"No answer yet," said Donahue, "but Shari suggested that they substitute what's on there for the genome for a rat, but I don't think those CIA types have a sense of humor."

"They're wrapped too tight," Thompson interjected.

In spite of himself, Elwood gave them a cautionary smile.

"Just don't lose sight of the fact that whoever these people are, they don't have much in the way of incentive to turn the family loose once they get what they want."

Donahue nodded in agreement. If they didn't want the world or the US to know what they'd done, they certainly wouldn't leave any witnesses behind.

She and Thompson got to their feet.

"I'll let you know once things are set up," said Donahue. "And you can thank your friend for us. If he or she hadn't given us the truth about Disler's work, we'd still be floundering around with no idea what the hell we're dealing with."

Elwood smiled. "I'll pass that on."

*****

FORTY

HERNDON, VIRGINIA
DAY SIXTEEN   11:00 AM

Chris Rooney sat in front of a small, flat screen monitor. He was in a basement coffee room in the CIA safe house in Herndon, Virginia. He was overseeing the implementation of the psychological stressors being used on Ali Niroomad, the First Colonel in the Iranian Quds, who was still under the illusion that he was being held as a captive by the Jordanian *Mukhabarat* at *Al Jafr* prison in the Jordanian desert.

To further break him down, they had kept the temperature in Niroomad's cell at close to one hundred and ten degrees. They fed him very little food to keep him focused on his hunger, and they demolished his sleep pattern by keeping him continually awake for nearly thirty-six hours before allowing him to experience a twenty-minute nap every six hours or so.

When awake, he was secured to a chair by his arms and legs, and through a set of earphones, they worked on his mind by subjecting him to piped-in music of the Beastie Boys that was broken up on occasion by the sounds of screaming from the room next door. The screams were part of a series of tapes made to sound like people who were experiencing the pain of physical torture. The tapes sounded so realistic that Rooney couldn't stand to hear them even knowing that they were faked.

He would have preferred to work on Niroomad slowly, stretched out for at least a couple of months. But time was of the essence in this case, so they would have to use whatever methods they could think of to speed up the process so that he would reveal whatever it was that he was still trying to hide.

Rooney was in his early thirties; a tall, imposing triathlete, who trained five days a week, fair weather or foul, as a biker and a runner on Herndon's backroads. His goal was to compete in the Ironman Triathlon at Kailua, in Kona, Hawaii, so in addition to the outdoor workouts, he also made
time every morning on a daily basis for laps in the pool at the local YMCA.

A bit of a serious health nut, he cooked all of his meals and spurned coffee and other caffeinated drinks in favor of bottled water.

He took a long series of gulps from a bottle of Arrowhead Spring Water before recapping what was left and getting to his feet. It was time to sit down with Niroomad again, and this time they were going to have a very far-reaching talk.

An hour before, Taylor had called him and filled him in on the reason behind Disler's kidnapping. Both men were convinced that Niroomad had been senior enough in the Quds chain of command to know exactly where Disler was taken and exactly what the Iranians had in mind. It would be Rooney's job to get him to talk, and if he couldn't, then it would be his call to make concerning the use of more aggressive, physical measures.

He had just spent the better part of the last hour figuring out the approach he would use on Niroomad, and now that he knew what he wanted to do, he was ready to make his move.

Because Niroomad was still convinced that he was in a Jordanian prison, Rooney had been handling the interrogation in a mask while posing as a member of the Jordanian secret police. But the time had come to level with him, and in his exhausted mental and physical state, Rooney hoped he would see the light.

He ordered the tech analyst to turn off the monitor feed and to shut down the taping system. He did not want any record to exist of what he was now about to do.

He entered Niroomad's cell, a dirty, hot room designed to look like a cell in the infamous Al Jafr prison. There was a strong smell to the room, a combination of perspiration, fear, and odors emanating from a bucket in the corner that Niroomad had been using for his bodily waste. Rooney wrinkled his nose and tried to breathe through his mouth.

Niroomad was asleep on a small metal bench. There was no mattress, no pillow, no blanket. It was intentionally designed to be about as uncomfortable as it could possibly be.

He walked over to the bench and gave Niroomad's shoulder a hard shove which quickly jolted the man awake.

"Sit up," he said in Persian. "We need to talk."

When Niroomad didn't stir, Rooney took what remained of the bottle of water and poured a bit of it into Niroomad's nose.

Niroomad bolted upright, coughing and sputtering.

"Are you awake enough to understand what I'm saying?" Rooney asked.

Niroomad nodded and slowly looked up at his captor.

Momentarily stunned, he couldn't take his eyes off Rooney's face. He recognized the voice. The man had been his chief interrogator, but he wasn't wearing a mask, and more to the point, he didn't look at all like a Jordanian.

This can't be good, he thought. Something must have happened.

"We've got a little situation here, Ali, so I want you to listen up."

"You're American!" Ali said, almost in disbelief. "I thought you were Jordanian?"

"That's right, Ali. I'm an American. And right now I'm sure you're wondering what's going on." He looked around the room. "This whole scenario is a fake. It's not real. You're not in Al Jafr. You're not in Jordan. You're in America, in a unique basement prison. No one knows where you are, and no one cares. Right now, it's just you and me, Ali. And you better listen very carefully to what I have to say."

Niroomad squinted his eyes. He was still a little groggy from just being awakened after so many hours of not getting any sleep, and in spite of his confusion over what the man was saying, he was focused enough to realize that something had changed, and it looked like the Americans were about to take things to another level.

So far he told them nothing of real consequences. He admitted his role in the kidnapping. Of that, he had no choice because they had him on the hotel surveillance tape. But other than ratting out Ansar al-Sharia as the ones who'd taken over her desert transportation, he'd said nothing else of importance, nothing that could have interfered with the completion of the mission. But he had yet to be subjected to physical torture, something that really surprised him considering his belief that he was in the hands of the Jordanian's. He wasn't sure how he would hold up to waterboarding, but he felt pretty sure he was about to find out.

"I've told you everything I know," Ali said. "I don't—"

"Quiet." There was a menace in Rooney's tone. "I told you to listen, not speak."

Rooney held his surprised glance.

"We know why she was taken, Ali. We are aware of her work and what your people plan to do once you get your hands on her research." He pointed at Niroomad with a finger.

"You still with me?"

For the first time since his imprisonment, Niroomad felt the cold hands of real fear.

If they know what we're trying to do, then they no longer need any answers from me.

He had just lost his trump card, his belief that they would keep him alive no matter what because they didn't have all of the answers worked out. But this man was telling him that they already did, and if that was true, and he had no reason now to doubt it, it didn't bode well for his country, and it certainly didn't look good for him.

"So here's where we're at, Ali. We watched your people move her through the desert, across the water, and deep into Iran. We could have stopped them if we'd known what you and your people had planned, but now it looks like it's going to be too late. If she gives up her information, it can be passed on the internet to others who will try to use it even if your country decides not to. And we can't let that happen, Ali. I'm sure you realize that now. So once Doctor Disler arrives at the place that your people are taking her, and before any of her information can go out over the net, we are going to bomb the facility and kill everyone inside. Mrs. Disler will be a casualty of war, but that's the price we're willing to pay to prevent her information from getting out. There will be no survivors, Ali, no information left in the hands of your people, and no one who can stop what we're going to do."

He leaned forward until he and Niroomad were nearly nose to nose.

"Do you understand what I'm saying? You waited too long, Ali. You could have stopped this madness, but you turned down our offer when we asked you to talk, and now that she's known to be in Iran, we have no choice but to launch an all-out assault that will destroy your country and send your people back to the stone age."

Niroomad's eyes grew wide. "You'll never do that. The rest of the world will never agree—"

"They already have, Ali. The world doesn't have a choice. And because you could have stopped it, I want you to know what's going to happen to your friends and your family." Rooney sighed heavily. "I think you have a right to know."

He took a step forward and lowered his voice.

"Right now, a large group of nations is planning a bombing campaign that is going to destroy the military infrastructure within your country, and they are going to systematically destroy all power plants, water systems, and transportation hubs in every major city in Iran. The idea is to bomb your country until it can never be a threat to anyone *ever again.* There will be no troops placed on the ground. Our coalition has secured the cooperation of the Jordanians, the Turk's, the Saudi's and the State of Israel. Russian, American, French, and United Kingdom forces will be sending missiles and fly heavy bomber sorties within the next forty-eight hours. Your country will soon cease to exist as a nation, and those who survive the bombing will be struggling to survive for the next fifty years."

Niroomad was speechless. *Could this really be true?*

Rooney smiled. "The people who don't die in the bombing will be reduced to cannibalizing each other just to survive day to day. But let's forget about that for a moment. I'm sure you're wondering what's going to happen to your family, so I'm going to tell you. When Angela Disler dies, a cruise missile is going to be dropped directly on your family's home. Your wife and children? They're all going to die. You are going to be kept alive for a few more weeks. We are going to make you watch the news and satellite films to show you what you've done to your country. And I promise you this. Before you die, I will get ahold of the satellite footage showing the incineration of your wife and children, and then, after you have seen what you brought about, you will be executed. My people are planning a death by hanging. It won't be pleasant, but at least it will be quick."

Rooney smiled tightly again.

"Enjoy what time you have left, Niroomad. I doubt that Allah or God or whatever you believe in will come to your rescue. You and your fellow co-conspirators have brought about the end of your civilization."

He turned to go, then stopped and turned back.

"At least you have the comfort of knowing that your wife and children will never know that you could have saved them, but that you chose to keep silent and let them die."

He left the room, walked back to the monitoring screen, and had the technician turn everything back on while several men got Ali up off the cot and securely strapped him to the chair before slipping the headset over his ears. One of the men signaled that they were ready, and the technician, who was also monitoring the room by video, turned on the Beastie Boys song "*Fight for your Right*" just as the two men left the room.

Rooney watched Niroomad for a while. He sat stone-like in the chair, eyes closed, and Rooney instinctively understood that in addition to dealing with the tormenting sounds of the *Beastie Boys,* he was trying to absorb what he'd just been told.

He walked over to a mini refrigerator and pulled out a bottle of cold water. He took a long drink, then spoke to the control room technician who was seated in the room next door.

"I don't want him to sleep. If he's gonna crack again, it should be soon."

Rooney sighed. He'd done what he could to get the man to talk. He'd constructed a scenario that sounded plausible on the surface, and he could only hope now that Niroomad's concern for his family, or his country, or his own neck, might somehow motivate him to talk.

All he could do now was wait.

****

To the north of the city of Mirab, Iran, less than twenty miles from the coast, the white van pulled over to the side of the road. The stop put everyone in the CIA Ops Center on high alert.

Once the President became involved, all pretense of confidentiality related to the search was discarded. There were now more than a hundred technicians, analysts, military planners, and no fewer than a half-dozen agencies involved in the monitoring of the van's whereabouts while others were gaming the possible scenarios once she arrived at her final destination.

Most of the people involved in the operation were glued to the many screens in the CIA's Ops center now devoted to the tracking of the vehicle, and collectively, they held their breaths, wondering if Angela Disler had reached the final destination.

Hamilton Granger sat in the small conference room reserved for senior management types involved in the search. He was seated next to Henry Creighton, who still had trouble believing that the CIA had waited so long before disclosing the true nature of the risk to the nation posed by Disler's kidnapping. He had yet to chastise Granger for this serious lapse in judgment, but his anger was simmering just below the surface where it threatened to blow up at any time.

Together, the two men watched as the driver stepped out of the van and walked over to what appeared to be a roadside stall selling fruit. He purchased several bags full of items, walked back to the van, then drove back out onto the highway.

"I guess he was hungry," Granger said to no one in particular.

Creighton frowned. He had reached a different conclusion. With plenty of food and their direction of travel to the north-east, the kidnappers seemed ready for a long road trip…one that would take them well into the interior of the country.

There goes our chance to send in the SEALs from the sea.

*****

FORTY-ONE

LANGLY, VIRGINIA
DAY SIXTEEN   11:10 AM

"Excuse me, Mr. Taylor. There's a call for you coming in from our embassy in Oman."

Taylor looked up at one of a series of world time clocks. The one for Oman showed that it was 10:10 p.m.

"Thanks, Ellen," he said.

He was still seated in the secure conference room, so he excused himself momentarily from the group, then made his way over to the Sensitive Compartmented Information Facility (SCIF), an enclosed room designed for unassailable security, where he took a seat and picked up the hardline phone.

"This is Taylor," he said.

"Sir, it's Bryan Harb. I'm here at the embassy and the line is secure."

"Thanks, Bryan. I wouldn't have asked you to go there unless it was important."

He leaned back in his chair and ran a hand through his hair.

"I wanted to tell you what I've learned about the reason for Disler's kidnapping. Apparently, she was working on creating a vaccine for the *Marburg* virus and hit upon a way to enable it to spread as an airborne disease."

If Bryan was surprised, he let on.

"Is the Iranian government responsible for her abduction?" he asked.

"We think so. The FBI is working on that."

"So where do they plan to take her?"

"We still don't know. The last report I got from Virginia was that Niroomad still isn't saying, so we're watching the satellite feed showing the van we think she's in moving inland from the Kolahi Marina."

"Do you think they're headed for Tehran?"

"I don't know, Bryan. Do you have a map of Iran handy?"

"Just a minute, sir."

Bryan opened his laptop computer and went to Google maps where he punched in the name of Kolahi, Iran. He then enlarged the map which showed cities, towns, and highways.

"Okay, sir. I'm looking at one now."

Taylor said, "The van left the marina and went north through the city of *Mirab*, to Highway 91. It then switched to Highway 94, heading northwest, and just a few minutes ago, it merged with Highway 71, now going northeast."

"They might be heading up into the mountains," Bryan said. "Must be a military base up there somewhere?"

"You're probably right. We'll keep watching, and as soon as they get where they're going, I'll get word to you." He looked over at the map screen again. "In the meantime, did you get the package I sent you with passports, entry visa's, money, things like that?"

"Yes, sir, but the travel arrangements you made are going to take too long. We've been ticketed on a Turkish airline flight to Dubai, and from there to Tehran. At that rate, we won't be even close to being on scene for another twenty-four hours."

"That was done because we were trying to anticipate where they were headed."

"I know, sir, but I've been talking it over with my Israeli counterpart, and he says his people can put us ashore near Kolahi within six hours. One of his contacts there can arrange for us to have a car. I think that's the wisest course for us to take."

"But you'll need weapons, Bryan."

"The Marines here at the embassy are well equipped, sir. I'm sure we can find what we need."

Taylor thought it over. The Agency had arranged for prepositioned weapons to be available just north of Tehran. They'd been smuggled in by Iraqi Kurds who were watching over them still, but if the Israelis were going to put them ashore surreptitiously, they could get the Marine weapons in without difficulty and that would save a significant amount of time.

It had been a good idea to include Mordecai in the search. He was going to have to call Eli Ben-Jehuda, his boss at the Mossad, and thank him for their willingness to cooperate in the mission.

He should probably tell them about Disler, too. Taylor figured he owed them that much.

"All right, Bry. Go ahead. Let me know your detailed plans. In the meantime, brief Mordecai on what we've learned about Disler's work and let him know that I'll be talking with Eli just as soon as you and I are through."

"We'll need a plan for extrication, sir."

"I'll discuss that with Eli. We'll get word to you as soon as we have things worked out."

"Very well, sir. Is there anything else?"

"Yes, Bryan, once we know where they're taking her, I want you to recon the location. The Pentagon is working on an airstrike scenario as one of the options, and we'll need to know the risk to civilians if a missile strike is appropriate."

"But we plan to get her out alive, don't we?"

Taylor cleared his throat.

"So far as I know, we do, but all options are on the table. With what's in her head, this has become a major problem."

****

Taylor continued to watch the satellite feed for another couple of hours when the first major shift in the route took place. The van turned off Highway 71 about twenty miles past the town of *Baghat* and forty miles before the next large city of *Sirgin*. It turned east towards the mountains, and everyone monitoring the search realized that the van was not headed towards Tehran, but probably a military facility or a weapons complex somewhere away from a population center.

Taylor turned on the conference line and asked to speak with an Iranian analyst.

"Are there any bases located in those mountains?" he asked when the voice came on.

"Not really," came the response. The voice was female and young. It made him feel old. "It's a mining region. Gold, primarily, but they also mine tin and some copper."

He disconnected the call, left the secure room, then walked over to Henry Creighton, the FBI director, who was standing alone by a carafe of coffee, adding cream and sugar to his cup.

"Have you got a moment, sir?"

"What is it, Dan?"

"I was just wondering if we know yet how the Iranians learned about Disler's discovery?"

Creighton sighed. "The working theory is hackers. And by the way, our experts say the system at Zurich was penetrated a number of times. Fortunately, they had several layers of firewalls, and their data was encrypted by a source available only to the military, so my people don't think they got their hands on her work."

Taylor sighed, "That's comforting."

"We've changed the encryption for everything in Zurich's computers, so even if they force Disler to give up her passwords, they won't get their hands on what they're after."

Taylor scratched the back of his neck.

"Did you give any thought to the idea of seeding the computer with misinformation that we can let them have? It might buy us some badly needed time?"

"We did, and the President has given his approval. The only data accessible to them will be the genome for a phage."

"A *phage*?"

"It's a harmless virus that lives on our skin." He could hear a note of laughter in the old man's voice. "It has the natural ability to infect and kill the bacteria that causes acne."

Taylor laughed. If they were lucky, it might even keep them distracted for a couple of days.

"How soon will everything be ready to go?"

"It could take a few more hours. It's not just the genome they'll be after. They're going to want her notes, the ones that describe the process for identifying the DNA segments that need alteration and exactly how the changes were accomplished. To keep them busy, we're going to substitute notes involved in the genetic modification of corn. That should confuse them no end. "

Taylor shook his head slowly.

"Let's just hope she's smart enough to play along."

****

Several hours later, the white van turned off the highway and onto a dirt road that meandered through a forest and up to what appeared to be a manned security gate.

The people watching the feed came to life. It appeared as though Angela Disler and her kidnappers had reached what might be their final destination.

Taylor picked up a land line phone and punched in the open line to the Iranian analyst who was monitoring the satellite views from within an adjacent room.

"Is that a known base?" he asked.

The female analyst quickly responded. "Not that we're aware of, sir."

A secret base? He supposed it was a possibility, but if so, when was it built?

"I want someone to call up all the satellite photos we have of the area. Go back thirty years. Set 'em up in sequence, oldest first. I want to know if they built something that we never picked up?"

He glanced up at the current satellite feed and noted that the van had started up, passed through the gate, and drove the quarter mile to a small building set up against the side of a cliff. The two men and the woman got out of the vehicle and they carried the semi-conscious female over to the building.

Three armed guards came out of the front door of the building, all carrying what appeared to be rifles. They assisted the others, bringing in duffle bags they retrieved from the rear of the van. When all were inside, Taylor asked for an area wide view from the satellite.

The resolution of the camera was adjusted, and the view pulled back to display a canyon area well isolated from any other occupied property.

Taylor leaned over to speak into the intercom again.

"Have we got those photographs ready yet?" he said to the analyst.

"They're uploading now, sir. On screen in…five, four, three, two…."

The first photo revealed an isolated canyon with no sign of the building where they'd taken Disler. The next few photo's flashed across the screen as a slide show in three-second intervals, and Taylor and the others could see that there was construction in the area. One of the photos showed several dump trucks, apparently moving quantities of dirt.

As the years ticked by in monthly photographs, it became apparent that a large-scale construction had gone on directly under their very noses. It had been done very carefully and had stretched out over more than a dozen years.

The construction of a single building could not account for the amount of dirt removed from the area, as shown over time in the photographs. There must be more to the facility, all carefully concealed inside the mountain or below the flat surface, and because it was such a remote region—one involved in mining—it would have been easy to mistake the construction as part of an actual mining operation.

But the site bore none of the hallmarks of a mining operation. No heavy equipment, no piles of tailings, no sign of a working crew.

He thought they must have been working at night to avoid the eyes of the geostationary satellite. And if that was the case, it must be quite an important site to have hidden it so well.

Taylor picked up one of the phones and this time he placed a call to his boss, Hamilton Granger, who had gone back to his office during the long wait. This was something he was sure that the President would want to know.

"The van has stopped at a location in the mountains. I've gone over the satellite photos for the past thirty years. Nothing obvious, but an analysis of time-lapse satellite photos reveals that the Iranians have moved a lot of dirt out of the area, and I'm pretty sure they've built a secret base over a very protracted period."

"How long?" Granger asked.

"Years, maybe ten."

"A fortified base?"

"Looks like it, sir. Not much in the way of overt security, but I imagine that there would be electronic measures in place."

"Your recommendation?"

"I've got a ground asset on the way. He'll be with an agent from the Mossad. I'll have them do an eyes-on recon before I make a recommendation."

"Why so conservative, Dan? You know we're working against the clock."

Taylor could feel his blood pressure rising. Granger was clearly pushing him towards making a recommendation for an airstrike.

You'd like that, wouldn't you? It would clean up the mess you caused by not telling anyone about what she was really up to.

He cleared his throat.

"Before I recommend an action that could put our country on a path to war, I intend to make damn sure that she's really in there and that the location is a legitimate military target and not an abandoned mine where a land rescue would be a more appropriate response."

Taylor disconnected the call before Granger could say another word. He didn't have time for the man's conniving. He needed to contact Bryan to let him know what he was going to have to do.

He exhaled slowly to get his heart rate back down to normal. There was too much at stake now to make a mistake, and he was going to take his time and make sure of the facts before he put his name to a recommendation that might lead to a course of action from which there could be no return.

*****

FORTY-TWO

THE PERSIAN GULF
DAY SEVENTEEN   1:25 AM

Bryan was seated on the deck of a fishing trawler that flew the flag of the nation of Sudan. The boat was decrepit in its outward appearance; ragged netting, chipped paint, rust and other signs of disrepair. But beneath the exterior was a powerful set of engines as well as an electronics and communications system that could rival the finest available. The crew of four were Sudanese, but all had been trained and supported by agents of the Mossad for a minimum of fifteen years. Their loyalty was beyond question, as was their skill at working the international waters just off the coast of Iran.

Mordecai was below deck, seeing to the equipment. Their weapons were supplied to them by a Marine Corp Master Sergeant who oversaw the armory at the US embassy in Oman. They were issued two MP5's, two Sig-Sauer . 45 caliber handguns, one M40As sniper rifle, and a silenced M16.

The Israeli's were furnishing a motorized rubber raft for the last part of their infiltration. The trawler would make use of drone surveillance being supplied by the United States to monitor the Persian Gulf for any signs of the Iranian navy. An EC-130U *Spooky* Gunship, armed with a single 25 mm GAU-12 Equalizer (a five-barrel, Gatling-type rotary cannon, with a rate-of-fire of 3,600 rounds per minute), was also on station over the international waters of the Persian Gulf. It was there primarily to monitor, block and disrupt the broadcasts of the Iranian military should the incursion by Bryan and Mordecai be inadvertently discovered by the Iranians. In that eventuality, they would be able to provide *force protection* should the order to do so be given.

They were just about to penetrate Iranian waters—the all clear having been provided from the teams of air force personnel who were monitoring the surveillance equipment—when Bryan received a call on his encrypted satellite phone.

Taylor provided the necessary code phrase, and when Bryan answered in kind, Taylor spent the next twenty minutes filling him in on Disler's current location. Thy talked about what was known about the site from the satellite photography, and the order to have them recon the site for possible assault by SEALs or, in the alternative, should it become necessary, an air operation that would permanently destroy the base and everyone in it.

"How long a drive are we talking about from the coast to the target?"

"About four hours," Taylor said.

Bryan did the calculations in his head and checked his watch. If they made it to the shore without any delays and drove straight through, there might still be time to do a little recon under cover of darkness before the sun came up.

"I'll call you back once we're on scene," he said, then disconnected the call.

He made his way downstairs to where Mordecai was loading a rucksack with ammunition, medical supplies, and a minimal amount of food.

"You know where we're going yet?"

Bryan nodded. "We're headed for the mountains, about a five-hour drive. They want us to recon for a land or air assault."

Mordecai looked up from what he was doing, then frowned.

"What's the site look like?" he asked.

"Best they can tell, it's a concealed base of some kind, most likely military, built into the side of a mountain."

"Coordinates?"

Bryan handed Mordecai a piece of paper that he had used to write them down during Taylor's briefing. He had already placed them into a handheld GPS, and he knew that Mordecai planned to do the same with the one that he would be carrying.

Bryan reached down, picked up his rucksack, hefted it, then said, "I've got room in my pack if we need extra ammo?"

"Can you take a few more grenades? You never know when they'll come in handy—"

"Too heavy, and too limiting. I'd rather take a few more clips for the handguns."

He picked up another half dozen clips, stuffed them into his bag, then picked it up.

"I'm going up topside. You need any help?"

Mordecai shook his head. "I'm good."

Once Bryan left the hold, Mordecai picked up a satellite phone of his own and placed a call to Eli Ben-Jehuda, the head of Mossad.

"We've entered their coastal waters," he said.

Eli was at home, standing by the window of his walk-up flat that looked out over the Mediterranean Sea. Across the road, he had a view of *Tayelet*, a series of bikeways and footpaths that ran along the coastline of the Beach Zone. It was a warm evening and hundreds of Israelis and tourists alike were out strolling, jogging and cycling; enjoying themselves and living in the moment.

"I spoke with Creighton at the CIA," Eli said. "He told me what the woman was working on."

"I know," said Mordecai. "It's hard to believe they would let someone like that go to a conference in Egypt, much less go there without protection."

"The Americans are still finding their way when confronting these terrorist bastards," said Eli, "but they will learn soon enough that the unbridled violence shown by these criminals must be met with equal force if they want their country to survive."

Eli closed the window curtain, then said, "I trust that the Americans are handling the details once you reach the shore?"

"Not exactly, I took care of setting up our infiltration. I hope that was all right?"

"Could I have stopped you?"

"No, Eli, but in answer to your question, I've arranged for a car to meet us when we go ashore. I've got the coordinates for you, where we're headed. It's a base of some kind, built into the side of a mountain."

He then read the coordinates out loud and Eli, who copied them down, read them back to make sure that he had written them down correctly.

"I'll have our people check these out," he told Mordecai. "If we can be of any help, let me know."

"I'll tell you what you can do," Mordecai said. "Put together an exfiltration plan. The Americans have put one together, but if something goes wrong, we could use a backup plan."

"I'll take care of it. Is there anything else you need?"

"We are conducting a recon for them, Eli. They have yet to decide whether or not to attempt a land rescue or to destroy the entire base from the air. If they choose the latter, we might want to consider going after their nuclear facilities at the same time. It's just a thought, but the timing might be right."

Eli was well ahead of him, although he was not about to say so, even on an encoded satellite phone. When Creighton briefed him, he advised the Israelis to consider a simultaneous attack. Preparations were now well underway to work with the Americans towards a coordinated strike.

But Mordecai was about to enter enemy territory, and in the event of his capture, the less he knew about any possible attack, the better it would be for everyone.

"We'll consider that, Morty, but in the meantime, I'm sure I don't need to tell you to be careful."

Mordecai laughed. Eli was like his father. He would never forgive himself if he forgot to say *be careful,* as failing to do so might jinx the mission.

"I'll contact you as soon as we reach the coordinates I've given you."

Nothing further was said, and after Mordecai had disconnected the call, he carried his rucksack up on deck and joined Bryan and one of the "fishermen" who was getting ready to put the motorized dingy into the water. The fisherman was going to guide the boat into the shore and then take it back out to the trawler.

"Will the vehicle be waiting for us?" Bryan asked.

Mordecai nodded. "It's parked at a particular GPS location. Keys will be under the rear seat rug."

"Then I guess we're good to go."

*****

FORTY-THREE

THE ZAGROS MOUNTAINS
SOUTHWESTERN, IRAN
DAY SEVENTEEN   3:00 AM

She felt like she was dying. Her body was so weak that even turning over felt like too much effort. She could barely open her eyes.

She had no sense of time yet, but as her self-awareness returned, she began to remember things in brief flashes.

She tried to lick her cracked lips, but it did no good. Her mouth was desert dry. And the smell…*what was that smell?*

Oh my God! It's me!

Her eyes stayed open, and as her vision came into focus, she soon became aware of a shape…a human…*a woman* who was standing nearby.

She was staring at her and smiling.

"We've given you a drug to bring you up. You'll feel better in a few minutes."

Angela didn't speak. She had no idea where she was, but her thoughts were now coming at lightening speed.

Is this a hospital?

Is this woman a nurse?

I must have been rescued.,,that has to be it!

"My husband?" she croaked as she struggled to find her voice. "My girls?"

Her mouth was too dry to continue.

The woman leaned forward and put a glass to her lips.

"Here, drink this. Small sips. Take your time. You've been out for quite a while and you're very dehydrated."

Angela sipped at the water, taking bigger and bigger swallows until the woman pulled the glass away from her face.

"You'll get sick if you drink this too fast. Let's see if it stays down, and if it does, I'll give you some more in a couple of minutes."

She put the glass on a small table next to the bed.

Angela looked around. Cement walls, no windows, a single bed, a table, a chair. A door that was solid metal with a very small window at eye-level height. The room was sterile and had the feel of a hospital room, but the woman was not dressed like any nurse she'd ever seen.

"Where am I?" Angela croaked.

"You are a guest of the government of Iran," the woman replied. "I am Noor. In your language, it means 'light.'"

Angela closed her eyes. Her disappointment was overwhelming.

I'm not free. I'm still a captive.

She opened them slowly.

"Why am I here?" she asked.

"As soon as you are strong enough to walk around by yourself, it will be explained to you." She reached again for the glass by the side of the table.

"Let's drink a little more water, then I'll see about getting you a sponge bath, fresh clothes, and some food. You must be very hungry?"

Angela took the glass with a shaking hand and promptly gulped down what remained of the water.

****

After her bath and a meal of rice and curried chicken, Angela was able to sit up in a chair without slumping forward. Her energy had improved dramatically after food and water, and the sponge bath and fresh clothing made her feel almost human again.

Throughout the food and the ministrations of Noor, she found herself considering the seriousness of her situation. If Noor was telling the truth, she was in a kind of a prison-like facility somewhere in the country of Iran. There could be only one reason for her abduction, and that was the nature of her research. Somehow, the Iranians or someone acting on their behalf had learned about her discovery, and that troubled her greatly. She had presumed, perhaps incorrectly, that once she notified the Pentagon about what she'd discovered, the information would be kept a top secret. But clearly, it seemed that someone outside that limited circle had stumbled across or otherwise gained access to something they shouldn't have known. How they found out was a question that should be looked into, but for the moment, she had other, more pressing concerns.

She doubted that they could have gained access to her research. It was heavily encoded and protected by several layers of passwords. She had to conclude that it was very likely that her research was exactly what they were after, and if that was the case, how far would they go to get her to disclose the passwords to her accounts?

Would she be subjected to torture? She hoped not because she didn't think she had the strength to resist. She was not very strong when it came to physical pain, so she would likely give in the very first time they pulled off one of her fingernails.

Did they still do those kinds of things?

She was on the verge of panic.

She tried to remember what she'd seen in the movies and what she'd heard on the news. They might subject her to waterboarding. That would be awful. She would hold her breath as long as she could, but would it be long enough?

The door to her room was suddenly unlocked and a tall male walked in. Angela noticed that Noor took a step back in deference to his obvious importance.

"How is she doing?" he asked in English.

The woman said something in reply in a language she assumed was Persian. The man listened intently, then looked over at Angela and flashed a big smile.

Late forties, although he might be older, his kindly face was shaped by a well groomed, short beard. He wore a dark business suit with a white shirt and tie. His English seemed formal, almost British-sounding to her ear. He didn't seem to fit the vision in her mind of the typical Iranian male.

He walked over to her bedside and took her hand.

"Doctor Disler. I'm so glad you're feeling better. My name is Doctor

Ahmad Farazi. I am a virologist and the chief of this medical research facility. I hope that we are meeting your immediate needs."

"Why am I here?" Angela asked. "I was taken against my will from my hotel in Alexandria."

"I know, and that is very unfortunate, but we will try to make your stay with us as comfortable as possible."

"And how long will that be?" she asked.

"Ah! That is the question." He pulled up the one chair in the room and sat down to face her directly.

"How long you remain here depends on how cooperative you are?"

"What does that mean? What are you saying?"

Farazi smiled. "You are a very famous doctor, and I am very familiar with your research. I was hoping you could find it in your heart to demonstrate for us some of your remarkable techniques?"

Is this guy kidding? Does he have any idea what's involved?

"I'm afraid that what I do is extremely complicated. It's not something that can be accomplished with just a microscope and a pair of scissors."

"Ah… I'm sure you did not mean that as an insult, doctor, but do not let your current surroundings influence your decision. We have a world-class laboratory here, and if you are up to it, I'd be pleased to show you around."

She had no intention of showing him any aspect of her research techniques, but she did want to get a look around in case there was an opportunity for her to escape.

"I'd like to see the facility," she finally said. "Can you help me get to my feet?"

"Of course."

He reached out, took her arm, and helped her to stand up.

"Can you walk?" he asked.

By way of answer, she took several steps, tentative at first, but soon she was able to walk on her own.

Noor followed closely behind them.

As Farazi led her from the room, he said, "I received my medical training at the Army Medical College in Rawalpindi, and after that, I did the majority of my research in virology at the National Institute of Health in Islamabad."

She looked at him.

"Islamabad? Isn't that in Pakistan?"

"Yes, I am Pakistani."

She stopped in her tracks.

"But I was told that we're in Iran?"

"Yes, that's true, but the Iranians have paid me well to operate this facility, so here I am."

They started walking again, and soon passed a guard at a table at the end of the hallway.

Farazi called for an elevator, and when it arrived, the three of them got on. Angela noted they were on the third floor as Farazi pressed the button for six.

The elevator went down, and Angela was suddenly struck with a sinking feeling that the entire facility was underground.

"You said you're a virologist?"

"That's correct. My specialty is communicable diseases, but recently, I've done some work in genetics. I find the entire subject fascinating."

The elevator stopped at the floor marked six and the three of them got off. He led her to a laboratory that was effectively sealed off from the hallway by a decontamination room, but through a window in the inside wall, she was able to see an enormous laboratory staffed with what looked like more than two dozen people.

Farazi hadn't lied. The lab was on a par with the equipment they had at Zurich. She was very surprised.

"This is the primary lab. There are others on another floor where you will be working, too. And as you can see, the equipment will not be an impediment to your work."

She shook her head.

Does he really believe that I would show him how to make a direct contact disease into one that's airborne?"

"Doctor Farazi, I'm afraid I won't be able to work here. What I've done has taken years of research, and to duplicate my accomplishments, I would need access to my research materials, and that, of course, is impossible."

"I believe we can assist you with that," he said.

What? How would that be possible?

"I don't understand? My research is proprietary and belongs to Zurich Pharmaceuticals."

"We know you have access to your research over the internet, and we are set up to allow you to call up your materials."

Angela frowned. It was time to stop this nonsense. If they expected her to give them her password, then they had another think coming.

She was ready to push back.

"Look, doctor, if you think I'm going to download anything for you, you're sadly mistaken. I'm not about to cooperate with you or anyone else. You had no right to bring me here against my will." She folded her arms across her chest. "And by now, I'm sure my government has started searching for me, so you'd better let me go before you end up creating a lot of problems for your country."

Farazi looked over at Noor and the two of them started to laugh. He shook his head.

"My dear Doctor Disler, you *will* cooperate with us."

She tried to keep her voice from shaking.

"No, I won't."

Farazi shifted his glance back to Disler. The warmth in his voice was now gone.

"Your youngest daughter, I believe her name is Carrie?"

"You leave my daughter out of this," she said as a wave of anger passed through her body.

"I would love to, but if you fail to cooperate fully, she will be the first one to lose her life."

"What? What are you talking about?"

"We have your two daughters and your husband. They are being well cared for, but that can change with a single phone call. Do you understand?"

But she didn't, not really. How could they have Henrik and the girls? They were in Los Angeles, not in Egypt. There was just no way.

Farazi could see the disbelief in her eyes.

"Would you like to speak with them?"

Angela's eyes widened. "They're here?"

Farazi smiled. "No, but we can arrange for you to speak with them on the phone."

He had to be bluffing; she was sure of that. There was just no way they could have Henrik and the girls.

Or could they?

"I will let you speak briefly to your husband. He will confirm for you that we have them all. After that, you will use your password to gain access to your research which we will download tonight. Then tomorrow, we will set you up in the lab and you will show us the modification you made to the genetic structure of the Marburg virus."

Her eyes widened again.

"I can't do that unless I have a sample of the Marburg."

"That is not a problem. We have what you need."

Unknown to Angela, during the 1990's, specimens of Marburg were stolen from western laboratories and delivered by *Aeroflot* planes to the Soviet Union to support the Russian biological weapons program. To secure a sample, the Iranians paid several million dollars to Dr. Andre Petrov, the Bulgarian virologist, who provided them a sample that he stole from the Russian laboratory in *Irkutsk, Siberia,* where he worked on biological weaponry.

They've been working with Marburg? My God! These people are serious about weaponizing the virus, and they expect me to hand it to them on a silver platter. What in God's name am I going to do?"

Farazi motioned to a guard who was standing nearby.

"Noor and this gentleman will take you back to your room. I would suggest that you get some sleep. The drugs are still in your system, and it will take a full day for you to get your strength back."

"But you said I could speak with my husband?"

"And you will. I will come and get you once we are ready to make the call."

Angela frowned. If they really did have Henrik and the children, she would have no choice but to cooperate. But would they free them if she did what they asked?

She didn't think so, which placed her in an impossible situation.

She could only hope that her husband had reported her missing and that someone was actually trying to find her.

*****

FORTY-FOUR

THE ZAGROS MOUNTAINS
SOUTHWESTERN IRAN
DAY SEVENTEEN   5:00 AM

The drive into the mountains passed by quickly enough. Mordecai was behind the wheel while Bryan was focused on the GPS locator that overlaid the Google map on his small laptop computer.

The Toyota was two years old but serviceable. It was provided for them by an Israeli contact, a Persian businessman who was also a deep-cover intelligence operative. He had stolen the truck from the port city of *Bandar-e-Abbas* and driven it down to the port at *Kolani* where Mordecai and Bryan were put ashore under the cover of darkness. The plates on the truck were switched to disguise the fact that it was stolen.

The trip had been unremarkable. No police checkpoints to worry about. Once out of *Kolani,* they had driven through farmland, deserts, and now the lowlands leading up into a range of mountains in a district known chiefly for mining. There was very little traffic on the roads at night, so other than a few vehicles and a half-dozen trucks loaded down with produce for markets along the coastline, they saw no sign of a military presence.

They made their way into the mountains, and as they got closer to their destination, Bryan began to assess their surroundings. They were still within the tree line, making concealment of the truck a simple proposition, but there was no way to know if there were isolated homes or people about. That was a bit unnerving, but if they had the time, they could check things out later when the sun came up.

According to the map and the GPS coordinates, they were now within a mile or so of the turnoff that Disler's captors had taken to get to what the analysts were loosely referring to as a base.

"We're getting close," he said to Mordecai. "Let's find a place to hide the truck."

They had continued for another kilometer before Mordecai spotted a turnout. It appeared to be a seldom used dirt road that wound it's way up into a thinly forested zone.

He pulled off the highway, and at the first opportunity, he left the dirt road and parked next to a clump of scrub Oak trees that effectively shielded the vehicle from being viewed by anyone driving past on the road.

They put on their packs, checked their weapons, and slipped on night vision goggles. After carefully examining the immediate area, and finding no sign of habitation anywhere nearby, they used broken bushes to wipe out their tracks and the tire marks from the parked truck, all the way back down to the highway before setting off on foot through the mountains.

The map they were using seemed to indicate that the base they were looking for was just on the other side of the ridge they were parked on, and rather than take the highway to the turnoff to go up into the valley, they rightly concluded that they would be less conspicuous if they climbed the mountain directly. It might take a little more time, but it would afford them an overlook view of what lay on the other side.

The mountain was fairly steep, but the footing was firm and there were few obstructions. They were walking through a forested area, mostly scrub Oak, but they also encountered stands of Ash and Elm. It took several hours, but they arrived at the top while still under the cover of darkness.

They crossed over the top of the ridge, took off their packs, and settled in beneath the protection of a clump of trees. From there, they could take stock of their position and assess the layout of the valley below.

The first thing they noticed was that the valley they were now looking into was much higher in altitude than the bottom of the valley where they'd just come from. Bryan was surprised but quickly realized that it would make getting in and out of that valley that much easier to do.

Through his night viewing binoculars, he could see one warehouse type of building with what appeared to be a very large corrugated metal garage door, and a single regular sized door about thirty feet farther to the North. Both the garage door and the regular one could be used for access into the warehouse, which appeared to be built right up against the side of the mountain.

He did not have a frontal view of the building. It was facing east, and they were to the Southwest. But given the location of the building, its proximity to the hillside, and the fact that this was a mining region, he suspected that the building just might conceal an entryway into the mountain.

The building had the appearance of a very large storage garage, and if this was, in fact, a mine, then the building was probably being used to store trucks or other heavy mining equipment.

From the building out to the security gate was a large, flat, graded pad that formed a level plain. From the guardhouse out to the highway, the road was downhill, about a three percent grade. A large number of trucks or vehicles could easily be parked on the pad, which was unpaved dirt, and it struck him that whoever had done the construction had most likely used the dirt from inside the mountain to backfill this portion of the valley.

Very clever, he thought. They could conceal the construction work by dumping the soil in such a way as to gradually fill up the canyon, and unless the satellite photos of the site were compared to each other over long periods of time, the gradual change in the landscape would not stand out.

He estimated the distance between the warehouse and the security gate to be about 150 yards. The gate itself was pretty basic. A single raisable arm, a security booth, and one man who was seated inside. A chain link fence surrounded the entire flat level plain, and it was topped by a coil of tight barbed wire.

It didn't have the feel of a military base. In fact, it looked more like the site of a typical mining operation with a single night watchman for security.

He could see the white van. It was parked in front of the building, so he was confident that they had the right place. But that little voice inside his head was telling him that there was more to this site than met the eye.

If this really was a mining operation, then why would they bring her here? Was this just a temporary stopover, a place for them to get some sleep before going back out on the road? Then again, if this was to be her final destination, and if it was the site of a military base, was the layout intentionally designed to conceal a secret base? If so, then it must be a base of considerable importance for the Iranians to have gone to such great lengths.

He suspected the latter was the case.

"Not much of a base," said Mordecai, who was still scanning the grounds. "Might be something tucked into the mountain."

"I'm going down there," Bryan said as he checked his watch. "We've got at least another hour before it starts to get light. I'll do a quick recon while you take overwatch."

Mordecai nodded. He would be taking up a sniping position to cover Bryan's incursion onto the site.

Mordecai said, "While you're down there, put this tracking device on the van just in case it moves again." He handed Bryan the device. "It's self-contained, battery operated and magnetized. Just slap it on the undercarriage and flip the switch. But try and conceal it on the inner side of the gas tank. Less chance of discovery if the van goes through a checkpoint."

Bryan took the device, slipped it into a pocket on his camouflaged cargo pants, shouldered his MP5, and using the night vision goggles, he set off down the side of the mountain into the valley below.

Mordecai broke out the M40A5 sniper rifle and mounted it on a tripod. The weapon came with a flash suppressor, to better conceal his position if he had to fire. From his vantage point, he could provide cover for Bryan while keeping tabs on the guard who was likely asleep at the gate.

He made an assessment of wind conditions using his night vision goggles by looking for swirls of dust on the ground and by watching the movement of branches in the trees between where he was crouching and where his possible targets would be. He paid particular attention to cross-currents that could shift the course of a bullet's trajectory.

He used a portable hand-held laser device to compute the exact distance from his perch to the front gate security booth; then he did the same for the distance between himself and the door to the building where Bryan was headed. He then made his adjustments to the *Leupold* scope—adjustments that allowed for wind, distance, the pull of gravity, and the rotation of the earth—before he settled in for what he hoped would be an uneventful recon.

Once he was ready, he spoke softly into his two-way communication unit.

"I've got you covered. Keep an eye out for electronic security devices."

Bryan double clicked his microphone to acknowledge that he'd overheard what was said without having to speak, which could give away his current position.

****

Bryan made his way slowly down the hillside, using the cover of the trees whenever possible. When he reached the chain link fence, he studied it briefly, decided it was not electrified, and then, after removing a pair of wire cutters that he carried in one of his pockets, he slowly began the process of clipping an opening in the base of the fence.

He slipped through the fence, then took a hard look around. There were no cameras set up, which likely meant that there were no sensors in the ground that would give away his presence. With a quick glance towards the guard shack, he moved quickly across the graded ground and towards the parked white van.

When he reached the rear of the van, he lay down on his back, slid under the bumper, and attached the tracking device to the side of the gas tank. He then took a handful of dirt and rubbed it on the device to do what he could to conceal it.

After sliding out from under the car, he made his way quietly and quickly towards the building. He crept over to the garage style doors, pressed his ear against the corrugated metal, heard nothing, then moved over to the regular door.

Again, he listened with his ear to the door, but there was no sound. He was tempted to try the door but quickly decided against it. There was still too much to do outside before taking that risk.

He slowly moved across the front of the building, noting the design and fabrication of the structure. It seemed weathered, and frankly, not very structurally sound. When he followed the building around to the side, he discovered that his first assessment had been correct. It was built into the side of the hill.

He also noted a set of vents, encased in cement, in the ground just to the north of the building. He made his way over, and upon examination of the vents, he discovered that they were about two and a half feet in diameter and covered with a thin, mesh, screen.

He smiled to himself. It had to be a ventilation system for an underground facility of some kind.

He continued his exploration, and he discovered a stairwell, partially concealed by bushes, and about fifteen feet down the flight of concrete stairs he found a single, metal door.

An emergency stairwell. He smiled to himself. *A possible way into the facility.*

He pulled out his GPS device, and within a few moments, he logged in a reading that accurately identified not only the location of the stairwell, but also the opening of the air vent pipe that extended down into the ground. He would pass that information back to Langley once he got back up to the top of the hill.

He made his way back to the single door on the front of the structure, and after listening again, he carefully tried the handle. It was locked, so he pulled out a small pouch and removed a lock picking kit. It took almost four minutes, but he finally got the tumbler in the right position and the lock slipped open.

It opened inward, and with a handgun in one hand, he opened it slowly. His night vision goggles were on, and a quick scan disclosed an enormous warehouse full of miscellaneous furniture pieces, a few vehicles, and some empty equipment crates. There were bins for trash, several exceptionally large ones, which gave him a hint that the below ground facility was quite large.

At the back of the building, set into the side of the hill, were two large metal doors. When he examined them, he realized that they were blast proof steel security doors, large enough when open to allow vehicles to be driven into the side of the mountain. A few feet away from a pair of elevators, he discovered a smaller door, also locked. It would likely be the door used by personnel to enter the stairwell that would take them down and into the facility.

He'd seen enough, and a check of his watch let him know that dawn would be breaking in less than half an hour.

He made his way back to the outer door, and after a quick peek outside, he shut the door behind him and quickly made his way across the graded plain and over to the opening he'd made in the fence.

He did what he could to obliterate his footprints, and after going through the fence, he again did what he could to re-attach the fencing before starting back up the mountainside.

"I'm through the wire and on my way back," he whispered into the mouthpiece.

The two clicks told him that he was understood.

When he finally arrived again at the crest of the hill, he took a seat on the ground next to Mordecai.

"It's a base of some kind," he said. "I think we should watch it for a while; see what's going on."

Mordecai nodded. "You want the first watch?"

"I've got to call in, so I'll take it."

"Wake me in two," Mordecai said. He lay back down, folded his arms across his chest, and closed his eyes.

Bryan smiled to himself. The guy was a soldier through and through. He didn't have to be told what to do, and he could sleep at the drop of a hat. It was somehow comforting to work again with a partner, one he believed he could trust.

He picked up his satellite phone. It was time to tell Taylor what they'd discovered.

****

Taylor hung up the phone and leaned back in his chair to consider what he'd just been told. Bryan had described the facility where Disler was taken, and there could be no doubt that the Iranians had gone to a lot of trouble to conceal a base of some kind in the side of the mountain. But what was the purpose of the base, and was it where they would continue to keep Disler, or was it just a way-stop of some sort on the way to another destination?

He leaned forward and picked up his secure phone.

****

Rooney spoke with Taylor for less than two minutes before signing off with a promise that he'd call him back within the hour.

He stood up, took a long drink of water, then turned to the on-duty technician and ordered him to turn off the recordings that were playing continuously into Niroomad's headset.

"Do you want me to record your session with him?" the technician said into the intercom.

"Keep it on," Rooney said. He marched out of the conference room where he'd taken the call, past the two on-duty security personnel, and into the room where Niroomad was being held.

He walked up to Niroomad and took the earphones off his head.

"Time's running out, Ali. We know about the base in the side of the mountain where your agents have taken Disler."

Niroomad looked groggy. The lack of sleep and the continuous screeching in his headset had taken a toll. Rooney decided he was on the edge and just might be ready to break.

"We want to know about the base, Ali. If you tell us about it, I might be able to convince my people to turn off the music and give you a chance to get some real sleep."

Niroomad looked up at him with pleading eyes. "Please! No more! I can't take it any longer."

Rooney reached out and placed a hand on his shoulder. "Then tell me about the base."

Niroomad closed his eyes, and Rooney thought he was falling asleep. He started to squeeze the man's shoulder, but it turned out that Niroomad was simply marshaling his thoughts.

"It's not a base," he said. "It's a laboratory."

"A lab?" Rooney felt his pulse quicken. "What kind of lab?"

Niroomad held his stare. "It's a biological and chemical weapons laboratory."

"And they want Disler for what purpose?"

A small smile appeared at the corner of Niroomad's mouth. "To get access to her research, of course. They want her passwords and security codes."

Rooney waited, but Niroomad's eyes started to close.

"Wake up, Ali." He shook him hard. "Did they want more than her passwords and codes?"

Niroomad's eyes popped open.

"They want her to demonstrate her technique..."

"Her technique for what?"

"Her technique for genetically altering the Marburg virus."

Rooney exhaled softly. Taylor had been right all along. Niroomad did know the entire plan, and it confirmed what Taylor's group had already deduced. They were intent on weaponizing the Marburg virus.

But how did they know about her work? From what Taylor had said, she notified her supervisor at Zurich, who passed it on to the Pentagon. Word of her discovery was made only a few days before she made the trip to Alexandria.

Rooney moved over to the door, opened it a crack, and asked the two minders to take off Niroomad's shackles.

They did, and when they'd left the room, Rooney said, "I'm glad you decided to cooperate, Ali. This will go a long way to helping you out. But I'm curious about a few things. First off, how did your people learn about her work?"

This time Niroomad made no effort to conceal his smile.

"With all your freedoms, we were able to monitor the research grants given out by your Pentagon. After that, our people monitored the emails sent back and forth between her lab and your government."

"So you intercepted word of her discovery in an email to the Pentagon?"

"It wasn't difficult," Niroomad replied. "Our people are very good at hacking into your government computers."

Rooney knew he was right. The state of internet security in the United States was scandalous. Billions of dollars of research and corporate proprietary information were stolen each year by hackers throughout the world. In fact, the problem was so bad that hackers of various nationalities from an assortment of countries were often hired by less sophisticated governments or private individuals to steal top secret information from their competitors.

"Did your people do it, or did they contract out the hacking?"

"I don't know," Niroomad said. "I was never told."

"We'll come back to that later." Rooney had another important question that he wanted to ask.

"Did your people give any thought as to what would happen if they weaponized the Marburg virus? I mean, your population would also be at risk if an outbreak was to occur?"

"My understanding was that a weapon would not be used until a vaccine was developed to protect our people."

Rooney was shocked. They planned to release the virus as opposed to using the threat of a release as leverage against their opponents.

"So the plan was to eventually release the virus?"

"Maybe yes, maybe no." Niroomad shrugged. "It would take years to get things into place, so who knows what the political situation would be at that time?"

"And where did they plan to release it?"

Niroomad gave him a curious look.

"Why, on Israel, of course! And after that, on the West!"

"And you went along with this?" Rooney asked, still trying to come to grips with the fact that the Iranians really intended to release a virus that could decimate the population of the entire world.

"I do not believe in what they're doing," Niroomad said, "but I have no choice. I do what they tell me to do, or my family will face the consequences." He glared at Rooney. "Same threat you made to me, right?"

Rooney sighed. He needed to call Taylor...*and fast.*

"Get some sleep, Ali. I'll be back later, and we'll talk again."

*****

FORTY-FIVE

THE ZAGROS MOUNTAINS
SOUTHWESTERN IRAN
DAY SEVENTEEN   9:00 AM

Angela awoke to someone shaking her shoulder. It was Doctor Andre Petrov, and he was smiling broadly.

"You?" she said.

She was thoroughly confused. He was the one who approached her that fateful day when she was kidnapped from the hotel lobby in Alexandria.

"Why are you doing this to me?" she said through clenched teeth.

"Does that actually require an answer, Doctor?"

She sat up straight and folded her arms across her chest.

"You're a bastard!"

Petrov smiled.

"And where is the other doctor? Farazi? What's happened to him?"

"Doctor Farazi is down in the lab making sure that we have everything you need to do your important work. He'll join us later." He studied her careful-ly. "Now, I trust you slept well, so as soon as you're up, we'll place that call to your family."

My family!

How she craved to hear their voices, to tell them how sorry she was that her work had put them in this position. She stared at Petrov. He and Farazi were men who were obviously motivated solely by greed. They cared nothing about the innocent lives that would surely be devastated once they had their hands on her research.

She softly cursed them both, and while she doubted that she'd ever see her family again, she vowed to make their efforts to get her information as diffi-cult as she could given her present circumstances.

She sat up on the cot, gained her bearings, then got to her feet. She felt considerably better than she did when she arrived. No longer dehydrated, she displayed a burst of energy that she hadn't had since Alexandria.

"I'm ready," she said.

"So I see." Petrov smiled again. "Before we make the call, I wish to show you something. Please come with me."

Angela started to walk, a little wobbly at first, but with the assistance of two of the Iranian military guards, she soon had her sea legs under her.

They walked to the elevator, and while they waited, Angela said, "So the Russians have teamed up with the Iranians? Your country must be getting awfully desperate."

"Oh, please, doctor. The Russians have nothing to do with this."

"But you said you work for them—"

"Not for them, doctor. I said I worked at *Irkutsk*. I've been on the payroll of the Iranians ever since I was in medical school. I spent my time in Siberia so that I could pass on what I learned about the Russians and their research discoveries."

"So you're a traitor as well as a kidnapper?" She shook her head. "And you call yourself a doctor?"

She was starting to get under his skin, but he held his temper in check. They needed her cooperation, but once they had it, he would address her insults the old fashioned way.

"I am a Bulgarian, Doctor Disler. I have no allegiance to the Russians. And besides, the Iranians pay me very, very well."

The elevator doors opened, and Angela noticed that they took it *down* to the fifth floor. At first, it was a little disconcerting, but then she remembered that she was in a below ground facility.

When they got off the elevator, Petrov and the two guards led Angela into a sophisticated workspace. Part office, part laboratory, it was equipped with a large array of computers, monitors, electron microscopes, and virtually everything else a sophisticated medical intellectual might need to perform state-of-the-art research at the genetic level.

"This will be your office during your stay with us. I sincerely hope you find it adequate?"

She noticed that he seemed pleased with himself, and she suspected that he was responsible for the selection and placement of the equipment and the design of what was to be her workspace.

But who did he think he was kidding? He's just shown me a glorified cell where I'll be kept as a slave until I die.

One of the guards whispered something into his ear and he nodded his understanding.

"Doctor Disler, if you'll come with me now, I believe we are ready to let you talk with your family."

Angela felt her heart begin to beat faster. Her adrenalin was pumping and her hands were starting to shake. She had hoped against hope that they were bluffing, that Henrik and the girls were not really being held as captives, but if this bit about calling them was just a bluff, then they were taking it right to the very edge. But if it was true, and if they were now being held by the Iranians, then she would have to use what leverage she still had to get her captors to set them free.

Petrov walked her into a nearby office. One of the guards was holding a phone in his hand. He gave it to Petrov, who spoke to someone in Persian, and after a few moments of conversation that Angela did not understand, he handed the phone to her.

"Your husband," he said, but before she could take the phone out of his hand, he added, "Do not tell him where you are or what we are asking you to do, or there will be repercussions beyond my control."

She took the phone from his hand.

"Henrik? Henrik! Is that you?"

****

Henrik had been completely surprised when one of their captors entered the room and handed him a cell phone.

He and the girls had been trying to sleep, but for some unknown reason, they hadn't been successful. What they did not know was that their captors had not drugged their dinner this time in anticipation of a call from Iran.

He took the phone, completely unsure what to do with it, but the man began to make the kind of gestures that indicated that he should put the phone up to his ear, so he did.

"Henrik? Henrik! Is that you?"

Oh my God!

"Angela? Honey? It's me. Where are you?"

"Oh, Henrik! Are you and the girls okay?"

"We're being held against our will, but so far they're treating us okay. How about you?"

"Same thing! I love you and miss you all."

"What's going on, Angela? Why is this happening?"

"I can't talk about it with you now, darling. They won't let me."

Henrik understood. He was astounded that they were allowing her to talk to him in the first place.

"The girls are with me. Can you talk to them?"

He heard her ask someone that question, and a moment later, she said, "Yes."

He turned to his two daughters who were now eagerly standing nearby. He handed the phone to Sienna, the oldest.

"Mom? Are you okay?"

"I'm fine, my darling. Are you guys doing okay?"

"No, it's horrible here. We're in this stinking bedroom in the Valley and they won't let us out—"

There was the sound of a brief scuffle and what sounded like her daughter pleading. Angela heard her daughter saying, "I'm sorry. I didn't mean to say that. Please let me talk to my mom. *Please!...*"

But whoever it was who took the phone from Sienna didn't give it back to her. Instead, the phone apparently was passed to Carrie, her youngest, because the next voice she heard was hers.

"Mom?"

"Carrie?"

"Mom! *Come home...*" She started to cry. "I want you to come home!"

"Oh, baby, I'll be home soon. You'll see—"

The guard standing next to Disler took the phone out of her hand and gave it to Petrov.

"No, *wait!*' Angela's gaze shifted to Andre Petrov. "Please let me talk to them? My kids are scared. They need—"

Petrov shook his head.

"They heard your voice, and you heard theirs. That is more than enough for now."

Angela was deflated. She shook her head, as though trying to wake from a terrible dream.

She tried to regain her emotional stability. If she didn't stay resolute, her family had no chance.

This doctor, Petrov, he obviously thinks I'll just go along with everything that he says. He thinks I believe they're going to let me go if I just do what they want. But they're not going to let me go, and once they have what they want, they'll kill my family, too. The only leverage I have at the moment is the research and my skills, and if they want to get the latter, then first they'll have to let my family go.

"If you let them go, I'll do what you want," she said in a shaky voice.

Petrov smiled. This was easier than he thought it would be.

"You've got that backward. Once we have what we want, that's when we'll let them go."

She shook her head.

"You know the work I've done is not complete. It could take several years to finish. I'm not going to do a damn thing for you unless you let them go right now."

Petrov shook his head. "Here's how it works, Doctor. No one knows where we're holding your family, and no one even knows that you're missing. You may think you can dictate terms to us, but you can't."

"Don't be so sure."

"But I am sure," he said with a smile. "You see, the people in charge have already determined what will happen if you refuse to cooperate. Your youngest daughter will be the first to experience our disappointment."

"You bastards would harm a little girl? How can you call yourself a human being? You're sick!"

Petrov held up his hands in a gesture of surrender.

"I'm not in charge, doctor. Between you and me, these men are evil. They plan to record what they do to your daughter on tape, and then they'll show it to you." He shrugged his shoulders. "I wish it were different, but there's nothing I can do. Everything depends on your cooperation. Please don't let them hurt your daughter. Just do what they ask."

"You listen to me, Petrov. I have no illusions about what's going to happen to me, so you go back to your master's and tell them this. If anything happens to any member of my family, you'll get nothing from me. If you kill or injure either one of my daughters or my husband, you might as well kill them all because once you take that first step, I won't do a thing."

She realized that she had been screaming, so she took several deep breaths to calm herself down.

"You let them go and I'll do what you ask," she finally said when she regained her composure, "but if you don't let them go, then I swear to god that you'll never get a thing from me."

Petrov studied her intently. She probably meant what she said.

"Okay," he said. "I'll tell you what. Once we have the information you stored on your computer, I'll arrange to have your family released, but we will continue to watch them, doctor, and if you do not cooperate fully, we will show them no mercy. Have I made myself clear?"

It was probably the best she could hope for, so Angela nodded.

"Fine," said Petrov, taking her nod for assent. "Then let's get started. Shall we?"

*****

FORTY-SIX

SANTA MONICA, CALIFORNIA
DAY SEVENTEEN   11:00 PM

Thompson cut the siren off about a block before she pulled up in the red zone in front of Zurich Pharmaceuticals, but when they locked up the car she left the red light flashing. They'd been summoned to the facility by a late night phone call from an agent at the NSA.

It seemed that someone was after Angela Disler's data.

Thompson picked up Donahue at her condo and the two of them went Code 3 through West Los Angeles and into the city of Santa Monica. Traffic was light, so the drive from Donahue's place took less than ten minutes.

On the way up the front stairway, Donahue said, "You think it's smart to leave our car in the red zone?"

"I left the flashers on, and if the pricks write me up this time, I'll file a formal complaint."

"Tempting fate...."

They showed their credentials to the receptionist and were quickly ushered into an office that had been taken over by an NSA data expert who was overseeing the government's monitoring of Zurich's computers.

Lum was standing behind a seated technician and both men were studying a computer screen.

"What's going on?" Donahue asked as she and Thompson peered at the screen.

Without looking up from his view of the computer screen, Lum said, "Someone has accessed the computer using Angela's passwords."

"Did they get anything?" Thompson asked.

Lum turned to look at them.

"They're downloading the phony data right now."

"Do we know where the data is going?"

The technician, who was monitoring the screen, turned his head and smiled. "We're running that down from another facility." He broke into a smile and extended his hand towards Thompson.

"I'm Sid. Sid Weber. NSA."

Thompson smiled. "That figures. Glad to meet you, *Sid, the Science Kid.*"

She reached out and shook his hand.

He was young, handsome, and military in bearing, not the usual perception of the computer geek depicted in Hollywood films.

"I haven't been called that since high school," he said with a smile.

"Who's *Sid, the Science Kid*?" Donahue asked.

"It's a cartoon host on a TV show," Thompson replied, who had shifted her gaze to give Donahue *that* look; the one that said, *"Back off! I saw him first."*

She returned her attention back to Weber, still holding on to his hand.

"She doesn't have kids," she told him by way of explanation.

Oh, brother, thought Donahue. She was playing the *MILF* card, and it was not very subtle.

As if reading Donahue's mind, Thompson let go of Weber's hand.

"My partner, Jen Donahue," she said with a smile.

"Nice to meet you," Weber said to Donahue, but he didn't shift his gaze from Thompson, and he didn't bother to extend his hand.

The boobs win out again, thought Donahue.

She struggled hard to repress a grin. He was certainly handsome, but probably no older than twenty-five or six. Too young for her taste, but he would fit right in for Shari, given her current penchant for younger men and completely inappropriate relationships.

While the two of them continued to lock eyes, Donahue directed her attention to Lum.

"Is there any way these people can get their hands on Disler's research?"

Lum shook his head. "We pulled all her data completely offline. We're undergoing a total security analysis, and before her data ever goes back online again, the protection will be state of the art."

"You'll never be completely protected," Weber said. He returned his gaze to the screen. "No matter what security system you end up with, if you're hooked up to the internet, someone, somewhere, will figure out a way to crack it." He glanced up at Donahue. "The best we can hope for is to stay ahead of the hackers by finding and patching the weaknesses."

Sid, the Science Kid, knew exactly what he was talking about. As a member of the NSA's *Red Team,* the fabled pro's known to be the stealthiest and most skilled firewall-crackers in the world, he was in a unique position to know exactly what was going on in the world of international hacking. In addition to wiretapping and massive data mining enterprises, one of the Red Team's primary functions was the protection of the military's secure computer networks. The apparent breach by the Iranians of the emails between Disler and the Pentagon had obviously become a major source of concern to everyone involved, hence, the use of the Red Team to sort things out.

"Can you bring us up to date on what's going on?" Donahue asked.

Weber nodded. Like any real geek, he was only too happy to talk about the nature of his work.

"Once we took the Zurich system off line, we created our own system using the Zurich IP address." Off their confused looks, he added, "All that means is that the hackers will crack into a system they think belongs to Zurich, but it doesn't. It belongs to us."

Thompson nodded. Weber seemed to be providing his explanation directly to her.

"We set up the same old security system, including access past the firewalls using Disler's security passwords. If someone tries to use her passwords, it triggers other members of the team in DC who have the capability to trace back the attack. But once the hackers get in, the only data they're going to find is what we want them to take at the request of the CIA."

"So they're downloading it now?" Donahue nodded towards the screen.

"We've made it particularly cumbersome for them. We broke the data up into hundreds of separate files, stored in such a fashion that's it's going to take some work to download it all." He looked over at Donahue. "Hopefully, they'll be online long enough to enable our people to track the signal back to its source."

"So what are we talking about?" Donahue asked. "Hours?"

"Minutes," Weber answered. "If we're lucky, maybe ten."

"And you can trace it back to the source that quickly?" Thompson asked.

Weber nodded.

"Our equipment and system are the best in the world." He looked back at the screen and frowned. "They're almost done."

All four of them stared at the scene in complete silence, and thirty-seconds later, the screen went dark.

"Well, that's it," he said. He looked up at Thompson. "They've just signed off."

"So what happens now?" Donahue asked.

"Well, my job here is done. The fish has taken the bait."

"How soon will we know if they successfully traced it back?"

Weber shrugged.

"If it gets traced back, the location will go to the DOD. They're our client."

"DOD?" Thompson was intentionally playing it dumb.

Donahue smiled.

"Department of Defense, Shari."

To Weber, she added, "Poor thing never did finish high school. Started pumping out kids instead. That's how she knows about *Sid, the Science Kid.*"

Weber's eyes had widened before he realized that the two women were having a little fun at his expense.

He blushed, but Thompson was undeterred.

"Any chance they'd tell you if you asked?" she said.

"They might," Weber replied.

Thompson smiled. "If you do find out, can you give me a call?" She handed him her business card.

"Yeah, sure!" He placed it into his upper breast pocket.

Donahue smiled. Thompson was truly on her game. If they had to wait for the information to filter down through channels, it might never make it to LAPD. But because of Shari's not-so-subtle interest, Weber would be chewing at the bit to impress, and she was willing to bet that they'd get a call before they even made it back to the station.

She turned to Lum.

"Thanks for the heads-up, doctor. Let's hope this helps to get her back."

Lum nodded and shook her hand.

"You ready, mom?" she said to Thompson.

Thompson smiled tightly, then looked over at Weber.

"I'm always ready," she said.

****

"No ticket," Thompson said as she unlocked their Crown Vic.

"Could you be more obvious?"

"What?"

"You know exactly what I'm talking about."

Thompson rolled her eyes.

"You can't play hard-to-get with these younger guys. It takes initiative to get them to call."

"You're incorrigible!"

"New world, Jen, you should try it sometime. Young guys can be a lot of fun."

Before Donahue could respond, her phone began to ring. She recognized the ringtone as the one she'd set for her former partner, Ulysses Gibson.

"Hey, Gibby! What's up?"

Gibson was quick to respond.

"The NSA says the Iranians called the people holding your victims."

"No kidding?" She turned to Thompson. "They called." Then back to Gibson. "Did we get an address?"

"The closest they got was a cell phone tower. Elwood wants you back here Code Three. He's calling in the bosses from Metro and SWAT for a meeting that's set to start in about an hour."

"We'll be there in twenty minutes."

****

Farazi smiled at Petrov, The two of them were watching the screen while a technician completed the download of Angela Disler's research materials.

He turned to Disler who was standing next to him. She was also watching the screen.

"That wasn't so bad now, was it?" he asked.

Angela didn't respond. She'd been watching the screen, too, and she couldn't imagine what the heck they'd been downloading for the last twenty minutes. Her data at Zurich was all stored in one file, but these people had downloaded many dozens of files, stuff that hadn't been part of her research. And since she didn't have password access to other research projects going on at Zurich, she couldn't understand what was going on.

And then it hit her.

Someone at Zurich must have anticipated an attempt to steal her data, so they removed it from her computer and substituted other files in its place. That meant that the Iranians did not have her research notes.

Maybe someone is trying to find me?

But how would the Iranians react when they found out what's been done?

She shuddered to think that they might try to do something to her husband or her children.

If she and her family were going to get through this, she had to buy time. She might be able to fool them for a couple of days at most, but when they found out what was going on, she knew there was going to be hell to pay.

"There's a lot of data there, doctors," she said. "I can start going through it tomorrow, but it looks like it's rather disjointed to me." She looked Petrov in the eye and held his glance. "Might take me a couple of days to sort through it, to get it organized into workable shape."

"Just remember, my dear Doctor Disler, there will be severe consequences if you fail to carry out your part of our agreement."

"I understand, and I'll do my best." She looked from one to the other. "So now that you've downloaded my research materials, is my family going to be released?"

Petrov looked uncomfortable.

"We'll be going through the documents for a while to see what we've got." He cleared his throat. "I spoke with my superiors, doctor, and they've decided that we must keep your family until you've demonstrated to us that you will work diligently to complete this project. I'm sorry to have to tell you that, but they insisted."

She held Petrov's glance and came to the slow realization that he never intended to release her family even after downloading the information.

She stared at him with undisguised hatred.

"So, in addition to being a traitor and a money grabbing whore, you're also a liar." She shook her head. "Why am I not surprised?"

Later, when she was back in her cell, and when no one could see her, she broke down and cried for the sake of her children and her husband.

*****

FORTY-SEVEN

LOS ANGELES, CALIFORNIA
DAY SEVENTEEN   11:30 PM

The meeting at PAB took place on the fifth floor in the conference room used exclusively by the Robbery-Homicide Division. By the time Donahue and Thompson arrived, most of the others invited to the meeting were already seated around the table; drinking coffee, telling stories, and itching to get going.

Elliot Davis and one of his cohorts from the FBI's HRT (Hostage Rescue Team) were present, and Donahue took a seat next to him while Thompson ran off to powder her nose.

After the introductions, Davis told Donahue that LAPD was going to take the lead while the Bureau waited in the wings. That suited Donahue just fine. She had no prior experience with the FBI's HRT, but she had worked with LA's SWAT team on many occasions, and they had always been careful and patient when hostages were involved.

Captain Tommy Elwood walked in and right behind him was Ulysses Gibson, one of the acting Lieutenants in RHD. Gibson smiled at Donahue, then called the meeting to order.

Thompson arrived a short time later, a coffee in hand, followed by Mitzi Roberts, who flashed a smile to Donahue. The seats around the table were already taken by the representatives of the Metropolitan Division and the SWAT team leaders, so the two female detectives found spots where they could stand along the wall.

One of the Metro supervisors got to his feet and offered Thompson his chair. She gave him a tight smile and accepted his offer. There was a long moment of embarrassed silence as everyone waited to see if any other male at the table was going to offer his seat to Roberts.

Donahue closed her eyes and shook her head. She knew exactly why Thompson had gotten the chair.

Once again, men's fascination with female boobs!

The FBI's HRT team leader got to his feet and gave Roberts his chair which finally put the awkward moment to rest.

Elwood began, "We've been advised by the NSA that a call was placed from a location in Iran to our missing family. The call was long enough to trace it to a cell tower in the city of Reseda, just north of the Ventura Freeway."

"How big an area is served by that tower?" a Metro Lieutenant asked.

"Four square miles," Gibson replied.

Donahue sighed. That was a fairly large area to canvass, but not impossible.

"How do we know that the call was to the missing family?" asked a SWAT team leader.

"As I understand it, the NSA computers were set up to identify any calls emanating from Iran where certain words were spoken. And thanks to the work done by Detectives Donahue and Roberts, the names of all four victims were spoken which the NSA feels makes for a hundred percent identification."

Elwood looked around, but it seemed that the questions, if any, were now going to wait until he finished his presentation.

"We've been given a copy of the call. It's short, so we're going to play it for you now."

He nodded to Gibson, who turned on a digital recorder. The quality was crystal clear, and for the first time, Donahue and Thompson were able to put a voice to the mysterious Angela Disler.

Donahue was struck by how nervous Henrik Disler sounded, and her eyes began to tear up when she heard the pleas of Angela's youngest daughter who just wanted her mother back.

Elwood glanced around the room. He now had their undivided attention.

"Detective Donahue and I have discussed our tactics from this point forward, and since we don't have a location for our suspects and victims, it has been suggested that we flood the area with Metro teams to preclude any possibility of the suspects moving our victims. I want Metro teams to stop any suspicious vehicles or trucks. Do ID checks and car searches. Pay particular attention to anyone who's license does not confirm their residence in the affected zone."

"Hold on, Captain." It was the Lieutenant from Metro again. "Your victims could be taken out in the trunk of a car. Are you suggesting that we stop everyone?"

"Not everyone, but we need to concentrate on vehicles driven by males, Caucasian in appearance. That's the best we can do for now."

"That's a tall order, Captain. It's really hit or miss."

"I know, Lieutenant. But while your people are doing that, we're going to assign twenty detectives from RHD to go door to door in the area to see if anyone has noticed anything unusual that might tip us off as to where they're holding the victims."

He looked over at the SWAT team leaders. "We've identified a shopping center on Ventura Blvd. with a parking lot that's not visible from the main street. We're going to ask your teams to stage from that location. A Deputy District Attorney will be with you, and if we identify a location, she'll get a telephonic search warrant which will allow you to take it down."

He glanced over at Donahue. "Do you have anything to add?"

Donahue glanced over at Roberts.

"Detective Roberts suggested that we start phoning realtors in the area to see if anyone recently rented a house or an apartment to someone of Persian descent. Given the fact that some of the conversation we heard on that tape was in Persian, I think it's worth a shot."

"Good idea," Elwood said. He turned to Gibson. "See if you can get a couple of detectives from Sex Crimes to help Mitzi make the calls."

"What time do we want to kick off this operation?" asked the Lieutenant from Metro Division.

Elwood looked over at Donahue. "What do you think?"

"We can't get anywhere calling real estate offices until they open up in the morning. I guess we can get started with the calls at about eight a.m."

Elwood nodded. "Then let's put Metro out in the field starting around seven. We can get the detectives out there at the same time, maybe catch people in the door to door interviews before they leave for work."

There were nods from the representatives of the various units.

He looked around the room. "Okay. If that's it, the address of the Command Post and the staging location has been written up here on the blackboard. Let's keep this operation as low key as possible."

There was brief laughter from the group. Everyone knew that as soon as Metro started to make their traffic stops, the news media would know that something was up, and after that, so would everyone else.

Donahue walked over to Gibson.

"I'm gonna go home and catch a few hours sleep."

He nodded once. "Okay, so I'll see you back here at seven. 'Capish?'"

Donahue nodded, then joined Mitzi and Thompson.

"Gibby wants us here at seven. We can put together a quick list of brokers so that we can be ready to start calling at eight."

"I'd rather be in the field," said Thompson while eyeing the Metro supervisor who'd given her his chair.

Donahue rolled her eyes in exasperation. "Have you ever considered getting spayed?"

Thompson gave her a curious look. "*Spayed?*"

"Yeah, spayed. As in removal of your ovaries, uterus and fallopian tubes."

"I know what spayed means. Why would I want to do that?"

"'Because you're just like a cat in heat, Shari. Don't you get sick and tired of men turning to mush just because of your boobs?"

"Actually, I don't." Thompson flashed her a smile. "You work with what you've got, Jen, and in my case, I've got a lot, and it works."

Donahue chortled. "You ever hear the adage...*What goes up must come down?*"

"Meaning?"

Donahue winked at Roberts who said, "What Jen's trying to say is...*the bigger they are, the harder they fall.*"

Donahue smiled.

"And in your case, Shari, I think it's safe to say that the fall is gonna be a real doozy."

*****

FORTY-EIGHT

LOS ANGELES, CALIFORNIA
DAY SEVENTEEN   8:15 PM

Mitzi Roberts leaned back in her chair and waved a piece of paper in the air. She was still on the telephone, profusely thanking the voice on the other end of the line. As she hung up the phone, she spun in her chair and quickly got to her feet.

"Hey, Jen, I got a hot one!"

Donahue was on her own phone call. She and Roberts and Thompson had just started working the phones. They'd split up a surprisingly large list of realtors who handled rentals and home sales in the San Fernando Valley, hoping they might find something that would tip them off as to where the Disler family was being held.

It was more than likely they'd end up with nothing, but they had to try something. The report from the field was that officers from Metro were stopping everything that even remotely fit the description of a possible Iranian male, but with the exception of a half a dozen arrests for outstanding traffic warrants, nothing suspicious materialized. Detectives were now going block by block, talking to residents, trying to see if anyone noticed anything suspicious. But so far, no one had.

Roberts stretched out her hand and waived the piece of paper in front of Donahue's face.

Donahue tried to brush her hand away. She was still in the middle of a call.

"Yes, Mr. Fond," she said. "If you come across anything at all, please give me a call as quickly as possible."

She hung up the phone, then turned to Roberts.

"I was on the phone, Mitzi. What is it?"

She took the paper from Roberts and looked it over. It contained a single address.

"So? What is this?"

"It's a home that was rented to an Iranian male one month ago. He paid cash up front, a six-month rental. The agent who handled the sale, one Patricia Powers, described him as being in his early thirties, about five foot ten, 170 pounds, with dark hair and very smooth skin. The name on the lease is Farid Hemmati."

Donahue looked up from the paper and smiled.

"Wow! This might be it. How the hell did we get so lucky so quickly?"

"Who knows? Maybe we were just due for a break."

Donahue nodded in agreement. "Can you run Hemmati through the system, Mitz, and see if he's got a rap sheet?"

"Right away," Roberts slid her chair back and rode it towards her cubicle.

Donahue picked up the phone and placed a call to the command post. Her former partner, Ulysses Gibson, picked it up.

"Gibby, we've got a good lead."

She gave him the address and back story, and Gibson said, "This looks promising. I'll put SIS on the location. In the meantime, run this guy Hemmati and see what we've got."

Donahue looked over at Roberts who said, "He's got no record, but according to Immigration, he's here on a six-month visa. Three more months to go."

Donahue passed the information on to Gibson who wrote it down and got off the line.

"What do you want me to do now?" Roberts asked.

"Call the rest of the names on the combined lists. I'm gonna grab Shari and go out to the CP."

Roberts nodded.

Donahue got to her feet and walked over to Thompson's cubicle.

"You ready?" she asked.

Thompson was attaching her Sam Browne belt around her waist.

"You think this is it?"

"God, I hope so! This family is running out of time."

****

The two detectives arrived at the command post just ahead of an LAPD SWAT team that had been mustered out to the CP pursuant to a call from Ulysses Gibson. Thompson parked the car in the lot behind the designated supermarket parking lot that was earlier commandeered by the police for use as a staging area.

They got out of their car and took a quick look around.

There were several fire engines, a couple of ambulances, and dozens of undercover units parked side by side. Several tables had been set up near the back of the market building, and large coffee percolators were brewing fresh coffee for officers coming in from the field as well as for the SWAT team members and administrative and support staff who were standing around, waiting for something to do.

Donahue and Thompson made their way over to a specialized trailer used exclusively as a command post for important operations. Inside was the latest in electronic communications equipment, a small conference room, and an area manned by three uniformed officers who monitored field communications and assignments while keeping track of everyone involved in the neighborhood searches.

Gibson was standing outside the door to the command post, drinking a cup of coffee. He waived them over and quickly started to fill them in.

"The address you gave me turned out to be a single family dwelling at the end of a *cul-de-sac*. I put several teams of SIS into the neighborhood, and I pulled Metro out of there so as not to alert our subjects that we're snooping around."

Donahue nodded. Using the Special Investigations Section (SIS) was always a smart move. SIS officers, both men, and women, were masters of disguise. They sometimes posed as city road workers, meter readers, gardeners, and on more than one occasion, as homeless derelicts. They specialized in surveillance of violent offenders, often watching their subjects commit a dangerous felony before taking them down by surprise. Once in a while, the people they focused on ended up dead, but the Division rarely ever had what was considered to be a bad shooting.

"Any intel from the surveillance?" Thompson asked.

"A rental car and a van are parked in the driveway. The car comes back to your guy Hemmati, and one of the SIS guys got a look at the house from a neighbor's backyard, and he says the windows in the back bedroom are boarded up on the inside with plywood."

"Holy cow!" Donahue looked over at Thompson. "There's only one reason to board up the windows! It must be where they're holding the family!"

She turned back to Gibson. "Is the house within the service zone for the cell tower?"

Gibson smiled. "It is."

Thompson asked, "So what's the plan, Gibby?"

"I've got Rick Jackson and a lady DA getting us a telephonic search warrant right now, and we've got a SWAT callout in progress, so as soon I hear that the warrant is approved, we'll hit the place hard and fast."

Donahue sighed. The lead was a good one, but the info they had was not conclusive. This might not be where the family was being held, in which case, she was worried about tipping off the subjects who might be living some-where nearby.

"Don't pull the others out of the area until we know for sure that we've got the right place."

"I've got it covered, Jen," said Gibson. "I've got thirty detectives out there still going door to door, and Metro is bringing in a second platoon. Nothing stops until we know if the family is in there or not."

He shifted his weight and looked around.

"And just so you know, I notified Davis, and he's on his way out here with a dozen or so units from the FBI. I'm gonna put them on canvassing duties until we resolve the situation with Hemmati. He said to tell you that he'd notify the task force in DC, so you don't need to worry about that."

Donahue couldn't help but chuckle. "As if I was worried about that."

"I don't know why you're so surprised," said Thompson. "He's a typical fed, Jen. They don't do anything without getting a signed permission slip from their mommies."

Gibson laughed. "Play nice, ladies. Play nice."

Donahue reached out and squeezed Gibson's arm. "I should have known you'd be way ahead of me, Gibby. Thanks for running this op."

Gibson shot her a quick smile, then turned to greet a Lieutenant who had arrived with the SWAT platoon.

Thompson took Donahue's arm. "You want to get a cup of coffee?"

"No, but I think I'll find a restroom. Nothing worse than having to go in the middle of all the action."

"Good thinking! Maybe I'll join you."

They walked to a nearby store, and after flashing their badges to the store manager, they got permission to use the employee's bathroom. Once they were finished, they made their way back to the Command Post trailer which was set up in the parking lot.

There was nothing more they could do except to wait for the search warrant and for SWAT to make their play.

*****

FORTY-NINE

RESEDA, CALIFORNIA
DAY SEVENTEEN   9:30 AM

Thompson was seated in the portable Command Post bus at a station set up with a computer terminal and a phone. She was on the phone with Rick Jackson, a senior detective in the RHD. He had just sent her an email complete with attachment, and as she printed it out, she smiled.

She quickly looked it over. It was a search warrant signed by Judge Robert Schuit who had reviewed it, added a signature page, then sent it to Jackson who had just forwarded it on to her.

"We got it Rick. Thanks for the help," she told him as she hung up the phone. She turned to Donahue.

"We got it. You wanna tell Gibby and the Captain?"

Donahue nodded. She stepped outside the bus and walked directly over to Capt. Tom Elwood who was standing under an awning, drinking a cup of coffee with a couple of senior agents from the FBI's HRT.

"We got the green light, Captain."

Elwood poured out what was left of his coffee and pitched the cup into a nearby trash can.

"Okay," he said. "I'll notify SWAT and Metro. Are you and Thompson gonna follow them in?"

"Yes sir. You wanna ride with us?"

"No, I'm gonna hang here where I can get a better sense of the scope of the operation."

He turned and walked towards a knot of officers who were dressed in full battle gear. As word spread throughout the parking lot, officers from all of the various divisions present in the lot began to head for their cars. Trunks were popped open, vests put on, and weapons were checked. Within a couple of minutes, the teams were all seated in their vehicles, engines running, waiting for SWAT to lead the large convoy to the possible location of their kidnap victims.

While Donahue waited behind the wheel of their car, Thompson, ran over to the lead vehicle and handed the warrant through the passenger window to the SWAT Lieutenant who was now running the show.

As soon as he got it and looked it over, he signaled to his driver to move out.

Car after car, more than twenty vehicles, pulled out from the lot in single file procession behind an armored truck that contained the SWAT's entry team. All were flashing their red and blue lights, but there were no sirens going, as they wanted to make their approach without warning anyone that they were on their way.

During the preparations for launching the assault, the SWAT teams had download photos of the property and surrounding buildings from Google Maps. A check of the building with the city's Building Department had enabled them to get a floor plan of what was a fifteen hundred square foot, single family, three bedroom tract home.

The SIS teams in the neighborhood were advised that the raiding party was on its way, so they began to break cover to go to the houses of the neighbors adjacent to the target home for the purpose of moving out anyone they came in contact with. Those they evacuated were taken to a designated location of safety several blocks away, and by the time the SWAT vehicle finally pulled up one house away from their target, the immediate area around the property was free of all neighborhood civilians.

The Metro units blocked off the street at both ends, and other units positioned themselves on the streets surrounding the area, effectively putting a ring of officers around the entire neighborhood. If it was the right house, and if the suspects and victims were inside, no matter what happened, the suspects would not be getting away.

Donahue picked up Thompson who'd been waiting by the parking lot exit for Donahue's car to pull up. They joined the convoy, pulling in behind the last Metro car, but in front of the Fire Department Paramedic Unit that always accompanied the raiding party on occasions where violence was a high probability. Neither detective would be going in with the entry teams, so they were free to focus on what would happen if this turned out to be the wrong address.

"I hope we got this right," Thompson said. "If we've got the wrong place, it's going to be hard to keep this out of the press, and that won't bode well for the Disler family."

"I know what you mean," Donahue replied. "I can't help thinking about the two Disler daughters and what they must be going through."

They followed the caravan for almost two miles through intersections full of traffic. It was the kind of force not usually seen in Los Angeles, and both women knew that passers-by were filming the caravan on their smartphones and that it would only be a matter of time before the local news channels were broadcasting the downloads and dispatching their news helicopters, thereby putting the lives of the Disler's at even greater risk.

One block from the location that they wanted to search, the caravan came to a halt. Four members of the SWAT Team whose job it was to approach the location from the rear got out of their two vehicles and made their way to the back of the property. A plan had been worked out to use flash bang and stun grenades through the front windows to enable the primary entry team to get the upper hand. No one would be coming in from the back, thereby eliminating the risk of a crossfire situation.

One member of that group of four carried a large metal battering ram filled on one end with cement. Referred to as the *key to the city*, it would be used to bust through the plywood covering the windows of the bedroom where they suspected the Disler's were being held.

Once all the teams were in place, the armored SWAT vehicle left the rest of the convoy behind and drove the final one block to the front of the residence. They would be striking fast, in concert with the other SWAT team members, so the rest of the units in the operation were ordered to stay put to reduce the risk of getting in the way.

Donahue and Thompson waited in their car with the windows rolled down, glued to the frequency being used by the entry teams, and even though they were a good two blocks away from the scene, they heard the muffled explosions of the flash bang grenades going off while the entry was being made.

****

Inside the front room of the house, the one used by the kidnappers as a living room, two of the Iranian males were sitting on a couch, glued to a movie on the television screen. They were watching *Argo* on Netflix, and both were transfixed by the audacity of the hoax the American's were attempting to pull off in their efforts to spirit their embassy workers out of Tehran.

"We should blow up a car bomb in Canada," said the taller of the two in Farsi to his companion. "What's the old saying? Revenge is a dish that's best served cold?"

"Shhh," said Farid Hemmati, the titular leader of the group. "If you're going to talk all through this movie, leave the room."

Both men returned their undivided attention to the television, completely unaware that their lives and the lives of the two men eating in the kitchen were about to change forever.

****

Inside the back bedroom, Henrik Disler and his two daughters were lying on the floor, sound asleep. They'd eaten their last meal about an hour before, and what they didn't know was that their kidnappers had been spiking their food with *Ambien,* a little tiny pill that promoted sleep.

It had been going on like this for days, but the Disler's were so bored by the extended captivity in a room devoid of any form of stimulation that they weren't even the least bit curious about why they'd been sleeping so much.

The first explosion in the front room woke them all up, and it was followed seconds later by a second one. Groggy with sleep, Henrik's first thought was that they were experiencing an earthquake and that the house had somehow shifted.

A large crash was followed by the sounds of men shouting which was quickly drowned out by the rapid firing of many shots.

While this was happening, the plywood on one of the windows suddenly splintered with a force that shook the outer wall. A second large crash dislodged what remained of the screws that secured the plywood to the window frame, and the room was suddenly bathed in sunlight, something they hadn't seen for more than a week.

Disler shielded his eyes, as did his daughters, who by now had crawled over to where their father was seated. With one hand, he put his arm around the youngest, Carrie, and tried to pull her closer to shield her if possible from whatever was going on. His oldest daughter, Sienna, had gotten to her feet, but was now screaming in confusion and temporarily blinded by the light coming in through the open window.

Henrik leaned over towards the sound, felt one of her ankles, and yelled at her to get down. Sienna dropped to her stomach, grabbed for his hand, and crawled into his waiting arms.

From where they were on the floor, if they'd been able to see anything, they would have spotted helmeted heads in the window, along with an assortment of guns with flashlights attached, probing the darkness inside for any sign of a hostile response.

The first two officers came in through the window, yelling *"POLICE"* at the top of their lungs. One covered the still closed door to the hallway while the second reached the Disler's and pulled Sienna to her feet.

"It's okay," he said. "No one's going to hurt you. I'm going to hand you out the window to other officers."

Sienna's eyes were blinking, but she was now finally adjusted to the daylight. She allowed the officer to lead her to the window where he scooped her up and handed her out into the waiting arms of a uniformed Metro officer who hustled her away through the neighbor's yard.

Carrie was freed the same way, but Henrik was treated differently. Other officers had climbed in through the window, and they had him on the floor, cuffed behind his back, while they patted him down. He tried to protest, saying his name and that he was a victim, but they didn't waiver from their procedures. There would be time enough to sort things out once the house was finally secured.

****

Internal communications between SWAT team members were on a frequency not used by the rest of the department, so when the call came out for the paramedics to respond, Donahue and Thompson feared the worst.

They arrived in front of the residence right behind the paramedic unit. Donahue jumped out of the car, followed by Thompson, and they rapidly walked up to a member of the SWAT team who was coming out of the house.

"Are any of our people hurt?" she asked.

He shook his head. "Two suspects down, two in custody."

"And the victims?"

"Let me check."

He spoke into his mouthpiece, received an update, then gave the detectives a thumbs up.

"The two young girls are being held in the yard next door. They've called for a paramedic unit to take them to the hospital for observation, but I'm told they're both fine. Their father was detained per our protocol, but he's been ID'd, so he'll go with his daughters and get checked out too."

Donahue turned to Thompson.

"Get Metro to transport the two arrestees down to PAB. Maybe they can tell us where the mom is being held?"

Thompson nodded, then Donahue added, "Make sure they transport them in separate cars. I don't want them talking to each other."

While Thompson walked off to find a Metro supervisor, Donahue entered the house.

In the front room were two men, both in their thirties, lying on the floor, face down, hands bound behind their backs with metal cuffs. Their feet were also bound with flex cuffs, and both looked none the worse for wear.

A Sergeant from SWAT approached her and gestured towards the two men.

"We took 'em by surprise. They were watching TV and didn't have a chance to go for their weapons."

Donahue looked him in the eye.

"I was told there were two suspects down?"

"In the kitchen."

He gestured with his head towards a nearby door. "They were partially shielded from the flash bangs, so both were holding firearms when we reached the doorway."

"Either one survive?" she asked.

He shook his head, then said, "Your victims were all in the back room. It's pretty bleak in there, but all three are in good shape. They were lucky."

She headed towards the back bedroom, looked inside, and saw Henrik Disler talking to two of the SWAT team officers. The room was now flooded with sunlight from the destruction of the plywood, so Donahue could see that it was completely devoid of any furniture, save several blankets and pillows in the center of the floor.

She walked over to Disler and his eyes went wide. He recognized her from his initial reporting of his wife's disappearance.

"They've got my wife, detective," he told her. "She's alive! She called us yesterday, at least I think it was yesterday? I don't really know how long we've been here."

Donahue gave him a pat on the arm.

"We intercepted the call. It's my understanding that the NSA has a pretty good fix on where she's being held. Once they finish checking you out at the hospital, we'll bring you down to our office and perhaps we can get you an update."

Disler was so grateful to hear that there was a possibility that his wife would be found that he made a grab for Donahue and gave her a hug.

Donahue said, "I'm sure your daughters would like to be with you, so if you go with these nice gentlemen, they'll take you to the girls and we'll get you all down to the hospital for a checkup."

Disler reached out for her hand and clasped it in both of his.

"Thank you, detective, for saving our lives." His eyes teared up and his voice began to break.

"I'm sure these men never intended to let us go. The last two days, they made no effort at all to conceal their faces." His voice cracked again and he began to cry.

"They made my daughters use a bucket in the closet…"

Donahue gave him another hug.

"It's over now, doctor. You go and take care of the girls and let us do what we can to get your wife back."

*****

FIFTY

THE ZAGROS MOUNTAINS
SOUTHWESTERN IRAN
DAY SEVENTEEN   11:00 PM

At night, the mountainous region of Southwestern Iran tends to get very cold. In contrast to the temperate climate during the days, the nights can be counted upon to be in the lower forties or thirties (Fahrenheit) for months at a time.

Bryan was wide awake, still scanning the area around the base while Mordecai slept nearby.

It had been a long day. He and Mordecai had carefully noted the routine at the base. They watched the comings and goings, the guard shack change-of-shifts, and the miscellaneous workers who arrived by bus in the early morning and left the same way in the afternoon.

They'd been there now for almost eighteen hours, so he was comfortable that they had a pretty good sense of how things operated on a daily basis. He checked his watch. It was time to check in with Taylor.

He pulled out his satellite phone, plugged in the earpiece, and noted as he did so that he could see his own breath when he exhaled. He pulled his jacket tight around his neck. They'd come prepared for the cold weather, but when you were out in the open throughout the night and not moving around, the cold seemed to get right into your bones.

He called the number he knew by heart, and when Taylor answered, he said, "Greetings from beautiful Iran."

"You guys okay?"

"Affirmative! It's a base of some kind, no sign of mining operations at all. We've done a recon, and it looks like it's built right into the side of the mountain. A single, warehouse type structure conceals access to the inside of the facility through two large steel doors, large enough to give passage to a good size flatbed truck. Also, there's an elevator inside the warehouse that only goes down."

"What about security?" Taylor asked.

"About 7:00 a.m., a military jeep and a bus pulled up. We counted twenty soldiers, automatic weapons, no sign of vests. A rag-tag group, one step above security guards. They drove up to the building and went inside. A different group came out about thirty minutes later. Same size. They boarded the bus and drove off. The jeep left with them. It remains to be seen how long their shifts are, but I'm guessing they're on for twenty-four hours before being replaced."

Taylor nodded to himself. That was a fairly logical, educated guess.

"Any civilians around?"

"A bus full of men and women, twenty-four, arrived about a half hour before the soldiers. Looked like medical technicians. Mostly young, although there were a few older ones, too. They went inside the building and came out again about 1700 Zulu. They left by bus. I think they'll be back again, same time tomorrow."

Taylor was absorbing the details, and his mind was racing.

"Any guards on the civilian bus?"

"Negative. Unless they were dressed like tech's, but there was no sign of armament."

That was good, Taylor thought. It meant that there were likely no more than two dozen armed combatants at the base, assuming they didn't make an assault during the change of watch. A SEAL operation would have no problem handling a group twice that size, particularly if they were as rag-tag as Bryan was describing. It also seemed to validate what Niroomad was saying.

"Any other access points?" he asked.

"Just the outside stairwell, but I did locate an air vent, 24 inches in diameter, covered with a flexible screen like material. Not sure how far down it goes, but several stories at least."

"You have the coordinates?"

Taylor was thinking about an entry point for a SEAL operation, but he also knew that a vent system, if it went down far enough, might make a good entry point for a JDAM missile or a bunker buster.

"Yes, sir."

Bryan rattled off the coordinates and Taylor took them down.

"Have you got our exfiltration set up?" Bryan asked.

"We're still working on it, but I've got some intel to pass on to you. The facility is exactly what we thought it would be. It's strictly for biological research. They plan to build and release once they've got their own protection. You copy?"

Bryan shook his head in disgust. They were actually contemplating building a biological weapon to release on the world. *Incredible!*

"I copy," he said.

"Also, the family of the victim was snatched last week. NSA has intercepted a call made from your location to the victim's family. No hard intel on the tape, but it's obvious they used the call to convince your subject that her family was still alive and under their control. We think they were leaning on the victim to force her to give them access to her computerized research."

"They're moving that fast?"

"Within an hour of that call, the employer got hacked, but all they got was junk. We locked down what we think they were after."

Bryan was relieved that they didn't get their hands on Disler's research, but he couldn't help but feel that there would be hell to pay once the Iranians knew they'd been deceived.

"That makes our timetable critical," he said.

"I know," Taylor replied. "We're doing what we can to speed things up, but I'm sure you know that any decision in this matter will come down from the man himself. As soon as I know what's up, we'll be in touch."

When Bryan hung up, he turned to Mordecai and gave him a gentle shove.

"Wake up, sunshine. Nap time's over."

Mordecai was instantly awake. He rubbed at his eyes, then tightened his coat against his chest and took a careful look around.

"Seems a lot colder," he said.

"Seems like it." Bryan pulled off his night viewing goggles. "Turns out the facility is a research lab."

Mordecai tucked his chin even deeper into his jacket. "You went down there again while I was asleep?"

"No, but you remember that Iranian Quds? The guy the Jordanians put us on to?"

"He's talking?"

"Apparently so. He told them the Iranians want to make and release the virus once they have a vaccine."

Mordecai sat up straighter. "And I'll bet we all know where they're going to release it first." He sighed, "So what do we do from this point on?"

"We wait and watch."

Bryan put his hands deep into his pockets.

Mordecai took out his night viewing goggles and put them on, took a careful look at the base below, then took them off.

"If the call were mine, I'd bomb the hell out of this place, then do the same to their nuclear facilities."

"They've got seventeen that we know of," Bryan said with a chuckle. "You'd hit them all?"

"In a heartbeat. They want to wipe my country off the map."

"How do you feel about the people?" Bryan asked.

"I don't hate the people, just their government. I'd hit them too if I had the chance, their whole fucking command and control structure."

"A lot of innocent people would die," Bryan cautioned.

"Even more would die if they got their hands on that virus or got themselves some nukes."

Bryan nodded. He had a point.

"You married, Morty?"

"Not yet, we had a little falling out."

"About this?" Bryan asked, referring to his work as a spy.

Mordecai shook his head in the affirmative.

"She's a nurse. She wanted me to be more than a tour guide, but I wasn't allowed to tell her until our relationship was more finalized."

Bryan raised a brow.

"You're speaking about her in the past tense?"

"She wasn't pleased that I was only a tour guide, so she gave me an ultimatum, and when I didn't respond, she broke things off." Mordecai shifted his weight to get more comfortable.

"So what about you? Have you managed to move on?"

Bryan was initially taken aback, then he remembered that Mordecai was briefed about the events of 9-11 and how they'd affected his personal life.

"Not yet, I haven't met someone who could take her place."

"No one will ever take her place. You need to realize that you're searching for someone new, someone just as wonderful, but different." Mordecai smiled. "My ex-girlfriend has a friend, well actually, it's her younger sister. Maybe I can get her to hook you up?"

"Tour guide, spy, and a matchmaker. That's some resume." He shook his head. "Thanks anyway, Morty, but I think I'll pass."

"You might want to reconsider." Morty pulled out his iPhone, scrolled for a moment, then pulled up a photo which he showed to Bryan.

"Twenty-three and she's studying medicine." He winked. "Last year's Miss Israel."

Bryan studied the photo for only a moment.

"I guess it couldn't hurt to meet her," he said with a grin. "But you really got dumped by her sister?"

"As I said, that may change. I have it on pretty good authority that if I give her a call she just might consider taking me back."

"Oh? And that authority is…?"

"My boss."

Bryan laughed.

"Well, I'll tell you what. If we get out of this okay, I'll take all three of you out to dinner."

"That works for me."

Bryan slipped on his night vision goggles and began to scan the terrain below.

"You gonna call your people?" Bryan asked.

"Guess I better. My boss always likes to know when we're one step away from world War III."

He pulled out his satellite phone, and Bryan got up and walked a discrete distance away to give him a measure of privacy.

He couldn't help but wonder if they really were on the precipice of another World War?

The Mideast, for all of its talk about the *Arab Spring*, was in a period of persistent turmoil. States were breaking down, becoming little more than autonomous zones controlled by tribal warlords. Weapons of war were more plentiful than food, and religious hatreds had spawned an endless series of mass killings that threatened to keep the region destabilized for many more years to come.

So where did the idea of spreading a plague figure into the Iranians long term plans?

Well, for one thing, they had no intention of giving up their goal of obtaining nuclear weapons. To be certain, they acquiesced in the short-term to international pressure to put a halt to their development plans in exchange for the lifting of sanctions. But to Bryan's way of thinking, that was just a short term concession. Their desire to obtain nuclear technology was a key part of the hard-liners strategy for obtaining power over the region and retaining control over their own population.

If they could build their own nukes, it would make them the second most powerful nation in the region, right behind their arch enemies, The State of Israel. And rather than square off with the Israelis in a face to face confrontation for dominance, the use of a biological weapon would be an untraceable way to strike a blow without firing a single shot or risking a nuclear confrontation.

And if that virus were to spread beyond the borders of Israel to other hated neighbors that the Iranians felt were in league with the West, like Saudi Arabia, Jordan and Egypt? Well, that would be a welcome bonus.

But the Iranian plan was entirely dependent upon releasing the genetically altered virus without anyone knowing the source of such a horrible contagion, and now that the cat was out of the bag, it was probably doomed to failure, for retaliation for such treachery would surely be on the horizon, and Bryan could only imagine what it might be.

He involuntarily shuddered.

Mordecai was absolutely right. The world, as he knew it, was squarely on the edge of the abyss.

*****

FIFTY-ONE

WASHINGTON, DISTRICT OF COLUMBIA
DAY EIGHTEEN   10:00 AM

The White House Situation Room was set up to provide current intelligence and crisis support to the National Security Committee staff, the National Security Advisor, and, of course, the President. The room was staffed twenty-four hours a day, seven days a week, by five shifts composed of approximately thirty senior officers, all of whom were members of various agencies in both the intelligence community and the military. They continuously monitor world events and keep the senior White House staff apprised of significant incidents.

The room was five thousand square feet in size, with five secure video rooms, a lead-lined cabinet near the reception area for the deposit of personal communications equipment upon entry, and glass-encased booths for safe and private telephone calls. There were two tiers of curved computer terminals that could be fed data and video from around the world and six flat panel display televisions for secure video conferencing.

A large conference table dominated the center of the room, and for this particular meeting, the President requested the presence of the National Security Counsel, the Director of Homeland Security, the White House Chief of Staff, Vice President John Dabney, and the Directors of both the CIA and the FBI. Dan Taylor's image was prominent on one of the flat screens, as was the real-time satellite feed overlooking the research facility in the mountains of Iran.

Taylor had taken a CIA jet back to Cairo earlier in the day to be closer to the action in the Middle East. Besides, he felt that the farther away he was from Hamilton Granger, the better it would be for all concerned. He wanted to remain clear headed during the duration of the operation, and being anywhere near Granger was just asking for trouble. He now despised the man for his incompetence, and he wasn't sure he could control his temper if the man made another major mistake.

When the President entered the room and took a seat at the head of the conference table, those in attendance immediately went silent.

He turned his chair towards one of the flat panel screens, the one show-ing Taylor from his conference room in Cairo.

"Where are you, Dan?" he asked.

"Cairo, sir."

The President nodded. Dan Taylor was proving to be an intelligent leader who valued the core principle of being closer to the action. Having him in the Middle East, available to meet with his counterparts in other services on a face to face basis could end up being critical if the current operation was to sud-denly go sideways.

"Can you give us a brief summary of where we are, Dan?"

"Yes, Mr. President. Angela Disler was abducted in Alexandria, Egypt, more than a week ago. She was transported by freighter to Yemen where she was transported east across the desert to Oman by members of the Ansar al-Sharia. From the coast of Oman, she was taken by a small power boat to the coast of Iran, then driven by van to a secret research facility in the mountains of South-western Iran. According to an informant, the Iranians want her to provide them with the research she's been doing on the Marburg virus, and they plan to have her demonstrate her technique for making the virus airborne."

"Airborne?" The question came from the Director of Homeland Securi-ty.

"That's correct, sir. She was working on a vaccine for Marburg when she realized that the disease could become airborne with one or two genetic modifications."

"Why in God's name would she be working on something like that?"

"Apparently, it was part of a research program the Agency and the Army were funding. As I understand it, the idea was to develop vaccines through genetic alterations to protect our military, and our civilians should an enemy discover a way to weaponize deadly viruses."

"So she found a way to weaponize Marburg?" the Vice President asked.

"That's correct, John," said the President. "I've been assured that it was not our intention to weaponize any biologicals, but she stumbled upon a way to do it, and now the genie is out of the bottle."

The Vice-President said, "Well, I suppose if someone had to find the way it's better that we are the ones rather than our enemies."

"That's the problem, John," replied the President. "The Iranians learned about her discovery, and they're trying to duplicate her results." He looked back up at the screen. "Please continue, Dan."

Taylor cleared his throat. "To get her research off the computer at Zurich Pharmaceuticals, where she was working, the Iranians kidnapped her husband and two children. Earlier this morning, the NSA intercepted a call from Iran. Angela Disler was briefly allowed to talk to her family members. We believe this was a proof-of-life call because a short time later, the computer system at Zurich was entered and her passwords were used to get through various levels of security to obtain a significant amount of data that we substituted for her actual research."

"You mean they didn't get her work product?" asked the Vice-President.

"That's correct, sir."

"Well, thank God for small miracles."

"But we're not out of the woods, Mr. Vice President. In a very short time, the Iranians are going to discover that they've been duped. But even without her research, our analysts believe that if they have a sample strain of Marburg on hand, and if they have the right equipment, they will likely be able to force her to duplicate her work."

"Do we know how the Iranians found out about her discovery?" The President asked.

"Yes, sir," said Hamilton Granger. He leaned forward in his chair.

"Our informant says a memo she sent to the Pentagon about her discovery was hacked."

"Are we doing anything about that?" The Vice President asked.

"We are," Granger replied. "We've identified the source location in Iran where the hacking call originated. From a satellite overview, it appears to be a high-tech building located on a Quds military base just outside of Tehran."

The President shook his head. This was getting more complicated by the minute.

"What about the Disler family? Is there a status update on that situation?"

"The NSA was able to trace the incoming call to a single cell tower in the city of Reseda, a suburb of Los Angeles. The LAPD and the FBI moved into the area, and the police detectives assigned to the case found a real estate broker who recently rented a house to an Iranian male. The house was raided and the family was rescued. Two of the kidnappers were killed and the other two were taken into custody."

"Thank God!" said the Vice-President.

The Director of Homeland Security asked, "Do we know what the Iranians plan to do with the virus if they find a way to get it to go airborne?"

"Yes, sir," Taylor replied. "Our informant says that once the Iranians have an airborne supply of the virus, and once Disler helps them make a vaccine, they are going to inoculate their population, then release the virus in Israel."

"Jesus, Christ!" said the Vice President. "They're insane! It's Nazi Germany all over again."

The President let the reference to Germany go. From time to time, the Vice President was known to make politically incorrect statements, but this time the analogy seemed to be spot on. He looked back up at the screen.

"How reliable is the information being provided by the informant?" The President asked.

Taylor sighed. He had hoped he wouldn't have to reveal his source, but now was not the time to hold back.

"The informant is a high-ranking officer in the Iranian Quds. He played a significant role in the kidnapping of Angela Disler, and we've had him in debriefing since we picked him up in Yemen."

"Coercive interrogation?" The SOC asked.

"Psychological only," Taylor replied. "But he told us about the facility where she was taken and their plan to download her research by hacking the Zurich computers. We've been able to corroborate the location by satellite surveillance and from a report provided by our men on the ground. And, of course, the unsuccessful effort to hack Zurich." Taylor took a deep breath. "Given the pressure the Iranians have been feeling from the slow pace of the easing of the sanctions and their increasing isolation from the world community, we believe that the current regime wants to push forward their position in the region as a power to be reckoned with. Since they have agreed to desist with their nuclear program in exchange for an easing of the sanctions, we believe that the pursuit of biologicals is their response to their loss of face in the region."

The President had heard enough.

"Has your task force drawn up the options I requested?"

"Yes, sir, we have."

Taylor went on to explain the list of options, including diplomatic, a land assault, and a missile strike. When he was finished, the President said, "You've got boots on the ground already, don't you?"

"Two men," Taylor replied. "One is a CIA field agent, and the other is an agent with Mossad." He looked around. "Using them for a rescue is another possibility, but we believe that the likelihood of success for that course of action would be all but impossible."

"Mr. President, we should probably notify the Israelis," said the Vice President.

"I've already spoken with them, John. The Prime Minister is reviewing their options and he will be getting back to me within the hour."

He turned back to the group, and for the next hour and a half, they debated the pros and cons of all three options. The consensus was that a diplomatic approach was not likely to get Angela Disler back. The Iranians would never admit what they'd done. Instead, if past history were any indication, they would claim that a rogue group within the military might have done it, and they would claim to "investigate thoroughly." But they would move Disler to some other location, and once we lost track of her, no one would ever see her again.

A SEAL assault was considered, and while it was the option of preference from most of the people at the table, they knew they were working against the clock. Once the Iranians discovered that the material they'd downloaded was not her work, they would have to assume that the US government was on to them. They would probably move Disler before the SEALS and JSOC could put a raid together, and if they tried to rush it, the end result would likely be US casualties, and the President was not inclined to send men into harm's way when there was another, albeit, more serious option still on the table.

A missile assault would take the life of Angela Disler, thereby guaranteeing that she could not provide the Iranians with the information they needed to weaponize the virus. It would also destroy their research facility, and if they launched the attack during the day, it would also kill all or most of the researchers involved in the project, a benefit that would likely put their biological program back to square zero. A missile assault would also send a message to the Iranians that there would be immediate and severe repercussions if they tried to pursue the development of biological weapons.

The military men at the table all wanted to do an additional strike on the Quds command and control structure, arguing that taking out the lab was not enough and that the Iranians needed to see that there would be severe consequences for even contemplating such an offensive weapon.

They also argued that the Israeli's would have a stake in what happened, and considering that they were to be the first intended target of such a weapon, a number of the people at the table argued that this operation should be made into a coalition of the willing, and expanded to include Iran's nuclear facilities as well.

The President listened to everyone's opinion, then thanked them all for their input. He got to his feet and promptly announced to the group that he would need a few hours to make his decision.

As everyone stood and prepared to leave, he asked his Secretary of Defense, the Secretary of State, and the Vice President to remain behind. He also asked Taylor to remain on the line.

The three men then moved closer to sit next to the President who'd returned to his seat.

"I received a phone call about an hour ago from Shimon Peled. The Israeli's want to take out Iran's nuclear facilities, and given the Iranians intent to attack their country with a virus, they feel, and I believe rightly so, that if the Iranians were reckless enough to pursue biologicals, then their nuclear agreement with us is not worth the paper it's printed on. They insist that this new provocation, if not dealt with now, would leave them no recourse but to launch a future nuclear strike before the Iranians can do it to them."

He looked over at the Secretary of Defense.

"Have we got enough assets in the area to hit the lab and a half a dozen of their nuclear facilities?"

The Secretary of State said, "Do they want us to join them in this madness?"

"They're waiting for my decision," replied the President.

"We have two carriers and three nuclear subs in the area, sir," said the Secretary of Defense. "We can easily hit this research facility and all of their nuclear labs."

The President held his glance for a moment, then looked over at the Secretary of State.

"At some point, I believe we need to advise our allies in Europe, the Middle East, and Asia what the Iranians are planning to do. I want to nail down their public assurances that they support our action, whatever it is, and I want their assurances that should the Iranians attempt a retaliation anywhere in the world, they will join us as full participants while we go back and finish the job."

"So we're going forward with a possible attack on their nuclear facilities?" the Vice President asked.

"I've not made a decision yet," the President replied.

The Secretary of State leaned forward.

"With all due respect, Mr. President, if I start consultations with our allies, word will get out, and the Iranians will have time to prepare for an attack."

"I'm aware of that, and I'll take that into consideration before I make my final decision. But once that decision is made, I want you to make the calls."

The Vice President shrugged. "I'd hate to see us do anything that would force us to put boots back on the ground."

The President shook his head.

"We didn't start this, John, and frankly, the threat is such that we can't ignore it. I don't plan to put more American lives on the line. If we go forward with this, it will be a surgical strike against a criminal government, and if it brings about an *Iranian Spring*, then so be it. But if they don't take this warning, and if they attempt any form of retaliation for what we're going to do, we will go back in there and completely eliminate their government and all aspects of their military capability without ever putting a boot on the ground."

"What are we talking about in the way of causalities at the lab," the Vice President asked.

The President looked over at the screen. "Dan?"

"Before 6:30 a.m., the total would be twenty military. Between 6:30 a.m. and 7:30 a.m., there would be forty military present and twenty-four civilians, thereby driving the total up to sixty-four. These numbers do not include Disler, her kidnappers, or any others in the facility that we've yet to see."

The Vice President folded his arms across his chest.

"If we do this, Mr. President, what about the Iranian civilians? Do we really want to take out the non-military technicians?"

"If they're engaged in research designed to wipe out the population Israel, and we have to assume that such an attack would spread throughout the world, then they are more culpable than the soldiers who are simply guarding the base."

"And if this attack doesn't dissuade the Iranians from resuming their biological program?"

The President looked around the room, locking eyes individually with the other three.

"If we have to go back in, we will eliminate the present government, and then we will help the citizens of Iran to reorganize their new leadership in a manner that no longer presents a threat to the rest of the world."

There was complete silence at the table as the members of the group considered the ramifications of the President's words.

When the meeting broke up, the President went over to his desk and sat in his chair. He called his secretary on the phone and informed her that barring any emergencies, she was to hold any calls for twenty minutes. He then leaned back in his chair, put his feet up on the desk, shut his eyes, and began the process of sorting out the facts before making his final decision.

Thirty-five minutes later, after carefully weighing the pros and cons of everything that had been said, the President arrived at a decision. He pulled his feet off the desk and sat upright in his chair.

When his secretary answered the phone, he said, "Amby, can you please get the Israeli Prime Minister on the phone for me?"

In less than a minute, Shimon Peled was on the line.

The Israeli Prime Minister was a tall man: late seventies, bald on top with long white hair on the sides of his head that he liked to wear combed straight back. The effect was to create what was unkindly referred to by his critics as *Shimon's angel wings*. His face was heavily lined, showing the wear and tear that one would expect of a man his chronological age; a man who had served with honor during three ground wars, followed by a distinguished career in the Israel Defense Forces.

He first came to the attention of the Likud Party during a *Hardline* interview on national TV. He was a recently retired General at the time, and he had a very strong opinion about the state of Israeli security and the threat posed by the Islamic Republic of Iran. From that point forward, he successfully navigated his way through the political ranks, and it certainly didn't hurt that he'd had combat experience and command responsibility during three wars and both of the Palestinian *intifadas.*

"Yes, Mr. President," Shimon said when he came on the line. "Have you made a decision?"

"Not yet, Shimon, and please call me Jamison."

"I appreciate that, Jamison. How may I help you?"

"You're in harms way no matter what option we pursue, so I wanted to discuss this with you before I formalize my decision."

The Prime Minister settled back in his chair.

"I have Eli Ben-Jehuda with me, Jamison. May I put you on speaker phone?"

"Certainly," the President replied. He knew Ben-Jehuda was head of the Mossad and therefore would be in a position to help evaluate the plan.

"Shimon, I'm thinking of a measured response. I want to launch a surprise attack on the research facility that we've discovered in the mountains in Southwestern Iran. I believe Eli has an agent on the ground at that location with one of ours."

Eli nodded, and Shimon said, "We've been getting reports from our agent, but what about your researcher? Isn't she being held there?"

"She is, but the risk to the entire world, if she is forced to show the Iranians how to alter the virus, is just too great to ignore. Believe me, I hate the idea that she's going to lose her life, but I see no other way to quickly and easily eliminate this threat."

Shimon understood the President's dilemma. On more than one occasion, he had to order men on missions where their deaths were all but certain. It was something you never got over, and he was sure that the likely death of this woman would likely haunt the President for the rest of his life.

"You've ruled out a land assault by Commandos?" he asked.

"I have, for a couple of reasons. It's pretty far inland, and it would take too long to detail out the mission. We're up against the clock, Shimon. Once the Iranians discover that the data they've just downloaded is junk, they might decide to move Mrs. Disler, and if we lose track of her, we might not get a second chance to cut off the source of her information."

"I see your point, Jamison, and I appreciate how difficult this must be for you. But you must do what is best for your nation, and sometimes that means that innocents are sacrificed by necessity in the process."

"Thank you, Shimon. I was sure you'd understand."

The Prime Minister was dying to ask the next question, so he did.

"Have you given thought to my suggestion that we take this opportunity to wipe out the Iranians nuclear facilities?"

"I have, and this has not been an easy decision."

The Prime Minister looked at Eli, but neither man spoke. They still had no idea how far this President was willing to go.

"Once again, I'm going to opt for a measured response. I don't want to kick off another full-scale war in the region, and as I understand it, the Iranians have seventeen nuclear facilities. If we hit them all, it's effectively a declaration of war, and we could be paying a heavy price for generations to come."

"But once they get their nuclear capability, and they will, Mr. President, even if they wait for ten years, they will get it and they will use it against us, and

I can't afford to let that happen."

"I know that Shimon, and that's why I'm going to ask you to hold off on any direct action on your part until we can see just how effective this measured strike will be." He shifted in his chair. "I suspect that up to this point, the Iranian perception is that the West does not have the stomach for another conflict in the Middle East. That may have been partially true, but I can't help but believe that our sudden and decisive action in this current matter will cause them to completely rethink the commitment that stands behind our previous statement that if they cross the line, we will act without hesitation."

The President used the next few moments of silence to gather his thoughts.

"I don't think I need to tell you Shimon that I'm a man of my word, and whatever it takes, the Iranians will *never* possess a nuclear weapon."

Shimon looked over at Eli who smiled. Both men knew that they'd just been given a firm commitment from the President of the United States that all military options remained on the table. And while they felt comfortable with accepting the President at his word, they also realized that such a commitment could easily vanish with a change of administration during the next Presidential election.

"I agree with your assessment, Mr. President," said Shimon, "and I welcome your restatement of the American position on the Iranian nuclear situation. However, since we are both pragmatists, I feel I can be frank with you at this particular moment in time.

"A future administration might not share your enlightened position, and this could end up leaving my country in a rather precarious position. If the Iranians were to move forward with their construction of a nuclear weapon, we might find ourselves backed up against a wall. Military action directed towards a facility where components were being assembled is far easier to accomplish than having to use a nuclear strike on our enemies to prevent their getting the opportunity to act first." Shimon looked over at Eli who was nodding slowly. "That position is a very real possibility, Mr. President, and setting aside the moral implications of such an action and the toll it would take on innocent human lives, it is also one that would be guaranteed to kick off a nuclear arms race throughout the Middle East."

The President sat up straighter and leaned forward in his chair.

"Where are we going with this, Shimon?"

"Ah, Mr. President, I can tell from your voice that you believe I am trying to intimidate you into an immediate strike against their nuclear facilities. But that is not the case, I am only projecting ahead to look at what I believe are the uncertainties of the political climate in both of our countries, and I think that the outrageous actions on the part of the Iranians now presents us with a unique opportunity."

"Go on," said the President.

Shimon took a deep breath. "I would like to suggest that as soon as this demonstration of American willingness to take military action is completed, that representatives of our respective countries put together a formal, binding treaty. One that expresses in no uncertain terms that should the Iranians get within months of completion of a nuclear device, that we would jointly engage in a military action that is designed to eliminate forever the ability of Iran to assemble a nuclear device."

The President's first thought was…*What a crafty son of a bitch!* He wants me to obligate the United States to a military action based upon an observable timetable. His second thought was…*If we attempt to put such an understanding into a binding document, it would require an act of Congress to make it official.*

The President had no illusions that the more conservative members of both houses would likely welcome such a treaty. And given the current crisis spawned by the biological warfare misadventure, such an agreement would likely sail through both houses, thereby guaranteeing that the policy would survive any change in administration.

The President closed his eyes and gave it some real thought. Always a man who was not afraid to make a quick decision, it did not take him long to recognize the wisdom of Shimon's proposal.

"If such a treaty were to be drafted, Shimon, I would think that it would be to our advantage to bring our European partners into the discussions."

Shimon balked. "But Mr. President, *too many cooks might spoil the broth*."

"That may be, Shimon, but given the risk that Western Europe was facing from Iran's biological plan, I suspect that even the Russians would have to acknowledge once and for all that Iran is a pariah state. We will stress that we were ready and completely willing to act at this very moment, but that we deferred doing so to allow the rest of the world to weigh in one more time with the Iranians on the advantages of peace over guaranteed physical destruction."

Shimon looked at Ely who was again nodding sagely. If a current war and its inevitable fallout could be forestalled with a united commitment to guarantee the safety of Israel and the region from the possible nuclear armament of Iran, then they had nothing to lose by giving it a try.

"Your suggestion makes very good sense, Mr. President," said Shimon, "and who knows? Perhaps this type of approach might become a template for a unified front in the face of future terrorist threats."

The President smiled. "I'm thinking about asking the British and French to provide some logistical support, post attack, of course, and I'm going to request the Saudis, the Jordanians, and the Egyptians to join us in immediately condemning the Iranians for their reckless biological intentions."

"What about the Russian's and the Chinese, Mr. President?" Shimon knew that was a potential problem. "Both have significant economic ties with Iran."

The President smiled to himself.

"I will speak to their leaders personally, once the attack is underway, I will stress the danger they were facing to their own survival if the Iranians were permitted to go forward with their plan to release a virus that would decimate the world's population. I'll convince them that our current restraint took into account their economic positions, but in exchange, I will insist that they put pressure on Iran to refrain from their nuclear and biological ambitions before we are forced to go in with massive force to bring about a change in regime."

For the first time during the conversation, Shimon allowed himself an unguarded smile. The plan was measured and very unlikely to plunge the region into an all out war, and while the viral threat could still be controlled by a decisive action, it was the nuclear threat that was proving difficult to conquer because of Iranian intransigence.

Well, perhaps that intransigence was about to get a good swift kick in the ass.

Shimon leaned forward in his chair.

"Can we be of any assistance to you in your mission to destroy the research facility?"

"I think we can handle it, Shimon. But perhaps your people can be of some assistance with the exfiltration of our two respective agents from the Iranians territory."

"I'll put Eli right on it, Mr. President, and we'll coordinate an operation through the usual channels."

A few grateful tears welled up in Shimon's eyes.

"Thank you, Mr. President, for your understanding of our dilemma. Safeguarding my country has always been my utmost concern, and being able to rely upon your friendship is a real godsend. We will carefully monitor the pulse of the Iranians after your pending action, and we look forward to joining with you to negotiate our mutual assistance agreement."

After a few additional, mutual pleasantries, the President hung up, took a deep breath, then rattled off a set of instructions to his personal secretary about the sequence of notifications he would now have to make.

*****

FIFTY-TWO

THE ZAGROS MOUNTAINS
SOUTHWESTERN IRAN
DAY EIGHTEEN   2:00 AM

Bryan stirred slowly. Mordecai was tapping him on the shoulder. His eyes popped open, and he was instantly awake.

"Your satellite phone is vibrating," Mordecai said softly.

Bryan sat upright and pulled the phone from the leather case attached to his belt. He plugged in the connector on the earpiece that was still in his ear and gave the opening of the coded phrase which Taylor finished correctly.

"What's up?" he said to Taylor.

"I need the two of you to make your way back to the following location where you'll be met by friends." Taylor rattled off a series of coordinates.

Bryan took them down on a small notepad he carried in his shirt pocket. There was a prearranged group of numbers that would be subtracted from the coordinates that Taylor had given him, producing the true location.

Even though the satellite transmission was encoded and supposedly foolproof, neither man wanted to give too much information out over the air. You just never knew what new technological breakthrough would come along, so neither was willing to take unnecessary chances.

"What about the package?" Bryan said.

"Out of the question," Taylor replied. "Time's run out."

"I'd like to take a shot, sir."

Taylor figured he'd make that request. The man was fearless, and if truth be told, a little reckless, too. Taylor had recently gone over Bryan's most recent psychological profile, and he had come to the conclusion that Bryan had a bit of a death wish which he suspected stemmed from the loss of his parents and fiancee during the tower collapse on 9/11. His time in the service in the high-risk role as a sniper, his work undercover in the Middle East hot spots, all pointed to a man who was still working out his anger and grief, one who wasn't afraid to take chances because he didn't fear the consequences of making a mistake.

"Too risky," Taylor said. "You need to be clear of your current location by seven a.m."

Bryan understood what Taylor was referring to. The President had apparently chosen to take the facility out with missiles at a time that would have maximum causalities. He couldn't fault him for it, it was a logical choice given the geographic location of the facility and the risk of mounting a manned operation. But it grated on him that Angela Disler was going to be an innocent victim of the ongoing tensions between the United States and Iran. She deserved a better break.

He studied his watch. It was 2:00 a.m. Five hours until all hell would rain down from the sky.

Bryan sighed. "Just so you know, the location I'm sitting on won't be easy to take down."

"The boss is prepared to do what it takes. You just worry about getting yourself out of there in time."

"Okay. Later."

Taylor sighed with relief as he disconnected the call. He had expected Bryan to put up more of a fight about trying to get Disler out. And while he'd put him in country to track her down, it was never his intent to have him get directly involved in her rescue. He was much too valuable an asset to jeopardize in such a risky operation, and now that a rescue was out of the question, he wanted him out of the country as quickly as possible.

****

"So what's going on?" Mordecai asked. Bryan had just unscrambled the location of the extraction point and was now packing up his gear and double checking his weapons.

He said, "You need to get yourself out of here. At 7:00 a.m. this place is going to become a crater."

Mordecai didn't need to be told twice. He began collecting his gear.

"And Disler?" he asked.

Bryan held his glance. "Officially, she's on her own."

Mordecai could only stare. The Americans were going to let her die instead of mounting a rescue? It didn't seem right. His own country would have mounted a massive operation, even if it was only to save a single soldier. The Americans used to have the same policy. What had changed?

"That doesn't sound right," Mordecai said as he broke down his scoped sniper rifle.

Bryan said, "Once the base gets wiped out, it will significantly narrow the escape window. Checkpoints will likely go up all over the country. You're gonna have to be very careful making your way down to the coast."

"You mean *we,* don't you? *We* are going to have to be very careful."

"Not we, *you...* "

Bryan got to his feet and slung his pack over his back.

"I'm going down there to get her out."

"But you said—?"

Bryan gave him a wink.

"I'm doing this on my own, Morty. You go back to the truck and get your ass down to the pick-up spot."

He handed him the note containing the scrambled coordinates.

"What's this?"

"The coordinates for the pick-up spot. Memorize 'em, okay?"

Mordecai nodded.

"Good, and if I get lucky and can get her out of here in time, I'll hot-wire the van they left down there and we'll meet you at the extraction point."

Mordecai checked his watch.

"You've got just under five hours until this place goes up. That gives you about four hours to get in and out."

"Then I better get going." Bryan reached out his hand. "I'll catch you on the other side."

Mordecai shook his hand, then watched as Bryan started off down the hill towards the plateau below.

He's crazy. He'll never get her out of there alone.

Mordecai shook his head. He must have a death wish...one of those guys who wants to save the whole world…

Oh, hell! I can't let him do this without help.

He got down on his knees and began to reassemble his silenced sniper rifle, and once it was set up, he scanned the hillside below and spotted Bryan moving towards the hole in the fence.

He turned on his communications headset and whispered, "I've got your back." And after a short pause, Mordecai heard two clicks on the radio that let him know that Bryan had heard the message and that he was going to maintain radio silence to avoid possible detection.

Mordecai swung his night viewing scoped rifle over towards the security gate. Since the last time he checked, the guard hadn't moved from his chair. His feet were up on the counter, and Mordecai suspected that he was sound asleep.

Sweet dreams, soldier boy. But don't wake up. I'd hate like hell to have to put you down.

*****

FIFTY-THREE

THE ZAGROS MOUNTAINS
SOUTHWESTERN IRAN
DAY NINETEEN   3:30 AM

Bryan reached the bottom of the hillside and made his way carefully through the cut in the fence. Before heading over to the building that concealed the entrance to the facility, he made his way to the front gate to deal with the man in the guardhouse.

He crept up using his night vision goggles and was clearly able to see the shape of the man in the darkness of the booth. He was sitting in a chair, apparently asleep.

Bryan slid open the door to the guardhouse and struck the guard along the side of the head with a sap, which immediately rendered him unconscious. He used a pair of flex cuffs to secure the man's hands behind his back and a second pair to secure his legs.

He took a moment to look around the guard shack before he noticed a landline phone on the counter. He knew that the phone could be used to communicate with the people inside the facility, so he tore the wire out of the wall, effectively rendering it inoperable. He then went through the man's pockets, located his cell phone, and removed the sim card which he snapped in half.

The booth was small, only large enough for two people to stand side by side. Other than the phone, there was no sign of electronic surveillance or hot alarm buttons that would alert the security forces inside the facility that there was any kind of a problem.

Bryan smiled to himself. The Iranians must have felt that the location was not important enough to spend what it would take to secure the facility with a high-end electronic system. It was a mistake that would end up costing them dearly.

On the counter in front of the man was a small thermos bottle, a *Disney* product, *Donald Duck* motif, which probably contained tea or a broth of some kind. He didn't want to scald the man, so rather than pouring the liquid on his face in an effort to revive him, he leaned over and shook him, and when that didn't work, he removed a popper from his medical kit, an *amyl nitrite*. He snapped off the neck of the glass ampoule and held it under the man's nose, allowing him to inhale the vapors. He came around quickly.

Bryan noted that the man was barely more than a boy, maybe nineteen years of age. He was in uniform, Iranian military, but certainly not a hardened veteran, so getting what he wanted would likely require no more than a little psychological pressure.

Bryan spoke to the man in *Persian;* softly, but in a firm tone of voice.

"I'm going to ask you some questions, and if you answer me truthfully, you will live. Do you understand?"

The boy's eyes were wide with fear. He was looking up into the face of a uniformed warrior who's equipment and armament seemed otherworldly. He had no reason to doubt the man's words, and since there was no possibility of escaping from this nightmare, he made the instant decision to cooperate fully in hopes of surviving this ordeal.

He nodded that he understood.

"How deep does the facility go underground?"

"Six stories, sir."

"And the young woman they brought in, where are they keeping her?"

"What young woman?" The young man looked confused.

Bryan instantly recognized his mistake. Disler wasn't young, and this boy soldier might not even have known that she was in the van that delivered her to the base.

"The people who showed up in the white van? Where in the building did they go?"

"You mean the Quds?"

Bryan nodded.

"I don't know where they went in the building, but the guards inside might know."

This was going nowhere, and Bryan was losing his patience. He probably doesn't know about Disler. After all, he was just a low-level facility guard. But he must know about the facility itself.

"What's inside the mountain?" Bryan asked.

"It's a research facility, sir. I don't know exactly what they do, but I think it's medicine. Down on the sixth level, they have a very large laboratory. I've never been inside because they said it has to stay sterile, but that's where most of the doctors work."

"What's on the fifth floor?"

"Sleeping quarters; for the military personnel, the doctors, and a few smaller labs, I think?"

"Any cells inside the building?"

The young man took a moment to think.

"I believe they built one on the fifth level, but I'm not exactly sure."

It figured that she would be kept confined where the military was being billeted. This would not be easy.

"What about the other floors?" he asked.

"On the fourth and third floors are offices, and storage is on the second. The first floor is the garage and for stockpiling items that they need to move down to the second."

"Any guards on the upper floors?"

The boy nodded. "There are two guards at the elevators on each floor."

"How often are they changed?"

"That I don't know."

He asked other questions, but most of what he wanted to know were beyond the boy's understanding. The only thing of value disclosed during the interrogation was the fact that the emergency stairwell that he had previously discovered went all the way down to the bottom level, and the doors from the stairs opened directly into the main hallway on each floor. If he attempted to exit the stairwell on any of the floors, he would likely encounter two guards near the elevators, but he wasn't worried. His silenced MP-5 and the element of surprise should enable him to have the advantage.

The boy had done what he'd been asked to do. He'd given him all of the information that he had. It was time to live up to the bargain he'd made.

"I'm going to go into the facility now. You answered my questions, so when I return, I will cut you loose."

The boy nodded gratefully.

"But if you've lied to me about the building or the position of the guards, when I come back I will kill you."

"I told you the truth," the boy said, his voice shaking.

Bryan nodded. "And just so you know, if you try to get loose, I am not alone. Your gate is being watched by a sniper. So if you try to get up or get out of the building, you will be killed. Understand?"

The terrified boy nodded.

Bryan took off and headed for the facility.

****

Once he picked the lock on the exterior of the door that led into the emergency stairwell, he raised his night viewing goggles up on his helmet, then carefully poked his head into the hallway on the underground second floor. This floor had been described by the young man as a warehouse, and from what he could see, it was. But more importantly, there were no cameras set up to alert the security personnel to his entry, an oversight he thought strange but welcome. The young man had sworn that there was no surveillance monitoring system, and it appeared that he was truthful. The failure to spend money on such a system was likely the direct result of the sanctions imposed on the Iranians due to their pursuit of nuclear weapons.

He slipped back into the stairwell, and on his way down to the fifth floor, he decided to tackle the beast by the horns. Supposedly, there were two guards assigned to watch the elevator on each floor, beginning with the third floor down, so rather than going directly to the fifth, while leaving armed soldiers on the floors above which would place him in a vulnerable position should his presence be discovered, he decided to render the guards harmless on each floor as he made his way down.

When he opened the stairwell door on the third floor, he immediately spotted the two guards sitting in chairs behind a waist high counter. One was clearly asleep and the other was reading a newspaper. A radio was on in the background; music softly playing.

Bryan brought up the silenced MP-5 and slowly made his way down the hall towards the two men. When he got within twenty feet of them, he put two quick rounds into the one who was reading, followed by two more into the man who was sleeping.

He reached the desk, checked to see that both were dead, then studied the counter area to confirm in his mind that other than a telephone, there was no hot alarm button or hidden monitoring system that he wasn't aware of. Satisfied, he made his way back to the stairwell, and repeated the process on the fourth floor, where he discovered that both men were sound asleep.

He didn't relish the role of an assassin, but these men were soldiers, guarding a facility that contained a kidnapped American citizen; a facility that was operating with the expressed goal of creating a biological weapon that could potentially wipe out a significant percentage of the world's population. When he looked at it in that light, his sympathy for these men and their families quickly dissipated. The faces of his late mother, father, and fiancee suddenly flashed before his eyes, and what had been a moment of sympathy quickly turned to a moment of rage.

Pulling the trigger was easy…for now. Maybe sometime in the distant future he would come to regret his actions; that is, assuming there was a future for him?

He checked his watch again; time was quickly running down.

He reloaded his MP-5, checked the Sig-Sauer secured in the holster on his chest, then he slowly made his way back to the stairwell that led down to the fifth and sixth floors.

He carefully opened the fifth-floor stairwell door and peered out into the hallway. Behind a waist-high desk that matched the ones he'd seen on the other floors, there were three uniformed military personnel, none of whom were sleeping. This was going to be far more difficult to deal with, as he had no reason to doubt the information from the young man that the rest of the security force—perhaps as many as twenty armed men—were sleeping nearby.

He stood there for a while, behind the stairwell door, and considered his options. He still didn't know where Disler was being held, and that presented him with a serious dilemma. If he managed to kill all three at the desk without waking the others, he would have to conduct an exploratory mission, searching for her confinement cell. That would take too much time, and it would unnecessarily force him to expose himself to those who might wake up at a moment's notice.

When he finally worked out a plan in his own mind, he readied several CS grenades, slipped a gas mask over his face, and after counting to three, he entered the hallway and walked straight towards the men.

Halfway there, one of the three spotted him approaching. He tapped the shoulder of a second, and in a heartbeat, all three were suddenly watching his approach.

The fact that he was alone and that he was wearing a gas mask seemed to completely confuse them. His MP-5 was on a shoulder strap, in his right hand, but slung out of sight behind his waist. He approached at a steady rate, and the matter-of-fact calmness that he presented seemed to lengthen the duration of their confusion.

He could almost see the gears turning in their heads. They had to assume that he was a medical technician and that a leak of some kind had occurred, hence the need for a gas mask.

When he was ten feet away from the desk, he swung the weapon out from behind his back and quickly dropped two of the three soldiers. The third one was seated at the desk, and he held up his hand in surrender, a futile gesture that was also meant to shield him from getting hit with bullets.

Bryan raised the gas mask over his head and motioned to the man to step out from behind the desk.

In Persian, he said in a very soft voice, "I have come for the woman. If you are quiet and lead me to her, I will not kill you. But if you do anything to alert the others, anything at all, I will kill you without a second thought. Do you believe me?"

The man nodded. He knew he had no chance to escape or warn his fellow soldiers, and this man, whoever he was, had no compunction about taking human lives, so he came out from behind the counter and stood quietly, hands up, in the center of the hallway.

"I don't want to die. Please. I'll do what you say."

He too is just a kid, thought Bryan. *Eighteen or nineteen tops.*

"Where are the other soldiers sleeping?" he asked softly.

The boy pointed down the hallway to a set of double doors in the direction farthest away from the emergency stairwell.

Well, that's a break, Bryan said to himself.

"And where is the woman who is being held as a prisoner?"

The boy looked momentarily confused, and Bryan wondered for a moment if the men guarding the facility had also been kept in the dark. But that thought quickly vanished when he said, "I was told there is a prisoner on this floor, but I don't know if it is a woman. The guard in the back, he's a Quds. He's not one of us, but he would know."

It made sense that the kidnapping of Disler would not be common knowledge among the security guards at the facility. Why would they need to know anything at all about her? But if they were holding a prisoner, it had to be her. Who else could it be?

"Are you regular army?" he asked the boy.

"No, sir, we are private security."

That explained a great deal. Private security guards would have minimal training, so the odds for a successful rescue just went way up.

Bryan noticed that the boy was still armed. There was a pistol in a holster on his hip. Bryan had him slowly turn around, and one hand at a time, he slipped him into a pair of flex-cuffs, then removed and unloaded the handgun before sliding it across the floor and back down the hallway.

"Take me to her," he said.

The boy nodded, then turned and walked down the hallway away from the direction of the emergency exit.

They came to a closed double door, the boy stopped short.

"What's behind the doors?" Bryan asked.

"It opens into a short hallway, sir. Down at the end is the guard. The cell is to your left, just past the guard."

"Is he armed?"

The boy turned his head slightly to look at Bryan's face.

"Of course."

Bryan nodded.

"Open the door and walk straight towards him. I will be right behind you. If you try to alert him to my presence, I will kill you. Understand?"

The boy nodded as Bryan reached for the door.

*****

FIFTY-FOUR

THE ZAGROS MOUNTAINS
SOUTHWESTERN IRAN
DAY NINETEEN   4:20 AM

Bryan pushed open the doorway that led to a hallway where the security guard had told him that Angela Disler's cell was supposed to be. He pushed the reluctant boy in front of him, then walked through the door with one hand on the kid's shoulder, while the other held the silenced MP-5 against the small of his back.

As they approached the sitting guard, Bryan peered over his hostage's shoulder. The guard at the desk was looking at them. He was about twenty feet away, apparently confused, but not yet going for a weapon.

Just another ten feet! Bryan thought. Ten more feet and I'll have him alive!

It took about three seconds to cover the distance, but just before they reached the desk, the man reacted and reached for his waistband. Bryan came up with the MP-5 and fired a quick, silenced burst, dropping the man, who slid off the chair and down to the floor.

The noise, while silenced, seemed deafening, and both Bryan and the boy stood motionless, waiting for a sound, any sound, that would indicate that the shots and the crashing of the body had awakened the men who were sleeping down the hallway. But there was no sound, and after just about half a minute, Bryan breathed a heavy sigh of relief.

He continued to hold the boy's shoulder with one hand, but rather than push him forward any further, he asked, "Where's the cell holding the prisoner?"

The boy, still in shock after seeing another person cut down, pointed with a shaky hand to the end of the corridor.

Bryan pushed him forward, and when they got to the end of the hallway, he glanced to the left. There was a steel door with a small window. He stepped over to the window and looked inside. A woman was cowering in the far corner of the room. It was Angela Disler.

Bryan looked at the door. It required a key to unlock it. He told the boy to sit on the floor while he walked back to the desk and found the key in the top desk drawer. It was attached to a wooden stick. He picked it up, hurried back to the cell, secured the hands of the young Iranian guard, then unlocked the door.

"Angela Disler?" he asked, walking in.

She seemed surprised as if only beginning to realize that the man might not be there to harm her.

"I'm Bryan. I've come to get you out of here. Stand up. We don't have much time."

It took a few moments for what he was saying to sink in, but she quickly got to her feet.

"Are you an American?" she asked.

He smiled. "I am. And we need to get you out of here as fast as possible. Can you walk?"

"Oh, thank God!" Then, "Yes, I can walk. These people wanted me to show them how to make a viral weapon. They have my family back in L.A. They said they're going to kill them if—"

"We have people tracking them down," he said to reassure her, "but we need to get going *right now*."

"But they have a live Marburg virus in this facility! It's in the main lab, down on the sixth floor."

"Don't worry about that now," he said, taking her arm. "In a very short while, this place will no longer exist. Now, come with me. Be very quiet. We're going to have to sneak out of here."

They moved towards the open door.

"Where are the other Americans? They need to destroy the virus."

"I'm the only one," he said with a tight smile. "So let's get going."

He looked down at the boy he was holding as a prisoner. He was just a kid, and he posed no real threat. He reached down and hooked him under one arm and raised him up to his feet.

"If you want to live," he said in Persian, "you can come with us now. Once we get outside, I'll let you go free. Otherwise, you can stay in this cell and take your chances. Understand?"

The boy nodded. He had the sense that something awful was about to happen to the facility, and when it did, he did not want to be underground.

"I don't want to die in here," he said. "I will go with you."

"Smart choice. We'll go down the hallway to the elevator, then up to the ground floor. Stay quiet. If any of the others wake up, I'll have to kill you."

The boy nodded, and even though his hands were cuffed, Bryan could see that they were shaking uncontrollably.

They made their way to the hallway, and after slowly opening one of the double doors, Bryan looked out into the hallway.

Complete silence.

He gestured to the boy to start moving, and once he was out in the central hallway, he had Angela follow. The three of them made it to the elevator without a problem, and Bryan pressed the button for up.

Just then, a door opened up about ten meters from where they were standing, and into the hallway stepped Andre Petrov.

At first, he didn't see them, but Bryan saw him and raised his weapon.

Angela gasped, and Petrov looked over in her direction.

The elevator arrived, dinged once, and the doors quietly opened.

Petrov looked over in their direction. He continued to stare, completely confused.

"He's one of the doctors," said Angela. "He threatened to kill my family if I didn't cooperate."

Bryan pulled the trigger, dropping Petrov where he stood. He then pushed Angela forward into the elevator, and when the boy joined them, the three of them rode the elevator all the way up to the ground level floor.

****

Up on the hill, overlooking the research facility, Mordecai sat quietly, staring through the *Leupold* rifle scope, slowly scanning the land below him. It was already dawn, and he'd had no word from Bryan since the double click on his receiver in response to Mordecai's statement that he would have his back.

He was starting to get nervous, not so much because there'd been no word from Bryan—he figured if Bryan had been captured, someone would have come out of the facility to take a look around, or at least to confer with the guard at the front gate—but because it was almost 0630 Zulu. That meant that there was a busload of technicians who were due to arrive at the lab; that is, assuming they stayed on the same schedule as the day before.

He swung his scope back over in the direction of the gatehouse, but there was no indication of movement from within. Mordecai assumed that the guard had been killed by Bryan, but since he didn't know for sure, he couldn't resist the urge to keep checking.

He'd placed a call to Eli during the interim, filling him in on what was going on, and together, they agreed upon an exfiltration plan as a backup should Bryan not get out in time. Mordecai didn't want to believe that Bryan wouldn't make it, but as time ran out, it was beginning to look more possible.

He sighed, then shifted his view back towards the main facility.

His earpiece suddenly crackled. Included within a burst of static were several words, but all Mordecai heard was something to the effect of…"*coming out.*"

He was focused on the stairwell to the side of the building, so he did not immediately notice that the door to the outside yard on the front of the facility was slowly opening. When he finally did notice a small movement of the door, he saw a head stick out, then quickly pull back into the darkness inside.

The noise of an approaching vehicle suddenly got his attention. He shifted his view back to the front gate and waited as the noise grew louder. It sounded like a bus, and he was pretty sure it had to be the busload of technicians who worked at the base.

It was.

The bus came into view, quickly followed by a second bus, both of which came to a stop at the front gate guardhouse.

Damn it!

The second bus contained the guards who were scheduled for the change of shift. Either they were thirty minutes early, or they'd been thirty minutes late the day before.

He turned on his transmit button and said, "The technicians and a bus-load of the military are at the front gate. Can you get out in the next few seconds?"

He heard a double click in response, then Bryan's whispered voice was in his ear.

"I've got Disler and a hostage. We're gonna make a run for the fence."

"I'll pin them down if it comes to that," said Mordecai, "but hurry. I think they're just about to find out what you did to the front gate guard."

A military guard from the first bus got off in the interim and approached the guard house. He was inside for only a few seconds before emerging with a second man whose hands were bound behind his waist. Mordecai could see through the scope that the guard was using a knife to sever the gate guards flex cuffs. For his part, the gate guard was in a highly animated state, and Mordecai concluded he was likely describing what had happened to him while pointing wildly over towards the building.

"They know something's up," he said into his mouthpiece. "The bus full of soldiers is about to find out, too."

Mordecai swung his view back to the main building, and discovered that Bryan, the boy, and Disler, were already hurrying towards the hole in the fence. He swung back again to the gate, and to his dismay, he discovered that the soldiers were scampering off the bus like ants out of a nest, and they were running past the booth and through the front gate towards the lab.

One of the soldiers yelled out, then stopped short and assumed a firing stance. He let loose with a volley of shots in the general direction of Bryan and the others. More shots were fired from a second, nearby soldier, and Mordecai immediately sprung into action.

His was a semi-automatic sniper rifle, and he was using a clip that held five rounds. He took careful aim for the first shot, striking the soldier who had fired first. After that, it was open season on the rest of the guards, who by now were out in the open, completely unaware that he was firing in their direction.

It took a few seconds for the Iranians to realize that they were under a barrage of sustained and accurate fire. Four of the soldiers were now motionless heaps, and another two were writhing around, mortally wounded, their screams frightening their comrades and causing them to hit the ground as they tried to crawl for cover.

Mordecai didn't bother to check on Bryan's progress, as he was busy trying to pick off the targets that were closest to where Bryan and the others were headed. The Iranians still had no idea where the shots were coming from, but it was only a matter of time before one of them figured it out, so he was determined to eliminate as many as he could, starting with those who were closest to the hole in the fence.

He picked off five before he had to reload, and by that time, the Iranians had begun shooting in his direction. He kept his head down, crawled thirty feet to his left, making sure to stay concealed behind the ridge line, then popped up again and resumed firing.

****

Bryan, Disler and the boy security guard reached the fence and Disler was the first to crawl through the hole. The Iranians soldiers had fired shots in their direction, but Bryan could hear the steady popping sound of Mordecai's silenced sniper rifle, and he instinctively understood that each one was buying them time.

He pulled out his knife and cut the flex cuff that kept the boy's hands behind his back.

"Crawl through," he told him.

The boy hesitated only briefly, then did as he was instructed and Bryan quickly followed.

He then bent the chain link fence back into place, hoping that the Iranians might miss it on their first pass, thereby buying them even more time.

He got to his feet, then turned to face both Disler and the boy. To Disler, he said, "We will climb up to the top of the hill to join my partner. Once we get clear of the top of the mountain, we will be leaving this valley as fast as we can run."

He checked his watch then turned to the boy.

"You will follow us up to the top of the mountain, but once we get there, you must go your own way. Do not come back down into this canyon, for everything here will be destroyed in less than fifteen minutes. Do you understand?"

The boy nodded. His feeling that something awful was going to happen had just been confirmed.

"But what about the others?" he asked, gesturing with his head towards the facility.

"Don't worry about them. If they catch you now, they'll probably kill you. Just get yourself away from here and never come back."

He turned back to Disler.

"Follow me, and be quick. We're running out of time."

As he led them to the start of the tree line, he turned on his mouthpiece and informed Mordecai that they were on their way up. Mordecai responded with a warning.

"They've got reinforcements coming out of the warehouse. You better pick it up."

****

They met up with Mordecai twelve minutes later. All three were winded from climbing the hillside at such a rapid pace and using the ridge of the mountain top as cover, they crouched down while Mordecai continued to fire the occasional shot. But in spite of his best efforts, some of the Iranians had already made it through the hole in the fence.

Bryan was kicking himself for not tossing a few grenades into the sleeping quarters of the soldiers who were inside the facility when he had the chance. It was bad enough that they didn't get away without alerting the soldiers who'd arrived for change of shift, but once the ones below ground had been alerted to the bodies that he'd left behind, they would be in a position to mount a coordinated effort to track them down.

To get clear of the area, he, Disler and Mordecai would have to hike down the hill into the adjacent canyon where they'd left their vehicle hidden beneath the trees. Before they ever reached the bottom of the canyon, the Iranians would be on top of the mountain and would have the superior firing position. They might also have called in for reinforcements, and since he didn't know what assets they had in the general area, they could bring in helicopters or additional troops, and that would put an end to any chance of escape.

He thought it over, all the possible scenarios and permutations, and it didn't take long to realize that the only chance they had was to delay the Iranian soldiers from reaching the top of the mountain.

He turned to Mordecai. "Give me the rifle."

Mordecai shot him a questioning look and gestured towards the boy. "Who's this?"

Bryan said, "He's a security guard. He gave me good info, and in exchange, I'm gonna give him a chance to get away."

Mordecai looked skeptical. "But he's one of them?"

"He's a kid, Morty. Besides, in a few more minutes, none of this is gonna matter if you don't get going."

Mordecai looked at his watch, then handed the rifle to Bryan.

"You take Disler down to the car. I'll keep the wolves at bay until Uncle Sam drops in for a visit."

Mordecai shook his head. "You're cutting it too close, my friend. We need to go now."

But Bryan was not concerned about his own personal safety. Getting Disler out for him was paramount. She was a walking encyclopedia with a skill set that made her quite valuable to the Iranians who were now pursuing them, and since he'd made the decision to save her life against the wishes of his bosses, the pending air assault would be for naught if the Iranians got their hands on her again.

He could hear the enemy scrambling up the hillside below them. They were close, really close.

"Go now," he said to Mordecai and Disler, and he swung the sniper rifle over his shoulder. He then reloaded his MP-5.

He looked over at the boy. "You stay here with me."

"Don't do this," Mordecai said. "It's too risky. You're gonna get blown to pieces."

"I'll hold 'em here while you get her down the hill," he whispered. "Get going while I keep them pinned down."

"You sure?"

Bryan smiled and clapped him on the shoulder. "Don't forget you're going to set me up when this is all over."

Mordecai nodded, then turned to face Angela.

"This way, Doctor, follow me."

He scrambled up to the crest of the hill with Disler close behind, and then they were gone, scampering down the other side, helter-skelter through the tree line.

Bryan turned to the boy. "Your name?"

"Amir," said the boy.

"Well, Amir, in a few minutes, bombs are going to blow up this entire canyon. Go over the top of the hill and run as fast as you can to the East. The highway is down there, and if you get that far, keep going and don't come back."

"But they saw me running away with you?"

"They're all going to die, Amir," Bryan said flatly. "You keep what's left of those cuffs around your wrist and if the soldiers pick you up, you tell them that I took you as a hostage shield, but you managed to escape when the bombs started falling."

Amir reached out and took Bryan's hand.

"May Allah keep you."

He then turned and scampered over the crest of the hill.

Bryan turned back to face the pursuing Iranians who were still about forty yards down the hill. He could count a half a dozen, maybe more in the trees below them. It wouldn't take much to flank him, so he had to act fast.

He pulled a grenade from his belt, pulled the pin, and pitched it down in front of the leader of the group, then he brought up the barrel of the MP-5 and opened fire, spraying those that he could actually see.

The grenade went off, and when he looked up again, he could just make out four bodies on the ground, about thirty feet away. Several shots rang out, whizzing close to where he was partially concealed.

They know pretty much where I'm hiding, he thought. *Time to move.*

He slid on his belly, parallel to the ridge line, for about twenty feet. He then pulled another grenade, raised up enough to guess where the remaining Iranians had taken cover, then pitched it into the trees where he thought they might be.

The grenade went off, followed by screams. More shots rang out, this time from farther down in the valley.

The second wave, he thought.

He clicked on his radio and said, "Can you hear me?"

Mordecai double clicked to indicate that he could.

"I didn't want to say it in front of her," he began, "but if it all goes to hell and the Iranians are going to catch you, you take her out. Understand?"

Mordecai double clicked again.

Bryan checked his watch. Another three minutes and they would pose no threat to Disler and Mordecai.

He got to his feet, then fired another burst blindly down the hill to force them to keep their heads down.

****

Mordecai and Angela ran down the hillside, cutting in and out of the trees.

Angela was terrified. She was absolutely convinced that she was running for her life and that the Iranians were going to catch them before they got away. She thought about Bryan, about the risk he was taking by staying up on the hill to cover their escape. It was a selfless act, and if she managed to get away, she would remember his courage for the rest of her life.

Mordecai was leading the way.

"Stay with me," he told her.

He could hear the sound of grenades going off and feared the worst. He knew that Bryan was carrying some, but he suspected that the Iranian troops were also similarly armed, and if they were close enough to the crest of the hill to be able to toss them at Bryan, then it wouldn't be long before they crested the ridge and continued the pursuit of Disler.

In that eventuality, they would have the high ground.

He looked over his shoulder at Disler. She was starting to fall back, so he slowed his pace.

He heard the sound of the MP-5 as it rattled off another clip. At least he was still alive, but he had to be getting low on ammunition.

Bryan needed to break off contact with the Iranians if he was going to get out alive.

He said a little prayer, then turned to Disler, "We need to pick up the pace."

****

The first Tomahawk Cruise missile came flying in at 7:01 a.m. Designed to deliver a large warhead over long distances with high accuracy, it was traveling at supersonic speed and was self-navigating when it honed in on the coordinates that Bryan had provided for the air shaft that led down to the lower floors of the research facility.

Mordecai and Disler never heard it coming, but the ground shook violently, tossing them off their feet before the thunderous sound of the explosion managed to reach their ears.

Angela struggled to get back up. She'd known what was coming, but had no real idea how just how powerful and frightening the experience would be. Even with the protection of the mountain, the ground had seemed to shift and the sound of the detonation had temporarily dampened her hearing.

Mordecai got to his feet. He, too, was surprised by the strength of the explosion. But he knew one thing that Disler did not. He was aware that there would be more missiles on their way in, and if even one of them was just a little bit off target, they might end up as dust in the wind.

He grabbed her hand and the two of them resumed running down the hillside, and this time they were far more reckless in their efforts to get away. Disler fell once, but because he was holding her hand, he quickly managed to pull her to her feet.

"Come on. Keep to your feet. There might be more missiles coming in."

He didn't need to say it twice. She took off running ahead of him, pell-mell down the hillside. She was now more afraid of the missiles than she was of the Iranians.

The second one arrived a few moments later, but they were much farther down the hill, so the ground didn't shake as violently and the sound of the explosion was not quite as deafening. Still, they quickened their pace even more as a direct result of the terror the strike had instilled.

At the bottom of the hill, which was really a wide, expansive valley several miles in width, Mordecai pointed in the direction of the truck.

"We parked under those trees, over there," he said. "Head over there and wait for me. I'll catch up shortly."

"Please don't leave me." The anguish in her voice was palpable. "I don't know where I am or what to do. What happens if you don't come back?"

"You'll be fine. Just wait there. I need to go back for Bryan."

While Angela agonized over being left on her own in a hostile, enemy countryside, she understood the man's need to go back for his comrade. She couldn't fault him for that, and in her heart, she felt the same way. All the way down the mountainside, she had been praying for Bryan's safety. He had risked his life to save hers, and his death, if that had happened, was going to haunt her for the rest of her life.

Mordecai turned to go, then looked back over his shoulder at Disler.

"You're gonna be okay. The keys are under the front seat. If I'm not back in an hour, take the truck and head down the highway, going west, and you'll hit the coast. There's a scarf in the front seat. Wrap it around your head in the fashion worn by some of the women in this country. It will help deflect any curiosity. Once you get to the coast, stay with the truck. I've put a GPS tracking device on it, and I'll notify my command that they need to send a team in to pick you up."

She nodded her assent reluctantly, then said, "I won't leave until you find him and get him back."

Mordecai smiled, then began his fast-paced trek back up the side of the hill.

351

*****

FIFTY-FIVE

THE ZAGROS MOUNTAINS
SOUTHWESTERN IRAN
DAY NINETEEN   6:30 AM

Bryan lay in the dirt on the safe side of the top of the mountain, just below the lip of the ridge. He had just managed to get himself over the crest of the hill before the first of the Tomahawks hit the facility. The shock wave had been unbelievable; throwing him a dozen feet or so down the hillside and away from the blast. His hearing was all but shot, and when the second missile struck the same set of coordinates, the shock wave had not been as bad, but his hearing was definitely going to take time to recover, if it ever did.

He rolled over to his stomach and checked his limbs. Everything moved, and but for a splitting headache, he felt pretty good considering the shock to his system. He was more than satisfied that the Iranians were in no condition to continue their pursuit, if any of them had even managed to survive. He got up to his knees, felt a little dizzy, figured he might have a minor concussion, but decided that he wasn't about to let that hold him back.

He remembered his radio, and he clicked it on then spoke softly into the headset.

"Can you hear me?" he said, then almost laughed. He wasn't sure he'd be able to listen to a response anyway because of the possible damage to his hearing. When he didn't get an immediate response, he wondered if his earpiece might have been damaged by one or both of the explosions?

When he was ready to concede that something was wrong with his hearing, he heard two distinct clicks, which made him smile.

"I'm okay," he whispered, grateful that hearing wasn't completely destroyed. "I'm gonna start down now."

"I'm on my way back up to you."

"You don't need to," Bryan said. "Just get the woman out of here."

"She's fine, hero. Besides, you might need me to cover your retreat."

Bryan smiled again. If he was honest with himself, maybe he could use a little help.

He started down the mountain, and five minutes later, he ran into the smiling face of Mordecai Ben-Gurion.

"You okay," he asked.

"A little dizzy," Bryan replied, "and everything you say sounds like you're speaking underwater, but I'll live."

"Disler is waiting at the truck. We'll get there pretty fast. It's a lot faster going downhill than up."

"You take the lead," Bryan said. "But look back once in a while, just in case I fall over or walk into a tree."

Mordecai raised his eyebrows in concern, then noticed that Bryan was smiling.

"See if you can keep up with me, old man," said Mordecai.

He then took the lead and led them quickly down the hill.

****

While they were scrambling through the tree line towards their hidden vehicle, neither man was fully aware of what was going on behind the scenes.

In Washington DC, at the CIA's Incident Room, the President was joined by top members of the Pentagon, his Secretary of State, the Secretary of Defense, the Directors of the CIA and the FBI, John Taylor on the flatscreen, and his trusted advisor, the former Senator from Minnesota and now Vice President, John Dabney.

Before the missile attack, an Air Force Airborne early warning and control plane, called an AEW&C, flew a high altitude flight path off the coast of Iran. This sophisticated aircraft is used offensively to direct fighters to their target locations, and defensively to direct counter attacks on enemy forces, both on the ground and in the air. Its radars were able to allow the operators to distinguish between friendly and hostile aircraft literally hundreds of miles away.

Also in the air were two carrier based EA-68 prowlers. The Prowler was a twin-engine aircraft used to jam enemy radar and to gather radio intelligence from the skies. Each one was armed with HARM missiles, designed to be used against enemy radar systems. The HARM hones in on electronic transmissions coming from surface-to-air radar sites. They also carry SHRIKE missiles which are also used to disable enemy radars.

The AEW&C assigned to coordinate the attack on the research facilities was controlling the skies along the Persian Gulf coast of Iran to monitor the possibility of any Iranian response to the Tomahawk attack on the research facility.

Initially, the skies were clear. The Prowlers effectively disabled the Iranians coastal radar sites, electronically destroying three of them, but sooner or later, word would get out about the attack and the Iranians would launch planes to assess the situation and to counter the assault.

Six navy F-18's, on station just off the coast of Iran, were there to fly support for the two Stealth bombers coming in from Tierra del Fuego, an archipelago province off the coast of Argentina. Because the Iranian radar systems were disabled, their presence went undetected. They were armed with an assortment of air-to-air missiles, air-to-ground missiles, and air-to-ground guided bombs.

In addition to the USS Enterprise and the rest of the carrier's support ships which were sailing just to the south of the Straits of Hormuz, a second carrier, the USS Ronald Reagan, was steaming into a support position just off the coast of Yemen to backup the Enterprise should anything go wrong.

Once the radar facilities on the western coast were neutralized by the Prowlers, the Ohio-class nuclear submarine *Georgia,* situated in the waters twenty miles off the coast of Dubai, fired off two of its Tomahawk cruise missiles without ever breaking the surface of the water. These were the two that struck the research facility. The *Georgia* carried a total of 154 Tomahawks, so they were ready to fire more if asked.

The geostatic satellite over Iran was still focused in on the research facility. The missile strike initially obliterated the attempts to do a damage analysis, due to the extensive amount of dust and dirt thrown up by the two big explosions.

As the dust cleared, an analysis was conducted, and the result was presented to the President by an Air Force General assigned to the Joint Chiefs of

Staff.

"Both missiles hit the target, Mr. President, but the depression created by the explosions is not deep enough to enable our analysts to conclude that the structure is completely destroyed."

"Your recommendation?" the President asked.

"We have two Stealth B2 Spirit's coming in from Tierra del Fuego to finish the job. They're each carrying two MOP's, so we can easily drop one or two which will likely do the trick."

The MOP's, or Massive Ordinance Penetrators, were commonly called bunker-buster bombs. Each one was designed to blast through up to 200 feet of concrete, so it was highly likely that only one would be needed to do the job.

"Would a few more Tomahawks do the job at the research lab?" the President asked. He hated to send the B2's into country if the use of more missiles would do the trick.

"Possibly," the Air Force General replied, "but considering the nature of the threat that their research facility presents, it wouldn't hurt to make sure that everything is completely obliterated."

"Any negatives," the President asked. He looked at the faces around the table.

The Secretary of Defense shook his head. "With their radars down and our F18's in the immediate vicinity, the risk to our bombers will be minimal to non-existent."

The President sighed. "Very well. Let's do it."

****

Ahmad Farazi, the Chief Medical Researcher at the facility, was running late. He'd overslept, something he abhorred when it was an excuse used by one of his subordinates, but after all, he was the Chief, and if he was a little late, then who was going to complain?

Petrov might. He'd been so eager to start going through Disler's research that he'd taken the unusual step of spending the night in a bunk room that was located in the same hallway several dozen yards from the site of the small lab that had been prepared for Disler to do her work. In fact, it wouldn't surprise him if Petrov had already started to work with Disler, just to get an early start on the day. If he had, that would likely temper his annoyance with Farazi's tardy arrival.

Once Farazi came to grips with the idea that he was entitled to be late if he wanted to, he decided to stop off for a late breakfast at a roadside grill where he lounged around for a while, thinking about how he was going to get Angela Disler started with the genetic alteration of the DNA of the Marburg virus.

He was convinced that the call he allowed her to make to her family had affected her in a way that would assure her cooperation. She had demonstrated that much by giving them the password that enabled his superiors to gain entry into her corporate computer. They'd downloaded quite a bit of material, so the first thing he would have her do is sort through the data, which he would then turn over to his research team. After that, he would have her suit up in the big lab on the sixth level to formally work on the molecules themselves.

But he had another, more pressing concern. They still had to deal with the sticky issue of Disler's family back in Los Angeles.

Farazi bore no ill will towards her husband and their children. They were just pawns in a much bigger game. And while he didn't have children of his own, he did have nieces and nephews, most of whom still lived in Pakistan, and he found himself here in this present situation in part because of the implied threats to hurt them by the ISI.

The murder of Disler's children was not something he wanted on his conscience, so if she did cooperate and didn't hold back, he would do everything in his power to get them released, even if it later incurred the wrath of those in the Iranian military who were funding this particular venture.

Up until now, he felt pretty good about the way things were going. The Iranians were paying him very handsomely for his work, as were his secret masters in the ISI (Inter-Services Intelligence) in Pakistan. They knew what he was doing for the Iranians, so as long as he passed on the information gleaned from Disler to the ISI, his extended family back in Pakistan would be left untouched, and he would end up being a very wealthy man.

He felt sorry for Disler herself. The Quds had no intention of freeing her, and once she revealed her genetic technique, keeping her alive would no longer be important, and if that gave him pause at all, it only served to convince him that his particular standing with the Iranian Quds was nothing to be taken lightly.

He didn't trust them at all, and he'd been working on an exit plan that would go into place should he get even a whiff of a hint that his services were no longer needed. He had secretly arranged for a fishing boat to be ready to transport him to Dubai with little or no advance notice. Once in Dubai, he would turn himself into the American Embassy where he hoped that he would be given asylum in exchange for the details about the Quds plan to turn the virus loose on Israel and the western world.

He left the roadside restaurant and made his way through several small villages until he came to the turnoff for the research lab. He wound his way up the road, listening to music on the radio until he suddenly became aware that something was terribly wrong.

There was an awful lot of dust in the air, and up ahead he spotted the burned out remnants of what remained of a bus. It was lying on the side of the road, and the guardhouse that protected the entrance gate was nowhere to be seen.

He recognized what was left of the bus. It was the one that brought in the morning change of guard.

Had it caught fire? If so, why was it lying in pieces on its side? And where in the world were the people?

He pulled over to the side of the road, jumped out, and ran the rest of the way up the hill to discover that all that remained of the guard house was a cracked slab of cement that had served as its foundation.

What registered next were the remains of a second bus. It was no longer a bus but rather a mangled hunk of metal slabs torn apart by what must have been a massive explosion.

In his state of immediate confusion, it didn't register at first that the building that concealed the entry to the underground facility was also missing, but when his gaze finally strayed over in that direction, it started to register that the base was no more.

In its' place was a massive crater.

He stood frozen to the ground, unable at first to move. It was incomprehensible that the lab that he had so carefully designed and equipped, and the people he'd chosen to work with were now completely gone.

He nervously ran his hand through his hair, then finally managed to get his feet to start cooperating. He walked towards the spot where the building used to be, the one that fronted the base by the side of the mountain. Aside from a very large crater and a rockslide that had covered the spot where the outbuilding used to be, every trace of the building—the elevator system, and even the cement encased emergency stairwells—were completely gone or buried under tons of rock and slag from the mountain above.

What happened? An earthquake? An explosion from within? What if it was—"

He stopped in his tracks again, paralyzed by the thought that the base might be gone because of an airstrike.

It then occurred to him that if he hadn't overslept, he might have been down in the bottom of the facility when whatever had happened took place.

He dropped to his knees and prostrated himself face down in the dirt. Through uncontrollable tears, tempered by fits of almost hysterical laughter, he gave thanks to *Allah* for sparing his life from whatever catastrophe had befallen his companions.

****

The satellite view of the scene in the situation room revealed the arrival and presence of one man at the research facility. Those who were seated at the table seemed to hold their breath. They watched as the man began to wander around near the side of the mountain where the entrance to the lab once existed.

"He can't believe his eyes," said the Vice President who watched as the man fell to his knees, then prostrated himself in the dirt.

"It looks like he's praying," said the Secretary of Defense.

"Can you blame him?" replied the Secretary of State.

They watched with interest as the prostrated man quickly got to his feet and ran back to his vehicle. Throwing caution to the wind, he sped away from the base and backed out onto the highway, then drove off at high speed in the direction from which he'd arrived.

"Lucky son-of-a-bitch," said an Air Force General who was watching the real time ticking away of the clock that was monitoring the arrival of the diverted B2 bombers.

Vice-President Dabney chuckled.

"Perhaps Allah was listening to his prayers."

****

Bryan and Mordecai reached the truck in just under fifteen minutes. It took a little longer than Mordecai had expected, but he knew Bryan was hurting, and he had to stop several times to wait for him to get past his dizziness.

There had been no more missile strikes, so both men assumed that the facility was destroyed. They threw their packs in the back of the truck, reloaded their weapons, then climbed into the cab where Angela was patiently waiting.

"Thank God you made it," she said to Bryan. She gave him a hug. "I was afraid—"

But she didn't say more. She didn't need to. Her gratitude for what he'd done was apparent, and he considered himself lucky that he'd been able to get her out.

They drove down the highway, heading west, and within thirty minutes they were making their way out of the mountains. They'd seen no sign of a military call-up, so they could only hope that it remained that way.

Angela had been squirming around in her seat, and finally, she decided that she had to speak up.

"Any chance we can pull over to the side of the road for a minute. I have to relieve myself."

Mordecai looked over at Bryan who cracked a smile. This was something they'd never even thought about.

"No problem, Doctor." He pulled over to the side of the road. "Just stay close to the truck in case another vehicle happens by. I promise we won't look."

They were next to a patch of desert scrub, so they were pretty much out in the open, but because they'd seen no other cars since they came out of the mountains, he was willing to take a chance and let her take care of her business.

Angela climbed out of the truck and disappeared behind it.

Mordecai turned off the motor and rolled down his window. It was then that he spotted two high altitude jet contrails.

Both he and Bryan climbed out of the cab and looked up into the sky

"What is that?" asked Mordecai.

"My guess would be a pair of B2 bombers," Bryan replied.

"You think they're headed to the research lab?"

"Looks like it."

They continued to watch as the bombers passed over the nearest range of mountains, and as Angela came around the side of the truck, a large mushroom cloud suddenly appeared in the distance, rising up into the sky from behind the highest ridge of the mountain range.

"My God!" said Angela, Her hand covered her mouth in a gesture of fear. "What is God's name is that?"

The sound of an explosion, like distant thunder, finally reached their ears.

"That's the end of their plan to create a biological weapon," said Bryan. He watched the cloud rise further; then he opened the door of the cab.

"C'mon, let's go. Get into the truck. We need to get out of here before the military starts closing the highways."

****

The apparent rescue of Angela Disler by the two field agents was greeted with genuine relief by President Lindhurst and the other members of his select group who received the good news from Taylor in Egypt who had just gotten off the satellite phone with Bryan Harb. The destruction of the lab and the rescue of the hostage triggered a few moments of backslapping celebration.

During the final hour before the destruction of the laboratory base, the

Secretary of State had been working the phones with American allies and others throughout Western Europe. Once these countries were briefed on the Iranians intent, even Russia and China were forced to concede that the Iranians posed a threat to the entire civilized world. With promises of support coming in from all over, the President felt confident that the action he'd authorized would have the support of all concerned.

At the last minute, the President authorized the use of a single Cruise missile to strike the Quds compound in Tehran where the hackers who intercepted Angela Disler's email to the Pentagon were located. This center had previously been involved in other hacking attacks of US military facilities, and since it was confirmed to be an Iranian military facility, it was adjudged to be a legitimate target for aggressive suppression. No accurate intelligence information on fatalities was ever released by the Iranian government, but Israeli sources on the ground put the casualty figures at somewhere in the neighborhood of fifty.

Once the raids were concluded and all forces returned safely to their bases, the President held a private meeting with a senior Iranian diplomat who was summoned from his government's special interest section which was housed within the Pakistani embassy in Washington, DC. Called a *protecting power*, the Pakistani's had agreed to represent Iranian interests within the United States. Conversely, the United States had a similar arrangement with the Swiss and operated their own special interest section within the Swiss Embassy in the city of Tehran.

In no uncertain terms, the President advised the diplomat that the United States, with the cooperation of more than a dozen nations, and acting with a mandate approved by thirty-two more countries, including Russia and China, had destroyed the biological research facility and the Quds hacking operation as a warning to Iran that they would never be allowed to develop or possess any weapons of mass destruction. He went on to state that the penalty for any retaliation by the Iranian government or any of its surrogate terrorist groups against the United States or any of its Allies, in particular the State of Israel, would be considered a declaration of war and would be met with the harshest of responses; responses that would include, in part, the complete destruction of its civilian government and its military capability.

But the President was not a foolish man. He knew that he had backed the Iranians into a corner, so he offered an olive branch as a way to possibly diffuse the situation. He told the diplomat that if the Iranians publicly renounced any future biological weapons development, and if they cooperated unconditionally and fully with unannounced and unfettered inspections of all military and civilian facilities by the IAEA, as well as inspections conducted by experts in biological weapons, then the United States and it's Allies would be willing to speed up the timetable for withdrawal of the remaining sanctions that had so paralyzed the general population of Iran.

The President didn't hold out much hope that the Iranians would quickly agree to the offer, but he did believe that there was a chance that the suddenness of the attack and the completeness of the devastation inflicted by the bombers would convince the Iranian government that any continuation of the same course of demonstrated recklessness would surely result in the destruction of their civilization.

*****

FIFTY-SIX

Amir, the young Iranian security guard, did exactly as he'd been told to do by Bryan. He ran for his life.

He sprinted down the hill as fast as his feet would carry him, stumbling once, scraping his right arm from wrist to elbow, and painfully bruising his hip. But he kept on running, convinced that the Iranian soldiers coming up the hill from the base on the other side of the ridge would conclude that he had willingly helped the American soldiers. Because of that fear, he had no doubt that they would likely shoot him dead or torture him until he confessed to whatever they wanted him to say.

He tried to use the trees for cover, zig-zagging like a madman, but never losing site of the direction he was headed. He would do what the American told him, stay to the East until he reached the highway, then head to the North and keep on going. He was mulling over what he would tell his parents when the first explosion hit.

The ground shook violently, causing him to lose his balance and throwing him to the ground. When the sound wave struck a moment later, he grabbed his ears and screamed, sure that the world was ending. When he didn't immediately die, he rolled over and saw a massive dust cloud that seemed to him to blot out the sky.

He'd been right in his assessment of the situation. Something awful had actually happened. He got to his feet and slapped the dust and dirt off his clothes, took a few moments to examine a scrape on his arm, then slowly walked down the hillside, no longer worried about the pursuing soldiers who were now more than likely on their way to visit Allah.

The second blast was not as traumatic for him, likely because he was much farther down the mountain and more sheltered from the shock wave. But the third explosion, the one caused by the MOP, nearly gave him a heart attack. The force of that explosion was so great that he wrongfully concluded that the American's had dropped a nuclear bomb. He started running again, worried about nuclear fallout, and praying to Allah to spare his life.

When he finally got to the highway, he stayed hidden for several days until a military response to the bombing had come and gone. Hungry, cold and tired, having lived only on water from a tiny creek, he got back out on the highway and caught a ride with a local fruit vendor who took him to the outskirts of the village where his parents currently resided.

His welcome home had been a joyous occasion, as his parents had believed that he'd been killed in the blasts. He told them what had happened, and because the Iranian authorities believed that he had been one of the casualties, his father wisely concluded that word of his survival would get around and that remaining in Iran was no longer safe.

Two days later, Amir and his parents, as well as his three sisters, all crossed the border from Iran into Turkey where they planned to start a new life.

****

After an uneventful nighttime exfiltration from Iran by a rigid-hulled boat that transferred them to an American submarine, Angela and her two rescuers were then taken to the USS Enterprise, a carrier on station just outside the Gulf of Oman, in the Arabian Sea. After clearance from a navy EMT, Angela, Mordecai, and Bryan were flown from the carrier directly to *Landstuhl Regional Medical Center* in Germany, the largest US medical center outside of the continental United States.

All three were subjected to extensive medical testing before being pronounced well enough to travel. Angela and Mordecai were released within forty-eight hours, but Bryan was kept an additional week because of his concussion symptoms.

Angela was flown from Germany directly to *Joint Base Andrews* in Washington DC, where she went through an extensive debriefing conducted by the CIA before being allowed to meet with her husband and children. She gave them explicit details about the research facility, and what doctors Petrov and Farazi had said to her during her incarceration. She confirmed that Bryan had shot and killed Petrov, but she had no idea whether or not Farazi had been killed when the lab was destroyed.

When they finally decided to allow her to rejoin her family, the joyous reunion took place in a suite at the Willard Hotel, a famous DC landmark. A lot of tears were shed, but all in all, it was a time for the family to decompress and to take a very hard look at how their lives were about to undergo a dramatic change.

The first order of business for the government to deal with was the future risks to Angela and her family. Discussions were held about the situation at the highest levels of government, and it was decided that Angela's possible Nobel Prize nomination should be quickly nipped in the bud. Given what already happened to her and the fact that there was always a chance that she could be a target again, it was decided that it would be better for Angela and her family if she didn't receive the type of press attention that a Nobel nomination would garner.

At first, Angela was opposed to the removal of her name as a candidate. She argued that her work had been legitimate, and despite the fact that she'd accidentally made a very uncomfortable discovery relating to the potential weaponizing of the Marburg virus, she stressed that the good that would flow to cancer patients from her technique for piggybacking chemo to an ordinary flu virus was undeniably ground-breaking, and therefore, worthy of Nobel consideration. But when it was pointed out to her that the limelight would make her a target of certain countries and terrorist groups that would love to get their hands on her and her knowledge, not to mention the lone wolf fanatics who might attempt to come after her in retaliation for the risk that she'd created to all of mankind, Angela quickly had a "*Come to Jesus Moment*" about her personal safety and the risk to her husband and children. She agreed to forego a nomination, preferring instead to enter herself and her family in the Federal Witness Protection Program.

Her passport was taken, as was her husbands, and the entire family was given new identities and sufficient time to learn their backstories. When at last they were ready to adopt their new personas, they disappeared completely from public view and were relocated by the United States Marshall's Office to a very small town in the state of Maryland.

The children were home schooled for a year by a government approved private tutor to give them an opportunity to mentally accept their new names and identities. Henrik established his medical practice in the local community, and the only concession he demanded and was given was hospital privileges at Johns-Hopkins under his new identity.

For her part, Angela resumed her genetic research into developing viral vaccines at an undisclosed CIA research lab located in Northern Virginia. Her previous research was scrubbed from the Zurich computers, and it was filed away in Utah, at the Intelligence Community Comprehensive National Cybersecurity Initiative Data Center, an impossibly long name for a data storage facility for the United States Intelligence Community. And while the NSA oversees all operations at the installation, the precise mission of the facility itself remains a classified secret to this day.

It took almost a year, but eventually the family's new life established a degree of normalcy.

*****

Bryan spent two weeks in debriefings at a CIA facility in Maryland before being given a forty-eight-hour pass to get out and unwind. He spent the two days in New York, visiting the 9-11 Memorial, eating at a couple of trendy restaurants, catching a Broadway show, and walking for hours, embracing the freedom to do so without having to look over his shoulder continually.

****

After speaking with Eli by phone, Mordecai left Germany on a flight to Switzerland where he switched to an El Al commercial flight that took him home to Tel Aviv. The longer, indirect route home was a standard technique for covering his tracks in and out of Israel, and even though he was using a passport with a false identity, new facial recognition cameras at certain Middle Eastern airports made international travel even that much more difficult.

Once he was back home in Tel Aviv, Mordecai met with Eli Ben-

Jehuda, the head of the Mossad. He also went through extensive debriefings, but during the process, he was allowed to stay at home and to renew his relationship with Rachel.

After consultations initiated by Eli with the Prime Minister and selected members of the Knesset, it was decided that a commendation was needed to recognize Mordecai's actions during the course of the hunt for Disler. In a very private ceremony, attended by selected members of the government, Mordecai was awarded the Israeli Medal of Valor, the nation's highest military decoration. Along with the medal, he received several privileges such as tax reduction and the right to be buried in the *Helkat Gedolei Ha'Uma* cemetery on Mount Herzl. The medal was designed in the shape of the Star of David, with a sword and olive branch on the left side. It came attached to a yellow ribbon, a reference to the yellow star that Jews were forced to wear during the Holocaust.

His now fiancee Rachael, her younger sister and the sister's new fiancee—a development that Mordecai had not foreseen when he first spoke about her to Bryan—were all present at the ceremony. They celebrated the occasion afterward by inviting close friends and relatives to join them for dinner at a restaurant overlooking the beach in Tel Aviv.

The guests were led to believe that the event was a celebration of Mordecai's engagement to Rachael, but Mordecai and Rachael paused during the festivities to pray together while they watched the sun set over the Mediterranean Sea, knowing full well that but for the grace of God, he could well have died in Iran.

****

President Lindhurst did what he could to keep the wraps on the details surrounding the destruction of the Iranian research facility, but within a few days of the bombing, word of the raid leaked out into the public domain.

At first there were strong public condemnations based on the initial reports that the Iranians had been after American research directly related to biological weapons. Most of it was directed at Iran, but a groundswell of anger began to build when journalists began to question what the Iranians were after and why was the US in possession of biological warfare information in the first place?

President Lindhurst took the unusual step of holding a press conference that was addressed directly to the nation. He explained that an unnamed researcher had been working on a way to genetically alter viruses in order to develop vaccines for viruses known to present the possibility of mass casualties in the event of a pandemic outbreak. He stressed that the research was in response to global warming and the understanding of experts that a warming of the world's climate would hasten the mutation of certain viral diseases which might then enable them to develop new pathways for transmission. He went on to explain that the researcher inadvertently hit upon a genetic alteration which would allow the airborne transmission of an unnamed but particularly deadly virus.

He advised the nation, with great sadness, that the researcher in question had been kidnapped by the Iranians and that she died during the bombing raid which destroyed their research facility. He assured the country that her research was destroyed during the attack.

He went on to advise the nation that he intended to present a proposal to the United Nations that an agency be established under the auspices of the UN to keep track of all governmental and private research being conducted on deadly viral strains in order to assure the world that there would be no risk of the unlawful spread of similar future discoveries to hostile parties or governments intent on using such knowledge to create biological weapons of war. He conceded that the establishment of such an agency would likely require a UN resolution, but in talks with more than a dozen nations, including all of the member countries of the UN Security Council, he was optimistic that such a resolution would face very little in the way of opposition.

*****

The day after his press conference, he accepted the resignation of CIA Director Hamilton Granger. The official explanation for his departure was for personal health considerations, but insiders in Washington understood that the

President had been extremely disappointed by Granger's inability to make important decisions promptly.

*****

The following day, Dan Taylor entered the Oval Office where he was warmly greeted by President Lindhurst. The two men took seats in the middle of the room with Taylor on the couch and the President in his usual chair. Coffee was served by a steward, and once they were past the small talk, the President got directly to the point.

"As you know, Dan, Hamilton has submitted his resignation, and I've accepted it, and frankly, between you and I, his failure to advise me of the Marburg discovery at the time it was made was a breach of his primary responsibility... and that made him unfit to serve."

He held Taylor's glance before going on.

"The information he sat on was a matter of national security, and from where I'm sitting, that action was inexcusable."

Taylor nodded imperceptibly. He wasn't quite sure why the President was telling him all of this. He'd had no role in the resignation, and although he believed that the change was completely necessary, it was definitely beyond his pay grade to be privy to this type of information, and for a moment, he wondered if he was about to suffer the same fate.

Lindhurst noticed a flicker of concern on Taylor's face, and it caused him to smile.

"You're no doubt wondering why I'm telling you all of this?"

Taylor nodded. "Yes, sir, I am."

"Well, you can rest assured, Dan, I'm not asking for your resignation."

Inwardly, Taylor felt an enormous sense of relief. He'd never before had a personal meeting with the President, and in the back of his mind was a nagging fear that heads would roll after what had happened and that his would be on the chopping block.

"I'm very glad to hear that, sir."

"Instead, it is my intention to appoint you to fill the Agency vacancy." He smiled broadly. "I'd like you to become the next Director of the CIA."

Taylor couldn't believe his ears. He hadn't seen this coming and as the President's words sank in he couldn't suppress his smile.

"I'm very flattered, Mr. President. I'd be honored to serve my country in that capacity."

"That's just great, Dan!"

Lindhurst got to his feet and extended his hand, and as Taylor rose and shook it, Lindhurst added, "You showed great intelligence, calmness and foresight during the Marburg crisis, Dan. You're just what the Agency needs in the form of good leadership."

"Thank you, sir. I'll do my best to live up to your expectations."

"I'm sure you will, Dan."

The President gave him a wink.

"Just remember to keep me in the loop and we'll get along just fine."

*****

Three months later, at the invitation of the State Department, Jennifer Donahue, Shari Thompson and Mitzi Roberts were invited to the White House for a private meeting with President Lindhurst. When the three women were taken to the China Room to await their audience with the President, they discovered a young man standing there who was engrossed in a conversation with his Secret Service escort.

Bryan smiled when they entered the room. He'd been told that they would be present as part of the Presidential audience.

"Hello!" he said when they approached. "I heard you were responsible for tracking down the men who were holding the Disler family as hostages."

Thompson flashed him a smile and quickly spoke up.

"That's right. Of course, I can't take all the credit, but we did catch a few breaks." She studied him carefully then held out her hand. "Shari Thompson, and you are…?"

"Bryan Harb," he said with a guarded smile as he shook her hand.

Donahue and Roberts exchanged a glance. Thompson was moving in on this poor guy like a lioness in heat.

He let go of her hand and turned to Roberts. "I'm Bryan."

"Mitzi," she said, smiling. "Mitzi Roberts."

"Nice to meet you." He shook her hand briefly, looked over at Donahue, then grinned.

"By default, that makes you Jennifer Donahue." He shook her hand, but this time he didn't let go.

"Congratulations, Detective," he told her. "Your idea to monitor all calls coming into LA from Iran was brilliant. I was told that you narrowed the search down to the area served by a single cell tower."

She smiled as he slowly released her hand.

"We got lucky. It was Shari and Mitzi who found the broker who rented the house to an Iranian male."

Thompson, who could already sense his obvious interest in Donahue, smiled tightly. She and Roberts were out of the running.

She winked at Donahue, then turned to Roberts.

"Hey, Mitz, let me show you the Kennedy dinner plates. That Jackie really had great taste when it came to decorating this place."

She took Roberts by the arm and together they walked off leaving Donahue alone with Bryan.

"Your partners seem to have abandoned us," Bryan said.

"Embarrassing isn't it?"

"I'll have to thank them later," he said with a grin.

They spoke for almost ten minutes, a conversation that was free flowing, comfortable, and full of laughter and smiles. Both of them seemed to realize there was an undeniable mutual attraction, so when he asked her to join him for dinner that evening, she found herself saying she would.

When a burly Secret Service agent who'd been watching them all from a post by the doorway advised them that the President was ready for them to go in, they made their way to the door of the Oval Office, and once inside, the President regaled them with praise and thanked them on behalf of a grateful nation.

*****

Ali Niroomad was eventually tried by a US military tribunal at an undisclosed military facility in the state of Georgia. For national security reasons, the trial was never made public, so no mention of it ever made its way into the public domain. He received a life sentence to be served in the United States Disciplinary Barracks at Fort Leavenworth, in Leavenworth Kansas.

At his request, his family back in Iran was never notified that he was still alive, out of fear that they would be retaliated against by the current Iranian regime if they ever discovered that he wasn't dead.

*****

In the weeks that followed the attacks on the research laboratory and the Quds facility, the Supreme Leader, Grand Ayatollah Seyyed Ali Hosseini Khamenei, ordered a complete shake-up within the Iranian government. Claiming that the plan for biologicals was a plot hatched by certain dissident members within the Quds force, and seeking to deflect any blame from himself, he ordered more than twenty senior officers within the Quds to be taken into custody.

The Quds, of course, to no one's surprise, were rapidly restructured with a leadership that was completely loyal to Khamenei.

*****

As the months went by, global attention shifted to the conflicts in Syria and Yemen, and while the bombings and the Iranian plans for a biological warfare attack had dominated the news cycle for a solid month, it soon became apparent that the entire event was destined to become just one of many footnotes in the continuing struggle between Iran and the West.

The United States and Israel signed a new mutual assistance pact which was publicly supported by more than twenty-five countries. This had a profound effect on the Iranians, particularly after a visit by the Russian Ambassador who privately insisted that the Iranians cease their plan to develop nuclear and biological weapons.

The message previously delivered by the President to the Iranian Foreign Minister apparently had the desired effect. The Iranians made no overt effort to retaliate against the US or Israel, and surprisingly, they accepted the proposed offer by President Lindhurst to renounce any future nuclear and biological weapons development in exchange for a faster withdrawal of some of the more meaningful sanctions that had paralyzed the Iranian population for such a long time.

Of course, the Iranians couldn't be persuaded to admit any of this publicly, so in exchange for their agreement to cooperate unconditionally and fully with unannounced inspections by the IAEA, the United States agreed to let them move forward at a face-saving pace.

This process began with an announcement by President Lindhurst that the United States and it's allies would immediately remove the sanctions on Iran as they related to medical pharmaceuticals. In return, the Iranian Foreign Minister publicly referred to the gesture as a concrete first step towards a reset of the relationship between their two countries.

*****

POSTSCRIPT

Eleven months after the decimation of the Iranian's biological facility, two Israeli *Shayetet 13* Agents silently slipped into the waters of the Mediterranean Sea from a Morena-class, rigid-hulled inflatable boat that now floated just about a mile off the coast of *Byblos sur mer,* in Lebanon.

The S'13 was one of Israel's special operations units; part of the Israel Defense Forces, and among other responsibilities, the men of this unit specialized in sea-to-land incursions as well as counter-terrorism. The S'13 was one of the most secretive units in the Israeli military, and their expertise and heroism were considered to be on a par with that of the US Navy Seals and the British *Special Boat Service.*

Using a portable GPS device that was fitted with a low light illumination, the two commandos silently made their way through the warm, dark waters towards the shore. They wore dark black wetsuits and custom-made scuba gear that was designed to diffuse their breathing exhales so as not to leave a trail of bubbles across the water's surface.

The waters of the Med were crystal clear, but the nighttime sky was moonless. This had been a critical requirement for going forward with the mission, as were several other events that had fortuitously come together on this particular evening. They carried small handheld lights, but they were only for use in an emergency. Each man was armed with an M24 sniper rifle and a holstered Glock pistol worn across their chests.

Their destination was the city's small marina, one that was filled with fishing and pleasure boats. Byblos was about forty-two kilometers north of Beruit, and the site was first settled approximately nine thousand years BC. It still carried the reputation of being one of the oldest cities in the world.

Along the coastline was a two lane road that was separated from the beach by a waist-high stone wall. On the land side of the road was a hillside that was covered with historically beautiful, mostly renovated homes, which were owned by some of the wealthiest families in the Middle East. Most of them had large stone patios that took advantage of the view of the sea.

The particular residence that the commandos were interested in was three stories in height. The lowest, first-floor level sat just about twenty-five feet above the highway. It was where the kitchen and the living room were located, so it was natural that the patio would be located there, too.

A twenty-foot table sat out on the deck of the patio, surrounded by more than a dozen chairs. The table could easily seat sixteen people, and the current owner frequently had parties where every chair was spoken for.

The S'13 had been tapping the owner's phone for several months and had kept the house under around-the-clock surveillance by a team of watchers. The surveillance had gone on for more than a week, and during that time period, they discovered that the owner was planning a dinner party, so the timetable for the operation was moved up, and plans were made in Tel Aviv to push forward with the mission.

Outside the residence, on the front of the house, members of the surveillance team kept track of the comings and goings of the inhabitants. And while there were any number of ways they could pull off the objective of the mission, they wanted their actions to make the statement… *"Israel never forgets."*

On this particular evening, the weather was still quite warm, and the patio was filled with a group of revelers who ate a long, slow meal while consuming more than a few bottles of imported chardonnay.

One of the men stationed out in front of the house took a look at his watch. It was five minutes after eleven p.m, and the streets of the neighborhood were still quite busy. Lebanon was known to be a country that liked to party, and after all the wars for so many years, the inhabitants lived life as if there was no tomorrow.

What time to make the approach had been the topic of many discussions before a final decision was made. It was felt by the powers back in Tel Aviv that late at night would be best, but not so late as to leave the street side watchers as the only people out and about. For them, it would be far easier to escape from the scene on foot if there were others around to confuse the police who might respond if something went wrong. So eleven-fifteen p.m. had been chosen as the time for the mission to go forward. It would be late enough to minimize foot and car traffic out on the street in front of the house, while affording the watchers a chance to get away without detection.

The commandos popped their heads up out of the water just outside the point where the breakers began. Bobbing quietly, the two men scanned the beach on both sides of the target residence. God seemed to be with them, for there was no one down on the beach, and while lights were on in some of the houses, there were no people outside on their patios who might spot them when they came up on the shore.

The taller of the two commandos used a pair of binoculars to get a good look at the party guests. There were men and women of various ages, all of whom were nicely dressed as befitted a dinner party at the home of such a generous host. He directed his attention to the head of the table and a very small smile crept over his face. Their target was seated in his usual seat, deeply engrossed in a story being told by one of the guests sitting farther down the table. A chorus of laughter was heard from the group as the tall commando tapped his partner on the arm and the two of them swam silently forward in their approach to the target.

When they arrived at the shore, they slowly crawled up onto the beach. Neither one stood up, and from where they were lying, both of them knew that they were virtually invisible to anyone who happened to be passing by.

There were several small clusters of rocks on the beach, and if the frogmen had been casually spotted, they would have appeared to be nothing more than one of those clusters.

In knee high water, both men removed the waterproof rifle cases that were strapped to a sling that covered their backs. Each one opened their respective cases, and both of them produced their high caliber M24 silenced sniper rifles with *Leupold* scopes that were already attached.

Safety's on; they once again scanned the beach for any possible spectators, then each man took a few moments to make the necessary adjustments to their scopes: adjustments designed to take into account the earth's rotation, gravity, temperature, distance, and the wind.

Doctor Ahmad Farazi, the Chief Medical Researcher who escaped from the Iranian research facility just before the arrival of the B2 bombers was the owner of the house and the host of this particular dinner party.

Several months after the destruction of the lab, the Mossad was given a copy of the film from the satellite camera that was taken of the base just after the initial missile strike. They saw the man who arrived at the base, the one who looked around before dropping to his knees and fleeing. They took the time to run the man's face through their own facial recognition software, and once Farazi's identity was confirmed, and once they learned from the Disler debriefing about his role in the Marburg scheme, a worldwide search was conducted for his whereabouts.

When the lab was destroyed, Farazi apparently decided to use the opportunity to extricate himself from his Iranian masters and from the Pakistani ISI. He knew that they would assume that he had been killed along with all of the others in the bombing, and since he had plenty of money carefully salted away, he decided to let them accept that conclusion.

He fled from Iran on a boat to Dubai where he caught a flight to Lebanon. He used a false passport to make the journey—it was easy if you had enough foresight and money—and since he was pretty sure that no one was looking for him, he set up a residence under the name he used on the phony passport.

Unknown to the doctor, the Israelis had been monitoring his relatives phones in Pakistan, and when he finally called to let them know that he was alive and would eventually send for them, the Israeli's were listening. They tracked him down to his new residence in Lebanon, and they watched him sporadically for almost six months. It gave him time to get settled, while giving them the opportunity to monitor all of his calls and emails to determine who his associates might be. And when it became crystal clear that he was no longer connected with either the Iranians or the Pakistani ISI, the decision was made to deal with him for his prominent role in the threat to release a deadly virus on Israel and the rest of the world.

Farazi laughed loudly at the punchline of a joke that was told by a man who was two seats away. He picked up his wineglass, gulped down a final swallow, then asked the pretty young woman seated to his immediate left to pass him a half-filled bottle.

He poured himself another glass of the Sonoma Chardonnay, then took a healthy sip. He placed the glass on the table, and then, with one elbow on the arm of his chair, he rested his chin in the palm of his hand while he listened to the start of another interesting story.

The two commandos fired simultaneously, and both shots hit their target.

Farazi's head exploded like a ripe watermelon, and the immediate reaction of those at the table was both shock and disbelief. It took almost a dozen seconds before the woman seated next to him suddenly began to scream.

A full-scale panic ensued at the table, with people yelling and scrambling to get inside to a place of perceived safety.

Their screams could be heard all the way down to the waterline, but there was no one still there to hear them.

*****
*

Other Novels by Peter S. Berman

HIDDEN AGENDA

WEB OF BETRAYAL

MONEY FOR LOVE

This book and others by Peter S. Berman are available at amazon.com
and other retail outlets and online stores.

IF YOU'RE SO INCLINED, PLEASE CONSIDER WRITING A REVIEW OF
THIS NOVEL ON AMAZON. I WOULD BE VERY INTERESTED IN
KNOWING WHAT YOU THOUGHT OF THE STORYLINE, THE CHARAC-
TER DEVELOPMENT, AND WHETHER OR NOT YOU ENJOYED
THE BOOK?

THANKS

ABOUT THE AUTHOR

Peter S Berman became a Los Angeles County Deputy District Attorney in 1973. After ten years as a trial attorney, he was promoted to the position of Head Deputy District Attorney, a senior administrative position. As a Head Deputy, he oversaw the daily operation of several geographic courthouses, as well as specialized divisions, including the Hardcore Gang Division, the Sex Crimes Division, and the Career Criminal Division. He retired from the office in 2002.

While working as a prosecutor, he lectured for the National Prosecutors College in Houston, Texas; the California Department of Justice; the LAPD Training Academy, and numerous other groups. He was a technical advisor on a Paramount/NBC Movie of the Week that recounted one of his sexual assault cases. His work has been profiled on a number of television shows, including CBS's Sixty Minutes.

He has received Citations of Recognition from the Los Angeles County Board of Supervisors; the United States Secret Service; the Association of Deputy District Attorneys, and numerous other law enforcement agencies and groups.

He currently works as a Specialist Volunteer with LAPD's Robbery-Homicide Division, Cold Case Specials Unit, where he investigates unsolved homicide cases. He was honored by the LAPD's Robbery-Homicide Division as their 2008 Reserve Officer of the Year.

*****

ABDUCTED

Printed in Great Britain
by Amazon